ORACLE OF RUIN

THE KING'S QUEEN
BOOK TWO

HAYDN HUBBARD

These scars will lighten and pain will turn to prose.
For Belle and Brett. I love you endlessly.

THE INN
REBELLION BASE

THE ORACLE
HILLS OF SIVA
E WOOD
MAVIS' COMPOUND

CONTENTS

CHAPTER I

PROLOGUE

Everyone always talks about death from a distance. They say you'll be okay with time, but they never talk about what happens when you aren't.

They tell you about the moment it happens, and if you're lucky, what comes next. They never talk about those of us who get left behind. Where *we* go next. Nor about how someone can go from warm and breathing in your arms one moment and then the next, you never see them again. Death is final. The poets never seem to consider that. Not *truly* consider it, anyhow.

The gods never give me enough time to think upon it for long, not with death coming for me next.

"How many do you think there are?" I shout towards the blond mercenary to my right.

His long legs match mine stride for stride, his chest rising and falling quickly beneath his leather vest. He turns his red face towards me and stares incredulously. "Less talking, more running," he barks between breaths.

Behind us, the growling grows, its guttural sound somewhere

1

between a moan and a raspy cry that sends terror curling around my spine.

"I am just saying, if there aren't too many, I would prefer fighting to running."

"Dammit, Vera, there's at least five too many to fight, so shut up and run!"

By five too many, he probably means five total, in his signature Rowan way.

The snapping of tree branches grows closer. They're practically on our heels at this point. I bite back a groan of frustration. These things are nearly impossible to kill, let alone five of them. Then again, when have we ever shied away from the impossible?

Up ahead, a clearing promises a fairer fight, and we both double our efforts. The wind whispers around us, chanting and pleading to not shed more blood in their forest. I cringe as my legs burn. With each inhale, I focus on pushing the oxygen through my muscles and calling on my pureblood strength to last me just a few paces more. Three more. Two, one...

We enter the clearing at the same time they do. Rowan dives to cover my body with his own, but I am quicker. Leaping around him, I turn to face the beasts with my hands raised.

They pause, sniffing the air as if looking for something—no, not something. *Someone.* Their gaze stops on Rowan.

The Kijova. A creation of pure death.

The five of them form a circle around us, oddly calculating, considering their usual instinct is to dive headfirst into the attack. My stomach drops at the implication. They're evolving. He is getting stronger.

The largest one rears its ugly head, its elongated fangs dripping with blood, silver and gold alike, its rotting gums speckled with human flesh. It stands on its hind legs, bent backwards like a horse's, its lengthy arms brushing against the forest floor. At the end of each of those arms are spindly hands with claws that were made for no purpose other than death. I've watched their razor-sharp points skewer a man in under a second.

The worst is the eyes. Their eyes are the only remaining human part about them, despite being completely soulless. From their black rotting skin to their form, nothing on the Kijova even resembles a human anymore, save for their eyes.

The creature of dark magic has an insatiable hunger for blood and whatever purpose their master gives them. Luckily enough for us, their creator—the man I once called Father—has decided he wants them to find his son and lover. That means we're running for our lives daily.

The first Kijova lowers his nose directly towards Rowan and takes a slow step forward.

I step between them and stare into its eyes. I nearly sob when I see that they aren't hers, that so far, she hasn't been made one of them.

All we know of the Kijova is from the banned ancient books of dark magic and our own experiences. The most pressing concern when dealing with them? They're nearly impossible to kill. Nearly.

Much like a blessed, who can only be killed by dark magic, the beast cannot be killed by anything other than light magic. There's just one problem—all the blessed mages are dead.

The monster opens its throat and screams, an ear-piercing sound that is all too familiar. Tears prick at the corners of my eyes, blurring my vision. My own scream comes from its throat, reverberating through the air, the sound of their creation—the day they were born of my best friend's blood. My Tanja, who gave her life for mine.

"You sick bastards," I grind out, digging my heel into the dirt.

It mimics my action before charging. Its trap opens wide to bare its teeth, planning to clamp down on my throat once their claws finish the job. I wait a moment longer until I can smell their distinct reek of death before I open my palms.

White light shoots forward, burning the creature straight through. It screams again, but I tune it out as the others advance. I pour every ounce of rage and grief within me into the light. The searing stench of burning flesh grows more bearable with time, and before long, I'm surrounded by six dead bodies.

"You miscounted," I say as I offer Rowan a hand up from where he still lays in the dirt.

He rubs at his hip where he made contact, but says nothing as he pushes himself up off the ground and starts towards our camp. I follow close behind, my eyes staying trained on the dead beasts around us.

Ophelus never should have let me live, not after he killed her.

The skull of a Kijova squishes easily under my heel as I walk over it, the undead creature dead once more.

I said before that all the blessed mages are dead.

I lied.

All the blessed mages are dead—*except for me.*

And I am going to kill every last one of these fuckers.

CHAPTER 2
VEROSA

The sun has fully begun her ascension to the sky as Rowan and I return to our camp. The first rays of daylight stretch across the gold and pink expanse of the sky, slowly giving way to a bright and clear blue. The crisp mountain air stings my skin and I inhale deeply. Pine and fresh dirt flood the air and my olfactory senses while I sigh into the autumnal chill. The morning dew clings to our boots and the hems of our pants as we trek through the grassy Hills of Siva. The wet of the cloth sticks to our warm flesh beneath, our skin still cooling from our early morning exertion. Few birds sing in the mornings these days, but one whistles in tune with our steps as we march towards our temporary home.

We chose the hills when we fled Ophelus's dark army. Only a day's ride from the palace if on horseback and a few days on foot, the mountains have been our shelter for the past few months. Our makeshift camp sits nestled in a small clearing of trees within the mountains. Most of the grass is dying out and crunches beneath our boots, but a few sparse patches still struggle to spring up from the ground. I step to the side—it would feel wrong to trample them.

A semicircle of tents forms around a firepit. The tents are comprised of a thick, red wool, blankets we stole from an abandoned inn and stitched together. They do a good enough job of keeping the chill out on nights we can't risk a fire, but fail miserably on days where rain overtakes the mountains. Under other circumstances, a cave would be preferred, but given our enemies and Ophelus's tracking skills, we all sleep a bit more soundly at the thought of having more than one exit to our campsite.

Ophelus—the man I thought was my father and now know as the fallen king. Five months ago, when he and my fiancé, Lucius, attempted to take my life, they failed. The blade meant to sacrifice me for my blood embedded itself in another's chest, and from her blood, Ophelus's dark army was born.

The Kijova are something none of us were prepared for, nearly unkillable creatures of shadow and death. Their one mission is to fulfill Ophelus's greatest desire—finding his former lover and son. Unfortunately enough for us, that would be the blond mercenary walking by my side, holding my hand, and his mother.

Rowan and I pass two familiar faces as we stalk by the firepit. Blaine and Emilie sit huddled around the pit, breakfast simmering over the open flame. We say nothing as we pass them, the morning brain fog too thick to form coherent thoughts and my unwillingness to disturb the simple peace preventing my tongue from moving.

Five months. For five months now, we have been on the run. All neighboring kingdoms have closed their borders and Ophelus has seized the harbors, leaving us trapped within a dying kingdom. Neva was the first, then Varium, soon followed by Tesslari, despite their crown prince's involvement in the atrocities that plague my kingdom. So far, we have managed to stay under his radar by hiding in these mountains where there is enough rock to slow our enemies' tracking. The occasional Kijova has made it this far, like the ones this morning, but they come in small enough droves that we can pick them off. We learned one eventful morning that the Kijova struggle to pick up our scent and sounds over rushing water. We attempted to make it as far as the port just above Varium and Neva, but Ophelus had all the ports destroyed or seized. No ships large enough to withstand the rough waters surrounding the continent were spared. Recently, we have settled for camping near rivers instead, far enough away to hear an attack, but close enough that it buys us a few more weeks of peace to make our next move.

But I know it is only so long before we run out of places to hide. One day soon, we will have to make a choice to run or fight. I can only pray we live long enough to make that choice.

From within one of the tents, someone swears.

I raise an eyebrow at Rowan. "Derrín?"

The mercenary shakes his head. "Derrín wouldn't swear."

We both come to our conclusion at the same time and follow the sound towards Kya and Amír's tent. The flaps of the thin tent are pulled closed, as if warning us not to enter. Per usual, we choose not to listen.

Amír sits hunched over a map when we enter. Her red hair is tied back in her usual braid, though a few of her white strands fall over her forehead. The gunslinger's calculating gaze slides over Rowan's form then to mine, and her eyes narrow. "I'd ask, but I think I already know."

Even as we've been in close quarters for five months, Amír's disposition towards me has yet to change. Cold. Standoffish. She would take a bullet for me, but it feels as though she would just as soon be the one to fire it.

Rowan offers a crooked grin and no other explanation as he settles on the dirt beside his second in command. The map before them has a multitude of red marks marring its crumpled page.

Rowan slides the piece of red charcoal from between her fingers and marks the spot where we encountered the Kijova. I stay standing silently, waiting for her reaction.

Amír pinches her eyes shut and rubs at her temple. Her headaches have become more frequent lately, and she fixes me with a stern look. I already know what words are about to leave her mouth before her lips even part. "We've been over this. Torin was in the palace when your father—"

"He's not my father," I hiss through clenched teeth. Ophelus has earned himself many titles throughout the past months after unleashing his dark creation upon the kingdom, and "my father" is not one of them. He himself cleared that up the day he intended to sacrifice me to create his Kijova, both by kidnapping me and then murdering my best friend.

Amír shakes her head then amends her statement, turning towards Rowan instead now. "Sorry. When *your* father unleashed the Kijova. We've all seen the report. There were no survivors."

Rowan scowls and my heart rate rises. The revelation of who his father is took us all by shock and led him to believe us to be siblings for a brief moment in time. However, there was something Rowan had forgotten to realize in his state of shock that should have ruled out this possibility instantly: Rowan is a hybrid and I am a blessed pureblood.

As a pureblood, my parents must have the same color blood—both blessed. This allows for my pure, golden blood, as well as certain advantages—increased strength, quickened healing, and my light magic being some of these.

However, Rowan's blood is flecked with both silver and gold, the telltale mark of a hybrid, something that has been outlawed for years. Previous kings feared a hybrid's power, given their innate abilities and lack of weaknesses. Hybrids are stronger, faster, and damn hard to kill. With heightened senses and lacking the weaknesses of a blessed or cursed given the combination of their blood types, all were to be put to death upon discovery.

Rowan's father, the man who kidnapped me, was cursed and his mother blessed. Somehow, the king had snuck through the royal line as a cursed, despite the law that has stood for centuries —that a cursed cannot even work in the palace, let alone rule. We've yet to uncover why, but it hasn't exactly been high on our list of priorities.

"That's not true. There were some," I argue, pleading with Amír to let me have this hope. *I was the one who ran and left Torin in that palace while I escaped. I left Tanja there to die. I let Seb hold the first Kijova off while I ran. I left them all there to rot. Laei, please don't let him be dead. Don't let his blood be on my hands as well.*

You run like a coward, that rebel boy said months ago, right before I killed him for it. He was right.

Amír, as always, refuses to give me such satisfaction or peace. "And they all succumbed to their injuries days later."

My gaze locks on the gunslinger's, two warring energies fighting for dominance in the battle of will. Her emerald eyes hold my blue ones, refusing to back down. Her anger radiates through the room, thickening the air with tension.

Just as Rowan is about to interfere, the scent of smoking meat wafts into the tent and Emilie calls for us to come eat breakfast. Nausea roils in my stomach and I press the back of my hand to my mouth as I start to dry heave. I haven't been able to stomach any food or many scents recently, let alone meat. The image of Raiko and his skin falling from his skull, raw meat hanging on his bones, flashes through my mind. Another retch rocks my form.

Rowan's palm presses against the small of my back, tracing soothing circles until the feeling subsides. My stomach uncoils and I hold my tunic over my nose, covering most of the scent.

Amír watches this all with something like pity before she

sighs. "I'm sorry you lost them, Vera, I promise I am. But we're going to lose so many more if this continues. We have enemies on all fronts! The rebels have taken over more than half of our territories to draw you out, Ophelus and his damned beasts are breathing down our necks every waking second, and meanwhile, Mavis is unrelenting in her search for you two. My hands are tied, and you two aren't helping by running off at your first chance!" She throws her hands in the air for emphasis, suddenly looking much older than her twenty-two years.

While half of her accusations may be unfair, they aren't exactly unfounded. Despite Rowan being the leader of the Nightwalkers, Amír is the one who has taken on the brunt of the work in an attempt to hold our small group together. We've been cut off from contact with the underlings of Rowan's mercenary kingdom, so for now, we're on our own. No allies, and enemies on all sides.

The soft susurration of a golden breeze caresses the back of our necks as Kya emerges from the shadows. All of us are used to the assassin coming and going as she pleases, and at this point, know that she could be there at any given moment. Privacy is a privilege not a right with the wraith of the Nightwalkers living only a tent over.

The Vari woman floats towards her lover. Her skilled hands make quick work of the muscle knots and tensions in the other woman's shoulders while she hums softly. Amír sighs into her touch and lets her jaw unclench. Kya is one of my dearest friends and the only one able to assuage Amír. On the outside, it is strange to consider the sweet woman could ever be with someone as hotheaded as Amír, but now knowing the lovers, it is impossible to picture them apart. Kya whispers something in Amír's ear while lifting her gaze to us. *Go.*

I nod gratefully, tugging Rowan with me through the flaps of the gunslinger's tent. The scratching fabric brushes across my forearms and I jump. Rowan settles his hands on my shoulders, both steadying and steering me towards Blaine, Emilie, and now Derrín, who has chosen to join them around the fire.

Blaine drops his gaze and takes another small sip from a cup in his hand. His motions are sluggish and his pupils dilated. In half a second, I have snatched the cup from his hand and raised it to my nose, gagging at the assault of the smell of cheap alcohol.

Guilt mingles with anger even as my friend and former love lifts his hands to request his cup back. I am to blame for his addiction and the thought haunts my every waking moment. Add it to the list of things to be guilty for. He turned to the substance to avoid his shame after he was bested by my fiancé in a duel for my hand in marriage in an attempt to win my freedom. Amír likes to remind me to be grateful he is a happy drunk rather than a violent one, or we would have a new slew of problems to deal with. My scathing response is always that there is nothing to be grateful for as I debate shooting the gunslinger with her own pistol.

Before I can say anything, the former captain turns his attention upon Rowan, who stands behind me, close enough that I can feel when he breathes. The Vari man sighs like a forlorn sweetheart. "I love you."

Without missing a beat, Rowan takes the cup from my hands and tosses its contents to the ground. "Say it when you're sober."

"Who let him drink this?" I seethe. "We don't even have alcohol at the camp. Where did he get this?"

Blaine's drinking habit would be problematic if we were still back at the palace, let alone on the run. With the Kijova tracking our every move, we are packing up camp and moving at least once a week. The thought of him being drunk during an attack... That foreboding sense of dread returns.

Not to mention the sight of him now, the way he slurs his words and stumbles, choosing oblivion over pain. Pain *I* caused him. *I* am the reason he left his only home. *I* am the reason his closest friends are dead. While it is not my fault I no longer love him, I suppose I can't blame him if he chooses to hold that over my head as well.

Derrín shrugs while Emilie stares at Blaine in disappointment. The disgraced captain doesn't bother to lift his gaze. Conveniently enough, a specific blade of grass has caught his attention rather than my ire.

"He said it was water."

"And you believed him?"

Derrín has the decency to look ashamed as I sigh.

"I don't know who I am more disappointed in."

Rowan shoots me a dry look of warning, but no one else makes any motion. The air around us hangs dry despite the moisture that clings to the grass and our boots. The silence permeates everything—my skin, my bones, my soul.

My lips purse when no one responds and my muscles groan as I sink to the wet ground. The morning dew seeps through my thin, cotton blouse, the garment courtesy of someone's laundry line a few towns ago. When I escaped the palace, I was wearing only a thin slip nightgown, which not only did nothing for my modesty, but did not protect my skin from the elements. I would've had frostbite by the first cold autumn night had Amír not loaned me a pair of trousers and a blouse. But supplies were sparse as we had to travel light. I have instead taken to raiding abandoned homes, noting the village and address of places we steal from in a journal gifted by Derrín so that one day, I can repay them.

I am especially grateful for the thick pair of pants I wear now that we have entered the wet season. Krycolis's extreme weather knows no bounds, and while it may be the end of summer, those withering heats barely reach us here in the Hills of Siva. Isolated by the coast at the northernmost tip of our kingdom, we receive the chill of the mountains and the wet wind of the ocean—a most "wonderful" combination. Besides, autumn only lasts a week or two here before the dead cold of winter sets in. In the mountains, autumn seems to skip over us entirely and go straight to winter.

Rowan settles beside me, an arm open for me to burrow into his side. I accept the invitation, letting my eyes drift closed for a moment.

Five months ago, Ophelus released his Kijova into the world in order to chase Emilie and Rowan. The aftermath of unleashing that kind of power was devastating. The palace cracked in half from the tremors, the splitting earth reaching all throughout the kingdom. Countless lives were lost from the earthquakes alone, and that was just the beginning.

The Kijova were born of human sacrifice, their first taste of the world being the metallic one of blood. This causes them to crave human blood, and the longer they go without it, the more rabid they become.

The fact that the six we faced earlier hesitated at all before attacking told me they had eaten recently. Bile crawls up my throat. The village we saw last night... the bodies...

I rise to my knees and retch up all the meager contents of my stomach into the grass. Blaine and Derrín recoil, but Rowan and Emilie kneel beside me. Rowan has one of his hands on my abdomen, holding me up so I don't face-plant into my own vomit, while Emilie dabs the back of my neck and my face with a damp rag. The feeling of their fingers and their body heat pressing against mine has another bout of nausea tearing through my body. I fight the urge to vomit again, gagging and holding my breath.

Rowan brushes my bangs from my face. "Let it out, love."

I spit into the grass and groan once the final wave of illness ceases. This is why I don't give myself time to think. With thinking comes memories, with memories comes guilt, and with guilt comes *this*.

"Have you been chewing your ginger root?" Rowan asks,

despite knowing the answer to his question. We both know there is nothing physically wrong with me and no ginger root will be able to take back the things I've seen. The things I've caused.

One of my mistakes sits opposite to us, biting his fingernails and eyeing the ground where Rowan just dumped out his drink. To say I wasn't pleased that Rowan had hid him from me is the understatement of the century. Imagine my shock when I woke up in the middle of the forest, surrounded by a gang of mercenaries and my first love, who was drunk out of his mind, all while wearing the blood of my best friend.

However, my anger was soon overridden by panic as the screaming started. I had been out for a few hours, just long enough for them to move us farther into the woods, closer to Belam and just far enough away to avoid their first attack. The Kijova didn't go for the decrepit cities that homed mainly the cursed. No, they went for the nobles—the nobles who were the blindest of all, sitting in their glass houses protected by the thin veil of monetary privilege. They never saw it coming.

The First Dark is what that night is now called. All the lights in the kingdom went out and the Kijova descended upon all—the elderly, the young, the healthy, the ill. None who were caught in their path were spared. The death toll of that night alone is estimated to be half the kingdom. Those who escaped went into hiding. The beasts went on the hunt.

We've been running for our lives ever since, just trying to live day by day. We haven't had a spare moment to think of a plan. Nothing goes past the consideration stage before it is scrapped to the bin. All possible answers are suddenly impossible in the face of this tragedy.

We've all settled into a semblance of a routine with minimal discomfort. We change our camp location every so often, either to avoid being found or because we have been found. Both leave us traveling by foot for miles through the harsh environment of the mountains. At most, we can stay in any given place for a month before they find us, but never much longer.

"Come on, let's get you cleaned up." Rowan offers me his hand, which I gratefully accept, when Kya steps out from the tent we just left.

She tuts her tongue and holds out her arms with a wicked grin. "No can do, lover boy. Amír needs to talk to you about our next move. I'll go with Vera." Kya pecks my cheek with a sly look aimed towards Rowan. "Don't worry, I'll take *real* good care of her."

I can't help but smile when Amír steps from the tent, her scowl matching Rowan's. My friend blows her lover a kiss before dragging me off towards the woods with her.

The assassin has a soothing presence. It is what makes her such a good friend to us and a threat to those on the awaiting end of her espas. Those long daggers bounce at her side now, their slender curve catching the daylight. If her aura doesn't loosen the lips of informants, then those blades will.

Kya walks ahead of me, her confident feet picking the best path as to avoid brambles and leaving footprints. I mimic her movements clumsily, fatigue causing the world to slightly spin and blur. A stern breeze props me up and Kya calls out ahead that she found it. The sound of rushing water quickly covers her voice and I pick up my pace.

Sunlight bounces off the crystal-clear river, scattering small rainbows and golden ripples on the surface of the water. Small schools of fish swim with the current, the silver of their scales blending in with the silty river bottom.

Kya pulls a minuscule blade from her hair, letting her dark curls fall freely to tumble about her shoulders. She slips from her crimson tunic and folds it neatly atop a tree stump. Her leather tights soon follow until she stands only in her undergarments.

When I saw Kya for the first time, I knew she was probably the most beautiful woman I had ever seen. Her curves look as if she has been carved to be the figurehead of a ship and her painted red swirls stand stark in contrast with her dark skin. She never shies from her beauty, but instead hones it as if it is nothing more than another weapon in her arsenal. She is art in its finest form—alluring, beautiful, and dangerous.

I know I look nothing like that. Any semblance of beauty I once held has been drained by sleepless nights and an empty stomach. I wouldn't mind if it didn't cause the others to look at me with such pity. My sickness is evident in my dull hair, my hollow cheeks, and knobby knees. Clothes that once fit just a smidge too tight now hang loosely from my frame to the point that Emilie has to fasten pins to keep them on.

I undo these pins from my top, allowing the fabric to slide from my shoulders. My trousers fall to the dirt without assistance and I slide out of the tunic just as easily before following my friend to the riverbank.

I don't miss the way Kya's eyes slide over my body. I don't mind. This gaze is different from the ones she gives Amír, not that I would mind either way. To be appraised by her might be like being admired by the gods themselves. But this look is filled with nothing but sorrow.

The cool water sends gooseflesh prickling across my skin as it rises to meet me. The bite of the cold is enticing and I allow myself to wander further in. The current isn't too strong, just enough that I feel a slight pull around my ankles.

"Come on in, the water is fine," I lie, knowing how sensitive Kya is to the cold.

Skeptically, she dips her toes in the water and promptly gasps at the sudden chill. I use the moment to strike, bringing my arm back and sending a wave of freezing water crashing against her sensitive abdomen.

The assassin shrieks and freezes where she stands. Kya holds her breath against the cold until she notices my devious smile.

Unable to hold myself back anymore, I burst into laughter, the joyous sound burbling between my lips and taking over my body until I lose my footing to the current and slip under the water. Coming up sputtering, I shake the water from my hair, the droplets splattering my friend.

With a mischievous grin, she forsakes her previous hesitance towards entering and instead dives my way. A large wall of water slams into my face, sending me into another fit of coughs.

"Gah, I think I swallowed a minnow!" Kya gags upon resurfacing. She pokes my side with a well-manicured finger. "You'll pay for that." Kya throws her head back, her dark hair catching fire in the sunlight, casting the slick strands a golden shade. She lowers her head and grins like she always would back when we were still in the palace.

"Patience, my little tyrant," Tanja laughs with a wicked gleam in her eyes. "It is something I have that you do not. Just you wait."

A large shadow darkens the sky, the sunlight disappearing just as quickly as it appeared. Kya's face comes back into view, her beautiful features pinched in concern. I shake my head, my grown-out bangs now falling to cover my face.

"Come on. We should go," she says softly, leading the way back to the riverbank. The water droplets slide from her body in small clusters, leaving streaks down her neck.

I swallow thickly and wade a bit further out in the river. "Okay, I'll meet you there. I think I've just got something in my hair."

Kya dips her chin in acknowledgment and continues further into the woods, clothes in hand. She doesn't quite believe me, but leaves me in the river anyway, silence confirming her departure.

A small splatter of a raindrop hits my face as I tilt my head skyward. The small pricks of water plop against my cheeks like tears before running down the length of my face, pooling at the soft skin beneath my chin.

Slowly, I sink beneath the water until I can feel the current's slight pull. The pressure builds the lower I sink, and my head begins to throb. When I am low enough that not even the sun can hear me, I drop my jaw and scream.

My eyes squeeze shut against the biting water that enters my throat as I expel all the air from my lungs. Bubbles float to the surface, the only proof of my grief reduced to small pockets of air, soon to pop and be washed away with the minnows.

No tears fall, even if there is no one to see them. I haven't cried since she died, haven't allowed myself to. But I see her every waking and sleeping moment. Her smile, her laugh, and her beautiful anger—all of it haunting me, but never blaming me. Somehow, that hurts worse.

I scream until the bubbles stop.

CHAPTER 3
VEROSA

The dreams always start this way—as dreams. Somewhere over the course of the night, the images shift and I am left where they always leave me: alone in the dark at the mercy of whatever horrors might await me.

Somewhere in the back of my mind, I am aware that I am dreaming, that when I wake, I will be in our camp, in Rowan's arms. Physically safe, for at least a moment. Yet somewhere in the haze, my heart considers the idea that I might never wake from the true nightmare.

Tonight, I await the usual demons—Irene and her taunts, Ophelus and the hollowness of his eyes as he watched Tanja bleed to death. Some nights, Torin or Blaine find me and scream until their voices are replaced with my own in the waking world.

Tonight, a voice I prayed I would never hear again speaks softly from somewhere within the darkness. The back of his hand softly drags across the nape of my neck, the other trailing down the back of my arm until it finds my wrist and squeezes. I can feel the ridges of his burn scars on both of his hands. The scent of charred flesh fills my senses and I hold my breath as long as I can before his thumb running along my pulse jolts me back to my senses.

I rip myself free of Lucius's grasp and whirl on him. My fists are raised at the voice, light begging to seep from my fingertips. Even though I cannot see him, I know he is there, lurking in the shadows. They cover for him, unlike Rowan. In contrast, the shadows greet the mercenary like an old friend, Lucius an accomplice.

I curl my fingers into a quivering fist. "I don't need to remind you what I can do with these," I warn, and send out a shot into the dark.

A low chuckle to my left echoes. "No, you do not."

His mirthless voice comes from behind now and I spin to be met with nothing but darkness. In my panic and rage, I lift my fist into the air, allowing a brilliant beam to cut through the blanket of darkness surrounding us. The sight of my once-handsome fiancé is undoubtably jarring.

His dark eyes are completely white and his eyelids are gone, scorched off where I drove the heel of my palms into them. I intended only to blind and impair him during our fight in the tower, but my rage took over and caused further harm than I intended. He now wears an open tunic with the sleeves rolled up, displaying every inch of where I burned him. The angry red ridges form a web of scarring up and down his muscled chest and arms. My handprints are distinct on his forearms, the imprint of my fingers where they dug in to push away.

Despite not being able to see where I am, he advances in my exact direction. Each of his footsteps hit the ground, rattling whatever plane of existence we occupy right now.

This isn't real. Wake up.

Wake. Up.

"This is all real, my love." He stops just a few feet from me and frowns. "Do you hate me so?"

The question causes a pause only momentarily. *Do* I hate him? I hated the idea of him when we first met, the man who would take away my future and what little illusion of freedom I had. Then he bloomed into a friend who granted me outings from the palace, allowed me to go further from home than I had ever been allowed before. Who sent flowers to my room every hour when he thought I was sick, and taught me archery.

Then he destroyed the only person that could make me forgive him.

"You killed her." I spit a large glob of saliva onto his face. I don't need to say who or why. Tanja will never be more than a servant to him, just as I have never been more than a step along the way. He loves me in the loosest form of the word.

Completely unbothered, Lucius lets my spittle slide to his chin before rubbing it off with an embroidered handkerchief. He tosses the used piece of cloth to the ground and grinds his heel into it. The shadows leap, and it is gone into the inky darkness.

"You killed her. You let her take that knife after you tried to kill me. If you hadn't done that, she would still be alive."

He steps forward, his straight brow furrowing. His hands seek my wrists, interlacing his fingers around them as I prepare to strike.

"Stop."

Still, he refuses to release me, holding me tighter to the point of pain as I struggle. His scars scratch across the smooth surface of my skin and I fight the urge to recoil. In truth, it is not due to him or the scars themselves. No, it is because *I* made those. Even as much as I despise him and blame him for all that has transpired, I still did that to another person. Feeling that proof against my flesh... I'm not sure which of us I hate more.

If Lucius's eyes could soften, they do, and he eases his grip a bit. His lips curve upwards in a smile that resembles something like pity, and his voice is gentle when he speaks again. "I thought you'd want to know that something went wrong with the spell. It didn't bring her back."

Her. His mother—the one he was willing to kill me for. From the outside looking in, it seems a noble pursuit. An honorable young prince willing to sacrifice the love of his life to bring his mother, the empress, back to life. He might even be the hero in someone else's story, or the villain only in mine. Rowan told me once that not everything in our world is black and white. I suppose the same goes for Lucius.

Then he smiles wickedly, an expression I've never seen him make before. "There must have been something wrong with her."

I know he is not referring to his mother now.

The single thread of restraint holding me back explodes and I unleash the last of my willpower that has kept me from hurting him. The light in my veins rages against my flesh, but I force it to die. I won't need my powers for this. With months' worth of caged grief and rage, I bury my fist in his face. The action splits my knuckles open, white bone protruding through my flesh as I repeatedly beat against him. My blood sprays across my face and I scream, but when my eyes open, it is not Lucius I have been attacking this whole time. It is an oak tree.

My blood drips down its trunk and I gasp when I see splinters of bark in my raw flesh. The edges are raised and form swollen peaks coated with my golden blood. Warm and sticky chunks of something I didn't know was in my body splatters across the trunk and my mangled hand. With a small whimper, I dig the splinters out, but not before noticing the warmth on the back of my neck. The dying sun warms the forest I'm in, but more importantly, I am alone.

Lucius is gone.

I bite my lip as hot tears prick at the corners of my eyes. Swearing under my breath, I cradle my injured hand, completely unable to use it.

A soft rustling of leaves and a low growling has my gaze shooting forward into the tree line. Instinct replaces fear and my weight shifts to my back leg, allowing it to take the brunt of my force for an attack.

A moment passes. Nothing.

Nonetheless, I raise my uninjured hand, fingers splaying painfully wide open right as the Kijova bursts through the foliage. The scent of death hits me like a wall, knocking me back. Every nerve in my body tenses as my instincts scream at me to run. I square my shoulders and brace for the pressure of my rising power.

The beast locks eyes with me and screams.

"*Vera!*"

My breath catches in my throat as my knees begin to shake.

No.

Gods, no.

"*Vera, run!*"

Don't look. Do not look.

It lowers on its haunches, staring into my face. My raised arm drops to my side as if lead. My eyes lift.

Golden eyes stare back into my blue ones. Tanja's eyes.

I sink to my knees, my body no longer able to hold the weight of my grief. The rocks hidden amongst the grass bite my knees and tear my linen trousers.

The beast makes no more sound, no more hint of recognition on its ugly face.

The lowering sun amplifies the odious scent of death that surrounds us. No breeze offers solace. Even the earth knows I do not deserve as much.

Tanja's eyes stare at my face as the Kijova rears an arm back, then buries its fatal claws in my gut.

And I let it.

I dart up with an inhuman noise that sounds somewhere

between a gasp and a scream. My hands fly to my stomach, but Rowan's is already there. His hair is mussed with sleep and his eyelids heavy yet alert as he steadies me. He reads my face carefully, something like sympathy masking his own.

I avert my gaze as I grip at my completely drenched sleep pants. The thin fabric clings to my thighs, practically see through at this point. It might have been embarrassing if this were the first time this has happened. Unfortunately, it is not, and I doubt it will be the last time. Rowan's hand rises and falls with my breathing under my shirt, allowing the feeling of his skin on mine to ground me.

I open my mouth to say something when I gag. Without hesitating, Rowan grabs the bucket beside my bed and holds my hair back as I vomit into the pail. He doesn't complain when some splashes on his arms or one of our only clean blankets. He simply massages the back of my head as he fists my hair, whispering soothing words and reminders to breathe into my ear. Slowly, the heaving subsides, and I fall back against his chest, exhausted.

Wordlessly, he lowers me back against the pillow and excuses himself to go empty my returned dinner outside. He returns a moment later with clean hands and a damp rag that he blots against my forehead with the utmost care.

Night after night, he cares for me, and every night, emotion fills my heart as if it were the first time.

I wrap my fingers around his wrist and he steps back to allow me to stand. The cool air assaults my skin and speckles it with gooseflesh. The sheen of sweat coating my body does nothing for the chill, and accepts the cold instead. This is our routine. I have a night terror that wakes up the whole camp, Rowan is there helping me, and then we all pretend like nothing happened the next morning.

In the beginning, it was different. Everyone would rush into my tent to find me screaming in my bed, thrashing as if fighting off an invisible enemy. They gave me my own tent back then, trying to allow me space to process. After a week of the same thing happening, Rowan moved in with me, and when the night-mares ceased, he would be there with a bucket and soothing smile. He doesn't ask questions—he made that mistake the first few nights, but now he helps wordlessly.

A breeze brushes against my feverish skin, slick with sweat. I use the rag to wipe down my arms before placing it on the back of my neck and tilting my head back.

The blond mercenary before me watches for permission before helping me step out of my pants. Once free of the soaked garment, he carefully helps clean my legs as well, then removes his shirt and hands it to me. Gratefully, I slip out of my shirt and into his, sighing when the fabric graces the middle of my thighs. I used to turn around, embarrassed and afraid of what Rowan might think. Now I just don't care.

No one has said anything to me. I know Kya and Rowan don't allow them to, but it is hard not to notice how my body has begun to waste away these past few months. Where I used to boast muscle and soft curves, there is now nothing but hollow shapes and protruding bones. I struggle to keep up when on the run and know that if my powers and pureblood strength weren't coursing through my blood, I would have fallen behind months ago.

I look as if I died in that palace and they dragged my corpse from the rubble.

Perhaps I did.

Rowan interlaces his fingers through mine as he walks back to his own bed and I follow closely behind. He sits first, propping his back up against the makeshift headboard Derrín made for each of us. I crawl in after him, settling between his legs with my back against to his chest. He presses a slow kiss to my temple, then pulls the covers up around us.

His heartbeat thuds against my skin, a slow rhythm that lulls my mind to comfort. I sigh as his arms wrap around my midsection, and bury my face in the crook of his neck.

"Will you remind me, please?" I whisper, my voice hoarse both from slumber and sickness. I don't need to elaborate for the mercenary to know what I mean.

Rowan flinches as my warm breath tickles his neck, but he nods. His fingertips press patterns against my side as we settle in. "When someone is used as a sacrifice for dark magic, the magic consumes their body. There is nothing left of them after the process is completed. They are completely erased from existence." He inhales deeply. "There was nothing left of her to be turned into a Kijova."

I hum sleepily. We never talk about Tanja unless we are alone. Emilie told me that the day Blaine found out Tanja was dead was the day he nearly drank himself to meet her. They found him convulsing in a puddle of his own bile, four empty bottles lining the wall behind him. We all know he blames himself just as much as I blame myself. Between his drinking and my night terrors, we have all resolved to never speak of her.

There are a few exceptions to that—nights like these, for example, when I beg Rowan to remind me that she hasn't been turned into a monster. It is a sick form of comfort, but he provides every time.

However, the thought of her being completely erased from existence has never sat well with me either. How could someone go from being so light, filling each room she wandered into, to having no place in this world at all? How could she be here one moment and then gone the next? It isn't fair. None of it is.

I bite back the sob that threatens to form in my throat. I haven't cried since that day, and I refuse to start now. It was my weakness that placed that dagger in her heart. I won't let it take anyone else from me.

Sensing the well of emotion rising, Rowan tightens his grip

and adds, "She's at peace. Her soul lives on. It lives in you." It is the most anyone has spoken of her in months, and his voice threatens to break. She had been a sort of friend to him too.

Someday, I hope to believe him, but I can't. Not now. Not while my every moment is haunted by the sounds of her screams, the image of her slit throat, her death rattle of a breath as she told me to run.

I squeeze my eyes shut and grip Rowan's shirt in my hands, causing the fabric to ride up my thighs. The mercenary pulls it down and lifts his fingers to my hair. He toys with the strands, listening to the hitch of my breath to know if he pulls or catches a hair. My muscles begin to relax and the bile lowers in my throat.

"You can sleep," he murmurs, his voice softly caressing the outer shell of my ear. "I'll be here all night, and forever."

"Forever? I like the sound of that," I offer with a small laugh.

Being with Rowan is comfortable and safe. Even as my world fell apart, he was the one I went searching for. He was the one to bandage my wounds and carry me to these mountains as the Kijova chased us from the palace. We came together quickly, and yet it feels as if he has always been there.

Yet he never told me about Blaine. He lied about who he was, even if I did the same. Our relationship was essentially built on a lie. That small voice in the back of my head is screaming *danger* and *slow down*, but I can't. I need him, now more than ever.

Even as we talk in hushed whispers, the heavy hand of sleep pulls at my consciousness. I still have tomorrow. I can think of the consequences of the world tomorrow. I allow my eyes to flutter shut and welcome the darkness of unconsciousness with open arms.

CHAPTER 4

ROWAN

The warmth pressed against my side is my only reminder of Vera's presence throughout the night. She feels so frail—no, so close to slipping away and never coming back. She murmurs occasionally, or calls for either Tanja or Torin. My own heart shatters with each of her cries while I lay here, helpless to stop it. All I can do is offer a warm body to hold her, and empty, placating words for comfort.

She hasn't slept well in months, and the lack of sleep and her inability to keep food in her stomach has been detrimental to her health. Jutting bones have replaced her hip dips, and perpetual dark circles halo the undersides of her eyes—her personal fallen crowns.

Yet aside from the state of her physical health, I worry about the war in her mind the most—the images that plague her in both the dream and waking worlds that I am powerless against. Her laughter—a sound I would die to hear again—is a rarity these days, and even then, it sounds hollow. Empty. A death rattle from her ribs.

She doesn't joke with Kya and Derrín like she used to. She

doesn't pick fights with Amír as often, or point out the beauty of trivial things to me. She's a shell of the woman I fell in love with, and yet I keep hoping... My fingers tangle in her hair, mussing the indigo strands until her soft whimpers subside.

Hope is a dangerous game. It is only a hurt you inflict upon yourself. I've seen this path before with my own mother and father, seen how their story ends. A part of me wonders if Vera and I are wandering down the same path, and yet...

The soft sound of light footsteps on the grass outside claims my attention. I stay rooted where I am as the flap of our tent is pushed aside by pale hands and my mother enters the room. Her shawl is tucked against her small body, her eyes heavy with sleep. She gently tilts her head towards the door of our tent. *Meet me outside.*

Slowly, I lay Vera back against my pillow, letting my hands linger on her shoulders as I pull the blankets to her chin before following my mother.

Emilie stands with her back to me, her golden hair that matches my own caught aflame in the rising sun. She hugs her arms to her midsection and shuffles on her feet. "It's getting worse," she notes without ever turning around.

I sigh heavily as I come to stand beside her. We have been over this multiple times as of late, and it always ends the same way. There is nothing we can do except wait.

"She watched her best friend die, Mother. That's something no one should see, let alone the *way* that she died. I..." My voice trails off, leaving the sentence open to the wind.

Purebloods like Vera and Tanja are more than rare. They're the exception to every rule our genetic code should follow. They are such an enigma that the best guess of a solution that our top scientist can provide is that they are a gift from the gods to those who are devout. For a blessed pureblood, they would need to come from a line of two blessed parents, and a cursed pureblood from two cursed. Not that anyone has seen a cursed pureblood in years. They, not too unlike their blessed counterparts, have been hunted to near extinction for their blood. While purebloods possess the power to heal anyone who descends from the same god, they also have the ability to poison anyone from the other divine bloodline. That kind of power isn't the type of thing to go unnoticed. Most purebloods go into hiding or seek the protection of the palace—or both.

Chances are, Ophelus didn't know Tanja was a pureblood. Judging by the records I studied while in the palace, the last recorded pureblood before Vera was Tanja's mother. Two purebloods in one family line is extremely rare. If I had to guess, Tanja's mother did her best to hide Tanja from the royals. Ophelus wouldn't have had any way of knowing there was an alternate sacrifice in the palace. All of that means that if I hadn't left Vera on her birthday, then Ophelus wouldn't have had a sacrifice and Tanja wouldn't have died. We also wouldn't be dealing with the Kijova, but I know which part of that narrative matters most to Verosa. The ever-growing pile of sweaty clothes and vomit-flecked pails tell the story for me.

My mother watches my throat as I swallow hard. Something might as well be lodged in it for all the struggle it takes to move my tongue in a way I have my entire life. Vera hates herself enough that she won't let anyone else be to blame for her friend's death, but that doesn't mean the thought of my involvement hasn't crossed her mind.

Emilie crosses two fingers over her heart and presses her lips together. "What *both* of those girls went through is horrible, Rowan." *Don't blame yourself.* "But Vera is letting her grief destroy her each day that she doesn't allow herself to process what happened. It's been five months, and she hasn't cried once, while these nightmares are only getting worse."

"Which nightmares? The ones in her dreams or real life?"

She pinches my arm. "I can see it, Rowan, the revenge blackening her heart. These night terrors aren't just from the trauma of all she's been through. Her soul is torn between what is right and what is revenge."

The air grows colder despite the rising sun. Goosebumps prickle my arms and the wind kisses the back of my neck. I wish I could say I don't see what she does, that I don't see Vera physically burning each time she eyes a Kijova, or feel the moment the darkness overpowers the light.

"What, are you saying she's like Father?" I growl out.

My mother watches the shift in my demeanor with something like pity crossing her features. She slowly rests her head on my shoulder, her hair tickling the side of my neck. "Your father was lost to black magic. Verosa is lost to grief. Thankfully for us, one is reversible while the other isn't. But this can't continue. Look at yourself, my love. Can you tell me that you both have forgiven so easily?"

She strikes a nerve, mostly because she is right. Ever since the day I met her, Vera's stubborn personality matched my own, stride for stride. She has never been one to forgive easily, and neither am I—if I forgive at all.

We haven't spoken about the things that have passed between us, the ways we have hurt each other. She screamed like I had ripped her heart out when I told her we should have stayed strangers and when Blaine left, and yet after she fell into my arms five months ago, none of that mattered. By the time she saw Blaine again and realized I had found him and never told her, she was too numb to care. She stepped over my slight as if it didn't exist. I do the same each day when she finally lashes out as a result of her anger and exhaustion. We cut each other deeper than anyone else can, and yet each night, she crawls into my bed and I hold her as if nothing else matters.

"Forcing forgiveness is just as bad as forgetting. Sometimes you need to be angry with each other first to heal." My mother slowly steers me back towards our tent. "Don't think you can outrun the day where you both suddenly remember the pain you've endured. It's better to release that anger before it turns to hatred."

By the time we return, Vera has kicked the blankets off the cot, seized by another night terror.

Mother sighs and hands me a mixture of ginger and mint, as well as a tonic. "Sleeping draft. Amír found it at last night's search," she explains as I take in the vile-looking liquid.

I pocket both gratefully as I pick my way to Vera again. The tent flap falls closed, encasing me in darkness.

I settle beside the disgraced princess and hold her to me until she stops flailing. Her breathing is shallow, but eventually slows. I sigh into her hair and kiss the top of her head.

She suddenly squirms in my grip and positions herself so that she is facing me. She looks up, her outgrown bangs falling into her eyes as she attempts a smile. "Hi," she breathes.

"Hi."

"Was that your mom?"

I nod.

"What did you talk about?"

My arm falls to drape across her hip and I allow myself to take her in. I love Vera in the mornings, still half drowsy enough to be at some semblance of peace. For a moment, she looks like the same nineteen-year-old girl who ran down an alley to save a man from a bar fight and wielded a butter knife against the king of mercenaries. She blinks the sleep from her eyes and it disappears. But for a moment, I hold on to that view.

"Nothing."

CHAPTER 5
VEROSA

Another Kijova attack forces us to pack what little we can carry and run not long after I wake up. I manage to take out most of them and we outrun the rest by dusk, when we stumble upon an abandoned inn. Derrín has qualms about sleeping in the same building as dead people, so Kya and Amír clear the property first. Surprisingly enough, there are no bodies to bury, or even signs of violence. Everyone apparently packed up and ran in a hurry, just like we did.

Sweat slicks the back of my neck and my stomach churns as I sink into a soft bed. I opt to lay on my back, as I have discovered laying on my stomach causes another roil of nausea to wrack my beaten body. The cheap sheets cling to my damp skin and I hold my breath in an attempt to cause the sickness to subside.

Blaine stands in the doorway, an eyebrow raised as my shoulders rise and fall rapidly. "Panic?" The bed dips as he sits next to me.

I shake my head, then immediately regret the action. "I think it's the running. Or my body has decided to betray me."

What is left of my meager breakfast threatens to resurface

when images of the Kijova dance across my vision. Then Tanja and that knife, then the bodies in the last town, and...

Something between a snort and a scoff escapes his lips. "It could be both." I notice the pale green color of his face and the way he pinches his lips together. He hasn't had a drink in a bit, and while he's sober now, it's only a matter of time before the anger and panic take him over.

Addiction is difficult to overcome in a fully functioning society, and a part of me hoped that at least the lack of resources would be a hinderance, but he always seems to find something to drink. I've learned to hold my tongue whenever he becomes aggravated or lashes out in his bouts of sobriety. The anger is at least a sign that he is still in there somewhere, that the alcohol hasn't stolen him completely.

Neither of us mention the duel or the fact that I am the one that lead him down this path.

We haven't been able to hold a full conversation yet. He's usually drunk or someone's health has taken a dip for the worse and our discussion is cut short.

His knee bounces up and down, rocking the bed and shooting dizziness straight to my head. I press my lips together to avoid snapping.

"Did you find anything?" he finally whispers. "This morning, I mean."

Did I find any sign that Torin is still alive? Always the same question, followed by the same answer. Each time, I get to watch the hope fade from his eyes and then I lose him all over again.

I drape my arm over my eyes and take shallow breaths. "No. We searched some new towns where we thought he could be. Some people have said they might have seen him, might not have. It was all dead ends again."

The bed creaks as he rises and sighs. His jaw clicks as he

clenches it, then he stumbles towards the door before turning around and speaking softly. "At least we got to say goodbye."

The door is shut before I can throw something, anything at him. Blaine got to say goodbye to Torin before he left the palace, while all he left me was a flimsy note at the foot of my bed while I slept. I hate how my own goodbye mirrors his.

Until we meet again, my greedy princess.

I love you. So live. Live, Vera.

I shoot to my feet far too quickly and clutch at the bedpost to steady myself. I need to get out of this room.

My fingertips trail the goosebumps and flecks of dry sweat and bile on my arms. I shout down the hall to let the others know where I am going.

Amír drops a hopefully clean towel in my hands and rings out her wet hair. With a small thanks, I step out into the chilly night air.

Kya and Amír found a functioning bathhouse while clearing the property, and after trying it out for a suspiciously long time, they deemed it safe and functional enough to use. It isn't anything like I expected it to be, especially not from the looks of the rotting wood on the exterior. Light floods the room as soon as I enter, tiny stars of golden luminance hovering in the air, attached to the ceiling by iridescent threads. The bath itself is made of chiseled cream marble, with small yet grand fountains every few feet shooting turquoise water overhead. A thin layer of golden lacquer coats the floor of the tub, causing the aqua-colored water to shimmer, as minuscule rainbows shower the fog that emits from the bath and fountains.

My body groans more with each step I take towards the water, begging for some release from muscle ache and fatigue. Slowly, I slip free of my clothes at the edge of the water, not bothering to fold them neatly or place them upon a stool. My sword hangs on a hook outside the door for fear that the steam may rust the worn blade. Besides, if a Kijova were to come, then the weapon would be useless. All I truly need are my powers.

My toes curl as I dip them into the water, warmth seeping all the way up to my ankles. My muscles slowly release all tension as I allow myself to sink fully into the water, the comfortable heat enveloping me completely. How long has it been since any of us bathed in an actual bath and not a cool river? These small luxuries I had before that I never fully knew the weight of. I'd give anything right now for Tanja to flick soapy suds at my face or push my head under the water.

Upon further investigation, I discover that the pool is quite deep, allowing me to swim across its width and dive below the waters without ever touching the bottom.

The door to the bathhouse creaks open slowly and I dip myself further beneath the waters. The warmth soaks up to my cheeks and I wrap my arms across my chest. The steps are too heavy to be Kya's or Amír's. They must be Rowan's.

Has he come here because I've taken too long? No, I've only been here for a few minutes now. Kya and Amír took an hour. I can only pray they had the decency not to do anything scandalous in the baths. I laugh, the action sending bubbles to the surface of the pool.

What if he came here for something else?

The water suddenly feels quite hot and I bring my full face into the cool air of the building. I breathe deeply. It has been months now since we confessed our love, and he *did* say he would wait... but have I made him wait too long?

"You'd better have your back turned," I call out teasingly, anxiety rippling in my stomach at the thought. "I don't think this is the right time."

I wait for the sarcastic quip or the shutting of the door, but instead, footsteps draw closer. Multiple sets of footsteps—far too many to be just our people.

The steam obscures my view, leaving only shadows visible. With stiff and slow paddles, I propel myself backwards, further into the bath, taking painstaking care to not send any ripples or splash the water.

"Don't make us come in there," a voice behind me warns. A male voice.

Some of the steam clears to reveal a heavyset man with a clean-shaven face armed to the teeth with cursed blades. I eye those dark weapons. They knew who they'd find here.

"I don't know what you've heard, gentlemen, but a lady is quite choosy about the company she keeps." I slip further under the water, using just my feet to kick through the current now. No splashing, no sounds or motions to give away my location. If I can hold out a bit longer, someone will come, assuming I've drowned. I hope it is Amír—she could easily take half of the masses forming by the lip of the bathing pool. Or Kya, who could kill them all in half a minute.

My legs already grow weary as I now begin to curse the depth of this pool. Maybe a few months ago, I could have tread water long enough for someone to come help, but now, my muscles are already feeling fatigued. Rage can only fuel someone for so long. The burnout comes eventually.

I count the heads to see about fifty men standing by the edge —heavily armed men who are much larger and far less wet. There's only one exit to the bathhouse and it's bound to be heavily guarded. I smirk. Evading the pursuit of a small army has never been a problem before.

Beneath my skin, power surges, sending my veins aglow. I call for the power, but do not allow it the release it craves, instead letting it build just beneath the surface. My skin heats and the water around me begins to bubble. My head swims as I call for more, and the steam rises.

Just a bit more. I'm too close to a burnout, and if I keep this up,

I'll boil my organs. One more push and the steam creates a thick wall between me and my assailants. One sense down, only four to go.

I move quietly while I still can. That pressure pleads to be released, but I rein it in. If my powers sound off, I'll be a walking lighthouse through this fog.

The men swear and scramble for their bearings, the exit temporarily lost. If they brought this many men, it's safe to assume they must have the others already and I'll be on my own to get through the remaining guards at the door.

I slip from the pool silently, listening carefully to make sure even the smallest droplet of water doesn't fall and give me away. I step into the thick of the steam.

My head spins as a fist encircles my upper arm, eliciting a small gasp of pain.

"Got the—"

He has no time to speak as I ram the heel of my palm into his mouth. His teeth scrape my skin, drawing blood, and he begins to gag and foam at the mouth. I notice a tinge of silver on his peeled-back lips and watch with a grimace as my blood poisons him.

I spare no time to hesitate as I sprint to the exit, the wind chilling my naked body. Another arm wraps around my midsection, someone's hand going for my face. I bite down hard and bump my rear against the man's crotch, using my momentum now to flip him over my shoulder onto the slick floor.

"By the exit! Through the steam!"

Shit. The open door is drawing the steam out. No time for fear or modesty, I sprint open-armed towards my one chance of escape. I unfurl my fingers and raise my palms, preparing for that release my body has been begging me for.

From my left, still obscured by the slight vapor of the air, an elbow rams into my jaw, sending me sprawling across the floor.

Before I can stand or even gather my bearings, another man grips my arms, pinning them painfully behind my back.

"Down, bitch," he growls out.

Some of the other soldiers wince as he hauls me unceremoniously to my feet. My head lolls back, a mix of pain and burnout dulling my senses. Panic fights against these bodily restraints, but in the end, yields as the world spins.

I don't see Rowan or the Nightwalkers as I'm pushed outside the building. They must have been moved to a secondary location already.

"Here." Another man steps forward, my crumpled clothing in his hands. With my arms pinned, I cannot take them, and the assailant holding me just shoulders them aside. I can't find it in myself to feel humiliation, despite knowing I am on full display. If emaciated young girls are their type, then I have bigger concerns, like freezing to death in this weather.

Without the sun to warm the mountains, the temperatures have dropped significantly. Goosebumps speckle my skin and my fingers go numb.

"Boss isn't going to like this, Argon," another man warns, his gaze averted to the forest floor as we move. "Give the girl some clothes. She's going to freeze to death before we get there." How considerate for a kidnapper.

The man immobilizing me, Argon, only grunts and picks up his pace. My legs have long since given out and he is practically dragging me through the trees. My bare feet snag on branches and stones, cutting their sensitive soles. Gold glints on the pine needles behind us. The tears in my flesh extend up my calves as Argon's arms grow tired of holding mine. His grip loosens as he senses I have grown too tired to fight back. Some boss wanted me, someone they were all too afraid of to harm me. Everyone except Argon, apparently.

But which enemy are they leading me to now? I've heard

rumors of nobles working for Ophelus and Lucius to find us, though these men look far from the nobility type. Are they rebels, or Mavis's?

We trek onwards through the night, and by *we*, I mean *they* walk and Argon drags me through the muck and mud. Small stones slice the tender flesh on my back to ribbons. I wouldn't be surprised if the stones cut to the bone for lack of fat and muscle to protect them. They ignore my shivering and the audible chatter of my teeth. Any protests or requests to Argon to allow me modesty and warmth are met with a glare of steel.

But this cold...

My lips sting with the cold yet burn when I drag my tongue over them. The night and chill have no end, just constant stabbing pain through my purple flesh. This isn't the kind of cold that can be solved with a blanket and a seat by the fire. No, this cold is wicked and cruel, and every breath I takes sends my lungs rattling within my rib cage. Pain surrounds me, my every unwilling motion and breath. My fingernails throb. I didn't know fingernails could hurt, but they do, and they hurt badly.

My body is far too frozen to even process panic. There's only been one time before this where I have felt such cold. Invisible snowflakes stick to my skin, my eyelashes. My leg screams with burning pain that even the freeze cannot dull. Howling echoes within my skull. I need to look away from the woods, but I can't blink. Can't move my gaze.

The cold nearly took me then, too, but that was nothing compared to now. Then, I at least was dry and wearing a thick nightgown. Here, my hair has frozen to my scalp and no scrap of cloth protects any part of me from the unforgiving freeze of the night.

"Y-you would've liked... my mother." I spit the word at Argon's feet with a painful grin. "You're both sadistic bitches."

"Shut your mouth before I show you how sadistic I can be."

Dawn etches the sky a rusty auburn color, mostly muddied by a thick layer of dark clouds. Fat raindrops plop against my face, streaming down my bare body in rivulets. Some of the men grumble something about rust, chafing, and chills. I don't care that the extra water freezes to my already frozen skin. I don't care that I probably already have hypothermia and frostbite. I grin into the cool precipitation. Serves them right.

My smile soon fades as I notice a hulking form before me, carefully hidden within the high arches of the mountains. I recognize where I am as a map flashes across my mind, marks surrounding this area, but never here exactly.

Argon notices the blood draining from my face and his lips curve upwards wickedly. "Boss has been waiting a long time to meet you, pureblood. Best not to disappoint her."

Her.

The last I checked, both the rebellion leader and my father are male. That leaves only one adversary willing to go to such lengths to kidnap me. But why? If she already has Rowan and...

The thought hits me harder than it should. They *don't* have Rowan and the Nightwalkers. They didn't bother to look. They only took me, and I haven't seen any sign of a second party joining us as we enter through the large gates.

Mavis's compound is larger than I imagined it to be. Carved into the side of the mountain, the safehold boasts tall, cavernous rooms, well-lit with thousands of oil lamps. Mostly women are seen wearing anything from a soldier's uniform to a fine gown. The few men either wear uniforms matching those of my kidnappers, or servants' clothes. I nearly sag further with relief when the heat of the space warms my bones.

The shattering of glass echoes through the entry room as a woman in a deep blue dress drops her drink. Her face is a mask of pure disgust and horror as her gaze falls to me. However, her disdain is not aimed in my direction, but rather at the man holding me up.

His face immediately pales, but he keeps his mouth set in a firm line.

Now that I notice it, everyone in the room has stopped to glare at him.

One woman in a highly decorated soldier's uniform steps forward. Her footsteps shake the cavern walls, her fury palpable, even from my spot on the floor. She brings her face close to Argon's, who, much to his credit, doesn't flinch.

"Have you lost your fucking mind?" the woman seethes, her slicked-back ponytail pinching her already intense features as she glares. Her eyes are narrowed to slits, her features that of a serpent ready to strike.

Argon says nothing but forces me to try and stand. The broken skin on my feet screams when it comes in contact with the pristine floors, and I cry out, falling to my knees. The woman is there in an instant, kneeling and shielding me with her cloak.

"It's not *that* bad. Stand." Argon hauls me to my feet again.

This time, I spit in his face.

Despite the situation, someone in the crowd laughs and his face reddens. Before he can lift his hand against me, a stern voice booms through the cavernous room.

"What is the meaning of this?"

I don't need to look to know who is speaking.

The female soldier smirks at Argon, who is growing ever paler, then bows deeply at the waist with dramatic flair. "Mavis," she croons, still in her bow. "We seem to have a problem."

CHAPTER 6
ROWAN

If Blaine breathes down my neck one more time, I might just reach back and flip the man over my shoulder and onto the table before us. We've been crowded around this round table in the inn's main room for just long enough that tempers have begun to rise.

"Dammit." Amír finally slams her palms on the table, pushing the map away from her. Whatever answer she thought was there originally has clearly evaded her.

Kya holds a candle closer to the map to light her view and swears as the paper begins to singe and the cheap ink bubbles. She pulls the open flame back and Amír carefully takes it from her hands while Derrín attempts to heat a piece of scrap metal over its burning heat. The map hisses as it cools.

I narrow my focus on a blur of red that streaks across the map. Amír has tracked each Kijova sighting for the past five months. Most of their patterns are predictable. Anywhere we are or have been prominently in the past is denoted with red, but the marked locations have begun trailing north recently—further north than we have ever been. They flock to a place under constant fog cover and ice, somewhere very few men have ever trekked.

"Anyone know what's there?" Blaine asks irritably.

I bite my tongue before I can offer a sharp reply that as former captain of the guard, he should know what is out there. He hasn't had a drink since we last ran, and we tossed all alcohol from the inn as soon as we arrived. His forced sobriety finally lights his face with rash irritation and pain. He runs his scarred hand down his face, pulling at his chin and jaw where faint stubble has begun to form. Vera has tried begging him to shave it, but he only fixes her with a look and raises his shaking hands as evidence of his plight. Her offer to shave it for him was also ignored.

"No, but we know what these are." Derrín taps a bandaged finger against the page.

We trace his gaze and Kya swears softly.

"Mages."

"Or at least where they *used* to live before the royals wiped them all out," I correct my assassin. "They're avoiding Ialenia."

Beneath Derrín's finger is a ridge of mountains at the northernmost portion of the Hills of Siva. The base of the ridge nearly crosses into Tesslari territory, but more importantly, a few days ride away from us. The Kijova have only been tracking me and my mother so far, so to see them head in a separate direction proves something: there's something else out there that Ophelus wants.

"How do you know what that is?" Blaine asks. He poorly masks his emotions these days, and his irritation at Derrín knowing something he doesn't is clearly written across his face.

Kya answers for him, her eyes narrowing to match Blaine's glare. "When you're fleeing a place that hunts people like you, one tends to look for places they might be more accepted. For example, chasing a legend of mages whose blood runs the same color. People who can protect you."

My second clears her throat at the frigid atmosphere and traces a finger down her lover's forearm. The assassin visibly relaxes under her touch, and something like guilt flashes across Blaine's features.

"So we have two ideas now," Amír declares. "One: they're drawn to dark magic in the same way they are repelled by light magic. Two: Ophelus is sending them to search for something."

Amír's reasoning seems plausible, but I am drawn to another smudge of red on the weathered map. There's another portion of the mountains they've been avoiding—the only mark of red on this map that was placed there originally, before it was at Amír's mercy.

I nudge my second with my elbow and she inhales sharply when she sees where I'm looking.

"Do you think…"

"It could be."

I don't want to think of what the implications are if the Kijova are also avoiding the Bone Wood.

"Vera is taking a long time. I'm going to go check on her," I announce, pushing myself away from the table.

Blaine stiffens, and Kya lays a hand on my shoulder. "She's probably unwinding. She's been taking this harder than the rest of us." Then she leans in to whisper in my ear. "It's probably best for everyone's sake that you give her some space. Especially while she's in the bathhouse."

The thought of her alone when we are potentially so close to another Kijova attack causes anxiety to surge in my chest. I move to brush past my assassin, but Kya's grip firmly stays planted on my shoulder and she shakes her head.

"I'll go," Amír groans finally. "Laei, just sit down and relax. You're going to give us all stress ulcers." As she leaves, she mutters something under her breath about how we don't need any babies while the world is ending.

Blaine leaps from the stool he was sitting on. His knee hits the table and the chair falls back.

I open my mouth to respond with a snide remark when I note the clarity of the man's eyes and the subtle shake of my mother's head. Her eyes beg me not to start another scene, not when we are so close to getting even a semblance of the old captain back. I ball my fists, but let the tension in my shoulders release. If the Kijova did attack, Vera is the only one who can kill them anyway. All we can offer is a distraction. She will be okay.

She *has* to be okay.

Not even a minute later, the thick walls of the inn begin to rattle. Pounding footsteps echo in the hallway and we leap to our feet just as Amír bursts into the room, her face pale yet flushed with exertion. Familiar fabric is bunched in one fist, a crumpled piece of paper in the other. "She's gone," she breathes.

Emilie pales and Blaine stalks towards my gunslinger. I snatch the note from her hands before he can, and my eyes race to scan the text. I find the familiar signature I was looking for and crumble the paper past legibility. The table rattles as I bang my fist against the aging wood and glare at a particular ring of red marks on our map.

Kya delicately picks up the paper from where it lay discarded on the floor. Her espas are unsheathed in an instant and the Nightwalkers stand at attention.

"Spread out and find an entrance to this point." My finger screams with pain as I jab it solidly against the area I was eyeing. "Someone find me a piece of paper. I owe Mavis a response."

Blaine stalks forward, his leg dragging slightly, resulting in an unpleasant scraping noise against the wood. I imagine the terror a soldier might feel hearing that sound in an echoey hallway, or a criminal in a rundown bar. His face is that of a seasoned warrior, and as much as I enjoy taking my jabs at him, it is hard to forget where he comes from. He places a pen and paper in my hand, a silent treaty. Despite our past, a spark of pride flickers in my chest. His eyes are clear and his motions precise. Consciously, he chooses to trust me. Consciously, he places her life in my hands. I do not need his permission, but what he means to Vera, and what this means to him...

I take the ink and parchment and scrawl out a warning. Three simple words that I nail to the door of the inn.

This means war.

CHAPTER 7
VEROSA

My first thought when I dare to lift my gaze is that Mavis may be one of the most beautiful women I've ever seen. Her tanned skin stands stark in contrast with her silver hair, highlighted by the occasional black streak. She stands tall and lithe, toned with years of muscle and scar tissue from a life of conflict. One eye is a warm, chocolatey brown, while the other a green that is a few shades darker than Rowan's. She wears a deep red cloak with a double-edged sword hanging at her hip, one side cursed, the other regular steel.

It isn't hard to see how Rowan fell in love with her. Confidence radiates around the woman, and each step she takes rattles the compound.

"Argon. Report while you still have a tongue." Her voice is rich and smooth, the timbre of a politician. A powerful weapon of manipulation to fit in nicely with her other blade: beauty.

The mercenary's face goes pale and his hands shake. I grind my teeth to stop from crying out in pain. Mavis's calculating gaze slides over to my pinched features and Argon quickly begins to ramble his recounting of last night's events.

He exaggerates the fight, stating I killed the men that he left behind. Some of the other soldiers blanch at his blatant lie, but Mavis's face remains impassive. His own face reddens as he speaks and he wildly waves his hands around, my body groaning in protest as the motion forces movement into my stiff limbs.

"We had no time to dress her. It was too much of a risk. She took out many of our best men on her own without a weapon. We couldn't risk freeing her hands."

A small swell of smug pride settles in my core. Even at my worst, I was able to take out some of her best fighters. I bite back a comment about how they had to wait until I was sickly and frail to kidnap me, but stop when I see Mavis slide her gaze my way.

The woman's face softens as if she is considering this, and the man visibly relaxes. Mavis's fingers tap the hilt of her sword and she steps within a pace of us both. Eagerly awaiting a reward, he holds me out to her, my shoulder protesting with a sickening pop.

In an instant, Mavis's eyes darken and her blade flashes.

Argon cries out in pain as his grip on me loosens. Warmth trickles down my arm. I look down, and to my horror, find his severed hand slipping from my forearm.

Mavis stands before us, her sword now wet with crimson and golden blood. "She is a woman, regardless of her affiliation, and deserves to be treated with respect. Now someone find her a cloak or it'll be your *head* rather than your hand."

Every goon of hers stands at attention, suddenly forgetting their sneers and their wandering eyes. Some rush off to find clothing, while others stand still in fear of retribution.

Instead, I step forward and wrap my fingers around her toned arm, eliciting a gasp from the mercenaries. "Why would you do that?"

Mavis eyes me for a moment, a predator deciding whether to strike, then shakes my hand off. Nevertheless, she takes a step closer. "Isn't it clear? Men are like children, they need discipline.

My dog knows how to sit on command. I expect the same from my soldiers."

"But he won't be as useful to you now!"

Mavis barks a laugh, her pointy and pristine teeth catching the torchlight.

Some members of her crew chuckle nervously, presumably not to lose their tongues, but I can't find it in my heart.

"*Useful?* You speak of usefulness? Here I thought you were a tender heart." She steps even closer. My breath catches in my throat as she brings a well-manicured hand up to brush stray hairs from my face. I can smell the spearmint upon her breath as she cups my jaw with her hand. "Rowan taught you well, I see."

With the hand not holding my face, she unfastens her own cloak, muttering about the incompetency of her servants, before tossing it over my shoulders. The crimson fabric is soft against my bare skin, embroidered with the finest gold thread. I find it almost a shame that my wet hair clings to it, ruining the cloth.

"Any soldier worth his salt learns to adapt." She tuts her tongue, a finger tangling in a saturated strand of my hair. "General Neris, show her to her rooms."

The kind soldier from earlier steps forward, her arm wrapping around my shoulders both in an act of steadying me and keeping the cloak around my shaking body. She frets over the blue hue my skin and lips have taken on and rubs her hands up and down my arms.

"Is she always like that?" I murmur through chattering teeth.

The other servants and soldiers clear the way as we walk down a long hallway.

"I'll pretend I don't know what you mean by that." She grins broadly and nods to a group of soldiers we pass. They bow their heads in respect and continue on their way without a single glance in my direction.

"All the high-ranking soldiers here are female," I note.

"Mavis prefers it that way. Men comprise our servants and foot soldiers that she sends to do the dirty work. Women are the only ones allowed in her inner circle."

I don't think too long on the information Neris hands me. The fact that I am walking and talking casually with the woman who oversaw sending out men to find and kidnap me for the past year is far more jarring. Luren pops into my head and my leg screams with the phantom pain of his blade skinning my calf.

"Do you know what she wants with me?"

Neris shakes her head. "I can't say, but your safety is guaranteed. No one here will harm you."

"I doubt they'd be able to if they tried," I respond swiftly, bunching my fists at my side. I don't mention to her that the deep calling of my power to my soul has dimmed since entering Mavis's domain. Even now, as I try to conjure even the smallest fragment of light, my fingertips only sizzle and sputter.

The guard smiles at my self-assurance, the toothy grin of a wolf as she continues to lead me down the hall. There is a multitude of doors on either side of the long passage, and I barely have time to marvel at all the carvings etched into the stone walls before Neris stops in front of one of the doors. Its wood has been etched with runes of some sort, and before I can protest, Neris shoves me through the entryway.

"No hard feelings, just Mavis's orders."

The wood slab slams in my face before I can respond and I am left alone in the chamber. I rest my hand on the doorknob. Locked. I swear softly under my breath, though stop when I catch sight of the large bed resting in the center of the room.

Reminded of my chill, I drag myself across the floor, my bare feet leaving wet footprints on the stone. The soft sheets are beckoning as I drop Mavis's cloak, then use it to dry myself before crawling between the covers, the warmth enveloping me almost immediately.

Sleep pulls at my eyelids until they close completely and I slip into the unconscious.

∾

SOMETIME WITHIN THE NIGHT, shuddering chills wrack my body, leaving me constantly switching between bundling myself in Mavis's cloak and throwing all the blankets to the side. My body is simultaneously on fire and surrounded by ice, my wet hair sticking to my sweat-slick face.

Drifting in and out of consciousness, I extend my arm, rolling to the side only to hit the floor. My body cries out in agony, the cold touch of the stone sending blinding pain through my spine and flesh. I can vaguely hear the door creak open and the rush of footsteps. Gentle hands cradle my body and lift me back onto the bed, the soft motions still enough to elicit a moan of pain from between my lips.

Someone murmurs a vehement curse as a second pair of hands press against my face. These ones are warm and scarred. They lift me into strong arms that carry me elsewhere before unconsciousness pulls me under once more.

The next time I am aware of anything, I feel something like warm water surrounding me, and a second body lay pressed against my back. Her arms rest over my waist, her hand pressed against the flat plane of my stomach. I lean into the warmth of the touch, the pain now gone. The body convulses, but stays steady as warmth settles in my bones. A strangled gasp escapes from the lips of whoever holds me, and I reach an arm around, grasping for them. My fingers brush across a soft face slick with sweat. My hand is batted away and someone covers my eyes.

"Sleep, little miracle," they purr.

My eyelids droop closed, a new sense of heaviness settling in my bones. Utterly weightless, I drift into oblivion.

CHAPTER 8

VEROSA

A dim light filters through the curtains that must have blown aside during the night. I stretch, hearing a satis-factory pop from my back and shoulders. Snuggling in further to the covers, I reach out, only for my fingers to graze cool sheets. My eyes shoot open and I sit upright in a panic.

The black sheets fall from my form and I wrap a fur around my shoulders. My bare feet grace the cold stone floor a moment later and I softly pad towards the window. When Neris, Mavis's general, brought me to my room early this morning, there wasn't much I could do but fall into the bed and let exhaustion guide my mind to sleep. Now, I can see how luxurious the room I've been placed in is, far too decadent for a prisoner. I walk to the door and attempt to open it. The knob jiggles, but stays locked in place.

With a frustrated groan, I trek the small journey towards one of the frost-paned windows, only for my hand to burn the moment it touches it. I yelp in shock, recognizing the overbearing power that coursed through me when I touched the glass—dark magic.

So much for not being a prisoner.

The door opens quietly, a woman I have yet to meet stepping in. My heart stops in my chest.

She's dead. She's supposed to be dead and yet she's here of all places. Tanja's chestnut curls are piled atop her head, highlighting her soft face. The gold of her skin should match her eyes, but rather than gold, they are a rich and deep brown. Sorrow pricks at my heart then turns to rage as Mavis steps in behind her.

The woman's eyes drop to her cloak that I left crumpled on the floor. "I thought a familiar face might help, however I couldn't get the eyes right. Purebloods are harder to replicate," Mavis croons, tangling a finger in a curl.

The woman smiles broadly and dips into a low curtsy, however the edges of her face begin to shift.

"Remove the glamour," I hiss, recognizing the ancient and rare magic Mavis is using. "How dare you desecrate her skin."

Mavis shrugs and the glamour drops, revealing a pale woman with flaming red hair and deep brown eyes. My chest physically hurts at the change and I clutch the fur closer to my body.

"Emi will be assisting you with whatever you need. She isn't a maid, so she might be lacking in some areas, however. All my servants are male and I figured you wouldn't be comfortable with that. Please excuse any of her discrepancies."

Emi crosses her arms over her ample bosom and throws her head back in a groan. A deep-seated scowl has etched itself across her otherwise pretty features. Gone is the twinkling smile that made my heart ache so. Cold sweeps through my limbs and I sit on the edge of my bed.

"I'll be back later," Mavis says, more to Emi than me. She tosses her crimson cape over her shoulder with extravagant flourish. The door slams behind her, leaving behind a heavy hollowness in the room.

Emi nods with a grunt towards a cushioned stool that sits

before a vanity. When I don't move, she roughly grabs my elbow and drags me there, all the while ignoring my protests. Her hands are rough as she sets to detangling my hair with a brush. I yelp as she snags one too many knots for this abuse to be accidental.

"I don't need a maid." I wince while using my fingers to knead my tender scalp.

"I'm not actually here to be your maid, but you're a smart girl, so I'm sure you've figured that out already." The sharp bite of her tone replaces any friendliness.

My blood boils beneath my skin as I think of how she wore Tanja's face only moments before. Where Tanja's playfulness hid kindness and her smile was genuine, Emi is cold and short. Each comment she makes is a thinly veiled insult.

"Well, you're a shit spy, so what are you really?"

"Just someone who owes Mavis a favor," she says, then throws a wad of clothing my way. "Put these on."

I find a thick pair of socks and roll the soft material over my cold feet first. I pull the leather pants and thick sweater on over these before shoving my feet into a sturdy pair of boots. I shift in the clothing, surprised to find how comfortable yet functional all the pieces are. If I have to plan an escape, I suppose at least now I know what I will wear.

Emi scoffs while I wiggle my toes in delight. The clothing still falls loosely from my shoulders, but they are warm and soft. More than that, they are clean, a luxury I haven't known in months.

"You were supposed to be the queen of this kingdom and yet here you are, wriggling like an insect over a pair of socks?" The girl's disgust is written across her face.

I maturely stick my tongue her way before flopping back onto the bed and curling up. With warmth in my bones, sleep calls for me again. I can feel my eyelids grow heavy when Emi rips me from my peace.

"Mavis expects you in the dark room," is all she says as she opens the door.

My lips part in shock when the door opens from the inside. "How'd you do that?" I ask, trailing close behind her.

"The door was enchanted to your blood. Anyone can open it from the inside."

"From the inside? What about the outside?"

"Only you and Mavis can open it from the outside. When you earn her trust or learn dark magic stronger than that on the door, you will be able to open it from the inside too."

Her steps are short, but I soon find myself falling behind as she scurries through the cavernous hallway. As we walk, the stone walls grow closer, the once-open space now hardly large enough for us to stand upright.

I duck as the top of my head scrapes the ceiling. "As if 'dark room' didn't sound ominous enough," I mutter.

The darkness grows around us and I find myself pressing closer to Emi. She scoffs and snaps her fingers. A whirring resounds in the hallways and suddenly, lights spark from the ceiling, lighting the torches.

"Don't walk too close unless you want to catch on fire." Emi speaks as if to a child, despite being many years younger than me. "Aren't you a mage? Make your own light."

"I can't. There's some sort of damper here," I respond, ignoring her slight. I can hardly feel the burning beneath my skin anymore. When I call or beg for release, it burns in my chest and steals my breath for a moment before sputtering and dying.

A door appears to our right and Emi sharply turns to open it without a response. The room is surprisingly well lit for something called the "dark room." The walls have been painted a deep red color and lined with a form of wood rather than raw-cut stone like all the other rooms I have been in this compound so far. I drag my fingers along the rough surface, a stray splinter snagging the pad of my index finger. I nurse the wound, popping it into my mouth while Emi stares on in disgust.

"Try to be cordial, Emi. She's a guest." Mavis appears from the shadows, not unlike how Kya often does. Something unsettling rises in my throat at the motion. It isn't hard to picture the two working together, teaching and learning with each other.

"What do you want?"

Mavis dips her chin. "Emi, leave."

I expect some form of snark or wit from the young girl, but she just bows shortly and walks from the room with the coordinated steps of a soldier.

Mavis returns her attention to me, her eyes painted dark with charcoal, her lips black to match. "I just wanted to get to know you better and give you the opportunity to ask any questions you may have." The woman snaps her fingers and a tea set forms before us. "Care for a biscuit?"

"I don't drink tea."

In an instant, the beverage turns a richer color, the steam from the cup wafting the sweet scent of chocolate to my olfactory senses.

"Molten chocolate, then?"

"I mean I don't drink with people who kidnap me from my friends and drag me naked through the woods." I fold my arms over my chest and bend at the waist. While I knew there was nothing much to look at anymore, the cold remembrance of those jeering gazes sends gooseflesh prickling over my skin.

Mavis runs a hand over her sleek braid, tugging a few silver strands loose. "Argon and those men have been dealt with accordingly. I apologize for their actions. They were sent by me, but do not speak for me." She speaks formally, her shoulders squared. Her etiquette is that of a noblewoman, not a mercenary.

Slowly, I take a sip from the cup before me. The rich liquid coats my tongue and I fold both my hands over the base of the mug, basking in its warmth. I allow myself another small sip. "You said I can ask you anything?"

"That is correct."

I know this should not be my first question, but I cannot help the gnawing jealousy in my gut. "Who broke off your engagement?"

"I did." Mavis smiles into her cup. "I stabbed him in the thigh and stole over half of his underlings as my own, then took the territory that was mine by birthright. I wanted full control of the Nightwalkers, but his inner circle—I think you've met them now —fought for him. They were the ones I was after. The gunslinger, the assassin, the mechanic. Each of them the best at what they do, I wanted them on my side. You can thank me for meeting Rowan that night, by the way. I'd been dropping false clues on where I was for months, and him being so hellbent on revenge, he fell right for it."

Kya was stabbed that night, I remember, all because Rowan was following her trail. I was cut and poisoned. I met Aiko and Finneas, too, that night, two people I haven't seen since my birthday. My stomach drops and I set the cup down with a clatter.

Mavis sips daintily. None of her lip stain transfers to the pristine cup. "How are they, by the way? I do miss them. Amír is the one who taught me how to shoot, and Kya taught me that fun party trick with the shadows. It does make the entrance more dramatic." Mavis throws her hand up with a flourish. "Derrín would run all his inventions by me, and oh! Emilie. Emilie was the mother I never got to have. I miss her the most."

I can feel my face growing hot as I stare into my lap. Mavis is only trying to get a reaction, I know this, but it is so easy to see her fitting in with them in all the ways I don't belong.

"I can see why they replaced me with you. You are everything they wished I was, and everything I am, too, but I'm guessing they try to ignore those parts."

The stool I sit on falls backwards with a heavy thud as I stand. Mavis crosses her ankles daintily. She looks so at ease sipping from a teacup despite being dressed in fighting leathers and undoubtedly armed to the teeth. I suppose that is what gives her comfort.

"What games are you playing?"

"I'm not playing any game."

I open my mouth to protest, but Mavis lifts a finger, effectively silencing me.

"As a show of good faith, allow me to answer your questions." The woman moves quicker than I've seen any other before. Quicker than everyone except one person—the person who taught her such stealth. Mavis's cape billows a midnight tide in her wake. It doesn't suit her as well as the red one did. She clasps her hands together before her and brings her face close to mine. "*Why am I here?* Because I want you to be. *Oh, but Mavis that isn't an answer.* Well, if you insist upon knowing, it is because I need you. *Need me for what?* To save us. *How?*" The woman pauses her charade and taps my nose fondly. "By teaching you dark magic."

My blood runs cold. *We need you. Save us.* Words that ring all too clear in my mind more often than I'd like to recall. Broken things torn from the throats of children who watched their parents be slaughtered in the night. Fathers who lost their children. Women who lost their lovers. Their homes. Their lives.

Dark magic is the cause of their suffering. The one I called Father is the guilty party behind all of this. I won't play into his hand and condemn my soul as well.

"No."

"Aw, cute that you think you have a choice. Your lessons start tomorrow."

I scoff. "Gods, you just like to hear yourself talk, don't you? I said no." I take a step back towards the door, feeling her piercing stare gutting through my spine. I ignore the foreboding feeling and close my fingers around the door handle. I swallow a whine of frustration when it refuses to open, then shriek when slithering dark flames begin to wrap around my arms, all the way to the base of my throat.

Mavis stands, her hands by her side and hips swaying. The steel toes of her boots clink against the floor, echoing in the barely furnished cavern. She pauses only a pace away. The powerful force intensifies, suppressing my senses and blurring my vision.

I fight the urge to fall to my knees as my legs begin to shake. "Why are you doing this?" I cry out, the tendrils of darkness flickering before my exposed flesh, though none dare to touch me.

Mavis watches curiously, her two-toned gaze cast heavily upon my face. "Because," she says, her voice barely above a whisper, "when I cut you, he bleeds."

The skeins of darkness rescind and slither towards the shadows where their master beckons. She watches my chest rise and fall rapidly, then flicks her wrist as if to say, *run along now.* Like I am but a child.

"As far as I am concerned," Mavis leaves me with a final warning, "you are the queen of this land. Learn to act like it."

The door squeaks, but opens this time when my hand closes around the handle. I turn back around briefly to see that Mavis sits with her legs crossed on that small stool, sipping from her cup. She smiles over the rim, her lips curling in a serpentine manner. I rush through, then close the door abruptly and press my back to the wall, tears pricking the corners of my eyes.

When I cut you, he bleeds.

Blaine told me when you find a Krycolian Viper, you shouldn't engage or turn your back. Your best chance at leaving alive is to either avoid or immobilize them. Don't let them cut or bite you. If you turn your back, they'll rip your throat out with their fangs.

I lace my fingers around my throat, feeling my pulse.

"What do I do if they attack first?" I asked him. "How do you survive?"

He pulled a flower from its roots then, and snapped the head from the stem.

"Bite first."

CHAPTER 9
ROWAN

Amír announces her return to our makeshift home base by tossing open the door and firing her pistol at the wall where we have pinned our map. The bullet lodges on the outskirts of an area marked in red, the exact location from which she and Derrín just returned.

"No shooting in the inn," Blaine snaps. He rubs at his temples with two fingers. His eyes are sunken in his head with fatigue, but clear and aware.

Mother places a steaming cup in front of him, which he gratefully accepts. She passes one to me as well, then offers one to Amír. The gunslinger shakes her head, but finds the cup pressed into her hands regardless.

"Nothing. We followed the blood trail and snapped twigs, but there's nothing. Either she's using a glamour spell or hired hunters to lead a fake trail."

"And who was the one who told you not to buy her that book of magic?" I note with a pointed glare.

Amír flips a vulgar gesture and holsters her pistol. "It was helpful before she stabbed you in the back."

"It was my thigh actually," I remind her, the scar suddenly smarting as if in remembrance.

"She should've gone a few inches higher," my second growls in frustration.

Blaine snorts and rocks his chair back on two legs. He flips a dagger between his fingers and aims for the portion of the wall right beside my head. I catch it between my middle and index finger, and raise an eyebrow. He only shrugs, as if he wouldn't care if he missed.

He's been sober since Vera disappeared a week ago. His headaches are common, and while Vera is gone, our rooms still smell of bile thanks to the former captain. Nevertheless, he hasn't touched a bottle.

"This isn't the time for jokes. This area isn't that large. Wherever they're keeping her is right under our nose." I slam my fist on the table, the old wood splintering and cracking throughout. Flecks of gold and silver line the splinters and I fall into the poorly cushioned chair behind me. It rocks as if debating if it should hold my weight, then steadies.

Mother lays a soft hand on my arm and brushes stray hairs from my eyes. "When did you last sleep, my Noiteron?" she murmurs. Her forehead crinkles in worry when I brush her hand away. We both know the answer to that question.

"I can't rest, not until she's back home."

"Mavis won't hurt her." Amír throws her head back against the wall. "She's more valuable to her alive than dead. She's all talk, anyway. She wouldn't hurt her."

"I wouldn't be so sure about that." Kya's voice is soft and unsteady as she enters the inn. Her golden skin has paled and unshed tears line her eyes. In her hands, she holds a small crimson box.

Blaine steps forward and gently takes it from her as her knees begin to buckle. Amír loops her arms around Kya's waist, holding her up with a soft curse. Blaine opens the lid. Before I can get there, he drops the box with a clatter.

A single finger falls out, the severed edges painted with dried, golden blood.

Blaine staggers back into the wall, rattling the ruined frames that are still hanging. He hits the ground retching. Derrín finds a bucket before the soldier's breakfast can splatter across our floor.

I kneel and brush my hand across the finger. It's cold and pale and undoubtedly Vera's.

"—owan. Rowan!"

Their voices blend as soft hands pull at my shoulders. The room spins. Edges blur into red.

These fingers which once laced through my own, touched my face, stitched wounds. She dared to sever it from such light.

Gentle fingers pry my own open and take Vera's finger from my hand. Mother's face pales and she quickly places it back in the box. I can see her internal fight and her struggle to hold back her building emotions to comfort mine. "Let it go, son," she says slowly. "You can't hold it if you want to save the rest of her." She places my hand over my own heart and holds it there, forcing me to breathe deeply.

The world slowly comes into focus, as does my rage.

My second's head snaps in my direction and her face pulls into a stern frown. "Don't do anything stupid."

"Was there a note?" I ask my assassin, who only shakes her head. With a growl of frustration, I start towards the door.

Blaine wipes his mouth with the back of his hand and stumbles to his feet.

Amír starts after us both. "Rowan, it's probably a trap. Mavis knows glamour magic. This might not even be Vera's finger. We need to think this through!"

"I am not willing to risk it."

The door closes in Amír's face before she can say anything else.

The message was clear. The longer I take to find them, the more parts Mavis will send until I do. If I don't find her soon, there might not be anything left of Vera to save.

"Wouldn't Mavis need Vera *alive*? She won't do anything that can kill her, right?" Blaine stumbles over a tree root before righting himself. He struggles but keeps pace with my quick walking.

I bite the inside of my cheek. "Not if she can't get anything from her. She would rather no one have her if she can't, and you know Vera."

Blaine swears. We both know Vera won't crack. She'll die first.

"Where have we yet to look?"

"The whole southern half, inner portion, and northeastern."

"Let's move inward then and cover the outer south tomorrow." Blaine's voice is commanding, and I oblige. We've grown accustomed now to staying armed at all times in case of an attack. Without Vera's magic, all we can do is slow the Kijova, but overall, we're powerless and defenseless in the face of their power.

I flip my dagger between my fingers and point it towards the inner southern portion of our boundaries. Blaine follows the pointed edge and we trek further into the mountains. We keep silent, even our breathing too loud as we await any ambush.

A scream rattles the trees moments later. Blaine rushes towards the sound, but I grab his arm in time and pull him behind a tree with me.

"It isn't her. Just her voice."

Moments later, a Kijova comes crashing through the brush, its jaw unhinged and snout in the air. It bares its teeth before screaming again. Months later, and the sound still wrenches my heart. The moment Tanja died immortalized in Vera's screams through them. I can see the gooseflesh prickling Blaine's arms. He inhales sharply.

Sometimes I forget he knew her too. Blaine, Torin, Tanja, and Vera. They knew each other for years, had helped each other to survive. Vera was his first love and all he has left. Now she's gone as well.

I wait a moment before the beast leaves before turning to him. "Are you okay?"

Blaine huffs, his hands on his knees. He fixes me with a strange stare. "Did you get hit on the head?"

"What?"

"You're not being an ass right now," he wheezes.

I focus on how disappointed Vera would be if I hit him to quell my rising annoyance.

"I'm fine, just..." He pauses momentarily. "When I was drinking, I never really heard it. Like, I heard it, but I never registered it was her. I hadn't realized that was the moment Tanja died. It's just hitting me now that Vera had to see that and be there when it happened."

Silence falls between us again as we continue onwards. Our breath crystallizes in front of us in short huffs, soon to dissipate into the crisp air. We follow any broken tracks we can find until we stumble into a small town that looks relatively untouched.

We pass an old tavern, the windows shattered and blood along the walls. There is every sign of a struggle and a fight, and yet something in off.

Blaine peers through the broken-down door into a home. "There's no bodies," he says softly. His boots crunch on broken glass behind me and he gasps.

Before I can turn to see what has happened, a cold blade is pressed to my throat and a low voice speaks from behind me. "Turn around slowly and show me your eyes," the voice growls. It is strained and yet familiar, though I do as it says. When I spin, I find a hooded figure, his face obscured by shadows. When he sees my face, he gasps and turns toward Blaine, who has now also turned, dagger to his throat.

"Rowan? Blaine?" he chokes. "Ruby, drop the blade."

Blaine and I look on in confusion until both hooded figures lower their weapons. The woman, Ruby, drops her hood, and I recognize her as Tanja's fiancée. Her once-beautiful face has been scarred by claw marks and she wears an eye patch, but there is no mistaking her.

"Who are you?"

The figure laughs, a strangled sound between a sob and a choke before lowering his hood. Torin grins ear to ear, that familiar loopy and boyish charm coating his weathered features. "You're alive," he breathes.

Blaine takes a tentative step forward, his eyes wide as if he's seen a ghost. Torin opens his arms for an embrace. Blaine stops a pace away, then whirls his fist into Torin's face.

Torin clutches at his jaw, laughing slightly sardonically. "Good to see you, too, old friend."

Tears stream down Blaine's face as he pulls Torin from the ground and crushes him in a hug. Torin's eyes squeeze shut as if he expected such a reaction and embraces him as well, as if nothing else matters to him.

"We thought you were dead, you bastard," Blaine hisses. "Five months. Five months!"

"I thought the same of you. We haven't found many survivors from the palace or the surrounding cities, so I assumed you'd either gotten out or died." When Blaine releases him, the man steps forward to briefly embrace me as well. "It's good to see you got out too."

Ruby steps forward, her eyes slightly hopeful. She fiddles with a sapphire ring identical to the one Tanja used to wear. "Has anyone seen her? Tanja? We haven't found her yet."

Blaine falters, and before he can even open his mouth, Ruby's face falls. Torin's gaze slides between the two of them. Only a choking sound leaves Blaine's lips as tears begin to slide down her face.

I place an arm around the woman's shoulders, stepping in for the former captain. He covers his mouth with the back of his hand and nods in thanks. Ruby's knees begin to buckle.

"I'm sorry," I whisper as she begins to break. "She was the first of Ophelus's victims. Verosa was there, so she will have to be the one to tell you, but she died a hero."

I don't dare tell the truth, that her fiancée's death was the reason for all this, that the screams of the Kijova that shatter the earth are actually the sound of her final moments. She died a hero to us, to Vera. To the world, she died a villain, no matter how pure her heart.

I hold her upright as her legs finally gave out, shattering sobs wracking her frame. Torin pinches his lips together and raises his hood. We can see his shaking shoulders, though we say nothing. Blaine clasps his hand in his. Something silent passes between them, and Torin nods.

"We need to go. We've been gone too long. It won't be long until they send out search parties looking for us."

"They? The other survivors?" I ask.

Torin's hood shakes. "The rebellion."

CHAPTER 10

ROWAN

Blaine and I pause for a moment, Ruby's quiet sobs fading into the background. Blaine raises his fist again and Torin dodges it this time.

"Let me explain!"

"There's nothing to explain, you bastard!" Blaine roars as his hands seek Torin's throat. "You're one of them? The ones that have tried to kill Vera since she was a baby? Who have killed hundreds of us? Do you forget Raiko and all the others so easily?"

If I wasn't the only thing holding Ruby up from falling, I would've gone in to separate them despite my growing rage. Instead, I watch as Blaine wraps his fist around Torin's throat, knocking his hood away from his tear-streaked face.

"Never." Torin's eyes blaze with fire. "But we thought you all were dead. We've been gathering survivors and placing a truce on our civil war to defeat Ophelus. We've been training an army."

Blaine pauses and releases his vice grip, though his hands stay on Torin's throat. "Explain."

The other man coughs, his voice strained. He turns to me, but Ruby speaks up.

"We've been looking for you."

I stumble. "Me?"

"News has gone around that Ophelus had a son, a hybrid. They plan on killing the king and replacing him with one of their own. You have a claim to the throne despite your cursed blood. They want you to take it and lead them."

"We have a cursed on the throne now and they still want to kill him. How am I different?"

"Ophelus enforced the prejudiced laws against the cursed to hide the true nature of his blood. His father secretly took on a cursed concubine, who had an affair with another one of the cursed. She fell pregnant with him, and once he was born and the former king realized he was fully cursed and not a hybrid, he killed the concubine. His wife had died and he was old with no heir, so he kept the nature of Ophelus's blood secret and named him his successor. They think you are the solution," Torin explains. A bruise has bloomed across his eye and brow bone, the whites of his eye now bloodshot. Blaine only looks slightly apologetic.

"And what of Vera?"

Torin falls silent, avoiding my eyes.

Ruby locks her eyes on mine and speaks solemnly. "They want her dead."

Blaine inhales sharply, then laughs, a dark and malicious thing. He runs his hand through his hair and Torin scrambles to respond.

"I—"

"I thought you were loyal, you dog." Blaine growls. "You're nothing better than those worms."

"I *am* loyal to her, and only her. We both are. She is my queen. I will serve her until my dying breath. We are only with the rebellion for survival and to convince them not to kill her."

Ruby pulls Torin out from under the former captain. "We have worked up to higher positions. Torin is practically second in command at this point. If we can get in their good books, we can form an alliance and not only stand a chance at killing Ophelus, but saving Vera."

"If she isn't dead already," Blaine spits at the both of them.

Torin pales and I snap my gaze to him. She isn't dead, she can't be. Blaine knows this, but that evil presence about him only grows as he watches Torin choke on another sob.

The Nevan man's hands begin to tremble as he clasps my knees. "She's not... She can't be."

"She isn't," I assure him.

"No, we are just being shipped pieces of her from Rowan's psycho ex."

"Blaine!"

"What?" Torin sways on his feet when he rises. His eyes form into steel and his knuckles whiten. "What has happened to Verosa." It isn't a question anymore, rather a command.

So I speak, explaining the kidnapping and our search, everything to receiving the finger and our search here.

Torin grits his teeth until his jaw pops. His muscles tense beneath his tunic and he listens intently until I stop speaking. "Ruby?" he finally says after a period of silence.

"Yes?"

"Go back and tell the others I will not be back for a while. Inform them of the location Rowan is about to give you. Tell them to meet us there. I will be going with Rowan and Blaine to find Vera."

"No, I am going with you. She's going to tell me about Tanja. Torin, I need to know."

"I will bring her to you eventually, but we need to make sure she is alive first." Then he adds under his breath, "Or there's no hope for any of us."

The woman waits a moment, inhaling deeply before shakily

exhaling. She nods and starts off the hill, kissing her ring and crossing two fingers over her heart. Blaine still shakes with rage, but allows the man to stay with us.

Torin silently picks up a long stick and begins to draw in the sand. He marks a circle and a few lines through certain areas when we tell him, then a few more where he has been. "We have occupied these territories in the south, so I can tell you she is not here. That leaves these areas. We can start here, then if she isn't found, I can deploy spies to search the other location. We have a few trusted members also working as double agents to find the rightful queen. One of them is your mother." He looks towards Blaine then.

The man's shoulders fall and he sighs in relief. I feel a twinge of jealousy and sorrow. He makes no note of Aiko and Finneas. I pause and wonder if I should ask, then think better of it as Ruby's face flashes in my mind. Sometimes it is better to have hope, even if it is false.

"Is she alright?" Blaine's voice is taut to match the fine lines of his face. Each motion of his is that of a calculating soldier—one who has seen death and did not run.

Torin nods, and he breathes a sigh of relief.

"Earlier, you asked to see our eyes. What was that about?" I ask, desperate to divert the attention away from the topic.

Torin glances over his shoulder as if expecting someone. "We've been finding survivors of Kijova attacks with some... interesting side effects."

"You're going to have to be more specific than that." I give him a sideways glance.

Torin runs his hand through his hair, flecks of dried blood streaking the strands. "They're blind. No pupils are generally the first sign. Trying to rip out your throat is the next."

Blaine grimaces. "Wonderful."

Torin nods in agreement. He looks years older, despite it only having been a few months. His bleached hair has grown out at the roots, revealing his natural darker color. "They can be killed, at least. We do our best to cut down their numbers, then give them a proper burial, but sometimes it is too overwhelming. The infection can be spread if you get wounded by them as well."

"So Ophelus can grow his army without having to do anything." I pinch my nose between two fingers. When did this all get so complicated?

Torin's face is grim, but no other words are shared as we begin our trek back into the forest.

The wood surrounding us grows thicker, the canopy above our head allowing even less of the sparse daylight through. We travel silently, listening for the sounds of our death.

Torin is the first to break the silence. "What do you think Mavis wants with her?"

"To use her, or to get to me. Or both. She renders me powerless while she has Vera, and Vera is the only one who can kill the Kijova. She makes Mavis the only one immune to this war."

"Stop talking like she's an object," Blaine growls under his breath.

My lips pull back in a snarl.

Torin places his hand on my shoulder. "It's getting dark. We can start again tomorrow with some more help."

The anger within my blood slowly subsides. The forest has grown darker and the silence is far too dangerous. Stepping on a single twig is as swift a death as any with the Kijova lingering around every corner.

Blaine grunts and leads the way back to town just as the first flake of snow begins to fall.

Torin and I lift our faces to the sky, the tiny crystals melting into our skin. Torin's face cracks into a wide smile and booming laugh. "Shit," he laughs drily. "Winter is here."

CHAPTER II
VEROSA

Snowflakes form a curtain outside my window, barring me from the small glimpse of the outside world that I am allowed. The flurries crystallize on my window. The smooth glass is cool to the touch.

I slowly work a brush through my hair and allow myself to gaze in the mirror. I've slowly put on more of my former weight. I am still far too thin and my bones visible through my skin, but my clothes do not fall from my shoulders anymore and I can sleep through the night.

A fire crackles in the corner of my room where Emi stoked it. She said nothing but a few thinly veiled insults before leaving me alone. I haven't seen Mavis in a week, and each time I questioned her whereabouts, I received the same answer: she's hunting.

A shiver works its way up my spine and I wrap my arms around myself. They never specified whether she was hunting beast or man. The former would be more surprising than the latter.

As if summoned by my thoughts, Mavis appears in the doorway. Her silver-streaked hair is coated in a thin layer of snow and ice. A halo for an ice queen.

I rise from the vanity, my brush clattering to the floor. Mavis's shoulders are squared as she tosses a glance over her shoulder. Two soldiers half carry, half drag a man behind them, his head lolling forward. Mavis drops a dagger and kicks it towards me, the iron blade skittering across the cool stone floors.

"What are you doing?" I hiss.

Mavis snaps and the soldiers drop the man. His clothes are tattered and his skin shares matching tears beneath the cloth. Golden-flecked blood gushes from the wounds—no, claw marks.

"Trying a new tactic." Her gaze drops to the man at her feet. Her features are aloof and unflinching. "Would you like to introduce yourself to the queen? No?"

"Mavis, he's dying."

The Nevan woman ignores me as I drop to my knees before him. Just before I can raise my flesh to my teeth and offer my blood, she speaks.

"I'll do it for you then. Verosa, meet the man who stole you from your parents."

My hand drops to my side and I stumble backwards onto my elbows. My parents. The one unanswered question I've been seeking the truth of. Are they alive? Are they in the kingdom? Are they looking for me?

Mavis watches with something like curiosity written across her features.

Conflict settles in my bones. He's dying. I should heal him. But I can't find it in myself to raise my limbs. They grow roots in the cracks of the stone floor and keep me there with them.

I find myself staring at the man's face. The man who stole my family, my chance at a happy life. His left eye is seated slightly lower on his face than the right, and the corners crinkle, even with his mouth firmly planted in terror. Laughter lines. His clothing is fine, deep purples and reds staining the velvet he wears, and his hands look soft. All the scars that lace him look years old—twenty years old.

Sorrow burns my throat. He's lived a life of luxury since kidnapping me.

Sensing the shift in the atmosphere, he attempts to bring himself to his knees, his blood-speckled hands clasping even as they press against the worst of his wounds. "Please, I thought of you every day of my life. I thought I was giving you a better life."

"Liar."

I am hardly aware I spoke the word until his face pales and he lowers his head.

"I was afraid," he pleads. "I was a coward. You knew the queen, you knew her. She was going to kill my girls, *please.*"

Of course Irene threatened him. That was just the type of thing she would do. The true strange thing of this ordeal is that he's still alive and she didn't kill him just to snip any loose threads. But he had met Irene. He knew just the woman he was handing my life to. He knew the torture and agony I would suffer at her hands. He knew and didn't care.

Mavis's face remains stoic as she surveys the scene. Her teeth capture her lower lip and she fakes a pout of pity.

Sympathy stirs within my heart, mingling with my anger at the sight. I knew the queen. I knew better than anyone what she had been capable of, what she had already done and what she was willing to do. Hardening my features, I set the dagger on the ground.

"Vera." Mavis's tone is stern, a teacher reprimanding her pupil.

Still, I scowl and raise my chin. "I won't kill him. He's dying—"

"Then save him! Don't you want to know who your parents

are?" The lights in the room flicker and Mavis kicks the back of his knees. "Speak."

I thought that there was nowhere further I could fall into my pit of misery. The Laei intend to prove me wrong, apparently, as the man opens his mouth with a whimper.

"Aiko and Finneas Iales."

Four words. Two names. That's all it takes for my final thread of restraint to snap. I've had my suspicions since Aiko mentioned having lost her daughter around my birthday. I'd have to be a fool not to have noticed the way I am a perfect blend of the two of them—my mother's dark hair, blue eyes, and round face, my father's freckles and soft mouth. Her wit and his heart—the two things that kept me alive those twenty years in the palace.

I hadn't let myself consider the notion, not since they were in the outer palace when the Kijova were released. Not since no one has heard anything from them and we've added their names to the list of the dead.

They died before knowing they had met me, their daughter.

With shaking hands and strangled sobs, I search for the dagger through a blurry gaze. My fingers wrap securely around the hilt and I feel its weight in my grip.

The man before me dips his head, accepting his fate. "Go on, child," he murmurs. "If this is all I can give you to atone for my sins, you shall have it."

I swallow thickly, my dry sobs slowly strangling me. Mavis watches intently as I lift the dagger from the ground and hold it above his head...

Then turn the blade around and bear it towards my chest.

Mavis shrieks, the most undignified she's allowed herself to be around me. Ripping something that looks suspiciously like a tongue from the pouch hanging at her waist, she raises a hand. The dagger dissolves right as it pierces my skin, leaving nothing but a trail of golden blood dripping down the front of my dress. A wave of dark power pulses through the room and Mavis pants. A silver strand of hair has fallen into her eyes and she spins on me with something like rage written across her face. She opens her hand and a new, smaller blade appears in it. In a deft movement, she reaches down towards the man and angles the knife to slice through the joint in his thumb. The blade sticks a moment before slicing through, and she lets his arm fall. It is as she tosses the severed digit at my feet that I notice he is dead.

"If you ever want to leave here, use it and escape." She speaks through labored breath and nods pointedly at the already cooling thumb. "He's already dead. No need to worry about offending the gods now."

A servant steps in, his face not nearly as shocked as it should be as he lifts the dead man under his arms and carries him out the door. I can hear Mavis tell him to bring the body somewhere I can't quite make out. I thank the Laei for that small mercy.

"You're a monster." I don't need to scream. I barely need to raise my voice above a whisper.

Mavis flinches. *Flinches.* "Maybe, but we become what we must to survive."

The door clicks closed quietly. She's gone in a breath.

I WAIT all night curled up in the corner of my room, my back pressed against the cold walls. As dawn breaches the sky, I hear the doorknob begin to jiggle, just as I expected it would.

Mavis eyes the severed thumb warily as she enters. A small spark of irritation lights her face but she doesn't look surprised by the outcome of yesterday's events.

Neris and Emi wait outside the door, but Mavis waves her hand and the slab of oak shuts in their faces. She groans wearily as she settles on the floor across from me, the thumb acting as the middle marker between us. Her knees pop as she crosses her legs and rests her elbows on her thighs, her face in her hands. "Why did you run away from home?" she asks suddenly. "I get the whole freedom thing, but you didn't need Rowan for that. You never needed to leave home anyway. You could have just killed your fiancé. I'm sure your knight lover would have done it if you'd asked. You could have even killed your father and assumed the throne so no one could make you marry again."

"I don't delight in killing," I spit.

Her lips quirk upwards. "No, but it's useful." Then her smile twists into something wicked. "Sometimes, the price of one life guarantees the safety of thousands. Just think of where we would be now if someone had killed those kings."

I open my mouth to retort, those memories still fresh in my mind when her choice of words sets my heart hammering in my chest.

Mavis leans forward, noticing the shift in my attention.

"What do you mean 'kings'?"

"I suppose you haven't heard..." She trails off, picking at an invisible speck of dirt under her nails. "Lucius killed his father and assumed the throne of Tesslari. I suppose I should have said king and emperor—my mistake."

Lucius murdered his father? Lucius is now emperor. We are no longer just fighting my father and a blind prince's monsters. We are facing the whole of the Tesslarian army.

"Why would he—"

"He and Rowan are quite similar, you know," she interrupts. "Ask me how. You know you want to know."

"How?" my throat traitorously croaks.

"Men only want one thing, Vera." Her crimson-stained lips tilt upwards in a wicked smile.

Heat stains my cheeks and I feel the urge rising to protect his honor, despite it being at my own expense. "Rowan and I haven't had sex. He'd never pressure me or be with me for that," I burst out.

Laei, please strike me down.

"*Power*, Verosa. I'm talking about power." She rises and stalks forward, her strides graceful and feline. "Sex is just an extension of that power. You can give it or they can take it, but either way, it gives them something over you. But sex isn't nearly a fraction of what power you hold. Owning you makes him the deadliest man alive."

"He doesn't own me."

"Sure, but what else could he need you for? Sentiment? Love?" She laughs, a cruel and sadistic thing. "Aren't you two only tied together by a deal that allows him to use you for his own revenge?"

"I used him too." I could have said anything else to redeem this situation. That was months ago, and things are different now. Anything other than the words that leave my mouth.

"How healthy," she croons.

I blow a stray hair from my face. My eyebrows knit together into a scowl as my glare settles on the woman before me. "And what of you? Why do *you* need me?"

"You're the only one who can save us, Verosa. I'm here to hone you into the weapon you were born to be."

"And before the world fell apart?"

"Men aren't the only ones who want power. Power is protection. I wasn't lying when I said having you makes one the most untouchable person alive." Mavis clicks her tongue, feigning disinterest. "At least I have been honest about my intentions from the start."

"I'm not a weapon."

Mavis crouches down to my level, her gaze searching my own with scrutinizing intensity. "No," she finally concludes with a wicked grin. "You are a woman."

"What?"

"An angry woman. That is as good as a weapon. You're using it as a shield right now. Isn't that stifling? Why don't you just let go? I can teach you how."

"I have my powers. I don't need dark magic. I'm not willing to pay that price," I bite back.

"And just how much, I wonder, would you be willing to pay to have your friend back?"

My throat constricts and I pause before the words leave my lips in a whisper. "I'd give anything."

This seems to be the answer Mavis wants because she smiles, her canines glinting in the light. She picks up the severed thumb and presses it into my palm. "Didn't your father promise to bring back the emperor's mother with dark magic? I wonder if that magic could be used for your sweet Tanja." Her hot breath caresses the outer shell of my ear, and a chill creeps up my spine.

I could bring her back.

In my dream, Lucius said that the spell did not work, that something had gone wrong. But I have what he doesn't—me.

I wrap my fingers around the bloodied base where the bone of the finger used to connect to the knuckle. The stiff edges scratch my skin and squish disgustingly. I bite back bile and focus on calling for my powers, only I reach further into my soul. I reach for those dark moments—Blaine screaming as he awoke, that night in the snow, Rowan leaving. Tanja's throat being slit.

Drip.

Blood slides from my palm where my fingernails have dug into my skin, the severed thumb no longer in my hand. It has been replaced with a dark flame that swirls and licks towards my blood. Each time it kisses my wound, a shiver of ecstasy rolls through my body so potent that my eyes roll back into my head. The shallow wound soon closes, but the flame remains.

I open my other palm, allowing the flame to leap to that hand.

Unlike my light, it does not wait for command, but jumps before I even think it. I realize with wonder that it is alive. It is alive and yields to me.

"It will last longer because it has fed on the blood from your cut. As a mage, you can sustain it longer without risking your mind."

Risking your mind.

The flame winks out immediately. A cold chill seeps into my bones and an emptiness settles in my stomach. I reach for that power again, but stop myself when I realize my hand is empty.

Images of my father absentmindedly pacing the throne room enters my head. His hollow eyes flashing as he lay me on that altar. Dark magic stole him from the kingdom, and stole a father from Rowan. A love from Emilie.

"Don't panic. The sacrifice pays the price for you. So long as you provide sufficient sacrifice, you will not be at risk of becoming... well..." She whistles and smirks. "I'm not crazy yet and I've been doing this shit for years."

Debatable, I think to myself as Mavis produces a stained pouch. She opens the sack to reveal eight other fingers—one thumb, one pinky, two rings, two indexes, and two middles. "For practice."

"Where's the ninth?" I swallow that sick feeling in my throat. It is soon replaced by that craving for the warmth the magic had filled me with. The pleasure.

Mavis only smiles.

CHAPTER 12
ROWAN

Kya sits on Amír's lap, her hair mused and dressed only in a robe she found in one of the closets. Amír's fingers trail up and down her lover's thigh, occasionally trailing too high, to which Kya nips at her ear. Derrín and my mother excused themselves at the beginning of our meeting to go gather some supplies.

I was reluctant at first to allow my mother to go on a supply raid, but Amír had been quick to remind me that she has now been trained in defense and weaponry—a gift from the lovers to my sanity.

"So last time, you went out and found a naïve woman and brought her home. Now, you've found a traitor and again brought him home." Amír rubs at her temples with her unoccupied hand. "I thought we talked about you bringing home strays?"

Torin flinches at the name *traitor*, his loyalty and pride at war.

Blaine advances, but Amír sets her gaze on him. *Don't start,* she seems to stay.

"Need I remind you it was *you* who found both Kya and Mavis? I'd say we are both collectors."

Amír picks at invisible dirt beneath her nails. "Perhaps." Her gaze narrows on Torin. "Speak."

"*Tch*, she always forgets who the leader is. We aren't interrogating you."

"I'd say Blaine already did that," Kya notes in response.

Torin inhales shakily and gingerly prods at his black eye. A blood vessel ruptured in it, leaving a harrowing red splotch painted across the white. His mouth opens and the full story pours out. The rebels finding them and offering them shelter. Being reunited with Blaine's mother. Secretly gathering intel from Seb, who has worked his way up to being Ophelus's second and is feeding him information. Then he turns to me, his eyes bright with new information. "Aiko and Finneas are alive. The rebels found them and they're bringing them to me. It'll be a few weeks of travel, but I thought you and Vera should know. I know you all are close."

My head swivels towards the door to find my mother's shaking hands dropping the supplies she and Derrín had found to the floor. She smiles widely and embraces Torin.

Amír rolls her eyes and murmurs under her breath. "So I guess we are just okay with him now?"

"Hush, love." Kya pecks her lips. "Don't sour it."

I step back towards the shadows, allowing them to cling to my skin and cover my trembling hands. *Alive.* They found them. Not their bodies. Not even their remains. *Them.* Alive. My eyes mist and I wipe at them with the back of my hand.

Blaine pats my shoulder gruffly. He says nothing.

My mother finally releases the Nevan man while Derrín settles silently into a chair in the corner of the room. He had stolen his twin's stealth to slip past during the emotional rush. The rickety seat groans beneath his weight. Torin's attention is dragged towards the sound and his eyes widen.

Blaine mumbles something under his breath. *Not again.*

Torin approaches the mechanic, his gaze lazily tracing his form. Derrín remains seated. He hardly notices he is being approached until Torin clears his throat.

"We haven't met yet. I'm Torin." His voice has lowered to a tenebrous growl I've yet to hear from the man, and Blaine rolls his eyes far back into his head.

Derrín looks the Nevan man up and down, before turning back and mumbling to himself, "Inadequate."

All the air seems to deflate from Torin's chest in one fell motion as shock registers on his face.

Across the room, Blaine startles us all by laughing.

Amír backs away from him slowly as he wipes an eye.

"This guy," Blaine chuckles to himself. "I like this guy."

"Don't take it personal." Kya pats Torin's arm sympathetically. "He doesn't like girls either."

"I don't like people," Derrín corroborates, not bothering to pick his gaze up from the mechanical device he's fiddling with.

Torin blushes to his ears and I clear my throat.

"What's going on with that thing?" I nod towards his invention.

Derrín perks up and lifts the creation into the light.

Kya leans forward and gently takes it from his hands. "And what does it do?"

"It's a communication device. Rowan and I have been testing it to see how far the distance range is for it to work. I managed to finish it before all this happened. I'm hoping with a few tweaks, it can reach anywhere within Krycolis. I just need to find a way to amplify its power."

"You could ask Vera when we get her back," Torin supplies. "*If* we get her back."

· · ·

"So what *is* our next plan? Mavis still has Vera, Torin is still with the rebels, and the Kijova are driving us further out. Someday, we will run out of land to run," Amír continues.

I furrow my brows. "What are you implying?"

"You know damn well what I'm implying," the gunslinger snaps. "That we stop acting like sitting ducks and do something about this. Mobilize somehow and take these fuckers down."

It only lasts a split second, but I can see the shift in Torin's gaze. He shoots me an apologetic look before turning back to my second. "That is what I've proposed to the rebels as well. They've agreed to work with the Nightwalkers to do such." He sucks in a sharp breath. "But only if Rowan agrees to be their leader and king."

Amír's gaze is serpentine. Her flaming hair frizzes and halos her face, her own living flame. With cold precision, she directs each word my way. "Interesting how you chose to leave that part out." She runs her tongue over her teeth as if tasting her rage. Not many possess the ability to make me uncomfortable, but it is a talent Amír has always possessed.

With one look, I shift in discomfort. "It wasn't important because I'm not going to do it. I'm not that type of leader."

"Bullshit. You're more than capable. You've led us for years."

I bristle and pick at an invisible piece of lint on my cloak. "This is different. I never wanted to be king. I don't have the training."

Amír lolls her head back and laughs, a dry, scratching sound that drags its nails down the wall. "Just say you are scared of becoming your father and get on with it."

"Amír!" Kya's shrill voice slices through the tension. Her face is a mask of shock and disgust at the gunslinger's implications. However, Amír's accusations aren't unfounded.

My hybrid nature allows me great advantages—the stealth, the strength, the cunning.

My blood boils in loathing.

It is not by my own merits that I have achieved anything, but the reaction of my mother's blood commingling with my father's within my veins. No matter the hours I work, the sweat I sweat, and blood I bleed, nothing I do will ever be a credit to myself. Deep down, I will always know it comes back to him.

The man who murders mindlessly, who stole not only my future, but Vera's and my mother's. He wholly stole the light from her.

Amír traces my gaze to my arms, to the first set of scars to lace my body—the ones I gave myself trying to claw my veins from my wrists when I was fourteen and learned what I was. And the truth of who *he* was.

"We can discuss this another time," my second concedes. "Right now, our priority is locating and retrieving Vera. Tomorrow, Kya and Blaine will take on our first quadrant, Derrín and I will take the third. Rowan, you will go with Torin and meet this rebel leader. I'm not saying you agree, just go feel it out."

"Absolutely not. Torin and I will take the fourth. I will see this leader once Vera is found."

"We could always go tomorrow night, all of us," Blaine interjects. "My mother is there. I should like to see her."

"Then it's settled." Amír extends her hand.

Kya gracefully takes it, color blooming in her soft cheeks. She allows the gunslinger's hand to rest comfortably on her hip, the two walking in step towards their room.

My mother smiles softly and squeezes my arm. "We will find her. I promise."

I allow myself a small smile and kiss the back of her hand. "I know we will."

It has never been a question in my mind whether or not we will find Vera. It is how much of her we will find. And that answer is what determines which part of Mavis I cut off first—and whether she will live to see the end of her torment.

CHAPTER 13

VEROSA

When Mavis returns a week later, I've long since exhausted my supply of sacrifices. She watches my hungry gaze dance between her face and the satchel she has hanging at her side.

"Don't spend it all at once," she purrs, tossing the blood-stained sack my way.

A small part of me recoils at the sight, though a greater desire calls for the power the horrible things within that bag will bring.

I pluck a thumb from the bag, my favorite sacrifice. They're large enough to last a while, but they feel normal in my hand. I've seen Mavis use a tongue. I don't think I could ever do that.

"Make an arrow," she commands.

She flicks a playing card in the air and I focus on forcing the darkness to take form. It bends to my will easily, and soon enough, a dark arrow impales the playing card just seconds later, the darkness piercing the dead center of the ace of hearts.

"Good girl."

Mavis's praise goes straight to my chest and wounded heart.

"Emi says you've been able to make a single sacrifice last for

89

over a day. Impressive. Mine only last one spell. I suppose that is the power of the pureblood."

In response, I conjure a small, dark snake that slithers around my neck. It leaps from the base of my throat and slinks towards Mavis before disappearing in a puff of smoke at her feet.

Her lips twist into a delightfully wicked grin and she beckons me forward. I smile and follow. Emi has been crooning about some reward Mavis has planned for us if I keep doing well in my training.

Training with Mavis is different from training with Rowan. Rowan hesitates. He holds back and pulls his punches as if scared he could hurt me. Mavis sees my strength and recognizes it. She doesn't hold back. She lets me fall and forces me to pick myself back up.

A pang of betrayal shoots through my gut. I miss Rowan daily, though never at night. These nights, I've been able to sleep, my body forcing me into a dreamless rest. The dark circles that used to permanently reside beneath my eyes have slowly dissipated, and my weight is slowly returning. I still have to wear children's clothing, as those made for women fall from my frame.

Despite sleeping and eating without throwing up, I haven't been able to gain back as much weight as I should have. It is as if something is stealing the nutrients from my blood the moment they enter my system.

Mavis's sultry voice draws me from my thoughts. "Neris will meet us in the living quarters. We figured it was time you saw the rest of our home."

"You trust me enough?"

"Neris trusts you, and if she does, so do I."

I can't help the beam that splits my face in two at the thought of someone trusting my capabilities for once. Trusting *me*. "You must respect her a lot."

"Of course I do. She's my second. She controls my soldiers and helps me run this place. If you can't trust your own people, who can you trust?"

The smile is immediately wiped from my face. "Right," I speak slowly. Darkness pools in the corners of my vision and panic licks at my heart.

Shut up, I silence the voices before they even start. *They trust me. I am one of them. They will come for me. I am only gathering information.*

"What will you do if Rowan comes for me?"

"*If?* Darling, I'm counting on him coming for you." Her gaze turns serpentine. "Do you think he won't?"

I feel the heat blooming in my cheeks and dip my head to hide my embarrassed blush. The last person I should confide my relationship troubles to is my lover's ex-fiancée. Still, my lips traitorously open and I amend my previous statement. "I'm sure he will. But what will you do when he does?"

"You'll have to find out. Now get ready." Mavis halts us before a wide set of engraved doors that resemble those that used to stand guard to our throne room. She spins on her heels to face me and tucks my cloak tighter around my shoulders, straightening the collar of my tunic. "There are many pieces at play, Vera. Just because I haven't made my move doesn't mean I don't have one."

"You two and your riddles," I grumble sourly.

Mavis barks a laugh before motioning to the guards who stand on either side of the door. They jut their chins downwards in respect and pull open the doors. I blink against the light that shines through before I hear it.

Laughter. Children's laughter. It comes from everywhere within the room. Some families walk hand in hand while other children roam freely on their own. There is music, food, and games throughout the large cavern.

Someone has strung candles around the room, the tiny flickering flames creating an ethereal glow along the walls. There's a ribbon tied to a pole in the center with some girls twirling around it in a strange dance I've never seen before. They giggle and place flower crowns on some of the boys present or dance around each other. The adults lounge in comfortable chairs and sip fine liquor or sample some pastries that have been laid out in baskets.

It reminds me of the village parties Blaine and I would sneak out to back when we were just kids trying to get away from Irene for a day. We'd sneak out at dawn and spend the day hiding from the guard, stealing baked goods from stands. He kept note of the names of the stalls we stole from and the owners would miraculously receive a large "donation" from an anonymous benefactor days later. I'd weave crowns like that for him and he'd retie the ribbons that kept falling from my fine hair.

Untouched. All of it remnants of a world I had forgotten could exist.

My eyes mist before I can stop myself, and I wipe at my face with the back of my hand. Mavis watches curiously before we are interrupted by a little girl tugging on the hem of my pants. She stares up at me with wide eyes before breaking into a toothy smile and dragging me back to her friends.

The girls speak so quickly I can't understand them, but soon, I am swarmed. I sit on my knees beside them while one braids my hair and another fiddles with my fingers, admiring the many scars that lace them.

"Pretty," she murmurs.

A little boy with green eyes like Rowan's plops a flower crown on my head. Buttercups, daisies, and orange lilies. I smile and pat his cheek, to which he blushes. They drag me to join a dance next, the beat foreign to my clumsy feet. They laugh as I bumble around, eventually inventing a new dance all together that is more hopping than dancing. I wave to a familiar face in the crowd and Emi hides behind Neris in embarrassment. The soldier laughs and mouths something I cannot hear over the roar of the music.

I haven't felt this light in months.

As the last song ends, I dizzily trip my way towards the two women I recognized. Neris has her fist digging into Emi's scalp affectionately, while the younger girl struggles to get away.

"Get off you oaf! I'll cut you!"

"Cute," Neris chuckles under Emi's furious gaze, as if she is nothing more than a kitten.

"I had no idea any of this was here," I huff between breaths. "It's beautiful."

"Of course you didn't know. We didn't tell you for a reason." Emi puts it plainly and rolls her eyes. Her gaze narrows in on a bag of blue candies in Neris's hands. "Those are for the children."

Neris brushes off the slight and extends the bag my way. "And adults. Try some 'Rosa."

I blush at the nickname and dig my hand into the bag, ignoring Emi's disgusted gaze. The simple taste of sugar explodes in my mouth the moment I pop one of the candies between my lips. My eyes widen and I eat a few more before laughing. It's so sweet, I fear my teeth may rot out.

"Your lips are blue," Mavis notes with an amused look as she approaches us.

I respond maturely by sticking my equally blue tongue out at her.

"Laei, your teeth too!"

My chest rises and falls heavily, but I feel light. If I wanted, I could run back into the dance circle and maybe learn the correct dance, or eat a few more candies and drink with the adults. My father, the Kijova, and Lucius all feel so far away. If only Rowan were here to...

Rowan. He's out there searching for me because I was kidnapped. These people are acting like my friends, but if I asked to leave, they would still tell me no. They're using me to hurt him.

I stumble and my smile falls. Sensing a shift in the

atmosphere, Mavis grips my elbow and leads me from the beautiful room without so much as a goodbye. She doesn't speak until we are back in my room and I settle for sitting at the edge of my bed.

"Out with it."

"If I asked to leave, you'd say no."

Mavis rolls her eyes. "Obviously."

My eyes water. Fake. It's all fake, just another ploy to use me. No one cares. My whole life, I've been viewed only as a weapon. A tool. A means to an end. Irene wanted me to compete with Emilie. Ophelus wanted me as a sacrifice. Rowan wanted me to kill Ophelus. Lucius wanted me as a trophy.

The only person who wanted me for me is dead.

Mavis watches my pinched face in her usual calculating way, and I resist the urge to drag my fingernails across her pretty face, to ruin her just as badly as I've been ruined.

"I'm heading out again in a few days." Mavis's voice is jarring enough to jolt me back into reality. "I want you to come with."

I raise an eyebrow in a calm façade. I pray to no particular god that she cannot hear the way my pulse races beneath my skin at the prospect of getting out from under this mountain. "Didn't you just say you wouldn't let me leave?"

"Only if you asked, but since I am the one asking you, I don't see an issue here."

"Why? What's your motive?"

"I just thought you'd like to get out of here." She shrugs so nonchalantly, as if she didn't nearly just read my mind. As if she isn't holding me prisoner.

My fists clench at my side.

She holds out her hand and I extend my own, only for her to grab ahold of my wrist and flip it so the underside is exposed. Before I can react, a sliver of darkness slices through her flesh, then my own. I scream and try to pull my arm back, but it only causes the magic to cut deeper. I can only watch in horror as my golden blood floats to mix with Mavis's own gold-flecked blood in the small space between us. The blood tethers us together before disappearing all together, leaving only two identical lacerations on our wrists.

"We leave in three days. This makes it so you won't be able to run away from me. Until I break that oath, you are tethered to me. You can go as far as I allow and stay as near as I want."

My stomach lurches to my throat and a dread settles in my bones. Mavis never intends to let me go. This is all for show, a display of power, a way to mark me as hers and to keep me tied to her. Even if the Nightwalkers found me, I couldn't leave. I'm trapped.

"You're a bitch," I seethe, frustrated tears pricking my eyes.

"Maybe. But don't forget I'm doing this because you're the answer. Anything I do to you is to save all of us. Don't you miss your life at all?"

My eyes burn at the question. For so long now, I've hated myself for loathing my life to the point where I forgot to love those around me. Those simple moments where Blaine was the only one capable of catching me when I ran. When Torin would flirt with the stable hands and Tanja would dig her elbow into his ribs. I miss our breakfasts we'd sneak before the rest of the castle was awake. Even through the lashings, the fear, and the pain, they were my constants. Now they're all gone. A shattered memory is all that remains and my filthy mind is the only one that gets to see it. They deserved so much more.

And yet I think back to sparring with Kya, trading insults over coffee with Amír, and watching Derrín work. The thrill of the chase back when Rowan wasn't afraid to knock me on my ass. Before he looked at me like I was glass that could shatter at any moment.

With a broken voice, I croak, "Do *you*?"

Mavis pauses. I swear I hear her whisper, "Always," under her breath before she closes the door with nothing but a soft click to remember her by.

I find myself curling up on my side, tucking my knees to my chest. The ghost of a breeze caresses my back, so soft that I check to make sure it is not a hand. It traces soothing shapes across my skin, and the sweet lull of sleep pulls me under.

CHAPTER 14
VEROSA

The snowstorm outside grows so intense that the stronghold is completely shut down. Mavis recalls all her scouts and sentries before the thick of it is upon us. Once the final men and women are through the doors, she bars all entrances and exits, windows and doors. Her dark power thrums in every crevice of the cavern. Even if anyone were to try to raise those doors, they would never be able to. Much like the magic surrounding my door, the handles and walls of any exit burn those with the intention of opening it. I've seen Neris lean on it and I've touched the handles and levers myself. They only burn when I try to leave.

The only advantage the thick blanket of snow provides is that my door now opens for me. Mavis locked all the weaponry away in an armory, the entrance sealed with the same dark magic that has kept me in my room these past few weeks. When I asked what she would do if there was a need for weapons, she just smiled and asked if I genuinely thought she would lock her people out of the armory. My cheeks burned with embarrassment and indignation as I read between the lines. Only I was barred from any form of weaponry.

However, with all dangers and exits locked away, Mavis felt it should be safe for me to freely wander the compound. I've taken full advantage of my newfound freedom, scouring every available room I can get to. Most of the doors have been locked or lead only to dead ends.

"Can we head back now? I already told you it's boring," the second stipulation of my freedom quips, her head lolling back with a groan. Emi's face drags with boredom as she trails behind me. For some reason, Mavis believes a scrawny fourteen-year-old —she finally confided in her age after my endless pestering—will be capable of stopping me if I decide to run away. I do not want to learn why she has such faith in Emi and choose to simply heed it as a warning.

"We can head back when you show me something interesting."

"Vera. It is cold, and I am tired. Dinner was hours ago and you've been forcing me to cart you around like a show pony. My feet hurt, my head hurts, my *brain* hurts," the teen drawls dramatically, laying an arm across her forehead.

Sighing, I allow her to lead me back to my room, apologizing on the way. She simply ignores me like she usually does. She is tired enough that as she closes my bedroom door, she doesn't notice my shoe sticking out the bottom, keeping it from shutting all the way. As soon as the coast is clear, I slip back out into the dimly lit halls. I cling to the shadows like Kya taught me. I know I won't be able to escape, but at least now I can find something interesting to occupy my time with.

As I walk, I survey the halls I pass through, noting my way home and which turns to take so I can slip back into my room, my little escapade unbeknownst to anyone else in the compound.

A small flicker of light draws my gaze skyward. There, I see a small candle in what looks like a window atop a steep stone wall. There. That is my target tonight.

I pop my hip out, resting my hands on either side as I survey the wall. The crags are jagged and some stones look loose, like if they were to bear any weight, they might crumble into dust entirely. The entire wall is ensconced in shadows, masking my trek but also myself, if I am to actually go through with this.

My eyes scan the rocky surface until I find a path. A few divots allow for a good route with crevices I can jam my fingers and toes into to grip the surface. Before I can talk myself out of it, I slip my fingers into the first crack and pull myself up. One foot remains on the floor while the second searches for a stronghold to rest on. Once it is found, I pull myself up further, the first foot now finding its home in a crevice on the rock face.

A thin sheen of sweat coats my forehead as I pull myself upwards, the muscles in my upper body straining against this obviously bad idea. My shoulders groan and pop in protest as I raise myself a few more inches, but I ignore the hot stretching sensation and focus on the small window at the top of the rock wall. Inside, a light flickers softly, casting a faint glow around the top of my trek. That may provide me with a bit more light, however, there comes the risk that someone will be able to see me.

Oh well, what are they going to do? Kidnap me again?

Only a few feet from the window, I push my fingertips into a jagged crack, the top portion of the digits straining and clinging to the rock even as it bites into my flesh. One of my feet slips and I hear my elbow pop as I hold myself up by one leg and my arms. Aching pain shoots from the joint and down to my shoulder. My muscles bark in pain from disuse.

I bet Kya could scale this wall in fifteen seconds flat.

I use the thought to drive energy into my worn limbs and jam my toes onto another stronghold. My fingers hiss with a slight sting as the stones scrape across the top of them, but I do not allow my body to stop moving. *Just don't stop moving.*

Slowly, the warm light at the top begins to grow until I can feel it across my face. My fingers hook over the lip of what feels like a small windowsill and I use the last of my strength to pull myself up and over the edge. My body moans in relief, invisible tension dispersing before ultimately disappearing from my body.

The room I have entered is small, and upon further inspection, I find it to be a study. A sturdy wooden desk sits in the dead center of the room, a rather inconvenient spot, I note, as I move around it. My finger traces along its worn edges, every ridge and splinter scraping against the pad. Sparsely decorated bookshelves line the walls, and much to my disappointment, they are filled with only droll documents and biographies. The brilliant glow that guided me up the stone wall comes from behind a barely ajar door and scatters across the threadbare rug that covers most of the stone floor.

I push the wooden door aside, and to my pleasant surprise, the hinges do not squeak. For as worn as the room appeared to be, it has been notably well kept. Stepping beyond the study, I stop in a hall much larger than the one I just exited.

Rows upon rows of books line the walls, the space between walls, and then the space between those shelves too. A winding staircase decorates the furthest corner of the room, leading up to what I can only hope is another room similar to this one. Ornate and plush rugs cover the polished floors, and if my feet weren't guiding me towards the nearest shelf, I think I might have laid down right there. My thumb brushes across the pristine and unbroken spine of the first book within my reach. Its teal cover is soft and decorated with the most intricate artwork I have ever seen. The one beside it is a deep crimson, the detail much the same.

I stare at the titles, all fiction and wondrously enticing. I glance over my shoulder to find myself alone. Surely it won't hurt if I borrow a few.

My hand reaches out of its own accord and my fingers wrap around a thicker novel, this cover made of leather and etched with an exquisite gold font. The first page promises tales of love, magic, pirates, and monsters. I tuck the book beneath my arm and continue to peruse the shelves, picking up about four more books of similar content before I find myself standing before that elegant staircase.

I grip my newfound treasures with one hand while the other goes to the railing. The steps creak slightly as I walk, but I pay them no mind, far too enraptured by the thrill of what may lay at the top of the staircase.

The room above exceeds my wildest expectations.

I knew that Mavis's compound is etched into the side of a mountain, but I suppose I always figured we were at the base of the mountain, not the tip. My eyes are met with twinkling stars as I stare directly at the glass ceiling, the moon boasting a full figure tonight. The steady snowfall obscures my sight only slightly, the fresh mountain wind blowing most of it away from my window to the outside world. Tears prick at the corners of my eyes. When was the last time I saw the stars?

Like an invisible weight has been lifted from my chest, I breathe deeply, then exhale and breathe in once more. I had almost forgotten how beautiful the world could be, trapped in dank caverns, no matter how luxurious the compound actually is.

The viewing room I have found myself in is no less ornately decorated or stunning. Hand-painted wallpaper lines the walls with large, green plants spiraling up the support beams towards the sunlight promised by the glass ceiling. Tiny purple and white flowers bloom from them, standing stark in contrast to the snow-storm raging outside. Four plush chairs, all jewel-toned and velvet, sit in a semi-circle in a corner near an ornate fireplace that flickers with golden flame. I find my feet moving towards the largest chair, curling my knees up the side, and resting my head on the arm of the chair as I open one of the books.

MY EYES ARE bleary as I flip to the next page. The first book is exactly as promised—pirates, monsters, love, and magic—and yet I turn the final page unsatisfied. So I start into the second book, hardly noticing how the moon has long since disappeared from the sky.

The second novel is a quicker read, the plot promising and the love interest charming. Before long, I flip to one of the last chapters, though my finger stills on the page.

I need you.

The words mark the page with promise and heat, and I feel my cheeks warm. A small voice in my head warns me to close the book or skip this chapter, especially as my eyes skim lower on the page, only to find toe-curling sin. Irene would have burned a book like this before she would allow me to read it. The thought makes me turn to the next page.

His lips are on her, tracing from her jaw to the slender column of her neck. Her voice is low and heady, his own equally thick with desire as he whispers her name against her skin.

His name is a forgotten prayer upon her lips as he trails lower, daring to pull the neckline of her dress even lower still. Every touch is electric and sends a pleasant ache through her core. Heat spreads between her thighs and she clenches them together, desperate to hide the evidence of her desire even as his presses against her thigh.

Then his mouth closes over her aching breast, the slightest flick of his tongue causing her back to arch off the bookshelves. He worships her with teeth and tongue, showing equal affection to the other.

She stiffens. This is improper for a lady of her title—any lady, really. And yet, she mentally begs him to continue.

"Anyone could walk in," she warns, pushing against his shoulders.

A low rumble of a laugh is all she receives in response against her skin. She doesn't need to bite back the whimper the action elicits, he can already tell the effect his actions have on her.

"All they will see is me worshipping you like a fucking goddess." His voice is low, smooth, and so goddamn filthy. It shouldn't excite her, it shouldn't make her feel anything. And yet as he pulls the top of her dress back up to conceal his handiwork, she can't help but feel disappointment.

My own legs press together as my body's reactions mimic her own. My eyes pinch shut for a moment as I try to steady my uneven breathing. I've felt like this before, generally while with Blaine or other passing flames, but never this intense, and sure as hell never from a book.

I turn the page, my fingers tracing the filthy words as I read. "Gods, not the bookshelves!" I gasp as I flip the page. The books surrounding me stand colorful in my peripheral, or it might be the blush that coats my face.

I hadn't known there to be so many words to describe the *length* of a man, nor for them to be so... creative. At some points, I have to bite back a laugh at the colorful descriptions. The character in the book is all but laughing as he rams into her repeatedly, his name drawn out from her lips as a cry.

I squeeze my eyes shut. In the book, they haven't been together that long, maybe a few chapters at most. How long would that be in real life? A few days? The characters seem so familiar, so willing and in love or lust that it doesn't matter the time. Is that how it should be?

Rowan and I have gone further in the past few months, though mainly we just kiss... fully clothed. There have been times his lips have trailed lower, though never beyond my navel. And he has seen me naked, of course, only when I vomit all over myself after a nightmare. Is that why we haven't gone further? I know Rowan told me he would wait for me, and he does every day, but some dark corner of my brain begs to know if it is truly because he doesn't think I'm ready, or if he thinks what my body has become is simply too repulsive.

Still, I allow myself to fantasize. What if we were back in the palace, sequestered in our usual corner of the library? What if he closed whatever book he had in his hand that day and crossed the distance between us? He'd lead me back into the darker corner, his breath a worshipping prayer across my neck before those lips trailed lower and—

"That's a good one."

My eyes shoot open at Neris's low chuckle that rumbles through the room. The book falls from my lap, my motions and reflexes sluggish. I scramble to recover the damning text only to fall from the plush chair, my legs long since having fallen asleep from hours of disuse.

Neris deftly picks the book up and dangles it by its spine before my face. "You know, if you are truly this... frustrated, plenty of the women here would be willing to take you, if you swing that way, that is. I doubt Mavis would allow any of the men to touch you, nor is your lover boy showing up any time soon."

I ignore the sting of her last few words and shake my head. Neris pokes my shoulder and smirks teasingly before helping me to my still-shaky legs. I fight the urge to fan my face and mentally pray to Deungrid to just end me now. Heat floods my cheeks and I refuse to meet her gaze. How long had she been standing there?

"Well, this is dreadfully embarrassing," I finally admit, tucking my chin to my shoulder in an attempt to hide my flushed face.

Neris only sets the books down and takes a seat on another one of the plush chairs and props her feet up on an ottoman. "Nothing to be embarrassed about. We are all adults, and besides, I already told you it was a good book, implying I also have read it. There, we both have sinned. That cancels all the embarrassment out," the woman says kindly in a tone much like one Torin would use. "I was going to ask why Emi wouldn't take you here, but your taste seems to be a bit old for the kid."

And I am blushing again. "I'll have you know this is my first time."

"Ooh, talk dirty to me."

Despite my blush and previous embarrassment, a loud laugh slips out from between my lips. It grows as the deliriousness seeps into my bones and mind. Gods, I truly am awful, and I honestly don't feel all that bad about it.

Neris chuckles behind her hand. She looks so small without her armor, sitting in the large chair. Or at least until she rolls up the sleeve of her tunic to reveal powerful forearms taut with corded muscle. Scars lace across her limbs, proof of years of struggle and turf wars.

Desperate for a change of subject, I lean back to stretch my spine. "So," I hum with a small groan. "Is there a reason you've interrupted my reading or is this just a pleasant visit?"

Mavis's general snorts. "Look up, princess."

My eyes trail to where her finger points at the glass ceiling, only to see the end of dawn's reign across the sky.

I gasp and whirl to face her. "I stayed up all night?"

"And scared the shit out of everyone," Neris adds.

I hadn't meant to stay up all night. I just needed a moment to unwind, and maybe do something that took me away from this gods-awful situation. Now that she mentions the passing time, my bones begin to ache for sleep and my eyelids droop right as my stomach decides to rumble.

Neris scoops my stack of books into one of her arms, then extends the other to me. "Breakfast is ready in the mess hall. You can take a nap afterwards. We can stop and leave these," she lifts the arm holding my books, "in your room. You might need these later."

CHAPTER 15

VEROSA

Neris piles a few other books into her arms before we leave the library, then shows me the way to the stairs. In case I want to come back without having to scale a wall, she jokes. Once we stop to dump the books on my bed and to allow me to change into new clothes, we begin our short trek to the mess hall. Mavis insists we all eat together now that she can trust me not to try and use magic on her soldiers. Not only is trust a factor, but I suppose the further knowledge she has on my magic now helps. Emi confided that there was a fear I could seduce her male soldiers into fighting for me using magic. I reminded her if I could do that, then Mavis's men wouldn't have been able to drag me here in the first place.

A few of the other occupants of the compound nod as we pass by, almost everyone bowing to the general, but some now acknowledge my existence as well. It would appear that they no longer fear me like they used to. Though I know the gesture is a far cry from acceptance, I still choose to dip my head in respect as we pass.

The action sparks a flicker of surprise on Neris's features, but she quickly schools them into a more amicable smile and we continue on with our pleasantries.

The mess hall is bustling with life and laughter by the time we enter, no signs of the turmoil Neris swears I caused by disappearing. I suppose word only got out to Mavis's best to track me down—her best being the general by my side, of course. The woman extends a tanned hand towards where I am to sit, even going as far as pulling the chair out for me. Emi sits to my left, Neris to my right. A few other faces I don't recognize sit across from me, the head of the table still remaining vacant. Mavis has yet to show.

A kind and round-faced woman sets a plate before me, offering the smallest of smiles as she departs. The dish is piled high with eggs, some thick piece of meat, and some fruit that I know wasn't naturally grown in this frigid winter. I stab the meat with the fork provided once I see everyone has dug in and is not waiting for their leader to arrive. It is too large to bite from, so I attempt to slice it with the fork, only to fail miserably.

A quick glance around the room shows that everyone has a knife—everyone except for me.

"Can I borrow your knife?" I try and nudge Neris's side, spearing the tough meat with my fork for emphasis.

Neris raises a single eyebrow and tightens her grip on the blade. "Can I trust you not to stab anyone with it?"

"Yes."

"Honestly?"

"No." I slink lower in my chair.

Neris barks out a laugh while Emi lets out a droll sigh. The general slides my plate towards herself using a fork, creating a gods-awful screeching sound that reverberates through the room. She slices my breakfast into thin ribbons before handing it back with a wink. I roll my eyes but accept it, nonetheless.

I take a bite of the savory meat. Its rich flavor coats my tongue and some of the juice drips down my chin. I swallow a moan with the bite, determined not to make a greater spectacle of myself. Some of the knights stifle their laughter as I'm sure my eyes have all but rolled into the back of my head. I'm usually not even a major fan of meat, but it has been so long since I've had anything this delicious. Not even in the palace did the food taste this good.

The taste turns to ash in my mouth as Mavis walks through the door with a small smile. The sight shouldn't send shivers down my spine, but it does. When Mavis smiles, someone either has died already or they are about to.

Silence envelopes the room within a breath of her entrance. With the prowl of an apex predator, she stalks towards the empty seat next to Neris's and pulls it back, the wooden legs not daring to make a sound against the stone floor. Even inanimate objects fear her presence, I note, with only a tinge of sarcasm in my internal monologue. That voice in my head has been witty and sharp recently, and the last thing I need is for my internal voice to become external and get me killed.

The mercenary pulls a crimson napkin out from under her plate and walks over to gently dab the mess I've made of my face. Her hand stills over my lips, a teasing glint in her eye. "The food is to your liking, pureblood?"

"You ask as if it wasn't already obvious."

"I want to please you. If it isn't to your liking, then I'll need to chop the chef's hands off, and that would make an unfortunate mess of the kitchen."

I flinch, but no one else seems to react to what she says. If anything, I think I hear someone laughing at the other end of the table. "You're sick."

"We've covered that already," Mavis replies smoothly, lowering her hand and retreating to her seat. She locks her gaze on mine, her hand reaching for her crystal glass. She takes a long sip, rolling the flavor over her tongue, all while staring at me over the lip of the cup. Her gaze softens to my glare and she breaks the stare to address the room. "Good gods, who died?" she barks out before digging into her own meal.

I'm not sure how that is supposed to be funny, but the whole room erupts with laughter, chasing away the silence that had thickened the air. The atmosphere feels almost familial, like what I imagine dinner in the knights' quarters to feel like. They always seemed so tightly knit. A sudden pang pierces my heart as I wonder what happened to them. To Seb and Torin, or that young healer who healed Blaine against the king's wishes the day of his duel. Are they nothing but casualty statistics now?

As if noticing the shift in my demeanor, Neris clears her throat and places her hand on my thigh. I jolt but stop when I feel the cold steel through my pants.

I pick up the knife with reverential hands. It is a thin and intricately carved dagger—not a dinner knife, but a real knife.

"Just don't stab anyone, please," she whispers with forced weariness.

Unable to help myself, I laugh, the intruding sound forcing its way through my lips as I accept the blade. "You're a horrible kidnapper."

"Smutty books, pretty daggers. We do it all here," she offers with a wink before turning back to her own breakfast.

Mavis quirks an eyebrow upwards with a sly smile but says nothing. The atmosphere returns to its previous joviality, and I feel the tightness in my chest subside just a bit.

"I can't believe you snuck out. Do you know how much trouble I'm in?" Emi protests loudly, drawing out her ire as she stabs at her breakfast.

A few of the seasoned soldiers and other people at the table chuckle under their breath.

Mavis clicks her tongue. "Not enough trouble if you're still whining."

"What's your punishment?" I ask with a shiver. The feeling of

Argon's severed hand releasing my arm on my first night here comes to mind. A quick once-over reveals that Emi still has all of her limbs and other extremities. Relief washes over me, strong enough that my shoulders slump over.

"Kitchen duty for a week!" She falls back against her chair with dramatic flair. Her freckled face flushes as she throws herself down.

"Enough of the dramatics." Mavis rubs her temple with her thumb and forefinger.

"When I snuck past the royal guard, Blaine used to make them run laps around the palace with their swords raised. They weren't allowed to stop or lower them until he said so."

Mavis's lips peel back wickedly at the same time that Emi shudders. "I like him," the mercenary purrs.

Something about the seemingly simple statement doesn't sit right in my bones. I set my cutlery down, the metal utensils suddenly feeling too heavy in my hand, my breakfast sitting like stone in my stomach.

"The snow has mostly cleared." Neris changes the subject quickly at the dip in my mood. "We should be able to head out in a few days."

Mavis nods, her gaze never leaving my face. "Yes, good."

"You haven't introduced us to the new pet yet," a voice calls from the other end of the table. Cheers of agreement ring out, some going as far as to bang their fists on the furniture. My glass rattles and nearly tips over, Emi catching it just in time. She looks over at Mavis to see if the mercenary noticed her quick reflexes, but the woman's eyes are narrowed on the source of the voices.

"I see no need. I don't like to share," she replies. A deadly edge rests in her voice, the same lethal precision used in each flick of her tongue or toss of a dagger. Her tone is clipped and sharp, daring any opposer to face down the blade.

Silence greets the hall again as we finish our meals. My hand shakes as my fingers wrap around the cutlery.

"Your wrists are so thin," Emi comments as if noticing for the first time.

I pull the thick sleeves of my sweater down and Neris shoots her a disapproving glare. She is right though. I sleep through the night now, my nightmares having ceased as quickly as they came and rarely plaguing my nights anymore. I have been eating food comparable to that served in the palace. Some days, I believe it may taste even better. Best of all, I've been able to keep all the food in my stomach after most meals. I have not missed the burn of my throat after retching until my chest heaves and my teeth feel soft. Nor do I miss the jog of shame to the bucket or toilet as I feel food rising in my throat just as quickly as it went down.

And yet I haven't gained much of my weight back. If Kya were here, she would remind me that any growth comes slowly, even that which seems easy to achieve, and yet I know I should have been at least a few pounds heavier than this by now.

Mavis has not withheld medics from my room, and yet each of them has said the same thing—rest, eat plenty and often, and give it time.

I've given time long enough and gotten nothing from it. I am still skinny and frail and have taken to covering mirrors when they are not in use. I walked by once and nearly screamed in shock. I thought I was a specter, come to haunt me for my sins. Sure, I'd seen myself in rippling reflections of ponds and rivers, but they cannot capture the crystal clarity of a mirror—each of my flaws and jutting bones grossly detailed in the reflection.

I push my chair back and excuse myself softly. My slippered feet hardly make a sound on the rough stone as I slip into my room silently. I hang my clothes back up where I found them before slipping into a soft nightgown. The silky fabric is semi-sheer and falls to my ankles, whispering about as I move across the room. The dress drapes across my body with a sultry flourish and I sit on my stool. After dipping my hands into a basin of cool water, I lift them to my face, massaging the water in circles, wiping away any remainder of breakfast or the night before. Once satisfied in my cleanliness, I slink back to my bed, slipping between the sheets and picking up the book that rests closest to me. The lavender cover is soft and I flip to page one, snuggling into the blankets and soft pillows.

I breathe a laugh along with the characters, allowing their story to take me away from my own. I think if I could live within these pages, everything would be simpler. Life would make sense and there would be a happy ending for everyone. I hum softly. Nothing but a silly dream, I know.

I don't blush at the romance this time, already desensitized to the filthy words. Somewhere along the lines, the characters shift into my friends. Rowan's face forms that Cheshire grin within the pages, and a low shiver cascades down my spine. I snuggle in closer to the blankets, letting the fluffy duvet brush against my chin. The warmth is so inviting, and the pillows so comfortable, I allow the book to lay open on my chest and my eyes to flutter shut. I dream of fantastical worlds where the conflict seems so much more manageable. I make all the right decisions and play hero. Stories meant only to exist in dreams before the blade of reality severs all ties.

CHAPTER 16
ROWAN

Blaine is sitting in one of the spare rooms of the inn when I find him. My mother sits across from him, one ankle draped over the other. She seems to be doing better since Torin told us that Aiko and Finneas are alive. Her movements are fluid again, like she is doing everything intentionally, no longer stiff, forcing herself just to breathe. The same could be said for Blaine. The relief of knowing both his mother and Torin are alive has taken a few years off his face and demeanor.

I suppose they are doing the only thing we all can be doing—surviving day by day and praying for the next scrap of hope when the first runs out.

Blaine dips his chin in acknowledgment and my mother rises to leave the room. She pats my shoulder as she passes and gives me a smile that says, *go easy on him.*

My smile answers. *I'll try.*

Blaine looks up as I settle down next to him. He is flipping a dagger between his fingers, the weapon looking rather small in the hands I'm used to seeing wield a sword.

I clear my throat. "You ready?"

He shudders in response. "Is it wrong to say no?" He elaborates when I remain silent. "I haven't seen my mother in six months. She's probably angry. I ruined her life and then ran."

Even hunched over and in his smallest form, Blaine's figure imposes on the room. He looks so foolish sitting on such a small stool, even though it would look normal if anyone else were sitting on it.

I hesitate before clasping his shoulder. "The world is ending. I think all is forgiven."

Blaine doesn't need flowery words or false promises. He needs the truth, and for perhaps for the first time in his life, someone is willing to give it to him.

His brows pinch and his lips form a hard line. He huffs softly but doesn't shrug my hand off. "That is certainly one perspective." Then he offers a half smile. "Thanks."

His sincerity is uncharted territory and I find myself shifting uncomfortably. I lower my hand from his shoulder to scratch at the back of my neck. "Yeah, don't worry about it."

"You two done with your bromance yet? We've got shit to do," Amír shouts through the thin walls. Seconds later, her boot all but shatters through the already worn-down door. She glares at the dilapidated wood like it insulted her first.

"We don't even get a hello these days."

"And you don't even have a concept of time these days. Off your ass and let's go," my second snips back in response. Her withering glare almost has me lurching to my feet, but I sit a second longer, basking in her ire with a smug grin. I finally rise when she fiddles with the holster that hangs at her hip. I have a feeling that Amír would have no qualms in helping me find religion if I test her patience any longer today.

"Maybe you should be the one going to talk to this rebellion leader. Clearly, you have no respect for authority, especially not mine."

Her gaze hardens and she all but hisses at me. "I respect authority."

"When it's your own," I say with a sardonic grin.

She tries to swat at my hand when I flick her forehead in passing, but Kya holds her hands down. Blaine snorts and is left scurrying to my side when the gunslinger flips her pistol from its holster.

I find Derrín and my mother standing in the kitchen. Her hands are shaking as she chops something, her face deathly pale.

I'm by her side in three paces, gently taking the blade from her grasp and setting it aside. "Careful, you'll hurt yourself."

I await the joke back that she is more than capable, that the knife should be more afraid of her, but I get nothing. She has that far-off look in her eye again, the one she had for ten years before Vera came into our lives.

Panic grips my heart and I grasp her shoulders. "What's wrong? Are you sick?"

She shakes her head. "Another box came," she croaks, her voice barely above a whisper.

Derrín is the one who steps forward with the package. His face a perfect mask of stone.

Anger lights in my chest. They weren't going to tell me until after the meeting. They wanted me to go, and knew I wouldn't if I saw whatever horrors this box contains.

"Show me," I bark.

Derrín stiffens, but lifts the lid regardless. My mother falls heavily into a chair and closes her eyes.

Four perfectly white teeth rattle around the center, their roots bloody and flecked with bits of pink gum. They stay tied together by a clump of black hair, gory skin still attached. Five fingernails lay littered amongst it all.

I'm not a good person. I have never claimed to be one. I have killed and tortured countless faces that I hardly remember anymore. A good man remembers the face of the life he took. For me, it is all a blur. But I know how to make someone hurt so it is swift or prolonged. How to meticulously cut the human body so it bleeds but breathes.

The finger was short-lived pain. She will miss it the rest of her life, but a large amount of the pain would have been gone in a few moments. The fingernails, teeth, and hair?

This was a methodical torture.

The rest of the Nightwalkers enter the room to the sound of the table splitting as I ram my fist into the worn wood. It splinters into my palm and drops of my blood splatter across her severed parts.

Blaine steps forward, swearing. His face has gone red as he reaches for the sword that hangs at his hip, but Kya stops him. She whispers something through gritted teeth. Anger. They're all angry. Verosa is one of us, and if Mavis is going to fuck with one of us, she is going to have all of us breaking down her door.

"We aren't going tonight. We are searching. We don't stop searching until we find her."

I expect them to argue, for Amír to call me a shit leader and throw this in my face. She stays silent.

It is Derrín who steps forward. With one look, he has the rest of them silently filing out, my mother in tow. He closes the box and puts it in a corner with the container that holds Vera's thumb. It is slowly beginning to rot and smell, but I don't know what to do with it.

What do you do when your love's body parts are being shipped to you one by one?

For now, we've elected to save them. Just in case...

Just in case we need something to bury.

In case it is all we have left.

Derrín sits beside me, his knees bumping against mine.

"What's it like to love someone?" he asks suddenly. "Romantically, I mean."

I jump but he says nothing else. He only sits, silently waiting for some answer. Derrín has never liked the unknown, and I suppose this is uncharted territory for him.

"It's like burning. Being close to them hurts and yet even when you're touching, you want to be closer than that. You want to be the air they breathe, their everything. You want to give them everything you can just for the off-chance of seeing them smile. It's all-consuming. And when they're in pain..." The image of her finger cold in my hand, her teeth and nails... I clench my fist. "It's like dying. And you would do anything, *give* anything, to take that pain away. To bear it yourself."

Derrín runs his tongue over his teeth, mulling over and tasting his response. His face pinches like it does when he is working on one of his projects. "So it is the same then. You forget I've loved two sisters and watched one die."

We don't really talk about Natara. Anytime we do, Derrín freezes and Kya gets this faraway look like she is still in that moment. Amír generally ushers her away somewhere and fixes us with a glare. She shot at me the first time Kya started crying. I haven't seen either of the twins cry about her since, and yet Derrín's eyes begin to water.

"The pain of love is the same, but the burning is a bit different. I don't know how else to explain it." I cringe at my broken words. How am I supposed to nicely say you'd never want to fuck your sister?

Derrín raises his hands in defense. "No need. I get a clear picture every time my sister and Amír are in the same room."

I wince, the image of my second and my assassin fresh in my mind. I made the mistake when we first went on the run to not announce my presence before entering their tent. I do suppose that one is my fault, however the mental scarring remains. Kya isn't even my sister and that image makes me feel a bit ill.

"I still don't know how that doesn't bother you."

Derrín shrugs. "She's my sister. I want her to be happy. If her idea of happiness is having Amír's tongue down her throat twenty-four-seven, then who am I to complain?" He fiddles with his newly wrapped fingertips. "She's lost a lot to love too. It's nice to see someone willing to remind her of the good parts. Even if that person is Amír."

I wonder if that is how Blaine feels about Vera now. If it is enough for him to see her be loved by someone, even if she will never accept him again? The unwanted twang of sympathy pulls at my heart and I push the thought to the back of my mind.

My fingers splay across the broken table. The splinters bite my calloused palm, itching more than creating any small hurt. I pluck the wooden chips out from under my skin in a sorry attempt to ignore Derrín's piercing stare. He hasn't been secretive with his intentions of that speech.

"Don't you think you could protect Vera a lot better if you befriended the people who want her dead? They can't kill her if they want something from you."

"You want me to sell my future to the enemy?"

Derrín shrugs. "You act like you wouldn't and haven't already done things much worse."

He's not wrong. I've already broken all my rules and walked among my enemies for months for her. I'd turn my back on heaven and walk straight into hell if she asked. I would kill the gods and raise her to the stars. If I need to barter my soul as the price of her safety, I will.

"You know I hate when you're right," I huff.

Derrín only grins. "You hate a lot of things a lot of the time. I'm not concerned."

Torin has joined the others by the time I make my way

outside. I can feel the heat of his oil lamp brush across my face as he swings it my way in alarm. The offending light perforates my vision despite raising my hand as a shield. Black spots dance across Torin, who shrugs sheepishly amidst them.

"Apologies, friend." His crooked grin gleams yellow in the light and for a moment, I'm transported back to the palace. I am watching Vera run through the kitchen as Tanja chases her with a handful of flour. Torin laughs and eggs her on, standing in the corner with Blaine, who is trying and failing to hide his smile behind his stoic demeanor.

My face softens and my hand reaches out to ruffle his hair on its own accord. He flinches at first before slowly, his shoulders droop and his face relaxes.

"Good man," I say, though I do take the lantern from him. "Let's go see what this rebellion is about."

CHAPTER 17
VEROSA

Neris all but drags me from my bed as the first rays of dawn seep through my window. The warmth leaves my bones the instant she rips the fur blankets from my sleeping body. Gooseflesh prickles my limbs and she dodges the pillow I throw with predator-like efficiency.

"Up and at 'em, princess!" She beams. "We are going out."

Days have passed and the snow has finally cleared enough that we can leave for whatever this expedition is that Mavis has planned. Sure, there will still be snow on the ground, I think with a queasy feeling, but not enough to hinder us from our travels.

"No, I am going back to bed." I pout like a petulant child. My heart raced with anticipation when Mavis told me we were leaving her fortress, however dread has seeped through my veins and shocked me back to my senses. I will be able to *see* freedom and yet it always stays just beyond my fingertips. I escaped the prison the palace presented just to be thrust into another.

My gaze drops to the thin white scar across my wrist.

Neris covers it with her scarred hand and without any warning, tosses me over her shoulder.

"Put me down, you brute!" I laugh, despite hanging upside down. "My head is dangerously close to your ass."

"Lucky you," she says with a wink before plopping me in the chair before my vanity. The soldier lays a sack at my feet and a pile of clothes in my lap.

I eye the thick woolen socks greedily before rolling them over my feet and quickly changing into the warm clothes. "Is Mavis okay? It's been kind of cold here."

It is no secret that Mavis's magic powers the entire compound. She keeps the warmth within the caves despite the biting cold, and I suspect she has been the reason I sleep through the night now.

Ever since I arrived in Mavis's compound, my nights have been dreamless. No night terrors or faces haunt my unconsciousness, despite the new terrors I've faced. I would like to think that despite how perverse my mind has become, the action of being dragged naked through the woods by kidnappers would be considered traumatizing, not relaxing enough to cease my nightmares.

"She's fine. Just tending to someone right now."

"Someone?" Not something. Someone.

Neris stiffens. "Emi was injured in the kitchens. Mavis is just making sure her injuries aren't too severe." Then she adds hastily, "We look out for each other here."

My eyes narrow at that final word. *Here.* Her tone is clipped as she says it and I don't miss the obvious verbal dagger she flings my way. The insinuation that Rowan and the Nightwalkers don't care for their own.

"So do we." I lift my chin, my eyes narrowing and my hand stilling on the sweater I've pulled over my head.

Neris holds my stare and a flicker of sorrow tightens the lines around her mouth. She can't be more than a few years older than I am, and yet she looks like she has seen lifetimes. Her mahogany brown hair is pulled back into a tight braid, similar and yet so different from the one Amír favors. Amír's frames her angular face, adding an alluring sense of danger to her beauty. Neris's hides her beauty, something that both ages her and creates a sharper fear. Instinctually, my stomach roils as we continue our stare-down, but the general drops her gaze first.

"Ask Emi about that then." I half expect her to stop, but she turns her face back to mine after a second of consideration. "They're not good people. Sorry to break that to you. Ever stop to consider how they gained their notoriety? It wasn't by holding hands and keeping promises."

My lips peel back in a snarl. "Stop."

"Don't tell me you've never heard the cautionary tales. The assassin no one can hear coming until your throat is slit? The tales of the red road the day their gunslinger was born? The innocents that were murdered in her slaughter?" The soldier laughs mirthlessly. "They teach children to fear the Noiteron's call for a reason. They don't warn us to stay inside after dark for fear of hidden monsters. No, it's the ones that walk among us and wear a pretty face. Be sure to ask your lover about my leg the next time you see him too. See if he remembers."

A sick tugging at my heart tells me to ignore her bitter words, but they're so raw from someone usually so composed... I find my gaze trailing down towards the foot that bears the least weight. Her pant leg has snagged on my bedpost, pulling the fabric away from a shiny metal leg. My breath hitches in my throat as I try to tear my gaze away, but find that I can't.

Neris doesn't balk or move to cover the appendage. Instead, something like pity flickers across her features. Her warm eyes bore holes in my face before I'm reminded to breathe again and greedily inhale the stale cavern air. Gooseflesh prickles along my arms and raises my hair. I know it is not from the chill inhabiting the compound.

Her hand reaches forward and ruffles my already mused hair. "You're loyal, that's a good trait to have. It's just a little misplaced right now. Finish getting dressed. I'll meet you outside."

I pull my remaining clothes on and my lips part to remind her I cannot go anywhere without someone else opening the door, but I stop myself. My outstretched fingers inch towards the door where it sits, shut after her departure. I wince prematurely and wrap my hand around the cool metal. It doesn't burn. I risk twisting the knob slightly. The door clicks and snicks open, baring the empty hallway to me. *Nearly* empty hallway.

Mavis crosses her arms over her chest with a knowing smirk. Neris leans against the wall beside her, too deeply engrossed in their conversation to notice my arrival. Or so it would appear. The general has keen senses and I know she knew the moment I laced my fingers around the doorknob.

Mavis wears her hair tightly woven to her scalp, small and intricate braids creating a pattern resembling that of a crown. Her skin is paler than her usual bronze tan, drawing out the severity of her two-toned gaze. Her emerald eye slides in my direction, freezing me in my spot. She raises a well-manicured brow as if to ask, *well, what are you waiting for?* "Took you long enough."

"Sorry, not all of us wake up perfect," I bristle under my breath, low enough that she shouldn't be able to hear it.

The mercenary queen's knowing look tells me she did.

Neris shoulders a large pack, her gaze never leaving Mavis's face. Her intense features soften to better match her personality. Something new flutters within my chest. She looks at Mavis like she hung the moon then gave her the stars.

I trail behind the both of them, feeling oddly upset and left out. I shake my head. I should have no desire to take any part in their twisted world. This trip is only to serve their wants. I have no choice in the matter.

The opening of the cave stands before us in mere moments. I hadn't had much time to look around as I was dragged in here, naked and bleeding, by Argon, may the gods damn his soul. The opening is guarded by a multitude of soldiers, dressed the same as Neris, though notably less well decorated. They bow deeply at the waist, their chests near brushing their knees as they do so. Some sit atop a large pillar that resembles the guard towers we used to have at the palace, before it crumbled and took those towers with it.

Large tapestries loom on either side of the entrance. Those, I am sure I have not seen yet. My neck cracks as I crane it to admire every stitch, the bold colors reflecting in the bright torchlight. Raon and Deun. Night and Day.

Usually, portraits and tapestries portray Raonkin with dark and muted hues, with no care made to provide her a face of beauty. Gilded colors, jewel tones, and other forms of glory are saved only for Deungrid—anything else would be considered blasphemy.

Yet this artist thought differently. Deungrid is portrayed as he usually is—intense and commanding, haloed by golds and reds. But Raonkin... Her usually stern face is soft and lovely, those hollow cheeks filled in and her scarred hands soft. Bright colors explode behind her, silvers, purples, blues, and the occasional tinge of pink. She smiles with her eyes closed, serene and caring. The tapestry portrays darkness as a comfortable blanket that covers all the world's hurt. Light illuminates, but darkness covers. Both serve their purpose and balance each other out.

"We don't worship either god over the other here," Emi sneers, suddenly appearing beside me.

My year of schooling my reflexes with Rowan is the only thing that stops me from knocking her out. "That feels like a pointed remark."

"Good," is all she says before stalking to stand beside Mavis and her general. No sign of injury on her body. I suppose it wasn't too serious after all.

I trail closely behind as Mavis raises a single hand. The sound of metal grinding on stones booms through the cavernous room, popping my eardrums and causing me to bite my cheek. Mavis doesn't flinch as the gates are raised, her soldiers saluting as we exit. Neris offers some command and a clap on the shoulder to one of them as she exits, and the blood bond tugs me forward silently, crawling under my skin when I dare to lag behind.

The cold stings my cheeks and brings tears to my eyes the moment I step outside. Winter has fully arrived in Krycolis, its biting caress tracing every inch of exposed skin. Neris extends a cloak my way that I gratefully slip over my shoulders. I burrow my face in the fur-lined hood, watching fascinated as tiny snowflakes and bits of ice stick to the fur.

Icicles sparkle in the midday sunlight, their frozen elegance gracing the branches of every tree we walk past, frost having frozen the moss on their trunks as well. The snow crunches delightfully beneath my feet, and despite the beauty of it all, nausea roils through my stomach.

I used to love the snow. Torin, Blaine, Tanja, and I used to wait by the library window every night leading up to winter, waiting for the first flurries to descend. We would burn through oil lamp after oil lamp, sneaking out with the help of my nanny, Tanja's mother. She would leave hidden sacks of goodies such as cookies or jelly tarts among the bookshelves. The librarians eventually caught on and would bring milk of molten chocolate that they had conveniently gotten too much of from the cook. If Irene ever knew of our rendezvous, she didn't say anything, which in itself was enough to make the first frost seem holy.

Until she ruined that too.

I can still remember the sting of the snow as it soaked my nightgown and froze my eyes open. Steam arose from my wound, the blood and flesh hot enough to melt a bit of the snow and ice, but not enough so to stop the hypothermia from setting in as the blizzard began again.

I'd read stories about monsters lurking after dark, how wolves can smell blood and search for the softest spots to attack. I was a child. I was easy prey, for both the wolves and my mother.

Blaine found me the next morning, and Tanja and Torin came to visit me, as well, while the healers did their best to save my young life. Torin's mother often visited Blaine's, and she allowed him to come into the palace despite the blizzard when news got out that the princess had fallen from a tower.

They all expected I would be afraid of heights, if anything, but it was never the fall that froze my senses with fear. No, the fall took me away from the horror. It was my mother waiting at the bottom, ready to leave me in the snow, that stopped my heart.

The frost came that next year, and when I pressed my face to the window like we had been doing for years, all I felt was cold dread.

That same dread settles deep in my stomach now as I stare down at the white powder. So clean, so pure, so evil. On instinct, I reach my hand out to hold onto... someone who is no longer here.

Mavis watches with feline curiosity, but says and does nothing. Neris kicks snow at Emi, who shrieks and throws a glob at the general's face.

"No rocks," is Mavis's stern warning, but otherwise, she lets the two play.

The feared general of Mavis's army, the queen of mercenaries's wolf, playing in the snow with a freckled teenager while the world falls down around us. Thankfully, neither of them includes me in their game. I am especially thankful when Emi doesn't heed Mavis's warning and includes pebbles and sticks in her snowball, a stray rock cutting across Neris's face. That puts an end to the game, and Emi is forced to carry the heavy sack the general has been carrying since we left the compound. She whines, to which Mavis launches into a long-winded speech on discipline, and Neris chuckles behind her hood.

We've been wandering for near two hours by the time I finally find my voice again. "Where are we going, and what the hell are we doing other than walking through a blizzard?"

Mavis groans and lolls her neck from side to side. "Don't be so dramatic."

"That's not an answer."

"It is if I say it is."

"Can you stop being a bitch for once and give me a straight-forward answer?"

"We are searching for someone, that's all you need to know."

I laugh mirthlessly. "You've brought me along to kill someone. Lovely."

"I brought you here so you don't kill *yourself*," she finally snaps. "So hold your tongue and keep walking."

Even if I wanted to fall down into the snow and let it finally kill me, I know I cannot. Even if I tried, she would force my blood to pump through my heart and my feet to move. She has effectively stolen any agency, even the sweet kiss of death from me. My feet move against my will and I follow her into the dark and snow like an obedient dog at the heels of a wicked master.

Spindly icicles dangle dangerously from tree branches, the scent of pine and snow hanging thick in the air. I allow myself to breathe deeply, the cold chilling my bones with each breath. The others press on ahead, Emi occasionally tapping the cold spires without the slightest flickering of fear across her face.

Tentatively, I reach out and wrap gloved fingers around the tip of one. The pointed mound breaks free from the branch and spirals downwards towards me. I shriek, stumbling back. Neris hides a chuckle and Emi sticks her tongue out, but I only stare at my hand.

I grabbed it. I wasn't thrown into it or forced down. *I grabbed it.*

No panic attacks. No remembrance of the howling wind or freezing snow. Any fear caused was from the jarring motion of the fall and not the ice itself. Pride swells in my chest, though the others only continue their walk.

Leaning forward, I scoop a fistful of snow into my hands, then throw the snowball as hard as I can at the back of Emi's head.

CHAPTER 18

ROWAN

Torin meets us outside just as he said he would, cloaked in midnight, illuminated only by starlight. He lowers his hood with a gloved hand, revealing his messy blond hair with the roots grown out. Dark circles crown his undereyes, but he still nods with a smile, allowing a bit of warmth onto his face. The three companions that flank his sides do not spare the same courtesy of allowing us to see who they are.

Blaine embraces the Nevan man, patting him firmly on the shoulder as they part. I follow suit, leaving my hood up as well.

"Noiteron." Torin dips his chin, plastering on a courtier's mannerisms.

I accept his hand in a firm clasp before stepping back. I turn my faceless hood towards the other travelers.

Each bows in reverence to a false king before spinning on their heel to lead the way.

The darkness was my first friend as a child. Even before Irene attempted to murder me and my mother, and my father lost his mind, I never had any friends that I could remember. I would play with other children, but never stayed anywhere long enough to remember names. I spied on them from locked windows, wishing desperately to be one of them. To be normal.

There was a girl I saw once after Irene shattered my semblance of a life. She and a boy ran into a clearing my mother and I were in. She was demanding, but possessed such commanding light that I found myself reaching for her before I was pulled back into the shadows.

I never wanted to bathe in the light so badly as then, until I met Vera.

But before Vera, there were shadows. They clung to me like a second skin, cloaking me in the night when the wind howled too sharply. Hiding my bruises from my mother when I first began picking up odd jobs to pay bills. I told her the sword was for safety. I told her I was simply an errand boy. It wasn't until Amír came home with me, splattered in blood with bruised wrists and ankles, did she realize what I was doing.

Then Amír found Kya and Derrín, and we amassed our army. Mavis was supposed to be just another recruit, another underling. Amír brought her in, trained her. I loved her, and part of me was killed by her.

Yet they still chose to follow me, even after I lost half our profits to a slit-tongued succubus and our kingdom began to crumble. To Amír's credit, I can see how I might have fooled others into believing me a fit ruler. I can see how the appeal of a hybrid who fought tooth and nail like them could paint a pretty picture upon a throne.

I stare at the scars lacing my forearms. They don't know the curse of this blood. They don't know like father like son. I may not be a monster yet, but by gods, I must be destined to be one.

I've never been a good man. I've never claimed to be. The poets say everyone has a villain in their story, and I have always been my own, happy to play the part. I try not to think of the innocent lives I've taken, whether they were caught in the cross-fire or used against me as leverage by Mavis or some other enemy. An indirect kill is still blood on my hands. The wicked that I've put down do not haunt my dreams, but the deaths that could have been avoided do. They scream in tones only I can hear, and when they threaten to rip me to shreds, the darkness shields me once again.

Torin and the rebels lead us into that darkness now, all walking in dead silence for fear of what monsters lurk in the trees. My eyes adjust quickly, outlining pines and other dead or dying foliage. Kya picks her way nimbly next to me. The assassin's fingers wrap around Amír's wrist, guiding her past tree roots and loose stones. Amír is more than capable of finding her way on her own, but makes no protest as the other woman leads her in the dark. Blaine keeps pace ahead with Torin. His hand never strays from the sword hanging sheathed at his hip.

One of the rebels leans towards the other, whispering something just out of my earshot. Kya is behind them in a second, completely undetected as they finish their conversation.

"That's not a nice thing to say," she whispers between them, making a shallow cut across both their thighs—far too close to something more valuable. She's back by my side by the time they turn around in bewilderment and fear.

Blaine stifles a chuckle while I lean in closer to the assassin.

"What did they say?"

"Oh you know, the usual." She shrugs, despite no one else being able to see her. "They expected me and Amír to be men. Thought we were just *company* at first."

"If you slit their throats, no one will know."

"You will."

"Sinners can't preach."

Kya snorts. "No, I suppose not."

"We're here," Torin whispers roughly. He knocks thrice on a hidden door against a wall of rock that not even I could spot, then kicks it once more when it won't open.

A thick voice speaks from the other side, muffled by distance. "Who is it?"

"Last I checked, Lio, the Kijova don't know how to knock," Torin drawls.

The door opens and a burly man with a ruddy face appears. He claps Torin on the shoulder hard enough to nearly knock the man over. "You can just give a name instead of talking out your arsehole," Lio answers, his voice thick with an accent.

Torin laughs, that bastard's grin still lighting his lips.

The large man takes that as a response and ushers us all in.

I take note of the seven bolts on the door and their locking mechanisms. A few pin locks, some that just slide into place. Get the top three loose and the final four will pop clean off with a soft enough hand.

Kya and Amír trail my gaze. I already know they've thought of every way to get them unlocked in the span of fifteen seconds.

"The boss is this way." Lio knocks my ribs with his hefty elbow. "He's been expecting ye."

"Good."

The others have lowered their hoods, but I keep mine raised. It earns odd stares, but I'd rather not make my face known to the entirety of the rebels until I've guaranteed Vera's safety. Only a few have seen the face of the Noiteron—my Nightwalkers, Mavis, and people who now lay beneath the earth. Anonymity is a luxury to keep in the fine industry of crime.

Amír and Kya wear their faces proudly during all our hits unless the particular heist calls for the thin cloak of stealth. Their faces are their own weapons, their objective beauty just as lethal as the gun and daggers hanging at their sides. Mavis's generals may not fall for that form of weaponry, but her foot soldiers—her predominantly *male* foot soldiers—fall for it every time. Hook, line, and sinker. They're still staring into Amír's green eyes with wonder as her bullet pierces between their brows.

They stand just slightly behind me now, their eyes constantly scanning. A few of the scattered rebels hunch their shoulders and drop their gawking gazes as we pass. I cannot feel the cold and yet some of them shiver. Gooseflesh prickles the back of Blaine's neck. He shoots me a sideways glance, the whites of his eyes peeking out from behind his lashes like whitecaps cresting on the ocean.

"We are here," one of the hooded figures says now, dropping their cloak to the side. His sandy hair falls out in waves, framing his freckled face. He clutches at where Kya sliced him earlier, blushing as he tries to hide the blood. The other does the same, too ashamed to explain how he got the wound.

Torin nods. "The mask goes on now," he whispers, just loud enough that I can hear it.

I dip my chin beneath my hood and the young man opens the door. I pinch my shoulders back as if a board is between them, flexing every one of my finely carved muscles. Amír scoffs.

The room is dim, but by no means is it poorly lit. No, the mounds of bodies piled into the small space absorb and block out the majority of the light, leaving only shadowy shapes along the walls. I bite back a grin. They let the king of night into their territory all while hiding in the dark—where I thrive.

The bodies part as Torin walks through, leading us. Some actually bow as we pass, their knees scraping on the floor, disappearing within the masses. A little girl looks up at me with wide blue eyes before she, too, is lost to the shadows.

A man stands in the center of it all, his hulking body seemingly absorbing the rest of the light in the room. A bold fur pelt clasps around his shoulders, the white fur shining brighter than the torches on the wall. His gray beard matches his weathered appearance, cut close to his jaw, just short enough to show off the thin white scar across his throat.

Amír steps forward, standing a hair's breadth before me. She crosses two fingers over her heart, a small slight that I will forgive for now. "Amír. Second to the Noiteron, the king of the mercenaries." There is no hint of a scoff or her usual blade-biting sarcasm as she speaks. Her voice is low and even-toned, just as it always is when the gunslinger's mask coats her mannerisms. She does not bow, just as I expected of her.

Kya steps forward, mimicking her movements, but without the warding sign. "Kya. Third to the Noiteron, son of the shadows."

A whistle goes out through the crowd and Amír's hand flies to her holster. The calling ceases immediately.

The hulking man's lips lift upwards in a smirk. He gesticulates in my direction with a large hand. "And the Noiteron, I presume?"

"Oh, don't presume things. I'd prefer a bit more conviction," I deadpan, smooth wit coating my throat like a fine liquor.

A small gasp of a laugh puffs from the man's nose. Not quite a laugh, but just enough effort to show he heard. "Why don't you take your hood down?"

"Why don't you tell me your name?"

"Roiden. Now, your hood."

Not quite a demand, but not quite a question either. His words are something else entirely that lays in the same domain of all other earthly dangers. Judging by the thin scar across his throat, as well as the multitude of others across his thick, tanned skin, this man is no stranger to danger. I doubt I am the first man he has attempted to anger to violence, and a lesser man might have fallen prey to such petty notions.

However, there is a difference between me and other men. If I had been holding the blade, that wound wouldn't have scarred.

I catch a flash of green from the corner of my eye. Amír's gaze burns into the blackness of my hood. Her gaze is questioning, rather than challenging for once. She dips her chin, feeling a shift in the air, and drops her hand from her holster. I reach up, my fingers snagging in the thick fabric as I pull it down.

An awed silence falls over the darkened room. Most are unable to see, but those in the front row look up in awe.

Until Roidan barks out a rough laugh like iron grating on iron. "Sorry," he grins, "I wasn't expecting a pretty blond boy. This famed killer, all along, was simply a boy."

I keep my features neutral, unlike his manic grin. Something tells me he doesn't wear a smile often, given the way his features pinch and his cheeks pull as if they've already grown weary.

Blaine covers a small scoff with a cough, the noise startling the rebellion leader's stare.

His gray gaze focuses on the former captain's face before his brows pinch together and he snarls in recognition. "And you've got some gall showing up here, captain. You've killed more of my men than all these criminals combined."

Blaine squares his shoulders. "You made multiple attempts on the heir's life. I was doing my duty."

"I wonder," Roiden drawls, his canines hooking on his lower lip, "if it was your duty you were thinking of and not your desire. We all know you had an affair with the bitch."

Kya's espa is pressed into my side before I can even lunge to finish the job of ripping that man's throat out. From the shadows, no one else can see the slender blade, but its sharp edge pricks my side with just enough pressure as to not draw blood. I ball my fists to the point of breaking skin. I'll kill him. Godsdamnit, I will use him as I need to and then I will take immense pleasure in tearing him limb from limb. I picture myself dragging a blade along each of his scars, using those as markers for points to dismember. Order be damned. Morals be damned.

Torin rests his hand on Blaine's shoulder, but the man shakes him off. He fixes the older man with an iron glare that would make any lesser man shrink.

"You should watch your mouth," he warns in a low voice I've only heard him use once. "Given the circumstances, I'll spare your life."

"As if you could take me." Roiden gestures to the scars tracing his flesh, to his broken nose and sword rusted from blood. His face says it all, pinched with glee. He finds a sick pleasure in the torment of rage. He wants a fight. He wants a mob.

A low rage boils in my core. He is exactly the type of man to lead a mob like this, inciting violence for the joy of it. He's a tyrant on some perverse power trip.

Blaine glowers down on the man and says in an even tone, "You've only faced petty criminals. You step foot into a pond and call it the ocean. You are a child playing with glass castles. If I weren't here to save a friend and the innocent people of this kingdom, you'd be dead in under a minute, and I am being generous. Sit down, old man, before I make you."

The older man goes red in the face in an instant, not because the accusations are untrue, but because Blaine has hit the hollow nail on the head. The fool can do nothing but crumble before he embarrasses himself. Or orders the mob to kill the former captain, though that wouldn't bode well for him. He would lose respect *and* his life. With the wicked gleam in his eye, I can only guess that he does not care about either of those things right now.

"You've got quite the tongue for someone who needs something from me," I offer, still masking my rage beneath a cool façade.

Roiden watches curiously before running a hand through his slicked-back hair. He sighs deeply, the motion causing his chest to heave. Before another word can be said, the man bows deeply at the waist, his belly brushing against his knees. "My people," he bellows, still folded unto himself. "I give to you the Noiteron, Rowan Krycolis. The world's only hybrid, son of Ophelus, and rightful king of Krycolis."

CHAPTER 19

ROWAN

Mavis. Mavis is the only one who could've told Roiden about what I am. My Nightwalkers know, but no one outside the inner circle has the right to that knowledge. Kya and Amír would die before they parted with it, and Derrín is far too loyal. My mother is my best kept secret from this cruel world and the Ialeses see me too much like a son to betray me like this.

And Vera wouldn't cave, not even under torture.

Mavis is the only one who had access to that information, to me, and would willingly share it. To get what she wants, she would do far worse things, so why should this one surprise me at all?

Perhaps because it was the only card she had yet to use against me. She has done all other evils under the sun, but this one felt holy, even to nonbelievers such as ourselves. To finally play this final card after all these years...

All the air leaves my lungs in one fell swoop. Mavis.

Amír jumps before me, gun drawn, her finger twitching on the trigger. She aims at the crowd. Kya stands at my back, ready to

139

protect me from the manic hands and frenzy of radicals who have gone far too long without a god to believe in.

But no one moves to swarm like a mob should. No, they stand utterly still and silent before falling to their knees and pressing their faces to the floor. They bow with sobbing breaths that pull them closer to the floor.

Roiden raises himself from his bow now, any trace of supplication gone from his rigid form. He raises an eyebrow in challenge. "Well, my liege, tell the people your demands."

A set up. Gods, he set me up. A traitorous bastard as he is, Roiden is cunning. He's raised me to a pedestal just a few feet below his own. He holds my head just above the hooves of the riot, letting me know he still is the one to hold the reins.

I drop my hand to my sword. "You will cease your attempts on Princess Verosa's life. Only then, once her safety is guaranteed, will I assume the throne."

I can hardly get the last words out before the mob surges, their cries of outrage echoing in the shadowy room. Their capes flutter in a mothy dust ball, swarming around limbs as if they have a mind of their own. Kya is whisked away with a shriek, and before I can reach for her, Blaine has rushed into the crowd after her.

A hand grips my forearm and I bring my sword down to sever it when a familiar voice shouts. The blade stops just a mere millimeter above Torin's wrist as he attempts to drag me towards an exit somewhere within the riot.

"They're rabid. You need to follow me."

"Kya and Blaine are out there."

"I'm more worried for the mob." Torin offers a weak laugh as he tugs. "You're the one they're after. Let's go."

Reluctantly, I toss a glance over my shoulder. The rebels are slowly getting closer, all of them shapeless forms moving in a mob. Some stand up to their brethren, blocking my body with their own, while the rest fight over themselves to get just a breath closer. Zealots, the lot of them.

Torin ushers us into a room and bolts the door, though the rabble stays contained outside. Not a single soul spares us a glance once my hood is up, allowing me to disappear into the shadows as I've always done. Amír does as well, her distinguishable features cloaked by darkness. I can see the turmoil in her motions without ever catching a glimpse of her face—her rigid shoulders and swift yet stern motions. My second is pissed.

"Kya will be fine. Blaine will bring her to us," Torin tries, noticing her distress as well. Poor lad.

"Kya will drag Blaine in here on her own once he fails. She could take that whole room with one hand if she wasn't holding herself back."

Amír is right, as always. Kya only holds back on missions because the rest of us are there and she would rather sever her own hands than risk hurting any of us. The first time I met her, Derrín found me and said his sister was trapped in a bar of angry men. They hadn't known the ways of Krycolis yet, but when we arrived, the floors and walls were painted red with blood. Despite there being many bodies in the room, only one moved—Kya holding a single dagger in the center of the bloodbath. If killing were an art, she is the master.

"Those radicals only want the Noiteron. Until Roiden can get them under control, its best that you all wait in here."

We swivel towards the sound only to find an older woman sitting on a rickety chair. Her sleek, black hair is peppered with gray strands and slicked into a low bun. Her angular features impose on the beauty of her face, but her gray eyes warn us not to come closer than she desires.

My eyes narrow. "You called him by name. Not one of those 'radicals'?"

"Who? My *darling* husband?" She drawls the word *darling*, those thin lips curving upwards in a wicked grin.

Amír's face turns to steel, colder than the frost outside as Torin bows at the waist.

The other woman scowls as well. "None of that, boy. Stand up straight. We all know your allegiance is a farce. Don't look so surprised. I won't tell."

"What's in it for you if you don't?" Torin rises nonetheless, but his posture stays rigid. "Lyra."

Lyra takes a long drag from her cup, frowning at something in the dregs. "We are all just trying to survive, boy."

Amír whispers something that sounds suspiciously like, "A tyrant for a tyrant," but Lyra says nothing, just motions for us to sit. All but the gunslinger oblige just as the door to the room is thrown open. The two missing Nightwalkers stagger in, Blaine leaning on a bleeding Kya's shoulder. The man looks worse for wear, as well, his high cheekbone already blooming with a violet bruise.

Amír rushes to her lover's side, cooing and fretting over the blood leaking from the assassin's hairline. Torin comes to support Blaine's weight while I remain seated, locking eyes with Lyra. I drop my hood, granting her access to the sight of my face.

She says nothing. No small inflection of her voice or flinch in her countenance. Nothing to give away any sign of shock or appreciation. She sips again, cringing now. "Dammit. Empty." She slides the cup across the table and nods towards the pitcher to my right. "Fill my cup, Noiteron?"

Unflinching, I pour the cup with steady hands. No foam rises and I catch a whiff of nothingness as I slide the cup across the table again. "It's water."

Lyra takes another sip and winks. "Still convinced we can do this without them?"

"They form quite the swarm. Maybe if we convince them that

the Kijova are secretly gods, then they'll tear them limb from limb for us." Blaine catches the ire of my gunslinger for his retort, but he has a point.

"How am I to lead a people who are hardly people themselves anymore?"

Lyra scoffs gruffly. "They're still people, little king. They've lost everything. Desperate times make more desperate people. They're all just clinging to something to believe in. Have you ever seen a sinking ship go down when there's only one life raft? Damned thing cracks and they all die anyway. We need another captain to come along with room on his ship."

"I'm not a captain."

"No. You're just a boy playing assassin. Soon, you'll have to play king too."

"And if I don't?"

"You cannot outrun fate, Rowan Banehart, just as you cannot outrun the mixed blood in your veins."

My wrists throb at her words, aching as if in acknowledgment. I steel my face against her scrutinizing glare, not a single flinch to betray my racing heart. She used my mother's maiden name. The burn from Amír's stare does all but draw sweat to the back of my neck. None of my Nightwalkers know my full name. Not Amír, who has been with me the longest, nor Vera, who holds the better half of my soul.

Torin breaks in now, his gaze softened from that sharp and calculating face he wore earlier. He shakes his head, his hair splaying out like some spaniel as he offers a crooked grin. "It looks like they've cleared out enough that we can get out unnoticed." Torin goes to bow, then catches himself, halting in a half-upright position. "Thank you for sharing your space with us, Lyra."

Lyra nods, her dark hair falling in her eyes as she dips her lips to her cup. She lifts those gray eyes to meet my stare and they slant into a smirk.

I brush it off and stalk towards the door, my hood already drawn. Blaine jumps when I appear behind him, his face flushing as he softly swears. Torin leads the way, with the captain trailing close behind him. Amír follows, Kya leaning her head against her shoulder for a brief moment. When she lifts it, a dark stain remains on Amír's cloak. The gunslinger's fingers tap furiously against her holster. I tighten my own into a fist as I step out into the hallway, but my feet falter when a lilting voice speaks from within the room.

"You have her eyes."

I shut the door and slip into the shadows.

CHAPTER 20
VEROSA

Dusk stretches across the sky as we crowd around a small fire, the heat melting the surrounding snow to reveal wet clumps of brown grass. Emi sits on the hem of Mavis's cloak, still gloating about her victory over the general in their snowball fight and remaining silent about the hits I landed. Every now and then, she rubs the back of her head, or her left arm where the second strike landed. She doesn't forget to throw a pointed glare in my direction before cuddling closer to the mercenary. Mavis hums in response, not mentioning anything about the young teen curled into her side, nor her sullied cloak.

I try to draw my gaze away from the muddy fabric, a streak of crimson across the white snow. My stomach churns and I swallow thickly. The howling wind weaves through the trees and I draw my furs closer. Neris returns at this moment, her arms filled with twigs and branches of varying sizes. The general drops them just far enough from the fire so that the embers cannot lick the wood into flame.

"Some of them are a bit wet so they won't catch flame easy, but still be careful." Neris settles beside me and plucks a few of the branches and begins to weave them together. She clears away some of the remaining snow and places her woven wood there. After she deems it acceptable, she rolls out a sleeping sack atop the frame and passes a few branches my way. "You'll want to make some sort of pallet to go under your sack or the ground will steal all the heat from you while you sleep."

I force a weak smile to my lips. "Not a terrifying thought at all."

"No more terrifying than Emi, and yet you took her on earlier."

"And won," Mavis notes in response to her general.

Emi rolls her eyes and snaps one of the twigs, much to Neris's joking ire.

"Ah yes, I beat the teenager. How mighty I feel."

Neris shoves me into the snow. "What are you saying about those of us who lost, you royal brat?"

I respond both by flipping her a vulgar gesture and jutting my tongue out like a petulant child.

This earns me both gestures in return.

I try not to settle into this sense of familiar comfort too deeply. It's difficult at times when it seems like they're opening their arms to their tight-knit group. Then I remember my own family waiting for me and that warmth freezes as a pit in my stomach.

They've yet to explain who they've brought me along to kill, nor have they admitted to their criminal intentions, but at this point, it is quite obvious. The only thing I have yet to figure out is why they need *me* to do it.

Since a cursed cannot kill a blessed without dark magic, it's obvious why they'd require me, if not for the fact that any one of them could easily do it. I'm not sure which god they each hail from, but I have to assume they have at least one person who is blessed among their ranks, so I cannot imagine they need *me* to kill a blessed. Not that consorting with dark magic is off the table for Mavis.

The woman occasionally tosses scraps of her sacrifices into the fire, her eyes lighting with primal delight as the flesh catches flame. Emi hardly looks bothered, not with her eyes closed and lower lip jutting out in sleep.

Neris swears and picks the teenager up, laying her on her own sleeping cot before moving to make a new one for herself across the fire. Emi's fiery hair pools beneath her, flicking like a living flame, no less real than the one before us.

Mavis snaps her fingers, and a sacrifice later, her bed is made.

"Show off," Neris whispers under her breath.

Mavis only smiles, the light catching on her canines.

I turn my back on them both as I sprawl across my own makeshift cot. We've agreed that Mavis will take first watch, her offer surprising no one. I wouldn't be shocked if it were revealed that she is some form of supernatural being, given her attributes —affinity for dark magic, perfect face of ethereal beauty, skills with all forms of weaponry. Not to mention her apparent lack of a need for any human necessities such as sleep.

The mercenary rises, her crimson cape swirling around her ankles in a dramatic flourish. All of us wear cloaks of neutral tones, meant to blend into the snowy landscape surrounding us. But not Mavis. No, she challenges the dangers of the world to face her. She dares them to try.

No Kijova have found us. Perhaps they realize there are greater monsters in our ranks. One that wears painted lips and has dual-toned eyes.

The crunch of the snow draws closer to my head and I pinch my eyes closed, my breath quickening. My newfound bravery from earlier in the day has completely vanished now that the dark has settled upon us. It blankets the forest, coating the trees and all but the stars in eternal night. Part of me— a younger part that has not aged in ten years—believes that if I were to place my hand amongst those tree trunks, it too would disappear. Lost forever to the void of night.

A heavy weight settles over my body, like a thick blanket or another's warmth.

"Sleep, Verosa," Mavis hums, her voice a steady thrum in my bones. "Sleep."

～

BY THE TIME I AWAKE, my peaceful sleep shattered by urgent, shaking hands, the others are alert and crouched by my resting form. A single look from Mavis is all it takes for every nerve in my body to alight. The hairs on the back of my neck raise as I hear the howling, a low and guttural sound unlike the one that haunts my nightmares.

Neris presses a sword into my hands, not a dagger—meaning I won't want to be in close range whenever that thing attacks.

"What is it?" My voice is barely audible over the steady hum of negative energy pulsing through the air. A deep sense of foreboding smothers my senses and I stagger. Dark magic. Its presence does not bother me as much while I am the one wielding the power, nor does Mavis's, for some unknown reason. But this... My senses are flooded with its heavy presence just as they were in the past, both in Irene's study and the tower when Lucius and Ophelus betrayed me. Raw and undiluted power.

Mavis drags her teeth across her lips. She looks paler in the dark, but by no means frailer. She is starlight, cloaked in silver light. She moves swiftly, the rest of us having no choice but to follow and abandon our camp. She raises three fingers and throws an unfamiliar gesture towards Neris. I drag two fingers over my heart. The general nods and grabs me and Emi by our elbows, hauling us after her. We leave Mavis within a circle of trees until distance and the dark swallows her.

Emi's face screws tight, her eyes prickling with unshed tears. She wants to protest, I can see it, but between Neris's firm grip and the howling that grows louder still...

I try my best to look confident. To look like I'm not about to fall over from fear myself. She's just a child who never should have been exposed to a world like this. No one should be, but a generation will grow up in this world. A broken world, riddled with monsters just waiting for the chance to tear them to ribbons. My heart gives a sudden twist. Emi should be playing under a bright sun with kids her age and studying for exams, not running for her life with a blessed mage and mercenary duo.

"Down," Neris grounds out, shoving both Emi and I down into a dying mound of foliage.

I land atop the teen, doing the best I can to cover her body with my own. Neris stands a few feet away, drawing the scent her way, her sword drawn. A crash later and a bloodied Mavis stumbles through the trees, her breathing haggard.

"What the fuck was that?"

"Emi!" Mavis admonishes, even covered in mud and blood. She accepts a swig from the canteen Neris extends. Her lips leave a bloodied mark on the lip of the container.

Emi's eyes widen and water at the sight of her idol beaten half to death.

I step forward, my shoulders squaring. "Kijova?" I ask, even though I know a Kijova doesn't sound like that.

Mavis shakes her head, dread settling in my gut. "Wraith."

"A wraith? Like the ghost things from those children's fables?" Neris supplies my question, her strong brow furrowing.

Mavis nods, a chill shattering my spine.

Wraiths were a warning against violence against children in fables. The tales spun were told in our primary school by teachers and students alike, each weaving a different image of the story. Still, the origin and ending remained the same.

Wraiths are the souls of children who met violent ends before their time. It starts with a man who lusts after a woman, only she refuses to marry him since her child is old enough to remember her real father. In order to have the woman, he steals the daughter from her bed and strings the child from a tree on his farm. Legend says that the wind took pity on the swinging girl and gave her three gifts: flight, transcendency, and the ability to take revenge. On their wedding day, the wraith stood at the altar behind the man, and her screams sent him spiraling to his death.

"Yeah, the stories didn't warn us about their fangs and claws though." Mavis gingerly raises a finger to her swollen and bloody cheek. "The poor thing's voice is the least of our worries."

"Where did they come from?" Neris muses aloud.

My heart turns to lead in my chest and I fight the desire to sink to the snowy ground. "Are there any towns nearby?"

Mavis nods, her gaze slanting in suspicion.

I inhale sharply. "The Kijova don't discriminate."

Mavis swears lowly and Neris begins to shake. Only Emi stands perfectly still, so unflinching that a stranger might have mistaken her for a frozen body or a statue. Her eyes are wide, that of prey cornered and staring into death's insatiable face. One terrifying question lay in the frosted air before us: if the unthinkable were to happen, if we were to lose her, would she turn into one of those?

Mavis's split lip dribbles, the blood marking a slow line down her chin before it drips into the snow. Gold flecked.

Emi's brown eyes watch each drip, her knees trembling in tandem.

Mavis turns, her dual-colored hair swishing with the motion. Her movements are languid, like a smooth river flowing peacefully under a full moon. Her footsteps crunch in the snow, the only sound in the evening as she approaches the girl.

Emi lifts her chin, defiant even as the first tear drips down her freckled cheek.

Mavis lifts her arms, her cloak like the fiery wings of a phoenix, wrapping around the teen as her shoulders begin to shake. Not shielding the world from Emi, but the girl from the world. For the fears she should never have been forced to have. She cloaks her in a darkness different from the one we stand in. This one is quiet, safe. Mavis is a fortress, the stones slick with rain and crumbling, yet impenetrable.

The wind refuses to whistle, that low howling no longer audible as well. Neris and I share glances, but neither of us dare to ask what happened to the wraith. Perhaps we both know our souls will never rest easy if we know. War can only take so much from a man before he breaks, and Mavis knows she is already gone. Neris, Emi, and I are still salvageable. Despite it all, I want to reach out and tell her there is something in her worth saving too.

Dawn etches the sky golden, roses blooming in the clouds. A hazy pink glow covers the mercenary and the child. In this moment, I wish I could paint, wish I could capture it in saturated hues forever. The viper and the canary.

Snow dusts the top of their heads and Mavis closes her eyes, the cloak falling to Emi's shoulder when the girl allows it.

They turn to us now, her arm draped protectively around the teen. "We need to move. There could be more and we don't have time to waste."

We wisely choose not to argue. Despite never having seen a wraith and apparently having a perpetual curiosity for things that spell detriment to my health, I would rather not see one today. My stomach roils with nausea at the picture of Emi's face, twisted in fear and horror. I've never been overly fond of children, but the thought of one dying such a violent death that their soul must roam for eternity, then that child being Emi? My fingers splay across my sternum and I focus on the rise and fall of my cascading breath. Pity will get us killed, just as much as panic will.

We only stop once to allow Mavis to tie a splint to her leg. She swears nothing has broken for sure, and if it has, it must only be a hairline fracture, but still. A weak leg will get us killed. Panic, injury, pity. Just existing. All of it spells death in these dire hours.

Emi stands close to the mercenary at all times, and if she isn't touching Mavis, she is touching her cloak, clutching the red fabric in her tiny, freckled hands. I never thought of fourteen as young before. With Irene as my mother, I never had the option of fully being a child and never understood the weight of childlike innocence. I can see it now, spelled with grief across the teen's face. I can feel it in the silence where her irate quips would usually occupy the air. Anger is her shield against her youth, and now with the snowy night having cooled it, there is nothing left but a wounded child.

"We are almost there," Mavis calls from ahead. She is slightly more winded now, but still doing far better than anyone else in her position would be. I would've collapsed in the snow and allowed the wraith to take me at this point. Even uninjured, I debate it, but Neris somehow has a sixth sense for when despair and foolishness settle in, always gripping my elbow in silent warning. *Don't you fucking dare.*

The general is the only one who doesn't look out of place in the snowy wood. With her fur hood up and stern face, she looks every bit the part of the borderline feral wolf that bites at Mavis's heels. Then a smile splits her face in two at something Emi says and that notion is gone with the howling wind.

"Now that we've almost died, can someone tell me where we are going?" I jog lightly to catch up to the other woman and fix her with a pointed glare.

She quirks an eyebrow skyward and I lift my wrist to show her the thin white scar that matches her own.

"And what would have happened if you had died? Would I have had to lug your body everywhere?"

Mavis rolls her eyes. "If you didn't notice, you were able to run off with Neris just then because I wanted you to. If I felt like I was going to die, I would have broken the bond. But if I didn't have time—don't look at me like that. I can see it in your face. You would have had to carry a vial of my blood with you everywhere. It's tied to blood not body, remember."

I can't say I'm fond of the idea of wearing a vial of Mavis's blood everywhere for the rest of my life, nor the idea of being at her disposal for all eternity. "You're removing this as soon as we get back."

"Aw, bitch doesn't like being on a leash?"

"You're fucking vile," I spit.

She responds with a wicked grin that tells me she knows and likes it.

Emi laughs, though, and despite the insult, some weight lifts from my lungs. All's not lost yet for the kid.

"And to answer your first question, we are looking for some-one," Mavis grunts as she marches through a deeper pit of snow. "A man."

"Is he a deserter or something? Is that why you need me?"

"Fucking hell, Vera, you ask a lot of questions."

"And you answer less than half of them."

Mavis lets out a frustrated growl that sparks a bit of pride in my chest. The ember flutters into flame as she runs her hand through her hair and finally answers. "He's an informant for the king. A noble who might have found out how to defeat him, except he's not capable of doing it alone, so instead, he's being a coward and informing Ophelus in exchange for immunity. He's on his way to meet Lucius now. We are intercepting him before all hope is lost. Clear enough for you?"

My brows furrow into a scowl. I can see how she and Amír got along so well in their time together. It must have been a constant pissing contest to see who could be the bigger bitch. I can't tell if Kya was in heaven or constant hell with the two of them. Or maybe they were great friends, I don't know.

But something she says bites at the corners of my consciousness, hard enough that I can't let it go. He's meeting Lucius. I haven't seen my former fiancé since he attempted to sacrifice me and killed my best friend instead. Does he consider himself my fiancé still? Does attempted human sacrifice constitute as annulling an engagement? If he is unsure, I will have to make it certain for him that we are done. And maybe send him to Tanja so she can tell him as well.

"Not really," I respond. "Why don't we just recruit him? I assume you're here to kill him."

Mavis laughs, a dry and hollow sound that chills deeper than the snow and ice surrounding us. "I don't spare traitors."

I can feel the ghost of a hand sliding down my arm and the wind begins to resemble Argon's screams. A sharp shiver licks up my spine and I rub my hands over my shoulders. "No, I suppose not."

Emi steps away from Mavis now, daybreak having fully crested the sky. She runs ahead a bit and Neris trails her, threatening to dump snow down the back of her cloak. Color begins to return to her cheeks and she laughs, the nightmares of last night chased away with the sun.

"Hey, I think we're almost here," Neris calls out from ahead. Her toe nudges a still-smoldering lump of wood, the bulk of the thing charred and warm.

Mavis nods, tracking her gaze to a set of footprints leading away from us. Emi takes this as her cue to fall behind, lest she damage the trail. I fall into step beside her, Neris leading the way now.

A brisk breeze of pine and snow brushes the hair from the

back of my neck. My joints ache from the constant pounding of trekking through the snow, but I remain silent. A part of me is more curious as to whether or not we will see Lucius, the curiosity drowning out any potential panic. The greater part of me wants to know who this informant is. What kind of rat is able to sell out humanity's only hope for his own life? Why wouldn't they bring it to us? Surely Mavis and the Nightwalkers aren't known to certainly be alive, but the rebellion clearly is. We could have stood a chance, yet he chose just himself.

Roughly an hour later, Neris lets out a pitchy whistle, the frequency high enough that the icicles tremble in the pine boughs and it is nearly lost to the wind. Mavis crouches, so does Emi. I follow suit. Neris, however, pounces into the brush. A few yelps later, she rises, holding an older man by the scruff of his cloak. When she turns to show us his face, my heart drops.

"Are you fucking kidding me?" I groan as I come face to face with none other than Duke Gadsden.

CHAPTER 21

VEROSA

Duke Gadsden is as slimy as he was when there was hot water and all the finest luxuries of life. In fact, seeing him now feels more fitting than seeing him squeezed into finery or in tunics with golden buttons popping off. His face when he sees me, however, is entirely different than how it was in the palace.

"Ver-verosa," he stammers, his composure slipping. "I thought you were dead."

There is no lust in his face or voice like there was when I was a child. Now there is only fear—a sickening and satisfying fear that reeks, especially when his eyes drop to the scars on my exposed skin and the weapon at my hip. The callouses on my hands tell him I know how to use it.

His face is more telling than his words, despite the obvious fear that laces each utterance. Out here, I am not a princess bound to the king, and he is not a duke protected by his title. His family's name and crops protected him, while my crown failed to protect me from his unwanted advances.

A laugh escapes my throat, dry and humorless. It rattles through the forest, bouncing off the trees. The birds fall silent and the others rise, watching me cautiously. I am slightly aware of a metallic taste in my mouth and something warm dribbling down my chin. My lip has split. And I'm sure I look fucking crazy. Blood coats my mouth and drips from my face as I dive into hysterics. Then I draw my sword, my face hardening to stone as I allow it to prick the soft of his chin.

"Of course it's you," I seethe through clenched teeth. "You've always been a slimy bastard, only concerned with yourself. Your wants—no, *desires*."

He must catch on to where I am heading because his hands begin to tremble as he claws at Neris's hands to no avail. "Please, princess. You are misremembering. You were a child. It is only natural that—"

"So you admit that I was a child."

All the colors drains from his face and he scrambles for his words.

I cut him off, pushing my blade further in to draw blood. "I should gut you like the pig you are."

"Vera." Mavis's tone is warning.

"*But* you have something we need. So you have until Mavis is done with you to convince me that you deserve to live." I sheath my sword at my side. "Start squealing."

Neris drops the man into the snow, and when he attempts to crawl away, she slams her foot down on his spine. He howls in rage and pain, swearing vehemently. His blood trickles slowly from the thin cut I made, but yellow stains the snow beneath him amidst the red.

Emi cringes. "Gross."

I would laugh if I weren't so fixated on trying not to kill the man currently laying in his own blood and piss. The man who haunted me my whole childhood until I broke his wrist in the back of a ballroom for trying to touch me on my sixteenth birthday.

"I'm assuming," he wheezes between breaths, "that you're here for the solution."

"Yes, you cryptic bastard, the solution. Humanity's last hope. The way to stop this damn slaughter. Whatever you want to call it." Neris smiles. There's no hint of a soul behind her eyes. She backs up, daring the man to run.

To his slightest credit, he has enough sense not to, and instead rises to lean against the thick trunk of a pine tree. The trunks of the Krycolian pine grow thicker in the mountains, leaving enough space behind him for his whole body to press against it and offer a minuscule amount of relief to his aching back.

"How do I know you won't kill me?"

"From where I see it, you have two options. One, you don't say anything and Vera has her way with you right here and now without even a second to plea your case to us or the gods." Mavis bares her teeth as she speaks and flips an arrow of dark magic in her hand. "I have ways of getting the information I want from your body just as easily dead as I do alive."

Gadsden licks his lips nervously. "And the second one?"

"You spare yourself a few more minutes at worst, a miserable remainder of your life at best. Your choice."

The sick fuck spills everything in a single breath. "I found an Oracle in the mountains, the Oracle of Raonkin. They claim to know the future and can gift their visions to men, too, but you have to pass some sort of trial."

Mavis brings the power closer to his eye, letting a flame lick his cornea.

His eyes water and he cries out.

"What type of trial?"

"I don't know! Something about the gods finding you worthy?

I just know that if you pass, you see the future, any future you need, but if you fail, you die."

"And you didn't want to risk your life for those answers, so you thought you'd sell this information to the king?"

"Yes."

"So he could wipe out this threat to his reign and you'd walk away with your life and immunity."

"Yes," he wails.

"And this is also why you tipped off Tanja as to where Vera was when they tried to kill her. Because you saw her bleed once while trying to spy on the princess and knew she'd sacrifice herself so you could steal Vera away."

"Yes," he answers before he realizes what he has admitted to. He slumps against the tree, his eyes widening to the point of near bulging from his face. "Wait, no, I— I didn't do that. Verosa, please, I didn't."

I cannot hear his pleas over the rushing water in my ears. Somehow, Gadsden knew the king had planned to sacrifice me, and if he knew, how many of the other nobles did as well? Or perhaps he got it from a maid—he had a nasty habit there as well. It doesn't even cross my mind that he knew where my room was in the giant palace. No, that thought is the least shocking of them all.

And he knew Tanja was a pureblood, something that even I hadn't known up until her death. Something her mother most likely died to keep a secret.

"How did you know?"

"What?"

"How did you know she was a pureblood?"

Mavis's face tells me she thinks I should be asking other questions, but I don't care. None of those answers can bring her back or make sense of it. This one, at least, leads down a path of revenge.

"I saw her cut herself picking some roses for that other maid one day."

"She wore gloves." Tanja always said her skin was too pretty to risk any scars or callouses when working near anything sharp or potentially harmful to the flesh.

"She took them off when she thought no one was around," he counters quickly. His voice is shaking with nerves, but he wouldn't lie. Not while his life is on the line. And Tanja was often reckless when she thought someone would turn a blind eye. It all makes too much sense.

So Tanja awoke to Gadsden in my room, who told her I was about to be killed. Tanja rushed in, knowing exactly what she would find. She had the whole run to the tower to decide or choose to turn back. She didn't. She knew the whole time she would die for me.

Emi's eyes widen with something like pity and she steps forward as if to deck the man, but Neris grips her by the shoulder. Her knuckles are white and her jaw set as she watches. Mavis traces a long fingernail down the length of her arm until she reaches the junction of her wrist. Then her fingers wrap around the hilt of her blade, her eyes challenging Gadsden to say anything else.

Red pricks the corners of my vision and I am vaguely aware of Mavis producing a map and having the duke mark it with where this Oracle is rumored to be. She rolls it up and safely stashes it in her cloak before releasing the man, who rocks his head back heavily against the trunk of the tree.

Then, so quietly I almost don't hear it, "I'm glad it wasn't you, princess."

I've read stories where the characters are so blinded by rage that they don't realize what they are doing until they've done it, or where love drives them to the brink of madness. I've never known the emotion for myself before now. My voice is a dead vapor in the chilled air, and Mavis extends her arm, shielding Emi and Neris. Shielding them from me.

"What."

Not a question. I heard him, I just need him to confess it again. To tell the gods as my pardon.

"She was just the help. If you're to be queen, it was better for you to live."

Gold flashes across my mind—her eyes, her smile, her love. Everyone says when someone dies for you, it is an act of love. All I can feel is hatred towards myself. It fills each crevice and void of my soul until there is no room left for this supposed love she gifted me.

My face is mere millimeters from his now. His scent of sweat and filth covers the earthy musk of the bark behind him, both overpowered by the distant scent of something burning. Someone swears low under their breath and I can feel something prickling my arm.

Skeins of black flame have wound themselves around my fore-arm, dancing upwards towards my heart. A glance downwards reveals the stains crossing the front of Gadsden's pants have grown.

"It should have been me."

"Princess, no," Gadsden rambles, his face slick with a sheen of sweat. "Why would you say that? Why?"

"Because she was all that was good and kind, and I'm stuck here rotting. It should have been me."

All the pain I've so poorly bottled up comes crashing through, so terrible it burns my throat raw. I dig my fingernails into my palms until they bleed. The dark flames lick at the blood and I can feel the heat from them drying the last wick of moisture from my face. My tears are nothing but salt in my eyes as I scream, "It should have been me!"

All the tears I refused to shed for months finally break

through the dam, and suddenly, I am choking on my sobs. Not because of the guilt in my chest or the truth the guilt bears. No, I sob because the fact that I am here means she is not. My existence is due to her death. If I am still here, I still have to live through the pain of her absence, I have to exist in a world where her laughter does not chase me through stone halls. I have to exist while she... she is nothing but a memory lost to the wind. There's not even a body to remember her by. Cruel—all of it is too cruel.

Pain like nothing I've felt before tears through my heart as I slam my fist into the tree trunk beside his head. My flesh splits open upon impact, bits of bark grating against bone. My other hand flies open on instinct.

Duke Gadsden stares at me, open-mouthed, barely a sound escaping his lips. A strangled, choking sob comes from somewhere in the back of his throat as blood burbles only for a second, though he stares at me as if I were the one making the sound. The top half of his body and the tree fall at the same time in one fluid motion.

The only sound in the forest is the sizzling of charred flesh and my own labored breathing.

Mavis kneels beside the body and peers closely before letting out a low whistle. "You cauterized the wound. That shouldn't be possible and yet..." She rises, mud drying and sticking to the knee of her pant leg. "You're incredible." She says it reverentially, as if I am something worthy of awe. Like I didn't just butcher a man in cold blood.

And yet none of that matters. The world is cold, so cold, and I am still painfully alive.

"I want to go home." I hate the way my voice cracks. Not with remorse for what I've done, but anger that I didn't do it until it was too late. "Please, just take me home."

For Tanja, I would have killed however many men I had to. I

would've stained my hands beyond repair. For Blaine, Torin, Rowan, and the Nightwalkers, I would do anything.

I will become a monster so they never have to meet one.

Mavis opens her mouth as if to argue, but one glare has her closing it. She flicks an invisible piece of lint from her shoulder, though completely ignores the mud caked to the lower half of her body. "Well, at least we got what we needed before you killed him. I suppose we could stand to gain a bit more though."

Mavis fishes a tongue from her pouch, and even I squirm at the sight when she crushes it in her hands. She snaps and a dark blade flies from behind us. A few seconds later, she opens her pouch again before ten new fingers and other body parts are deposited in by a dark breeze.

"Twenty or so for the price of one," she says with a wink.

"That's sick." Even as I say the words, I can't help the way the corners of my mouth begin to lift. My dried tears disappear on my bloody and crusted lips.

It isn't until we have been walking for a good fifteen minutes that Neris's gaze drops to my bloody hand and she swears under her breath. The careful fingers of a soldier who knows the delicacy of a hundred weapons lift my damaged hand by the wrist. Her callouses brush against the joint, the ensuing shivers sending a spark of pain through the still-raw skin. "This needs medical attention."

"I'm sure she knows that, Neris." Emi rolls her eyes. I purposely ignore the way her face pales and she glances nervously at the wound, even while the sarcasm drips from her lips.

My own gaze trails theirs. My hand should have at least started to heal by now. Generally, I hate these types of wounds because the skin heals before the muscle and tissue, causing all sorts of internal damage. Usually, it appears healed, then someone well-meaning pokes or grabs the wrong spot and the process starts all over again. But not now. Now, the wound is still as raw as it was a few moments ago when it happened, the only difference being some dried flecks of blood amidst the new running stream.

"Don't you have healing powers?" Emi's voice rises an octave. "Heal it!"

"I should." My brows pinch together and my forehead creases. "But I've had some sort of damper on my power since I met Mavis. I guess I haven't gotten injured enough to notice. Small cuts heal slowly but fine. I guess this wound is too much."

"Or the dark magic is suppressing it," Neris hisses under her breath, turning her face from Mavis's disapproving glare.

The notion takes me aback for a moment, the only time I've seen her unflinching loyalty waver. The thought is pushed to the back of my mind as she reaches into the sack that hangs by her side, rummaging through it until her fingers wrap around the neck of a bottle. She pulls it from the damp and molded cloth and uncorks it with her teeth.

I raise a single brow. "You didn't pack any medical supplies?"

Neris cringes and opens her mouth, but Emi cuts her off, her features narrowing in warning. "We figured with a pureblood who can heal herself, we wouldn't need any. The rest of us are competent enough to not get injured, or at least smart enough to not punch a fucking tree."

"Language," Neris warns. "This is going to sting."

The words barely register before pain sluices through my mangled hand. Red blurs the corners of my vision and a strangled cry tears through my throat and burns my vocal cords until nothing comes out but hoarse wind. Stars spot across Neris's concerned face. Emi's already pale face turns a horrid shade of green as she spots the white bone peeking out behind my ruined flesh. Mavis slings an arm around her shoulder and ushers her away while her general finishes bandaging my wound.

"You'll need to see a real medic as soon as we get back. Pureblood or not, I don't want you doing anything with that hand, you hear me?"

Emi murmurs something like, "Okay, Mom," under her breath and Neris shoots the teen a playful glare. My heart swells in my chest and fills just a fraction of that ever-growing ache.

Even if Irene was never what one would consider a good mother, I know what a real mom should act like. I have read of the warmth and love in the books I so cherish. I would hole myself up in the library, my calves still bleeding over the fine rugs and a book tucked to my chest with another stack beside me. I always sat on the floor, the cool stone grounding me just enough that I never drifted too far into fantasy. The return to reality was always worse than whatever drove me to books and the lives I could live through them.

Aiko was a better mother to me in the few times I met her than Irene was her whole life. Aiko didn't need to know I really am her daughter, she just saw someone who needed love and gave it freely.

Neris certainly isn't the mother of the trio, more like the older sister. She affectionately buries her fist in Emi's fiery red hair. The child hisses—actually hisses—at the grown woman, who only lets out a hearty laugh while Mavis swats at them both. I can see Mavis being the father.

My heart weeps only for a moment. Emi is truly cherished. No, they *all* cherish each other. All broken rejects from a world that turned their back on them, the perfect pieces for their puzzle of a family.

They aren't so unlike my Nightwalkers.

The bond in my blood tugs me towards Mavis as I fall too far behind. She glances over her shoulder as I stumble, then slows her pace to extend her arm. "A dead pureblood is no good to me." She juts out her lower lip. "And knowing you, you'll trip over a tree root and snap your neck."

"Just admit you like me already and get on with it."

Neris barks out another laugh from behind us, while Emi grumbles jealously. I extend a hand her way, but the teen only bats it away, an embarrassed blush coating her freckled face. The mercenary queen, her wolf, and lamb—then there's me. I know I am not meant to fit in here, nor should I want to. My home is somewhere out there, searching for me, trying to bring me home. Rowan is out there. My parents are out there. And somewhere, Torin lives, and I will find him. I will bring him home. I won't lose anyone else.

But for now, it cannot be too wrong to wish to be loved by these three. It can't possibly be wrong to find that I am enjoying my time with them as if they didn't kidnap me.

Gods, maybe there is something seriously wrong with me, I think with a wicked smile. And maybe I like it.

CHAPTER 22
ROWAN

Kya sits propped on a stump, Amír fussing over her head. It takes both Blaine and I holding the gunslinger down to keep her from storming back to the rebels and shooting them all once she discovers a sizable welt on Kya's temple. Her anger is hardly assuaged when she learns it is from a man kicking her in the head when she was knocked over in the swarm. Kya informs her that the man left with a broken wrist and dislocated shoulder, which does help a bit.

Torin offers a dampened rag, which my second accepts and holds against the Vari woman's bleeding head. Kya winces at the cold, but remains still as Amír's cautious fingers prod along her ribs, searching for soft spots to indicate any fractures. Once satisfied, she retreats a bit, contenting herself to wipe the blood from her girlfriend's face.

Blaine accepts no such tender care from me. He has a sizable gash on his arm and his limp is worse than it was when we entered, but he bandages himself and threatens to emasculate me if I attempt to nurse him. I bite back a quip that his former lover wouldn't be pleased if that happened. The peace we've established is still fragile, and while I don't detest the man as much as I used to, I hope Vera realizes this is all for her.

We are still a few miles from the inn, where Derrín and my mother wait. Derrín is probably asleep by now, but Mother won't rest. Not until we are home safe.

"Come on, we need to get moving before something worse comes along."

"Worse than what?" Amír snaps, nonetheless rising.

"Worse than *you*," Torin quips.

I bite back a laugh while Amír's face contorts with indignant fury, calmed only by a gentle touch of the arm from Kya. It has always puzzled me how soothing and motherly Kya can be when I've seen her laugh while ripping a man's spine out. A silent and unassuming killer.

We trudge onwards in silence, but voices ring clearly in my head as if they were still beside me. Roiden called me the rightful king of Krycolis, and somehow, that was almost worse than him exposing me as a hybrid. *King.* The title is one that has chased me since my teenage years, but it has always been followed with "of mercenaries." My people are small and ruthless and I can use whatever force I deem necessary to quell a threat. King of Krycolis isn't a title that allows that.

Not to mention the ties it has. Ties to my father, Ophelus. The man I swore to kill for forsaking my mother. But now knowing the full story and seeing the love my mother still harbors for him... Even if I held the blade now, I'm not sure I could ever force myself to still his heart against it.

Yet he's not the same man, I have to remind myself. Thousands have died and millions more will if he is not stopped. I have a duty, and those duties will only grow as king.

Then there's Vera. We talked about moving far away, living a simple life with no strings tied to the crown. We were going to escape these lives we have been forced to lead, and now we must willingly walk back into them?

Derrín told me the best way to protect Vera is to befriend our enemies and elevate my own power. Would becoming king be the best way to do that, or would I be placing her further in harm's way?

Would I be able to willingly watch her walk away?

Verosa made it clear that royal life is not for her anymore, and how can I ask her to return to a palace where so much has happened? Where she has lost so many?

You have her eyes.

Lyra. Roiden's wife. She knew my mother, though she didn't admit how. She could have taken a guess—plenty of people have green eyes, and given that my father doesn't, it is likely my mother would. It was a guess, simple as that.

Yet something in my gut tells me it wasn't. That there is more to the story.

Now that I consider it, the rebellion began about ten and a half years ago. The group existed before that, but they were stragglers, just barely getting by and often killed in mass executions for treason. They were lost to the wind, then ten years ago, that changed. They became organized and moved in groups. They became quick and their attacks ruthless. Verosa was eleven when the first attempt on her life was made. It was at the queen's funeral, nonetheless. The royal family did not issue a statement, but the rebels did. They pinned dark-haired dolls to the palace walls and painted, "The false heir is next" in pig's blood.

I shake my head. I will ask my mother about it in the morning.

Amír settles in step beside me, Kya finally shooing her off. "You're thinking too hard."

"How do you know?"

"You look like you're about to kill somebody."

"Isn't that my natural face?"

Amír snorts. "Touché."

We settle in step beside each other, her long legs matching mine stride for stride. She's always done this since we were teens, making sure when she steps, her foot lands just a bit before mine. It started once she stopped growing and was just an inch shy of being taller than me. Mother tried to console her and explain she was incredibly tall already, standing at six foot two. Amír now must prove how much better she is by having a longer stride than I do, the action now more of a habit than a conscious act.

Silence envelopes the group, a welcome change from the quick pace of the night. We have nearly reached the inn now and exhaustion weighs heavy on all of our limbs. I keep my face stoic in the dark and my steps brisk despite feeling like the tether of gravity is trying to pull me back down to earth. Just as we break through the thickest of the trees right before the inn, I halt.

Every muscle in my body stills. Where there used to be five sets of footsteps, now there are only four. Ever so slowly, I inch my fingers towards the hilt of the blade that hangs at my hip. Blaine and Torin pull to a halt before me. I raise a single finger to my lips, letting the silence fill the questions that linger. Amír's braid slaps my face as her head swivels, recognizing who is missing.

From behind us, a soft grunt and the singing of a blade disturbs the stillness of the forest. Our fifth set of footsteps reappear, something dragging behind them.

Kya drops the man's bound body at my feet, not so much as a stray hair out of place on her head. The man's skin is littered with small, deliberate cuts and bruises—just enough to subdue, not enough to gravely injure or kill. He never stood a chance.

"Found him stumbling around behind us. He wears Mavis's colors, but look." She crouches down and pulls his head up by his hair. Torin winces at the man's pained moans, but my gaze goes straight to his eyes. His pupils have shrunk to be nearly invisible.

"It's dark," Blaine notes and I nod. They should be dilated, even slightly.

"She's gotten better control over her blinding. She didn't burn his eyes out of his socket this time," Kya notes offhandedly.

With a snarl, I bring the heel of my boot down on his hand and grind it into the dirt. Mavis's soldier howls, the dismal sound mixing with the symphony of his snapping bones.

It has been nearly a month since Vera was taken and the man is in rough shape already. He shouldn't be alive, but almost as if a sick gift from the gods, he is. Crusted blood around his mouth and fingertips tells me it was not so much gods that let him live and more so an unlucky rodent and a tad bit of fortune on his end.

"Bring him in for questioning." My voice is cold and I can see the moment he recognizes it. The one voice you never want to hear while wearing Mavis's colors.

Torin and Blaine shoulder his body and drag it towards our makeshift safehold.

"Kya?"

The assassin pulls a small dagger from her bodice and flicks the blade with a wicked smile. "With pleasure, boss."

CHAPTER 23

ROWAN

By the time we reach the basement, Kya has made quick work of tying our prisoner to an old dining room chair. A thin sheen of sweat already coats his forehead, his face pale and bruised. He must have been wandering in circles since they took Vera, her gift of blindness prohibiting him from ever getting far enough to hope for a rescue.

Now he can die alone, gutted by my assassin like the pig he is.

"You're a foot soldier, right? So you've encountered the Kijova and seen firsthand what happens to traitors in Mavis's ranks. I can assure you, if you do not answer my questions, all that will seem like child's play."

"I don't fear you."

A dry laugh. "Fear me? No, darling, I *am* fear. If you walk away from this—which you won't—you'd spend your whole life dodging every shadow and sleeping with your eyes open, knowing I could be anywhere and you'd never know. Tell me where she is." Her voice drops to a sultry timbre. "Or I'll have you screaming, making sounds you didn't even know you could make."

The lines between pain and desire blur so seamlessly when the blade is in her hand. Those words could carry a different sort of weight coming from those painted lips at another time.

"You've taken someone I love, and you're going to tell me where to find her." Kya runs her finger across our prisoner's jaw, scratching him lightly with her nail. "Your boss has been sending her back to us in pieces. Why don't we take a note from her book? I believe she started with a finger."

Her eyes narrow, and in an instant, a sickening snap resounds in the small room as she bends his finger back just too far. With serpentine precision, she strikes so quickly, all we can see is the flash of her blade as it slices clean through the joint.

The man isn't finished screaming by the time Kya holds it up, the flesh still warm. She fakes a pout and taps the dagger against her lip. "You moved," she whines. "Now it's not nearly as pretty as Vera's. Let's try again."

She takes another and immediately staunches the bleeding with an alcohol-soaked gauze. His screams rattle through the floorboards, the vibrations shooting up my legs from the soles of my feet.

He spits a bloody glob at her, just barely missing her pretty face. "You bitch!"

"Laei, at least try to be original. You've been calling us that for years now," she purrs. "Still not ready to talk? Mavis sent us teeth and fingernails, but you'll need your teeth to talk."

Committing torture and watching it have always been two separate skill sets for me. When I'm holding the blade, I *am* the blade. I don't think, I just cut until there is nothing between me and the cool metal in my hand. Watching is the personal part. Standing and waiting. How do I usually hold my hands? Where do I look? I settle for letting my eyes roam the room.

I can guess what type of person the innkeeper was just by

looking at this basement, and suddenly, all guilt for ruining his rooms disappears from my conscience.

Kya's cuts on the man are precise. They bleed little and cause enough pain that the man is writhing when he hears her approach. She flicks her braid over her shoulder and selects a small, curved blade. Personal and wicked.

Blaine and I stay confined to the shadows while Amír watches the door from outside. The little light in the room gravitates towards Kya. She shines along with her blades as she painstakingly slides her knife beneath the man's fingernail. Just a bit more pressure and it pierces the sensitive skin beneath. He grits his teeth against a scream and I let out a low whistle.

Blaine's jaw clicks as it sets and his teeth grind against the sound of metal slicing through flesh. The man's fingernail comes clean off.

"Kya is your interrogator?"

"The best there is. We will have our answers in a few minutes." The stronger-willed villains can last hours, but with Kya in charge of interrogations, we never have to wait until the next morning for our answers.

"But she's so kind." Blaine runs his hand over his face and frowns. "I suppose when we were warned of the Noiteron's assassin, I pictured someone a bit larger, with sharp edges. I never thought she could be warm."

"That's because she likes you. Don't get her wrong, if you hurt Vera or any of us, you could easily be the one in that chair."

Blaine's warm skin pales almost to ash, but I continue nonetheless.

"You still haven't figured out why her tattoos go from fingertip to elbow?"

Blaine shakes his head as blood sprays from Kya's latest infliction. The crimson liquid splatters well past her forearm and Blaine's eyes widen.

"Now you know."

"Where is my friend?"

When the prisoner refuses to answer, another fingernail flies off, a bit of meaty flesh still attached. Blaine flinches.

Her usually sweet demeanor gives way to show the monster underneath. It's been clawing to get out for a while. I've been impressed by how clean her blades have been all these months.

I stalk forward and Kya steps back to switch blades and methods. Each of my footsteps grows in volume until the man is all but convulsing as he trembles before me.

"Just give us an answer and we will release you. Mavis hasn't come for you, and given the situation, I doubt she will. You don't need to protect her. Just give me a place." When he pinches his lips shut, I make a show of sighing. "Fine, I guess my assassin can have her way then."

Kya inspects a dagger, and I recognize the thin weapon. The tip nearly grazes my cheek as I step back out of the way just a second before the knife goes through where I was standing to slice the prisoner's ear clean off. He howls in fear and pain and rage, thrashing against the bonds. Kya makes a show of slicing into his final ear, pressing the tip of the dagger in just far enough for blood to bloom from the wound.

"Imagine being completely in the dark. Not knowing where I am, when I am coming for you. No sound, no sight. No hope." She digs deeper and twists the hilt. "I can make it all go away. Don't test my patience."

I step back into the shadows, their shifting forms covering me as they always have. Kya's eyes burn with golden flame as she lifts her espa. I inhale sharply. She never uses those blades for torture, only to kill.

"Kya," I call with a warning tone.

Her narrowing gaze is her only indication that she heard me. The tip of her espa slices a shallow laceration at the base of the man's belly button, his eyes widening with wild fear. Ever so slowly, she drags it downwards, a red and silver line following.

"You found her in the bathhouse. I'm sure you loved that sight. One woman against all of you. Naked and alone. What if I just..." She drops the weapon below his belt and Blaine swears. "Not even the memory of that sight would get you up again once I'm done."

She pushes the espa deeper and he bites back against the agony. With fury written across her face, she pulls her arm back, but as she prepares to thrust it through, the man pleas.

"Wait! Bring me a map! I'll tell you where, just bring me a map!"

I knock twice on the door and Amír answers, pressing the parchment into my waiting hands. I unfurl it carefully and hold it before the man. With a trembling finger, he points to a specific spot in one of the first sectors we searched. I recognize the cave system based at the foot of the Hills of Siva. Less than a day from here.

I mark the spot and nod to Kya before rolling the map back up.

The assassin's lips peel back in a truly cruel grin. "Pigs like you always squeal the loudest."

I beckon Blaine out with a finger. He follows, not sparing another glance at the unholy sight behind us. The screaming stops as soon as it starts and the door shuts behind us. Amír offers a brisk nod and nothing more as we ascend the stairs to the main level. Derrín and my mother sit with Torin around the broken kitchen table, the only sound being the scraping of spoons against a bowl.

"There's soup in the pot." Mother smiles with her eyes. "Torin is a wonderful cook."

Torin bows at the waist with his hand over his heart. "You flatter me." Blaine fixes him with a stern glance and he immediately stiffens. "You got her?"

"We've got her. Go get dressed. We leave now," I bark out. I have no more time for waiting or jokes or anything. The map crinkles in my hand. I've got her.

Torin swears and my mother bites her fist to stifle a sob. Vera is like a daughter to her, just as much as Kya and Amír are. She's adopted all of my inner circle, but Vera sits closer to the softer spot of her heart.

I kiss the top of her head as I pass. "I will bring her home," I murmur into her hair, the same golden tresses that match mine.

She looks up at me, her green eyes shining with tears that mirror my own. I thank the gods every day when I look in the mirror that I look entirely like my mother, and nothing like my father.

Kya joins us outside moments later, the blood on her clothes now dried. Amír wipes a smudge off her face before giving her a leg up onto her horse. She wears the blood as a warning, the rest of her figure ensconced in darkness.

Dawn crests the horizon as I spur my mare into a gallop. My sword hangs heavy at my side as I set my gaze on the Hills of Siva.

Amír shoots me a glance. Without words, I already know what she is saying. *She might not be alive.*

She will be.

She has to be, or I will tear this world apart with my bare hands to get her back.

CHAPTER 24

VEROSA

Never have I ever missed my powers more than I do right now. Mavis and Neris are seated close to our fire, crowing over the map Gadsden marked. Meanwhile, Emi is retying my bandages and placing snow atop my wrapped hand in hopes that the cold will numb some of the pain. It is a sweet gesture, but nonetheless, a bit pointless.

"You know, ice is good for things like muscle and bone injuries, not so much splitting your whole fucking hand open," I try to joke, even though my pinky finger is all but dangling from my hand. The sight makes my head spin and my dinner revolt in my stomach, so I try not to think about it. Emi complained enough, as well, that Mavis tore off some of her shirt for Emi to wrap it with. "If you don't want to see it, *you* treat it," she had said. Emi swallowed thickly, and even though I told her she didn't have to, she still did, pausing at any flinch or sign of pain.

"You should have thought of that, then, before wasting my fucking time," she snaps, her face flushing pink.

I offer a small laugh, but I note the silver lining her eyes. Then without warning, she plops down next to me and lays her head in my lap, curling most of her spine against my stomach. I turn to Mavis and Neris for help, but neither woman offers any words or even a glance in my direction.

I can hear Emi sniffle lightly, and on instinct, bring my good hand down to brush her hair away from her face. "What's wrong?" I try to make my voice as soft as I can, gritting my teeth through the waiver of pain.

She sniffles again, louder this time. "He shouldn't have said that, about your friend, I mean. And—" Her voice breaks and it takes several moments before she is able to regain it. "And I'm sorry you lost her."

My heart softens in my chest. Emi might be young, but she is no stranger to loss either, Neris having mentioned multiple times now that she lost her parents. I had thought as much when I met her and saw the way she clung to Mavis, but she was so young, I hadn't wanted to consider it.

"Thank you," I whisper, though the words don't feel like enough.

The girl doesn't leave me with much time to dwell on it when she bursts into tears. "I'm sorry for wearing her face when we met. I shouldn't have done that."

Pain flashes at the mention of our first meeting, but I push it down. "Hey now, that wasn't your fault. You didn't know, and besides, Mavis is the one who did that. She should be apologizing, not you."

"But I agreed. I knew I was pretending to be someone that you had lost. I should have said no."

I snort lightly. "You can say no to her supreme will? I wasn't aware that that was something you could do in this cult."

"They can, *you* can't."

"You're a bitch."

"Don't wear it out." Mavis winks. Her motions are always cold, but she's developed a bit more personality since we first met.

Our short-lived conversation seems to draw a small laugh from the teen curled on my lap and she finally stops crying. My fingers tangle in her curls and my heart physically aches at the familiarity of it all. Slowly, I set to detangling them, the task proving to be significantly more difficult with one hand. Emi sits silently as I work. Her hair is beautiful and soft despite her obvious lack of care. Slowly, her breathing evens out and she melts under my touch. It does some to soothe the pain in my chest, this new vulnerability to her. I keep playing with her hair, mussing then smoothing it, even as I call out to the other two women.

"Has the map spoken to you yet or have you finally realized you've lost it?"

Neris cocks her head to the side in mock pondering. "You know, it did just tell me to leave you out here. I wasn't going to listen, but now..."

Emi's tiny fingers dig into my thigh.

I smile and dip my chin towards the girl. "Alas, your child seems a bit attached now. Wouldn't want to upset her, right?"

Neris comes over at that, her hand reaching out to pinch Emi's cheek. "Oh, the shit I put up with for you, kid." She shrieks when Emi licks her hand, then dissolves into a fit of giggles. I can feel each one through my ribs. It is soothing almost, like the feeling of being rocked.

CHAPTER 25

VEROSA

We arrive back at the compound late in the night, a few hours past the moon's ascent into the twilight. The guards outside the gate bow before shouting something to the people inside. After a brief moment of stone grinding on metal, the entrance to the cave begins to open, allowing us into the warmth.

I don't realize just how cold I am until I step inside the cave and feel heat seep into my bones for the first time in days. Emi clings close to my side, holding my cloak like it is her lifeline. I let my arm loop lazily around her shoulder as we trudge the snow in with us. Only Mavis stops to shake off her boots before continuing.

"Where are you going?" I call after her.

"To eat and take a hot bath," she replies as if it is the most obvious thing in the world.

Neris seconds the motion, following behind her.

Emi tugs on my sleeve. "Aren't you coming?"

I ruffle her fiery curls, much to her ire. "I'll be there in just a moment. I want to drop my cloak off and change my socks. They got a bit wet."

The teenager follows after the other two mercenaries, leaving me to my devices for the first time. Quickly, I allow my instincts to guide me, rushing up the hall and past my room.

Mavis's office is not difficult to find given that it is one of the only rooms without any guards in it. I slip one of my boots off and leave it to prop the door open—just in case there is another incantation on the door and I will be unable to leave once I enter.

Pressed against the far left wall is a simple wooden desk littered with various papers. I can only tell that it is wooden by its legs, the only bit of the surface left untouched by the stationary. I knock on both drawers. Just as I suspect, the one on the right sounds hollow and is shallower than the other.

Lifting the false drawer, I spot what I am looking for. A small, leather-bound notebook with addresses scrawled across each page, along with names, some of which have been crossed out.

Mavis has been talking about these men ever since I arrived— those that use their power and wealth to oppress and have their way over others. Judging by the names marred by a red X, I suppose those are the ones she got to first.

A list like this could prove to be invaluable as queen, but not only that, to weed out those who have hurt others while this earthly form of hell still rages on. Blame it on a Kijova, a wraith.

I tear a few pages from the notebook, cautious to only take ones from the back. I pray this small action will give me time to get out of here before Mavis can realize they're missing.

A wave of confusion slams into me. Where is this sorrow coming from, and why do I feel it at the thought of leaving? I shove it down again. There's no good in it. Not now.

I'm cautious when I slip into my room, taking off my boots and leaving my wet socks to dry on a rack in my washing room. I pull on a fresh set with a pair of slippers, not caring how ridiculous I look wearing socks and slippers as well as my snowy winter gear. At the last minute, I change my sweater, attempting to excuse my lengthy absence. I pay no mind to which I throw over my body, just making sure it is thick and warm.

The other three are still seated when I return. No food is sitting in front of them, though a full set of silverware rests before all four seats.

Neris grins. "Nice slippers."

"Finally." Mavis lolls her head back with a groan. "Emi wouldn't let us eat until you got back."

I settle beside the young girl, smiling at her despite the weird feeling in my gut. A few days ago, she was hurling insults at me, and a month ago, she wouldn't care if I died. Now, she isn't allowing her idol to eat if I am not at the table. The shift feels too instantaneous to be comfortable.

A few servants step out, smiling as they lay the table with warm hunks of meat and bowls of soup. Our cups are filled with sweet wine that tastes like a watered down Tyjn. Either way, it is better than leeche.

The first spoonful of soup warms my bones, and soon enough, the bowl is empty and the servants are delivering mugs of molten chocolate and dolloping them with spoonfuls of whipping cream.

Emi has a cream mustache in moments, to which prompts Neris's teasing. The two of them get into it while Mavis and I watch in cool bemusement.

I take a slow drag of my mug before resting it on the table. "I'm exhausted," I admit, drawing myself up from my chair. "I'll see you all in the morning."

Neris lifts her mug in cheers and Emi's arms encircle my waist in a crushing hug. I pat the top of her curls, smoothing some of the living flame.

Mavis follows me out the door and delivers me to my own. "Give me your wrist."

I do as I am told, watching as she drags a long nail over the thin white scar on my wrist. I don't have time to flinch or even gasp before it breaks skin and draws blood. She whispers something under her breath and the pressure beneath my skin subsides.

"The blood tether is broken. You are free to roam of your own will."

"Thank you," I say, adding on *for showing basic human decency* silently at the end.

She nods with a mocking salute before stalking back to her own room—but not before I sneak my hand into her cloak and snatch a rolled parchment. The map burns behind my back as her footsteps echo further and further down the hall.

The silence is the first thing I notice after the door snicks shut. Without Neris and Emi's childish squabbles and Mavis's sharp reprimands, the room feels empty. Cold.

Fighting the shivers that wrack my body, my feet force me towards the washing room again, where I run a hot bath. The water does little to warm the chill in my bones and muscles, but it is nothing compared to the first night I arrived.

I can still feel the phantom pains of the stones that tore the soles of my feet and my legs to shreds. The immobilizing chills as the cold stole my breath and slowed my heartbeat. The first bit of true warmth that night was when Mavis cut off Argon's hand and his blood sprayed across my arm.

Then someone placed me in warm water and held me until the shuddering passed. A healer might have come in the night, I'm not entirely sure. I hope not, or I have another person to find and be indebted to. After seeing how things work in Mavis's territory, I hope that healers here have free will over when they use their abilities, but I cannot be sure.

The fluffy towel wrapped around my shoulders does nothing for the shivers I can no longer contain. There is something so miserable about being in the cold for days on end, only for it to truly settle once you are in warmth. It is a cruel form of relief.

I bundle myself in blankets and form a nest of pillows in the bed once I've dressed myself. Then, for good measure, I pull a different cardigan on over my sleep shirt before snuggling in.

My drooping gaze trails over to the stack of books on my bedside table. Most of them have been read by now, and the majority have admittedly been filthy romances, but I still debate picking up a new one. Despite my wishes, my eyelids grow even heavier to the point where I cannot hold them open, and I succumb to the warm promises of sleep.

"WE'RE UNDER ATTACK!"

Someone's urgent voice rouses me from my slumber. Panic pushes the sleep from my eyes. Attack? Who would attack? Rebels? Kijova? Or...

"The Noiteron," someone gasps in the hallway.

Rowan. My Rowan. He came, he found me.

In under a minute, I pull on a thick pair of leggings and a sweater, my sock-clad feet finding their way into the black boots I've come to love. I brush past the servants shaking in fear, past the screaming civilians and charging soldiers. Someone shouts my name, tries to pull me back, but I can hear him now, hear his voice for the first time in weeks. I run, the promise of finding him at the end of my trek pushing my legs to pump faster, my feet moving in a flurry across the stone floors.

"Give her back to me or I swear to the gods—"

"You don't even believe in the gods, Rowan."

Mavis's response causes me to stumble, the ground rising

quickly to meet me as I lose my footing. Rowan and Mavis, in the same room. In my head, I always knew that the two used to be lovers, and in my head, I was okay with that. But now, my heart cracks slightly, parting to make room for jealousy and fear to claw their way in.

"You should start praying if you still do," he snarls right as I rise to my feet and step out from the hallway.

Rowan looks exactly as I remember him, though a new, darker aura surrounds him. His already messy hair brushes across his brow, obscuring a good portion of his face in shadow. His knuckles are white as he grips his sword at his side, no need for him to draw it yet. His presence alone sent the majority of Mavis's people running. Clad in all black, Rowan cuts an imposing figure —even armed with only a sword, the soldiers in the room slowly shrink away. His eyes darken with rage while Mavis stands calmly before him, her arms crossed over her bosom.

Behind them stand my friends, my family. Kya, cloaked in shadow as she always is, stands at attention with her espas drawn, rusty blood flecked across her form. Amír stands by her side, guns drawn, her right shoulder brushing against Blaine's. His eyes are clear as he scans the room for any potential threat. Then Torin...

Torin, who is alive.

Torin, whose gaze locks with mine and his tired eyes light up. "Vera," he breathes. And then he is running, running right into my arms as we both sink to our knees.

My fingers weave through his hair, pulling his head to my shoulder as I cannot decide between squeezing my eyes shut against the tears or taking in every bit of his appearance. His face breaks into a smile, a face I thought I'd never see again. I sob as both of his hands cup my face and he kisses my forehead.

Behind him, Blaine staggers, and Kya rushes to prop him back up.

We rise to our feet and slowly, I take step after step, my feet guiding me to Blaine. Rowan holds the line, his sword now extended to create distance between me and Mavis. My fingers trace along Blaine's features, his straight nose and strong brow. Kya's hand finds my other one, squeezing it until I move to embrace her. Even Amír offers a small smile before she places her finger on the trigger of her gun, raising it level with Mavis.

My brows furrow in confusion until strong arms wrap around my middle, Rowan's face burying in my hair and the crook of my neck. His lips trail kisses across my neck and face until he pauses to inhale deeply. "I missed you," he whispers, his voice low and gruff with want.

My knees buckle, but as I fall back, his grip tightens to hold me to him. And gods above, never have I felt more secure, so safe. So loved. I melt into his touch.

Mavis says nothing as we turn around, one of Rowan's arms still securely fastened around my waist. His sword is drawn again before us all, the steel blade separating me from Mavis. Something feels wrong, though. My heart shouldn't hurt. I shouldn't feel anything but relief that I get to go home and yet...

Sorrow sinks its claws under my skin at the cool indifference in Mavis's face. She doesn't care, and *I* shouldn't care. But I do.

"You traitor!" The scream reverberates through the cavern, rumbling the ground and jarring Mavis enough that her eyes widen a fraction. Emi rushes in, still clad in her night clothes, her red hair unbound and streaming behind her like a living flame. Neris runs behind her, trying and struggling to keep pace with the furious teen. I don't know who I expected to find her glare honed on, but I didn't expect it to be on me. More specifically, at where Rowan's arm lays tight across my waist.

My eyes dart back to Mavis. "You didn't tell her?"

She shakes her head and mouths *no*.

Behind me, I hear Rowan's breathing hitch. "*You,*" he breathes, his voice barely above a whisper. "I remember you."

Fury burns behind the tears that shine in her eyes. Her features pinch in rage and her face reddens as she screams. The corded muscle in Neris's arms flexes and strains as she holds the smaller girl back. Guilt pulls the corners of her mouth down and she murmurs soothingly to the girl.

My heart pulls within my chest and my hand reaches out, reaches to her in pleading. "Emi—"

"I'll never forgive you. I hate you!" The girl thrashes more violently now and Neris hauls her further away from us. "I hate you!"

I know that Emi's rage is directed towards the blond mercenary who stands next to me, unflinching, however, I feel her heated gaze slide my way and feel her fury in my bones. Her shrieks continue to rattle the walls of the room as Mavis dips her chin towards one of the many halls. Neris nods back and begins to lead away the one I once might've considered my friend. Her tear-streaked face contorts and she rips into her flesh with her teeth before spitting a blood glob the ground, mumbling something indistinguishable.

"Emi!" Mavis shrieks, her façade slipping for just a moment.

Some of the crowd hisses and a murmuring goes about. Kya pales.

My scarred hand seeks her painted one and she responds by interlacing our fingers. "What did she say?"

"It's a blood curse."

"On Rowan?"

She swallows thickly. "On you."

Upon hearing these words, Rowan's hands shove me behind him and Amír cocks her gun, her finger trembling on the trigger. Kya reaches for an espa with her spare hand while Blaine and Torin step before me, shielding me.

When I cut you, he bleeds. Mavis wasn't the only one who believes that—Emi apparently does as well. Rowan stole the ones she loved the most, and now with this curse, she intends to do the same.

I thank the gods I never mentioned Emilie to the grieving teenager. Rowan, however, snarls and steps forward, sword drawn, towards the hall where Emi and Neris have just disappeared.

Mavis blocks his path.

"The only way to break a blood curse is to kill the witch that cast it," he grounds out, now pointing the edge of his blade just beneath Mavis's throat. "Let me through."

"I will deal with the curse and Emi," she says smoothly, her voice the perfect picture of cool confidence. The mask is back up, even when Rowan presses forward and draws a pinprick of blood. Her army surges forward, but she halts them with a single flourish of her hand. "I said I will deal with her. I don't want Vera dead any more than you do."

I break free from between Blaine and Torin, both of the men stumbling in surprise. My hand seeks out the coarse fabric of Rowan's black tunic, holding firm and bringing my pleading stare to his. "No more bloodshed. Not today."

"This curse will kill you."

"I'm not dead yet. There's still time. You don't need to kill her."

Mavis watches with feline curiosity as Rowan raises a hand to cup my cheek.

His fingers lace around the back of my neck and the callouses on his palm scrape against my jaw. "How many times do I have to tell you?" he responds gruffly. "I don't care how many or who I have to kill to keep you safe."

My heart traitorously flips in my chest, but I shove it down. "But *I* care. So please, let's just go home."

He searches for something in my face, a sign or any disgust hidden within my features. When he finds none of what he is searching for, he sighs and drops his forehead to mine. His hand squeezes at the back of my neck, the fingers lacing through the underside of my hair. "As you wish." He flips his glare towards Mavis. "You know this isn't over."

She narrows her eyes to slits and her lips twist into a wicked grin. "I'd hope not, pretty boy. Life would get rather dull."

As the Nightwalkers begin to file out of the compound, I stand still, waiting for... for what, I do not know. For them to stop me? Or perhaps a goodbye? That seems a rather silly thought now, but it still doesn't settle right with me to just leave after all we've gone through the past few weeks. In some ways, this place has become another home. I've grown to love these people—the same people who now look like they wish to slit my throat as I walk out hand in hand with the man who killed so many of them. That betrayal burns worse, knowing that it is me who does the betraying. They trusted me, and while they took me from my home, part of me wishes that wouldn't change now that it is time for me to leave. The line has been drawn in the sand, splitting us apart in more permanent ways than the ache in my heart.

I turn my face to Mavis, expecting a smirk or any form of acknowledgment. We lock gazes and she turns without another thought, trailing down the hallway where Neris went, the faint sounds of Emi's screaming sobs still echoing. Somehow, that stings worse.

I can't fault the girl for hating me, no more than I can help the ache in my heart at the thought. It is much easier to hate those who deserve it than it is to feel nothing but sorrow for the ones who want you dead. It is much harder to be the villain in someone's story when you know you weren't the one to do anything wrong.

Rowan places both of his hands on my waist as we walk. Half

of me expects to be unable to walk out of the cavern, for the blood tie to pull me back, but nothing burns and nothing stops me from leaving as I take my first tentative step into the sunlight. The snow is the same as the last time I stepped outside the compound, and yet everything feels different. I know deep down, it is not the world that has changed.

VEROSA

Emilie's face breaks the moment I walk through the door. Instead of embracing me like the rest, she holds my hands to the light, running her gaze over my fingers then plying my mouth open to look at my teeth. She murmurs a prayer in broken breaths before holding my face to her chest. "Thank the gods."

"You're alive," Derrín notes plainly, not bothering to rise from his seat by the window. "And in one piece, it would appear."

I offer a puzzled look but don't ask for any other form of explanation. Some gut feeling warns me that I don't want to know.

Derrín finally rises, choosing to answer anyway. "I'm going to go bury the body parts," he says as he brushes past me. I notice his eyes are red and slightly swollen, and I smile sadly to myself. The mechanic will never be able to find the words to say that he worried for me and that he cares, not for many years, no matter how badly he wants to. Some things don't make sense with Derrín, and many never will, but I know he cares, even if he never says it.

Emilie pulls a blanket over my shoulders and steers me towards a room, but Rowan stops her with a soft yet stern look. I can see him mentally pleading for her to take a breath, and to let me breathe as well.

She sighs through her nose, suddenly looking incredibly old and worn. "I'll be in my room. I'm glad to have you back safe, Verosa." She runs a gentle hand down my arm, pausing to squeeze my wrist before walking off down the hallway, her arms tucked into herself, and her shoulders shaking.

"You should've let her stay."

"She would've examined every inch of you to check for injuries and only stressed herself out more," Rowan replies softly. "I'll go check on her later tonight, I promise."

"I'll go see her too. I'd like to."

"Whatever you wish, love."

Warmth bubbles in my belly, spreading through my core and down my arms and legs before moving to my face. I rise up on my toes and press a kiss to his cheek. It feels hollower than when I left, and I can feel his jaw unclench as my lips brush across it again, slower now. His eyes darken, but he keeps his hands to himself as he escorts me to our room.

Back when we first found the inn, I'd hardly had any time to acquaint myself with the space. I was too thankful for solid walls, even if they were thin and splintering. Wood beneath my feet instead of soft earth. The relief was short-lived for the obvious reasons, but I have the time now.

The room Rowan leads us to is only a bit smaller than the one I had at Mavis's, with wooden walls and shaggy rugs covering the floor. A small and weather-beaten desk sits in the furthest corner of the room near a window. Torn curtains have been pulled over it, blocking the reminder of the darkness surrounding us and keeping my mind from wandering. I've been terrified since I was a little girl that if I looked out into a dark window, there would be a face staring back at mine, not that I would ever admit that to anyone.

But the best part of all is the tapestries. They cover nearly every inch of dilapidated wood. Torn, beaten, some with their threads picking, while others are pristine. Glorious stitches marking stories that someone once deemed important enough to tell. I can't help but let my mind wander. If we survive all this, if we win the war, will they tell ours? Tell mine? I've never thought myself one to care about petty things like pride or a legacy, but now... For the hell we've faced, I'd like to see my tale stitched in jewel tones somewhere, even if it is hidden away in some private collection.

A sudden surge of shame courses through me. Tanja deserves a tapestry. That will be one of the first things I do when I take back the throne. I will find all the artists left in the kingdom and commission the best, commission them all. I'll fill a room with her story, her life. Her love.

Rowan stands closer, his hand stone against the planes of my stomach, my back pressed into his solid abdomen. He rests his chin on my shoulder and I can feel where he has to curve his back to do so. "I didn't sleep well while you were gone," he admits unabashedly. "And Amír got tired of my pacing. So I collected any tapestry I could find and hung them here. Something about it felt almost symbolic. How art could survive in a place like this. It also made me feel closer to you, as silly as that sounds."

My heart does something funny in my chest, not quite a flip or a spin or a twirl. A wide grin splits across my face and Rowan presses a kiss to the hollow of my cheek. The sight of Emi flashes across my mind, her screaming face contorted with rage and pain. That, and Neris's warning of what these people—my family—did. I shove the thought down. I shove it somewhere dark and cold and pray it doesn't resurface. Not tonight. Tonight, I am home and

I am loved and nothing else matters. Tonight it is just me and him, no one else. Nothing else.

"I learned something while I was gone," I admit.

"I'd imagine you learned many things."

I smack his chest lightly and he laughs.

"I learned who my parents are." Then, unable to bite back my grin any longer, "Aiko and Finneas."

Rowan pauses, his breath hitching, and the first tear drips down his face. Then the second, and he is burying his face in my neck. "Gods," he breathes, and I can feel his smile against my skin.

"What? Mad that you didn't guess it before?" I tease through choking laughter.

"No, it's just perfect." He pulls back, his hand cupping my face as he studies me. "I see them in you."

The thought swells my heart. Before I let the emotion overtake me again, I lean forward, pressing my lips against his. Rowan smiles into the kiss, his tears pressing into my cheek. He has loved my parents as his own family for so long now. Seeing this chapter close for them must be the biggest sigh of relief he's had in years.

Rowan brushes my hair away from my neck with the back of his hand and presses another kiss, longer and slower now, against the slender column. I offer a breath of a laugh but he continues, his lips tracing feverish patterns across the sensitive skin. He nips slightly at the junction between my throat and my shoulder, and I bite my lip to keep from crying out. He growls out a low sound of approval that skitters across every nerve in my body and sends my knees buckling. His tongue flicks over the small hurt. Heat and desire creep up my neck to my face in a scarlet haze and I push myself off of him, spinning so my hands can rest on the plane of his chest. His answering lopsided grin is teasing as he loops his arms around my waist. He leans down and presses a quick peck to my lips, but I hold my hand up against his lips with a small giggle to stop him.

"Stop, you rogue," I laugh as he continues to pepper kisses across my ticklish palm.

"Never," he murmurs against my hand with a sly grin. "You were gone a month. I missed you."

"I missed you too."

"Then..."

"Get your mind out of the moat. I need a bath, and to be honest, I'm not fond of the idea of going alone after what happened last time."

Rowan mocks a gasp, his hand pressing over his heart as he attempts to ignore my insinuations. Whether that be to assuage my embarrassment or take things slow for my sake, I don't know. "Vera, are you making a move on me?"

My cheeks flush crimson and I desperately wish he would go back to playing nonchalant. "Please, just put me out of misery and say you'll go."

His face softens and he tightens his grip ever so slightly. "Relax, sunshine. Of course, I'll come with you."

His old nickname for me unleashes a new wave of giddiness upon my weak heart, but the implications lacing his tone send a tsunami of a different emotion through my system. Something hotter, headier. I swallow thickly, my mouth dry.

I pluck a clean towel from nearby and hold it to my chest when Rowan raises a hand to stop me. He pulls the cloth from my body and presses a cool piece of metal into my hands. I look down at the ornately carved dagger and my breath hitches in my throat. It is the dagger he gave me back at the carriage ambush, the one that I used to take my first kill. I hadn't noticed then how beautiful the weapon truly is. The iron is surprisingly light in my hands, the hilt worn enough to be held comfortably without slipping. A finely carved rose crowns the handle, which is woven with iron thorns and vines. Gilded leaves comprise the hilt, the blade itself resembling an elongated thorn. Beautiful and yet deadly. The two ideals coexist in harmony as if there has never been a question as to whether it is possible or not.

"Where did you get it?" I finally ask, my voice thick with emotion.

Rowan blinks in hesitance before admitting, "Torin. He said the rebellion leader had it and returned it as a peace offering."

A million questions swirl in my mind. Torin? The rebellion? How had they known it was mine?

"Torin and the rebellion?"

"I will explain everything tomorrow," and then when I raise an eyebrow in disbelief, "I promise." His hand finds the small of my back, a firm anchor against the storm of questions brewing.

Tension laces the air for a moment before I let it fall and walk with him towards the bathhouse, the dagger still clutched firmly in my hands.

Rowan leans down to whisper in my ear. "You look so beautiful holding such a lethal weapon."

"Darling, I *am* a lethal weapon."

"That's my girl."

His praise chases a blush to my cheeks and I fight the urge to physically shake the color from my face. I naively hoped that this embarrassing effect he has on me would fade after the first month of us being together, but as fate would have it, I was once again wrong.

The bathhouse looks nearly the same when we arrive. A new door has been screwed on to the hinges to replace the one I apparently splintered apart in the fight. The room has been meticulously cleaned, no sign of any disturbance or enemy in wait. Still, my heart thunders in my chest.

Rowan opens the door and passes me my towel and clean clothes. I hold on to the dagger even tighter as I stare up, wide-eyed.

"I'll be just outside the door. You know there's only one entrance, so no one can get in."

"No!" The word slips between my lips before I can stop it.

Rowan jumps as if stung, his dark eyebrows shooting upward. "No?"

"Please," I plead, "don't go."

Rowan follows wordlessly, his jaw set and mouth a firm line. His fists clench at his side as he takes my items from my hands again and rests them on a dry spot near the edge of the bathing pool. I dip a toe into the water, ignoring his stare boring into my back.

I am suddenly so much more aware of everything—how cool the breeze is on my skin, the warmth of the pool, the steam that would do little to conceal anything. Rowan makes a show of turning around as if he has never seen my body before, and I slowly slip out of my clothes and into the water.

The pool is warm, with a soft floral scent. Something tells me Kya had something to do with that, given her usual antics. I let the water run over my body, smoothing it over my shoulders before dipping my hair in. I reach for my shampoo, but Rowan halts me, now turned back around.

"Let me," he insists, and I do not argue as he pulls my back against his knees and begins to lather my hair with the suds.

I haven't let anyone wash my hair since Tanja. The thought of it nearly brings tears to my eyes, but I shove them down. This is not the time for regret, nor would she want me to think of her with Rowan only mere inches from my wet and naked body. "Are you insane? Pull him in the water, you dumb bitch!" I can practically still hear her voice shouting at me now. "You thought he was attractive *before*? Try now when his clothes are all wet and clinging to his body and you can see everything..." That's generally where I'd cut her off and blush to high noon while she laughed at me.

Rowan gently massages my scalp but says nothing as I tilt my head back onto his lap, letting my eyes shudder closed. I probably just ruined his pants.

Still, he says nothing. Not as he rinses my hair, nor conditions and rinses again. Even as I finally move to rise from the pool and he turns his back again. I sigh dramatically, but nerves nip at my stomach and I open my damn mouth before I can think twice.

"Am I that hideous?" I ask his turned back. It is supposed to come out as a joke, but the small laugh sounds broken even to my ears.

He turns around, his motions stiff. Rowan's gaze darkens and he swears under his breath. He stalks a pace closer to the pool, leaving my clothes at the edge of the water. "Get out of the water." His tone is commanding, yet not demanding.

Nerves ripple in my chest under his hot stare, but I find my body obeying. Slowly, I rise, walking to the edge and allowing the water to sluice down my body in taunting rivulets. Rowan traces each one's path with his eyes, his gaze hungry and dark. Suddenly keenly aware of his assessing gaze, I move to cross my arms over my chest but he is quicker, holding them to my side and finishing his sweep of my exposed body.

"You don't need me to tell you you're beautiful," he growls before dropping to his knees. "But just in case you still have doubts."

My knees buckle as he plants a kiss just above my navel, his hot breath skittering across my wet skin. One of his hands slides up to cup my breast, his thumb teasing the firm peak while his other clasps the back of my thigh. His kisses trail lower and a soft whimper escapes from the back of my throat. Gods, is this really happening right now?

Rowan looks up. Laei, he is beautiful, staring up at me from beneath those thick lashes and on his knees before me. He holds eye contact as he presses another kiss to me, this time just above the apex of my thighs. His approval rumbles through my core at the soft moan. He's barely touched me and yet I feel as though I could come apart just from that stare alone.

"You have to tell me when to stop."

"Gods, don't stop."

It is all the permission Rowan needs before standing swiftly and bringing me with him, my legs instinctively wrapping around his middle. I hardly have time to blush before he lays me down atop my towel, bracing himself above me. His shirt is off in a moment, tan, corded muscle now exposed and showing off just how powerful the man before me is. I reach a finger up and trace one of his scars, eliciting a small shiver.

Nerves settle in my stomach and I halt my hands on his chest. "I've never done this before."

"I gathered."

"No, Rowan, I—"

"Do you want me to stop?"

I shake my head, and he places his lips on my neck again.

"We don't have to go all the way. There are other things I've been dying to do to you, sunshine."

The things his words are doing to me couldn't possibly be healthy, nor is the way my heart flips at the sight of him over me. I feel... safe. Protected. And in a place where so much violence has occurred against me, he is like my miracle solution.

"Okay."

The word barely leaves my lips before a sharp moan escapes as Rowan lowers himself over me. His lips trail from my neck down to between my breasts before he takes one into his mouth, teasing the sensitive nub with tongue and teeth. Something new creeps into my body—a hot desire incomparable to what I felt while reading those books back at Mavis's. This is stronger, needier, and gods, it feels sinfully good.

Heat pools between my thighs and my head would slam

against the ground in pleasure if not for Rowan's hand. My hips buck off the ground as he takes my tender skin further into his mouth and gently scrapes his teeth across the tip. His fingers grind into the soft flesh between my hip and my thigh, pinning me in place.

"Gods... gods," I moan.

Rowan looks up with a devilish grin as his spare hand trails lower. "Yes, love?"

I would've retorted with something equally witty, I'm sure, if he hadn't swept his finger over the sensitive bud between my thighs. His fingers circle again, eliciting another moan from the back of my throat. I nearly whimper when his mouth leaves my breast, it suddenly feeling empty without his presence.

Never have I felt so lost in anything. This need clouds my every sense. There is no more bathhouse. No more Nightwalkers, no more war. There is only Rowan—Rowan and his wickedly talented tongue and fingers.

Then he hooks an arm underneath my knee and pulls my leg over his shoulder. I nearly shriek in shock and embarrassment, as I am now fully bared to him, but Rowan's not staring between my legs. He holds my gaze, his own predatory and ravenous.

"You're in control, Mei Reinha. Tell me how you want to be worshipped."

A choice. A choice to continue or leave things as they are. We've already crossed so many lines, pushed so many boundaries tonight. And yet the ache in my core is unbearable and desperate for his attention. I need him like I need oxygen. The way he claimed my title as queen rather than princess does nothing to assuage that heady need. No, it only grows. With no hesitance, I finally whisper,

"Take me."

The first flick of his tongue sends me reeling, my reality all but shattering as Rowan leads me towards the edge then backs away again. Desire thrums potent in my veins as he dips his head lower to get better access, his tongue flicking across my core, then lazily back towards my apex. I gasp his name, my fingernails biting into his muscled back. He groans, the vibrations sending pleasure rippling through me. My hips thrust towards him involuntarily and he laughs.

"Needy," he taunts, withdrawing just long enough for me to miss him. "Do you always want me this badly?"

"Yes," I breathe.

Rowan pauses his ministrations with a bastard's smile. Tension coils in my core and I gasp as he allows a finger to barely graze over my sensitive skin. So close to where I need him and yet...

"I can't hear you." He leans closer, his breath skittering across my exposed sex. "Tell me you need me as badly as I need you. Tell me I'm not the only one who died without you in my bed every night for the past month."

"I need you. Gods, I need you," I whine, the need for release clawing up my center.

"Good girl."

Rowan plunges his fingers into me as his tongue flicks, a shattered cry tearing loose from my throat.

Mavis was right in saying that sex is a power, because here, with Rowan on his knees and my back arched with pleasure, I have never felt more fucking powerful.

Rowan makes love the same way he does everything—perfectly. He molds himself to my body like an artist, his hands doing the gods' work with each flick or stroke. I can feel myself coming undone with each motion, each groan against my center bringing me closer to a release until my hips buck and I shatter with his name on my lips.

Rowan works me down slowly, his praises never ceasing even as his hands still and he lays my leg down beside my other. He rocks forward, taking my face in both of his hands. "I need you to taste how fucking sweet you are," he whispers before he crashes his lips to mine.

I don't know how he can expect me to focus on anything other than him. The gentle weight of his body pressing into mine. The scent of citrus and leather. The hard length of his desire pressing into my stomach.

I lean forward to take him, to make him feel as good as he has made me feel, but he stops me.

"Tonight is about you."

"But I want you to enjoy it too."

Rowan takes one look down my body, his gaze lazily trailing every mark he's left before he brings his eyes back up to mine. His tongue swipes over his lips and he brushes across my mouth with his thumb. "Trust me, I did."

Heat creeps into my cheeks, and the space between my thighs still feels... sensitive. Satisfied, but tingly. I slowly close my legs and rise to my knees, kissing Rowan's forehead then his nose. "I love you," I breathe.

His lips find mine again as he wraps his arms around me. "I love you." This time, his kiss is slow and sweet. I've noticed he never says, "I love you too," only "I love you." As if it is a fact and not a repetition of a sentiment. Like he does.

My heart swells as he pulls me to my feet and wraps the towel around my shoulders. My knees buckle as I stand and I brace myself against his forearms.

He chuckles, a low and dark sound. "Sorry," he murmurs, not sounding sorry at all.

I bite my tongue in order to keep from poking it out at him and instead reach for my clothes. I drop the towel slowly, making a show as I bend over for the discarded garments. I dress slowly, Rowan's gaze hot on my back. His hands find my hair the moment I am clothed, pulling me back towards him. His fingers weave through the inky strands, pulling gently until it is tied atop my head in a neat braid. I don't ask where he learned to do that.

As we walk, his hand lights on the small of my back. When it isn't there, it is on my elbow, my shoulder, my upper arm. Touching, always touching me, even as we settle in the main room of the inn. Everyone else gathers around an unlit firepit, bowls in their hands.

Blaine ladles the soup into a spare wooden bowl, chunks of tender white chicken and wild rice splashing in the broth. His hand stills on the spoon, his eyes trailing to my still-wet hair and skin and the door where Rowan and I just walked from. He notices the flecks of soap and water staining Rowan's knees. My cheeks flush as his stare turns hot and accusatory towards the mercenary.

I accept the bowl with a small, "Thank you." I inhale deeply and nearly moan, but stop myself as I catch Rowan staring at my face intently. Gods, he couldn't be more obvious if he tried.

"How did you manage to find chicken?" I ask, settling on the ground beside Kya. I withhold a flinch as I sit and curse Rowan's skill while trying to maintain composure surrounded by my newfound family.

A smirk lifts the corners of the blond's lips. He helps himself to dinner as Blaine recedes to stand by Torin, then settles beside me. His thigh brushes against my own.

Gods.

"They had some out back," Amír answers between spoonfuls.

Kya leans back, her inky tresses spilling over the gunslinger's shoulder. Amír brushes her lover's hair to the side, careful not to sully their silky sheen with her dinner. They are open with their affections and bedroom activities, yet there has never been any of this awkward tension. Maybe there was the first time. I'll have to ask Kya later.

"Very descriptive," Rowan drawls before dodging an expertly thrown piece of bread.

Emilie smiles behind her spoon, tucked into a worn blanket. She says nothing about Rowan's wet knees, nor the small water stain on his shoulder where my leg was. She avoids looking at us in general, actually, and I begin to wish that the earth would swallow me whole.

Silence aside from the sounds of eating fills the room until Derrín breaks the silence.

"You didn't do it in the pool at least, right?"

Blaine's knee hits the chair in front of him and Amír chokes back a laugh.

Kya stares agape, flinging her twin a filthy glare. "Derrín!"

"I'm just saying it is our only place to clean ourselves, unless you all were fond of the river."

"I thought the river was delightful." Rowan grins and runs a scarred hand through his hair. Bastard. He's actually enjoying this.

"No," I offer meekly, hiding behind my hands. All that confidence I possessed in the bathing house has disappeared instantly, and I set my empty bowl on the floor as my stomach turns.

Kya lays a hand on my arm. "I fucked Amír against that wall right there with the hilt of my knife. You might want to move over a little, Torin, unless you want to keep leaning on that holy spot."

"I doubt it's holy."

"The noises she made were."

Kya's reply shuts down Torin's dry response.

The words are so bold and unabashedly filthy that I find myself coughing, then near laughing as Amír's face blanches. Derrín groans and excuses himself while Torin hastily moves from his spot on the wall. Emilie keeps eating like she never heard anything.

Rowan sighs. "In front of my mother? Really, Kya?"

"You didn't seem to mind a minute ago." She sips her broth noisily. "Besides, it's just sex." The assassin drapes herself over her lover's knee now, their fingers interlocking as Amír regains some of her color.

The rest are too horrified by the new and explicit information they've received to remember what Rowan and I did. Everyone except for Blaine, who remains still, his eyes unfocused.

Rowan picks my empty dish up from the floor, asking in a soft voice if I am still hungry. When I say no, he carries the dish to the wash basin and rinses it clean before returning to where I sit, offering me his hand. The others murmur good nights, beginning to disperse to their own rooms with promises of discussions tomorrow. I leave the room hand in hand with Rowan, leaving Blaine alone to his thoughts.

Guilt gnaws at the edges of my consciousness, but nevertheless, I let Rowan lead me away, down the halls to the room we found before. He allows me into the bed first, letting me rest on the edge closest to the wall and furthest from the door. He settles in beside me, his presence all encompassing. A wave of citrus and leather washes over my system and I sigh. The darkness of his presence has never been the same sort of darkness that plagues my nightmares. His is warm and covers me with protection. There is no chill of terror or smothering. I settle against the solid plane of his chest, my face against his bare skin. I can feel his lips as he presses a kiss against the top of my head and wraps his arms around my middle. I drift off into comfortable sleep, the dark claiming my consciousness.

CHAPTER 27
VEROSA

Rowan shifts in his sleep, the motion rousing me from my own. I stretch my arms skywards, my every joint popping as they snap into place after a night of good rest. Rowan lays on his back, his face exposed to the light drifting in through a gap in the curtains. Tiny filaments of dust dance in the weak golden light, cascading around his face like a golden halo. I turn on my side, propping my face on his chest to study him.

My pinky traces the straight lines of his nose, his strong jaw and brow bone. My palm traces down his chest and abdomen, his scars scratching the surface of my palms. I lean forward to kiss one on his shoulder that I recognize. He got that one saving me a year ago from Mavis's goons the night we met. Its jagged, raised peaks etch the first lines of our story, and as much as I hate seeing or remembering him in pain, a small smile lifts my lips. Despite it all, that night brought me to him. It brought me to Kya and Derrín, and yes, even Amír.

A low knot forms in my stomach. It brought me to my parents.

Aiko and Finneas... I don't even know where they are right now. Don't know if they're alive or not. I won't think of that. They must be alive, just as Torin is alive. Everyone else thought that was impossible, and yet here he is.

Here he is working for the rebels, the people who want me dead. He swore he was loyal to me always, and yet...

Rowan's knuckles trail up my arm to the junction of my shoulder then back down again. He blinks the sleep from his eyes and nudges my face upwards with his shoulder. His lips capture mine slowly, and he keeps his eyes open a second before they flutter closed. "Good morning," he murmurs, his voice low and laced with sleep. The sound goes straight to my core.

"Morning, sleeping beauty." I prop myself up on my forearms. My bangs fall messily in front of my face and I attempt to blow them away before I give up.

Rowan chuckles, the sound reverberating through the bed. I rise now and Rowan groans, trying to pull me back down.

"Come on, I've got questions to answer, and a few of my own."

"Can't that wait? It's only dawn."

"If not now, then never." I smirk as I saunter towards the door. "Besides, they're all awake."

I'm not wrong. Amír stands by a griddle flipping grainy pancakes while Kya lays against her back with her arms weaving around her middle. A bowl of winter berries occupies the center of the table next to a plate of roasted potatoes. A pot of coffee sits beside the griddle, the black liquid less appetizing now with the absence of milk and sugar. Derrín sits at the table, popping a piece of meat into his mouth and sipping at the black coffee. Blaine and Torin sit beside him, completely engrossed in their conversation.

"Where's Mom?" Rowan asks through a yawn. He stretches and attempts to right his bedhead.

Amír nods to the porch out front and he follows it out the door. A few moments later, they reenter, Emilie greeting me with another hug. She smiles when she notes the less noticeable dark circles under my eyes and motions for me to sit beside her. Rowan serves us both platters of breakfast before going to serve himself.

"Where's this breakfast in bed for us?" Torin quips.

My eyebrow raises at the new closeness between him and the mercenary.

Rowan takes a slow sip from his mug of coffee. "Last I checked, they're not in bed."

"Touché."

Blaine remains silent.

Emilie coos over my hair, noting that she would have to trim the edges for me soon and asking when I last saw the sun. I swallow back the image of that man and his charred remains, split in half. I smile instead and tell her how I beat Emi at a snowball fight, leaving out names or identifying details, of course. Rowan and the others go rigid at the mention of my time with Mavis, but Emilie only smiles.

"We do need to talk about that, by the way," Amír notes, spatula in hand. "What happened with Mavis?"

"Laei, Amír, it is dawn. *Dawn*," Rowan groans.

I frown at his reluctance to discuss what has happened. The same way he has withheld the information on Blaine's whereabouts in the past, or why Torin is with the rebels now and yet sitting here at our table.

I clear my throat. "Actually, we do need to talk." I swallow a bite of food before swiveling towards Torin.

He pauses for a moment, then his shoulders slump in resignation. "I suppose I do owe you some answers."

"You suppose?"

"I do," Torin responds surely. He sighs deeply, his hands bracing on his knees. When he opens his mouth, he tells me all that I assume he has told the others. How the rebels found him half-dead outside the palace after a near-death encounter with one of the first Kijova. How Ruby was with them already and convinced them to save him. In turn, he was nursed to health and pledged his allegiance for pure survival, until he got the notion that he could work his way up the ranks to save my life. He tells me how originally, he planned to use them and leave, but has now decided to be a double agent to convince them to spare my life and unify all the survivors. He explains his guilt, his suffering, and begs for forgiveness.

But there is nothing to forgive.

Torin's eyes swell with tears as I squeeze his hand and tell him as much. Blaine stiffens but smiles a bit at that, some of the tension disappearing slowly from his face. Then their eyes turn to me and I divulge all that occurred at Mavis's compound.

"And there's another thing," I offer meekly. I spotted the teeth when I entered last night, figuring they were the pieces of "me" that Kya explained were shipped to the Nightwalkers. I stalk over and claim one before they can stop me and plead with the dark magic that has been lying dormant in my blood. It responds to my call and forms a small ball in my palm, dancing in contrast to the morning light.

I expect maybe awe or slight fear. I do not expect Emilie to go pale and clutch at her chest before excusing herself from the room. Amír swears and Kya's eyes widen. The others just stare open-mouthed until the darkness disappears, taking the tooth along with it. I wash my hand off in the sink before returning to my breakfast.

"Mavis taught me to wield dark magic without paying the cost. She said it would make me more powerful if I could wield both light and dark. It would make me the most powerful weapon in this war." I do my best to explain and wait for the relief to show on my friends' faces.

Pure disgust and horror show instead.

The worst of them though?

Rowan does his best to conceal his shock, which is horrifying given how well he usually hides his emotions. His throat bobs and his eyes widen, sending a knife through my gut.

Kya swallows thickly and is the one who tries to hide it the best. "Let's talk about this later," she says slowly, gauging the others' reactions like one would a wounded animal. "We've got more news."

I take a long sip from my mug, peering over the lip intently as Amír unfurls a long parchment. Names have been messily scrawled across, and she assesses each with a predatory gleam in her eye. "We didn't have a moment to fill you in on everything yesterday, given... everything. But the rebels will be here with delegates in roughly..." she glances outside, then back at me, "two hours to discuss the terms of our alliance and plans moving forward. Seb will be there too."

My heart rises as quickly as it sinks. Seb is alive and coming, but so are the rebels. Someone who was willing to die to protect me and a group of people who want me dead. I'd think that the two emotions would cancel each other out, but I am left feeling jittery and anxious yet relieved simultaneously.

"You just got back, so you don't have to come if you're not ready," Rowan says carefully, running his tongue over each word as if tasting their danger.

I can feel my eyes narrow ever so slightly at his words as I push myself away from the table and stand to get ready. "I'm ready. Or I will be in a few minutes after I get dressed."

I ignore their searing stares as I leave the room. Undoubtedly, questions will begin to swirl the moment I leave, about what truly happened while I was with Mavis, my new powers, Emi. They saw the way the girl's eyes drifted from Rowan's form to mine during her declaration of hatred, they've just yet to say anything about it. Amír usually would be the first to, but somehow, she's managed to show a modicum of restraint.

"If you come down in a crown, I'll shoot you."

Never mind.

I allow myself a bit longer in front of the mirror today, not looking at my appearance, just sitting still for a moment. This might be my last moment of stillness and quiet before my life gets shot back into hell, so I might as well take it. Savor it.

A low rapping sound comes from the door. Blaine peeks his head in, his knuckles still pressed against the wood as if poised for another knock. "May I enter?"

"If you must," I droll.

He hesitates, then sees the upward tilt of my lips and allows himself to step inside. He settles on the edge of my bed, now freshly made aside from his presence. His steely gaze traces over all the tapestries that adorn the walls before it makes its way back to me. "This is nice."

"Blaine, I don't mean to snap, but you're horrible at making small talk. What do you want?" I do my best to make my tone gentle. The truth is, my ire isn't directed at him, and it shouldn't exist in the first place. I shouldn't feel angry with Rowan at all, but a small rage simmers at the base of my throat. He is just trying to be considerate; I know this. I need to know this.

"I wanted to see how you are," he admits slowly. I note the clarity of his eyes and his voice. While he rubs at his temples now, he seems completely aware of everything. "We didn't have a chance to talk last night, and the Torin thing was a lot for any of us to take in."

"I'm guessing that's where that scar on your fist came from?" I bite back a laugh at his embarrassed flush. "It wasn't there when I left."

"You'd be right about both of those things. But Rowan was right—this is important and we just got you back. If you aren't ready, let us know."

"Blaine," I bite out, that irritation rising again, "if I wanted to be coddled, I would've stayed at the palace and let them kill me. If I'm going to stop this war, I need to partake in it."

Blaine's brows set in that scowl he always seems to be wearing, his features sharpening as if I flipped a verbal switch. "So now you want to be queen again? After you already turned your back on the people?"

The verbal slap slams across my face as if it is physical. My cheeks heat, embarrassment and rage commingling in the crimson flush. From anyone else, it might have been a backhanded insult, but from Blaine... His is so much worse because he actually means every hateful word. He has always thought of the people before me, like a good ruler, a good man. Meanwhile, I shut my eyes and left, leaving them alone. I tried to kid myself and say I was doing it for them because I would be a bad leader, but deep down, we know the truth. I feel guilt, yes, but my own selfish desires outweigh the consequences they would face.

"Do you always have to be such a dick?" I lash out. It is the only defense I can conjure. Pinning the blame on something else entirely, something unrelated to my sins.

But per usual, Blaine is not having any of it. "Did you really think he would let you go? Lucius would only lead Krycolis through marriage, so with both of you gone, there would be no heir. No one to take over. Enemies would get wind of this and invade; the rebels would have invaded, and I've met their leader. He would have been ruthless, the type to kill anyone in his way. Do you know how many people, innocents, would have died by his sword? What about other enemies? Or by the king as he sacked homes and tortured civilians to find out where you went? And if Tanya had lived, then he would've known to go after her first. Then when she didn't crack, Torin, and then me. None of us would have given you up, but our blood would be on your hands. Now tell me why you are fit to be queen?"

The rejection stings like nothing else. All my life, I have been raised and groomed to be queen. I've memorized every line and verse of law in the kingdom, now able to recite them upon command. I've had my wrists whipped if I held my cutlery at the wrong angle, or if my spine was not straight enough. I've been preened and polished until I bled, all to prepare for the weight of the crown.

"My whole life, I was raised for this."

"Your whole life, you were raised to be a figurehead. An image. Up until this year, you thought the cursed were literal monsters. You so easily forgot that they were your people too."

Tears of embarrassment prick at the corners of my eyes, but Blaine continues, his voice unwavering.

"I know you were kept in the dark on purpose. I know it is not all your fault, but by the Laei, at least take accountability for what was. You have always been so headstrong about everything and nothing. I never understood how you could sit silent as they lied to you."

My mouth clamps shut, and even when I try to open it, no words utter from between my lips, just a dry, croaking noise.

Blaine's eyes are dark and sorrowful and his hand twitches as if longing to reach for mine. Instead, his shoulders go rigid and he rises. "The rebels are cresting the hill. They'll be here soon. I just thought I'd let you know."

He closes the door on his way out. Gently, so gently. Like he was never here.

A dry scream sticks to the back of my throat. Not because he was wrong—Blaine is hardly ever wrong, especially when it concerns me. No, he's so right about everything that my heart burns with rage and sorrow.

Slowly, I smooth my dress. Darkness coils in my stomach, but I shove it down. The rebels are nearly here and if there is anyone I cannot afford to show weakness in front of, it would be them.

My fingers fly to the dagger at my hip, and I press the pads of my fingertips against the iron thorns. They are blunt edges, but the dull bite calms my senses just enough that I can clear the mist from my eyes and open my door.

Later. Everything that Blaine just said can be dealt with later.

Rowan's hand finds my elbow, the mercenary appearing at my side as if from thin air. I smile brightly at him, vanquishing any last trace of my sorrow or contempt. If he notices, he doesn't say anything, just walks beside me in silence until we round the corner that will take us back to the lobby of the inn where the others wait.

"So," I drawl, my feet suddenly dragging. "Any idea how long this meeting will take?"

His lips lift into a smirk. "Why? Do you have somewhere more important to be?"

"Well, I was in the middle of this book."

"A book?"

"Mhm, one of those filthy ones Kya likes." I near laugh at his darting glance. "I think I should like a whole library of them once this war is over."

Rowan pauses, glancing over his shoulder before pulling me down a side hall. His arm braces on the wall behind me, his lips dangerously close to my throat. "When we retake our kingdom, I will build you the largest library this world has ever seen, and I will take you against every bookshelf. Tell me everything that goes on in those dirty little books of yours and I will make it happen once you're on your throne."

My knees tremble as my breath hitches in my throat. I don't know where I find the strength to whisper, "Our."

"What, love?"

"I preferred it when you said *our* kingdom. Our throne."

My tongue feels heavy in my mouth, the words lazily being dragged from my hazy subconscious. Everything is Rowan. He caresses my senses, completely enveloping me in him. The scent of citrus and pine floods the room in a thick wave, and his emerald gaze pierces through what little bit of my sense of self that I have left.

His knuckles graze my side as he trails them from my hip up to my ribs, mapping the expanse of my torso. His warm breath kisses my skin and I am not ashamed to admit that my gaze has now settled on his lips.

His voice is low and heady when he chuckles. "I'll have you on our throne, as well, if that's what you want, sunshine."

Desire scatters across my flesh in the form of goosebumps and my back involuntarily arches off the wall. My chest scrapes against his as I breathe and his fingers raise to hook under my chin.

"What happened to your boldness? Were you all talk with that wicked tongue of yours?"

I feel the sudden urge to stretch up on my toes and press my lips against his, to show him just how wicked this tongue is, but my feet remain rooted to the worn wooden floorboards. He smirks knowingly, already basking in the victory that comes from my breathlessness. His arm wraps around my midsection in the gap between my spine and the bookshelf, his fingers splayed across my waist. With one deft motion, he hauls my form against his and crashes his lips down onto mine.

He is shadow and light. Sin and good. Pure bliss and eternal torment. Each time his lips close over mine, I feel as if I might die, and yet when he pulls away, I find myself leaning forward on my toes in search of him again. His mouth is warm, and he chuckles against my lips before lacing his fingers through my hair at the base of my neck. He pulls my face to his, leaving me no choice but to stay enveloped in him as he claims more of me. My body. My heart. My very essence.

I don't need to be the sun in his life. I don't need to shine like

Mavis shined to him. I just need to be the stars that reside in his darkness. Gods, just grant me that much.

Feeling emboldened, I step closer, hooking one leg behind his knee and pressing into his hips. He groans against my mouth and I repeat the motion, feeling heat settle low in my core. His teeth scrape across my lower lip and I gasp, one of his hands trailing up past my ribs. His thumb traces circles across my flesh. Gods, this is better than reading it in a book, this is...

"You're seriously making me reconsider going to this meeting." He grins against my skin. His lips move to trail up my jaw before he playfully nips at my ear.

"We could skip?" I offer helplessly as his ministrations leave me breathless.

"And what happened to that good girl act?"

"Fuck the meeting."

Rowan pauses, his chuckle a low rumble in his chest that vibrates through my palm. I fight the urge to whine when he steps back, pressing one last slow kiss to my swollen lips before smiling. His hand reaches out and smooths my hair where he mused it and brushes my bangs from my eyes. "We have to go. I've got to make sure this world is safe for you first, then I'm all yours."

My lips involuntarily form a pout. "You mean when *we* make sure the world is safe."

Rowan's breath hitches and his emerald gaze traces my entire body. His face softens and something like peace washes over his features. His touch becomes reverential, worshipping almost.

"What?" I breathe.

"Just making sure you're real," he whispers, pressing a slow kiss to my forehead. "You're perfect. Fucking perfect, sunshine."

I blush red to the tips of my ears, the back of my neck warming with humble embarrassment. I've been called many things in my life, some things more savory than others, but never have I been spoken of with such whimsical awe, such adoration.

Silently, I interlace our fingers and allow him to lead me towards the dining hall.

Kya told me on the way back that they've been holding all meetings in this room, the once ornate dining table now converted into a war table. The door squeaks as we enter, announcing our entrance to all the patrons inside.

Kya's descriptions haven't done the chaos in the room any justice at all. Maps have been pinned to the wall with carving knives, certain portions slashed through and marked up with charcoal and an assortment of colors of ink. They overlap, creating a grand depiction of the entire continent, an ocean of parchment, charcoal, violence, and blood splatter. The few chairs that are in the room are occupied, drawn into a circle around the war table.

I take a moment to register the unfamiliar faces. The Night-walkers clump together, Amír residing in the center, seated between Kya and Torin. Torin bridges the gap between merce-naries and rebels, the sight more jarring than I expected it to be. A woman sits to his right, the majority of her face obscured by her hood, but not enough so that I can't tell she used to be pretty. Her eyes are dull and red and her cheekbones sunken, but her face is kind. Her brows are soft even as they pinch together, and I gasp when I recognize her.

Ruby lowers her hood, her gaze finding mine immediately. Her jaw clicks as she bites her cheek, those pretty eyes filling with tears almost immediately. I find myself biting my lip, pain slicing through my heart. Torin dips his chin when he notices our inter-action and his hand reaches out to squeeze hers. She offers a small and appreciative smile before squeezing back and turning her face to the map resting on the table.

Another hand descends from behind the woman's head and points to a specific part. My lips peel back in a wide grin and before I can stop myself, my feet are pounding against the floor and I'm throwing my hands out towards the young knight.

"You're okay," I breathe into Seb's shoulder, cradling his head against my neck with a small laugh.

The last time I saw the young man, he was facing down a crumbling castle and Kijova with nothing but a sword after Tanja's death. The few times before that had been when he escorted me somewhere within the palace, our first meeting, of course, being when I jumped out of the palace window during his first week.

While his fiery red hair and freckles have remained the same, not much else has. New scars lace his pale skin, some still fresh enough to be red and fleshy. He's grown slightly taller, and while he is still young in age, he has the haunted look of a seasoned soldier. Blaine wore the same tense expressions when he returned from war, his face gaunt and his motions jittery as if anticipating the next attack.

Seb's muscles still to stone for a moment before he softens and allows his arms to tentatively wrap around my form as well. He holds me tightly enough that my feet lift from the floor and he grins. "So are you, Mei Reinhavich."

"Please, the world is ending. You don't need to use formalities anymore," I offer while I release him from my tight embrace. "Just Vera will do."

"At least let me call you Verosa instead. Vera might be too shocking right now." He blushes. "I'm still used to only seeing you in a crown or royal portraits."

"Fair enough, but you better call me Vera at least once before this war is over."

"I think I will manage."

Rowan clears his throat behind me, his hand snaking around my waist and pulling my back into his chest. A smirk fights its way to my lips at his blatant jealousy, but Seb only extends his hand.

"It is an honor to meet you, Noiteron."

I jab Rowan's side with my shoulder. "Just Rowan for him too."

"Noiteron is fine," Rowan responds coolly.

"Are you ready to start this meeting or are we going to dawdle around your pride all day?" Amír calls from her spot at the table. "We know your dick is bigger, Rowan, so just sit down."

A few spare laughs break the only slightly awkward tension before we settle around the table again. Some of the rebels eye me with disdain, the rest opting not to look my way at all as we sit.

Rowan smirks. "At least we all know it now."

I drive my elbow into the soft spot between his ribs and he chuckles, the sound and his breath scattering across the outer shell of my ear. I shove him back towards his chair, purposely sitting beside Kya instead of the seat next to his. He rises and follows me to my chair anyway, opting to stand protectively behind me and glower at any of the rebels who eye me for a second too long.

"Territorial bastard," I murmur under my breath.

Kya giggles while Rowan pinches my shoulder warningly.

An imposing man who sits across from us clears his throat, and my eyes narrow in on him. Truth be told, he was the first one my gaze went to when we entered the room. He wears all white, the material surprisingly comprised entirely of leather and fur. His gray beard matches the textiles, his pale blue eyes complimenting his appearance as a whole. He's burly, not unsimilar to the way Finneas is. However, while Finneas obviously could kill a man with his bare hands, he doesn't appear to be the type who would. This man is every cut and jagged edge of a killer, and the thin white scar across his throat shows all he is no stranger to the face of death either.

His gnarled hands rest folded atop the table, occasionally tapping the worn wood. His piercing stare sends a chill through the air that caresses my spine and licks at the nape of my neck. I force myself to hold his gaze. Slowly, his lips twist back in a wicked smile.

Amír's voice cuts through the tension. "—Verosa back, we can proceed with the next phase of our plan."

Everyone's attention remains rapt, hanging on her every word while the gray man and I continue our stare-down. How long has she been speaking?

Rowan squeezes my shoulders and Kya leans in.

"She's asking if you'd know any potential Kijova weaknesses to exploit," the assassin whispers.

"Which you'd know if you had been paying attention, princess." Amír sneers, leaning back in her chair. "But seeing as you're the only one who can kill them and save us from certain doom, I suppose I'll give you a pass."

Gods, she's a bitch.

"Thank you for your kindness," I purr.

The gunslinger mockingly salutes, her spare fingers fiddling with a loose thread in the stitching of her leather holster.

The gray man narrows his eyes on the motion before his attention snaps back to me, as if daring me to notice that our minds wander the same paths. He sits close yet ahead of the rebels, obviously their leader, and even more obviously the man who has ordered multiple assassination attempts upon my life.

My gaze trails to the knife at his hip, its dark black steel iridescent in the dim inn lighting. He smirks as if noticing where my mind is going.

A cursed blade—one of the only things that can kill me as a blessed. An object that allows the cursed to murder a blessed without any repercussions like the ones that come with dark magic.

"How did they forge your blade?"

The gray man laughs, a low, gritty sound of steel on gravel. "I'm not in the business of dealing out illegal secrets for free, girl."

I ignore the slight, even as Rowan's fists tighten and one of his hands reaches for his sword. Kya's face goes white with barely restrained rage while mine remains impassive.

"I'm not asking for names or places, just the process."

"Answer her, Roiden." Rowan's voice is a low growl, barely audible save for the three of us.

The gray man, Roiden, sighs for show before brandishing the blade. Torin and Blaine shift closer to where I sit and I force my body to still.

Roiden grins knowingly, then raises a brow with feigned innocence. "A dark mage blesses the blade as the iron cools. There's a specific incantation and the iron is mined from a particular mine within these mountains. I don't see how this information is helpful. We have cursed blades and they do nothing, just like everything but your magic."

"Exactly."

Amír's eyes widen as she tracks where my mind is heading. "You don't think..."

"The moon needs the sun to shine, just as the Laei designed it." I spell it out slowly and plainly, hoping wickedly that his struggling brain won't catch up. "If there are cursed weapons, there must be blessed weapons, as well, or a way to make them. We have a pureblood mage, that must be more than enough."

"So if we can find what incantation we need and obtain that iron, we can maybe stand a chance in this war." Rowan finishes my thought before turning to me with a proud smile. "Good job, sunshine."

Murmurs rise through the room, some questioning, while the others cheer early. The day stretches her rays of light through the window, warming our skin slightly even in the dead of winter. For the first time in nearly six months, hope flickers and jumps amongst us.

"As much as I admire your tenacity and childish naivety, there is no such thing. And if there were, what makes you think we'd have access to anything like this?"

Hope flickers out and I finally stand, towering over Roiden from my end of the table. Snakes like him were all too common in counsel meetings at the palace, but those snakes die off when you crush their heads. Roiden seems to grow a second one.

"You, of course, wouldn't. I don't doubt that you've never been given access to anything fine or confidential, but I have." I turn to Seb, Blaine, and Torin now. "Irene's study. The night I broke in, I saw she had books open by that hand and was catching the blood. Knowing the queen, she must have found some way to weaponize a pureblood or she wouldn't have bothered."

"Couldn't she have just sold the blood for profit?"

"Come now, Roiden, do try your best to not display where you are lacking," I sigh drolly. "Why would a queen need more wealth when she already had the king by his crown jewels? Irene was never interested in wealth anyway, only ever power. If she found some all-mighty power that she could weaponize for her own gain, she would've written it down somewhere. My guess is there's instructions somewhere in her study."

Blaine nods in agreement. "No one was allowed in or out, not even the king."

Even if Irene wasn't hiding blessed weapons, she was hiding *something*. Something that could turn the tide in this war.

"So we form a task squad to break into the palace and search the queen's study."

"Noiteron, if I may," Seb interjects. When Rowan nods, he unrolls another longer parchment. Guard rotations and labeled rooms. "I would like to propose a dual-purpose mission. Ophelus has been storing a group of knights here near the outer wall since he unleashed the first wave of Kijova. The numbers have been dwindling. I've tried smuggling them out myself, but I'm unable to get more than one out at a time. They can't get far on their own; their health is... deplorable at best. Ophelus and Lucius have been using them to raise their dark army. If we don't stage a rescue soon, there may not be anyone left to rescue."

"How do you suggest we accomplish this?" Rowan's voice isn't judgmental like Roiden's has been. His thumb and index finger pinch his chin in concentration as he traces the inked lines with his gaze. He analyzes for every potential weak point, anything to exploit or siege.

Seb points to the map, emboldened by Rowan's acknowledgment and respect. "We send two separate teams. One will break in and free the knights, while the others head to Irene's study. These are the exit points. We rendezvous at the western tower just below the study. If anything goes wrong, I'll send out a single blow from the war trumpet at the top of the east tower."

"That actually sounds reasonable." Amír scans the map for any signs of error with a faintly impressed expression coating her face. "Not too bad, kid. We will decide the teams at our next meeting after we've had a chance to fully flesh this plan out."

"In the meantime," Rowan continues, "be prepared to be called upon at any time given the time sensitivity of this mission. We can't afford to wait long, not with those lives on the line. Meeting adjourned."

I pull Seb aside as soon as Rowan finishes speaking. I ignore the pointed gaze of Roiden and the familiar pang of it. I've seen his face somewhere, I just cannot place where.

Seb follows along silently, watching my motions curiously. My hands are frantic, I know, but a low dread has settled in my stomach ever since he pulled out that map. Torin, Ruby, and Blaine trail not too far behind. Once I am sure we are alone, I set into the young knight.

"How would you know all of that?"

When Seb stumbles over his answer, blushing like he would in the palace, Torin steps in. "He's been working as a double agent in the palace." He speaks lowly, keeping his voice out of earshot of Roiden and everyone else. "He feeds information straight to me and I steer the rebels into making the right choices to see the means to our ends."

"What?" I whirl towards the redhead, my voice a hissing whisper. "Seb, that's incredibly dangerous."

"No more dangerous than what you've been doing," he retorts.

"Still—"

"Mei— Verosa," he corrects himself, "I took an oath. Those are my brothers in those walls, and my queen is out here fighting on the front lines. If I can save a few more lives, then it is worth the risk."

Of all the thoughts running through my mind, the most prevalent one is that Ms. Eida was wrong in her initial assumptions of the young knight that one sunny day when he escorted me back to my studies. She deemed him no one of importance, not even notable enough to know his name. Now, he may be the bravest, most important boy I know.

I throw my arms around him for the second time today, ignoring the jealous glare Rowan shoots our way. I inhale sharply, my shoulders falling heavily. "Don't get yourself killed for honor," I whisper fervently. "You're no less important than the rest of us."

Silence, then a strangled sob from behind me. I turn to find Ruby, her hood down and face pressed into her hands as she weeps. Behind her, the rebels have all cleared out, Amír emptying the room with nothing but a holstered pistol and the cold glare on her face.

The woman sinks to her knees, now clutching at a chain that hangs around her neck. Her fingers part to reveal an engagement ring. My heart catches in my throat when I glimpse that sapphire embedded within the gold. Soon, I am on my knees with her, reaching for her hands as I finally allow tears to slip down my cheeks. Blaine's breathing hitches and Torin turns his face towards the shadows.

"I want to hate you." Ruby chokes on the words, her sentiments strangled by grief. "But how can I hate someone that she loved enough to die for? How can I hate you knowing that she loved you enough that it would be easier to die than to live without you? I can't. *I can't.*" Her face crumples as she folds in on herself, her sobs now borderline screams as she pulls her face to her knees.

I cannot say for sure what possesses me to do this, nor why Ruby doesn't stab me. I lean forward on my knees, wrapping my arms around her shaking form, holding her tightly as grief wracks her body and shatters her voice.

"I'm sorry. Gods, I'm sorry. It should have been me. I wish it were me, every day. There isn't anything I wouldn't do to bring her back. I wish *I* took that knife. I wish..."

Ruby looks up, her chin propped up on my bosom. Tears stain her pretty face, a mosaic of sorrow plainly written. She clasps my wrist with both hands as I go to brush those silver tears away. "Tell me how they did it. Tell me how it happened."

"Ruby..."

"I need to know."

Darkness crawls into the corner of my vision. To her and to everyone else, I have come off as wanting to spare her from the horror of her fiancée's murder, but in truth, I selfishly want to spare *myself.* I haven't spoken about what happened, haven't dared to dwell on it too long in the waking world. Dreams are terrible enough reminders as it is.

But her face is so shattered, her eyes so pleading, that I squeeze my own shut and part my lips. I start from the beginning, from waking up drugged and alone in a cell, the ropes purposely biting into my skin. I tell them of Ophelus and my disgraced fiancé stepping from the shadows, how Lucius initially tried to bargain before giving in. I tell them how I thought I would die hated and alone, about the undead guards, and then how, at the last moment, a force pushed me from the altar. It was pure light and power that cut through the darkness, like nothing I'd ever known. How it felt to see the knife in her chest, her death rattle and final plea. I debate lying and telling Ruby that Tanja said she loved her before she died, but I cannot bring myself to desecrate her memory with anything but the truth. I choke when I tell them how they slit her throat. I pinch my forearms, trying to block out the thoughts of how horrible a death it was, how painful and terrifying. She died full of love, but she died alone while I ran.

I gasp at the end of the story, pinching hard enough to draw blood. I can't breathe. I can't breathe. I can't.

"Ver."

I blink at the softness of Blaine's voice as he kneels beside me, then shatter completely when he wraps his arms around my waist and lets me sob into his shoulder. I open my arms and Ruby crawls in, and Torin comes behind us all, holding the four of us together. The last survivors, her family, proof of the light she brought to this shadowy world.

For the first time since her death, I can feel a crack in the wall of despair that has encased my heart. The pain is still raw and fleshy like a new wound, but it's bleeding. It's bleeding out resolution and clarity.

The naïve remnants of who I was a year ago flow away completely as I allow myself to cry out into this entanglement of limbs and tears. Tanja didn't die so I could waste away like this. She didn't give her life for mine so I could disgrace her memory like this.

She gave her life because she loved me, and she believed in

me. Tanja always saw the best in me, even as I continuously proved to her that I was nothing more than a selfish monster.

My heart hardens to the light as the lingering darkness in my veins begins to burn. We cannot afford to wait for some magical solution of blessed weapons or fairytale promises.

Duke Gadsden spoke of an Oracle of Raonkin, something that could provide all the answers to my questions. Something that could save lives and end the war. Something only the darkness can find. My eyes narrow even as silver tears stream down my face. If Tanja was able to forgive me for the monster I was, then she will forgive me for the monster I am about to become.

Blaine stares at my face a moment longer, the fine contours of his own forming a hard line. Those gray eyes seem to stare through my skin to my soul and slowly blackening heart. He says nothing, per usual, but in the way his mouth tightens, I know he can see where my mind has gone.

Ruby breathes through a shuddering sob before grabbing my hand. She does this quickly, as if convincing herself to go through with this impulse before she can think otherwise. I feel a cool stone and metal band pressing into my skin.

"Ruby, no."

"Keep her memory alive," Ruby pleads, pushing the wedding ring further in my hand. "Keep her with you and keep her alive for me. Carry her to through this war and let her sit with you on the throne in your new kingdom."

My fingers curl around the gold band, my face reflecting back to me in the sapphire. It is identical to the one Tanja wore. The one she was wearing when she died. I can almost imagine her placing it on Ruby's finger, her smile when she did it.

My throat constricts with emotion and I nod.

"I promise."

CHAPTER 28

VEROSA

Once Ruby leaves, Blaine grabs my elbow and Torin by the edge of his cloak. "We need to have a talk. All the Nightwalkers too."

"I'll grab them." Torin eyes the tension between us and stalks off, more than happy to relieve himself of us, even if only for a few moments.

I cross my arms over my chest, sighing through my nose. "Want to clue me in to what this is all about?"

"I figured you would let us in on that," he presses, "given that your plan seemed to revolve around the others' capabilities and not your own. You haven't been back to Irene's tower in ten years and there's no way in hell you're going into the dungeons. That is too much of a risk. So where can you use those new powers of yours—which we aren't done discussing, by the way."

The air between us turns cold, lethal. His body mimics my own, all fine lines and hardened muscle. Defensive. Commanding. Another argument waiting to blow up.

At some point, the others file in silently, just watching the showdown until Kya raises her voice. "He's right. What aren't you telling us?"

I shoot her a betrayed look. Of all the people in this room to undermine me, she is the last on my list, even past Torin. Her face remains impassive, her assassin façade in place. Amír stirs restlessly beside her and Rowan's eyes bore holes into my face.

What aren't you telling me?

I sigh, obviously and miserably outnumbered. "Mavis took me on a mission right before you all found me. I thought it was a simple scouting mission or a test to see how my new powers hold up in a real-life scenario. In reality, we were searching for someone."

"Who and why?" Blaine presses.

"Just wait a minute," I retort, the darkness in my core snapping like a leash against my anger. "There was a man who had heard something about how to end the war. I didn't know the man was Duke Gadsden until we found him."

The scent of charred human flesh floods my senses for only a moment. The man who tormented me during my teenage years with marriage proposals and preyed on all the maids. The man who was partially responsible for Tanja's death. Perhaps he deserved what he got, but his blood evaporating from my hands is a feeling I won't soon forget.

Rowan emits a sound something like a squeak or a grunt which he covers with a cough. In any other situation, I might have offered a laugh. Such an odd sound for such a domineering man. His feet scuff against the floor and he nods, asking me to continue.

With a heavy sigh, I comply. "He planned to sell the information to the king and Lucius in exchange for immunity. Some of the nobles have been doing that, as we know—spying on the innocents, selling them out if they see a woman or young man with blond hair. Selfish bastards."

Amír slams her fingers against her holster before snapping. "And? Any day now, Vera."

"*And,*" I drawl out pointedly, "we got to him first. He spilled everything. Rumor has it, there's a being that lives in the mountains not too far from here that can see the future. An Oracle that knows how this war ends, and what must happen for it to come to pass." I draw out the map that I stole from Mavis and unfurl it.

A sharp inhale rings through the room. Kya drags two fingers across her heart and Derrín taps his feet against the ground, his toes making a mangled tune against the wood.

"That's the same place the Kijova were heading. Amír, your tracking..." Kya hisses.

"This is all speculation." Blaine pinches his brows together. "You're taking the word of a slimy pedophile who would say anything to save his life. You want to put your life on the line based on his word alone?"

"And what of the cost? There's always a price for these sorts of things," Amír adds.

"I know it's true because Irene had books on it," I snap finally. "In her study. To earn the truth of your future from the Oracle, you must be deemed worthy by the gods through a trial. Once you pass the trial, you are granted the visions of the future that you seek. Something like that could save so many lives, at the risk of only one."

"Yes, *yours,*" Rowan bites back, fear lacing his words.

"It's worth the risk! How many have died? How many *more* are going to die?"

The room falls silent. I can see it on their faces—they all want to beg me not to go, but they cannot argue with my words. A whole kingdom has fallen to the whims of a madman. Only one equal in power can take him out. If my soul is already damned, then why not give it to the one thing that might save everyone else?

"The people are expecting a miracle," Torin mumbles under his breath, worry lines now creasing his forehead.

"Then I will give them one." The sweet susurration of my power fills the silent room, the dark tendrils curling through my splayed fingers. I smile despite the pull at my chest.

"The miracle would be if we could pull this off." Blaine casts a pointed glance my way. "*Without* dark magic."

"We can't. We have exhausted all of our other options."

"Well, there is—"

"The power of a pureblood isn't what we think it is," I snap at Torin, who only shrugs. "*This* is the power. To master magic without paying the price, and to use it yourself."

"I wonder who has mastered who."

I whirl in a fury towards the source of the voice and find Blaine leaned over, his shoulders hunched and his handsome face contorted with worry.

"Do you have something to say, captain?"

He flinches, but squares his gaze to mine. "Do you hear yourself right now? There is a price, whether you realize it or not."

"Even if there is, we must pay it! For the people."

"It's the people I worry about, Vera, but none more than you."

The others fall silent, suddenly none of them looking me in my eye. It's been this way since I was returned from Mavis—a jab in my direction, then silence.

Fury boils in my gut. "Worry about the people, then. *That's* your job," I hiss, but it's not enough.

"We can't afford to have your hands tainted with such dark forces! You are the future queen—"

"Then you will listen when I tell you to stand out of my way, or suffer the consequences, captain."

The room is tense with apprehensive silence, the air crackling with anticipated violence, like the brief second before the blare of the war horn or the moment before the wave crashes into white, frothy sea foam.

Blaine rises and Amír's hand inches towards her holster. The former captain takes two sure steps forward, stopping about a pace away from where I remain seated. I raise my chin in defiance and he pauses only a breath.

Then he bows deeply at the waist, his nose nearly touching my knees. "A su sonji, Mei Reinha," he all but spits out.

As you wish, my queen. A mockery of the loyalty it is supposed to pledge.

The Vari man straightens, a purely murderous look painted across his handsome face, before he stalks from the room. Torin swears and follows behind him quietly. The others soon follow, dispersing to their own destinations while I am left seated in the room, rage simmering low in my veins. Somewhere outside these walls, a door slams.

My fingers fiddle with the ring around my neck. The sapphire bites against my palm as I squeeze it. Ruby gave me this ring because she understood. She knows Tanja's death was my fault, and that only I can fix it. She can't hate me only because Tanja loved me. But Tanja was far lovelier than I can ever be, and I no longer care how much I must sully my soul to avenge hers. Ruby knows this. Even this damn ring knows it.

The Oracle is the only answer. Ophelus and Lucius are constantly one step ahead, and something about the rebellion leader nags at my consciousness. I've seen his face before, years younger, though equally hardened with hate. He's in on his own schemes—he has his own plans, even if they are set late down the road. He's a snake, the lot of them.

Blood dots the blue gem as I release my grip.

"No, no no no," I whimper, wiping the blood off the jewel. No reminders. No blood. No—

The blue is clear and clean again when it falls against my

neck, shining just as brightly as it did when it hung around her neck, then on her finger. My own face reflects back, a hundred refractions of my own broken stare.

I have to do this. I have to.

Rowan steps back into the room a few moments later, the murmuring voices in the hallway ceasing at once. As if they were never there.

"Hey," he says, his voice barely above a whisper. His clothes are rumpled and his hands stained crimson, gold, and silver. The metallics catch the light and I fixate on it to ignore the iron scent that covers the citrus to which I am accustomed. "You've been in here for a while."

"Hmm?"

Have I? I glance out the window and notice the dying sun. It was noon when we all gathered. That was hours ago. Now twilight streaks across the sky, painting it in bold tones as the sun claims one last victory over the horizon.

"Everything okay?" he asks as if he doesn't already know the answer. The mercenary pulls a stool away from the table, its wooden legs screeching against the floor into the dead air. He settles atop it, his powerful frame making the stool look small. Like it belongs in a dollhouse.

He always sees through me and my lies. Not as quickly as Blaine or Torin do, but he is getting just as quick as them the more time we spend together. The pad of his thumb extends towards my face and smooths the crease between my brows. I force my face to relax, the muscles straining against my command before falling dormant. The action earns a small smile from Rowan.

"Why are you bleeding?"

"It's not mine."

"Oh. Okay."

Silence falls, a thick blanket over the two of us. The lack of sound, of anything, strangles me in ways I cannot understand. There shouldn't be this strain, not on us.

"A silver for your thoughts?" Rowan jests, flipping a coin my way. It falls heavily in my lap, a useless trifle from a bygone era.

"Come now, I hear you're to be a king. Offer me more than that and maybe you'll have a deal."

A bit of the tension eases when he laughs. It's a beautiful sound, and gods be damned if I've earned it. If I deserve to hear it. "How about a crown?" he murmurs, and I almost smile. "And a ring."

I stand immediately, the coin clattering to the ground and ringing through the room. Rowan stands as well. The stool falls and I jump. He's quick to rush to my side, but I hold up a hand.

A ring. *A ring.*

"You're thinking about her again." He stands a few feet away. I can see in his face that he is dying to reach out and hold me. He's never been good with words, not truthful ones anyway. He needs to use his hands, to work physically to fix things. The distance is smothering him just as much as the silence is me.

"I have to find the oracle." I have to, I *have* to...

"Ver."

"It's the only way to win this war. It's the only way to save everyone. I have to avenge her. I have to make this right."

I am aware I must sound slightly mad at this point, my bleeding hands reaching up to pull at my hair. It falls about my face haphazardly and I take to clutching at my trousers instead once I spot the pained look on Rowan's face. His eyes stare at the strands of hair I pulled out, woven about my fingers. I can't feel it, I can't feel any of it.

"You can't blame yourself." The mercenary speaks with such sudden clarity that it startles me from my stupor if only for a moment. His voice is soft and mollifying, as if comforting a wounded animal or a startled child. But this isn't a snapping twig or monster under the bed. The monsters are here and they walk among us. They always have.

And they're here because of me.

"I need to blame *someone*."

"So blame me." Rowan runs his hand through his hair, the strands already coated with drying blood as if he repeated the action earlier. "If I hadn't left you, then he wouldn't have had a sacrifice and we wouldn't be stuck living like this. Tanja wouldn't be dead."

"No."

"Her mother hid her tracks. The king didn't even know Tanja was a pureblood. She wouldn't have been hunted down like you were. She would be safe. She would be married. She wouldn't be dead."

"Don't say her name." My voice breaks midway through my words. "Don't you dare say her name."

Rowan presses on anyway. "She wouldn't be. But you can't blame anyone other than yourself, right? Anything to keep wallowing in your self-hatred and pity." His tone is soft, but I can feel the biting edge behind his words.

I love him for being willing to sacrifice my view of him and I hate him for being right. None of this is my fault, but if I let go of this self-hatred, I am left with nothing. A queen with no throne, a lover with no heart. A life without Tanja.

I am nothing.

"I think we need some space tonight." I grind out the words.

Rowan inhales slowly in near hesitance, but eventually nods. The only thing that conveys his hurt is a slight flicker of pain in his eyes, but he says nothing. Gives no indication of his inner turmoil. He hesitates before kissing my forehead and stepping out into the hallway. The shadows swallow him immediately, and Rowan is gone.

It almost seems unfair, how he can just appear and disappear whenever he likes. Some days, it is like he just forms from mist and shadow then disappears in the wind when he's done. It isn't like how Kya does it. Kya comes from shadows, yes, but she has always been there. You can feel her presence in the room. With Rowan, it is as if he was never truly there.

I wish I could disappear. That the wind could whisk my broken fragments away until I am nothing but a whisper of smoke and shadow. Then I could reappear whenever the gnawing hole in my heart has healed, and if it never does, I can stay among the clouds where the chill freezes the hurt from my bones.

But this is real life, regardless of the seemingly fantastical monsters that haunt our waking moments. Hell is here and it has brought all its pets. Rowan will never understand that weight, even if he claims accountability. Even as he gets to watch me break apart each day and fade before his eyes, even in sleep. He will never understand. None of them will.

My fury chases me to our room, where I half expect to find him waiting. He isn't, loyal even in his hurt. I slip my sweater from my shoulders first, relishing the frigid air that spills over my exposed flesh. Goosebumps prickle along my skin and chase the sweater downwards, then my trousers, greedily engulfing my skin as the clothes give way. I stand naked in my room, letting the cold bite to my bones and ground my feet to the broken floorboards. I wash my face the same way, my motions stiff and mechanical before I finally slip into a nightgown and creak the door open.

The chill guides me towards a door I haven't dared open since arriving. The night is silent save for the crisp cracking of the wooden floorboards beneath my feet. I step on any loose boards I can find as I approach Kya and Amír's room. The walls here are thicker than the cloth tents and open sky we had on the run, but not thick enough. My hand lingers over the brass doorknob. I can feel the heat start to slip back into my bones, sorrow chasing it the rest of the way there. I grasp the handle firmly and push the door open.

"Come in," Kya calls, even as I step inside.

My arm hits the door in my carelessness, a bruise already blossoming. I push it aside with a small flourish and enter the dim light. Amír has lit a candle beside their bed and neither of them bother to rise from their bed as I enter.

"Here comes everyone's favorite tyrant," Amír groans. Her head hits their headboard with a heavy thunk.

Kya jabs her ribs with her elbow before rising to greet me. Before she even reaches me, the Vari woman stops and sighs softly. She doesn't ask—she doesn't need to. "I'll grab a pillow." She smiles tightly.

Her lover slams a pillow onto her face and groans, the dramatics eliciting a small laugh from the assassin. Amír sinks further into their bed, her arms outstretched in a momentary softness. The two women whisper to each other in sweet voices until Amír says something that has Kya blushing red to her ears.

The assassin laces her nimble fingers through mine as we walk back to my room, a pillow stuffed under one arm, making small talk and commenting on things like the frost on the windows. She says nothing about the tightness of my mouth or the fact that Rowan is gods know where. Knowing the assassin, she probably knows about our fight—hell, our whole inn probably heard it.

Like I said, thin walls.

Kya settles herself on my bed, claiming the spot closest to the entrance. I try to hide how my shoulders slump in relief at the comfort her presence brings, but those golden eyes pierce through my thoughts anyway. The assassin says nothing about the arguments that transpired mere hours ago. Says nothing about the threat of doom hanging over us or my proposed self-sacrifice. She just lazily drapes an arm across my waist before making a show of placing a dagger under her pillow.

"If you're going to try and cuddle me, just don't put your arm under the pillow," she teases lightly, earning a small laugh from my lips that breaks the silence of the night. A smaller part of me hopes that Rowan can hear it, that he knows that I am fine. Completely fine, even without him.

I take the time to snuggle in closer, pointedly not sticking my hand under her pillow.

The assassin brushes her nose against mine, her breath tickling my upper lip.

"Can I expect Amír to come storm in here at any point? Or maybe a stray bullet on my pillow?"

"Nothing with Amír is stray," Kya offers with a wink. The threadbare blanket shifts as she wriggles beneath it to intertwine our legs. "Gods, it's cold."

"Your feet are freezing!"

In response, Kya allows her toes to dig into the soft of my calf and I squeal. The Vari woman shoves her freezing hand onto the back of my neck, as well, before finally retreating once she has sapped all of my bodily warmth.

"I should've believed the rumors about the Nightwalker's assassin. Your torture methods are inhumane."

"You should hear what they say about *you* these days."

"And what *are* they saying exactly?"

"Oh, you know, you're Rowan and Mavis's whore. It's a joint custody situation." She blows a stray hair from my face. "And that you're conspiring with the king to burn the world down." Her hand reaches out again to trace small patterns across my arm. The motions are precise, yet smooth and motherly.

I giggle softly at the absurdity of it all. If only the people out there knew the truth. Mavis kidnapped me and her men dragged me naked through the woods, while Rowan...

Rowan's words make me feel anything but filthy or whorish.

I turn my back to her and face the wall as to hide the hazy blush coating my cheeks. "What do they say of the rest of us?" And then when she hesitates, "Come on, humor me."

I can hear the telltale popping sound of Kya pursing her lips, but she relents nonetheless. "Derrín isn't my brother, but rather a Vari genius we kidnapped and force to make lethal weapons for us. Rowan is a womanizing murderer who bathes in blood and steals women from their husbands. Amír is a succubus that Rowan cut a deal with through the sacrifice of a hundred virgins. She is a soulless vessel with the war abilities of a god. Oh, and I am secretly a man. A little insulting that that's the best they could come up with for me, but those are the tame ones, as ridiculous as they may be."

I stifle a snort. "Amír's sounds accurate enough."

"Try not to fault her too much," Kya whispers with a faraway tone. "She's a dreamer born in the body of a nightmare."

My brows furrow as I try to think of Amír dreaming of something other than my head on the wall. Something tells me her dreams smell like gunpowder.

Kya only fixes me with a sad smile. "I think she's beautiful because of it."

I know now she isn't talking about something as superficial as her red hair or emerald eyes. Her beauty is something that runs in her blood that she hates so much, something in the broken bits that refuse to shatter completely.

All those gentle touches between the two of them have never been simply flirting or something as fleeting as love. Amír treads the line of wandering too far from the hope, and Kya tethers her to something worth living another day for.

Curling up on my side with my knees tucked into my chest, I turn my face towards hers. Her dark waves spill over the pillow and pool around her face, a dark and lovely frame for her pretty face. When I first saw her, I thought she was one of the prettiest people I had ever seen. That analysis still stands to this day. She claims Amír is beautiful, but I don't think anyone can hold a candle to her.

Silently, I reach a finger out and poke her cheek. "Are you sure you're real?"

"Yes, Vera. I think I can confirm that," she deadpans.

I blow a raspberry and snuggle in closer to the worn-in mattress. I rest my head on her pillow now, brushing our foreheads together. "Derrín was right."

"Hmm?"

"You really are Amír's bitch."

One hand snatches the pillow out from under my head while the other cradles my face away from the awaiting dagger. Her elbow pushes the weapon aside and off the bed so she can use both hands to bring the pillow down upon my face. My shrieks are muffled by the only slightly molded fabric, but the assassin doesn't relent. She knows exactly how long she can smother me before I lose consciousness. She presses down right until that second before releasing her vice grip.

I come up laughing between gasping breaths, eyeing her with mocking contempt. "You and your girlfriend need to work on your anger issues."

"She's angry because she is kind," she murmurs with the smallest of smiles. "There's nothing quite like female rage."

I mock a gagging sound. "Stop with this wise and poetic shit. You make me feel like an idiot."

"Well..."

"Good *night*!"

Kya's lilting voice chases me to dreams as my head hits the pillow and deep sleep envelopes me.

CHAPTER 29

VEROSA

In the next few weeks, Torin goes to meet with the rebels more frequently, and Rowan or Blaine go with him on occasion. They haven't allowed me to go yet, which isn't too much a surprise, given that the majority—if not all of them—still want me dead. So I've been left to my own devices for the most part, pacing the halls and reading, but mostly I spend my time with Emilie. When I go out on patrols, I do my best to find things for her to do. Last week, it was some colored charcoals and a pad of paper, and a few nights ago, Kya brought back some grains that we've been able to grind into flour.

Emilie loads a pan Derrín made into the oven, an oddly shaped cake sitting in the center. It has taken most of the morning to make, but the older woman smiles so softly that the trouble is worth it.

"Oh, and when your father brought out the flowers, your mom was immediately covered in hives. He panicked so badly that he tipped the boat and they both went into the water."

Emilie has taken the extra time we have together to tell me stories about my *real* parents and their lives before me. She's hesitant to say anything about what happened after my birth. Obviously, it is not a happy story, and I don't pry, but a part of me wants to know anyway. Maybe a bit of a darker part wants to know how hurt they were, and to dream of what it was like to have someone care about me so much that it pained them. I've never known that love before now, but I try to tuck that thought away.

"I don't understand. He's so..." I pinch my face together as I try to think of the right word to describe my father. My *father*. "Warm. I don't know how he killed anybody." I pick up a glass of water and move to bring it to where Emilie sits. Finneas killed my mother's suitor for the right to marry her. He was the last person to use that ritual before Blaine tried months ago for my hand.

Emilie brushes my comment off with a small wave, a mischievous sparkle in her eye. "Oh, he's killed many people. He was a soldier in the king's army, one of the first when Ophelus took the throne, actually. It is how we met."

I drop the cup to the floor, swearing as water splatters over my legs. Emilie laughs, a beautiful sound. The resemblance of the woman she was before Ophelus is starting to shine through again, now that all of us are here. It is almost sick how it took the world ending for it to begin again, and I can only imagine how lovely she was if this is what Rowan considers a shell.

"He *what*? And you *what*?"

"Oh yes, every noble had to do a tour of duty at first. He was just one of the better ones, and brought me along to the celebratory ball at Aiko's insistence. Your mother claimed that if he was to parade around with the other guards all night, she would need me for the company. At some point, the two of them snuck away and I met Ophelus on a balcony. I didn't know who he was, as I came from Adil, that poor town even less developed than it was a few months ago." She stands and takes the cup from my hand, refilling it and coming back with a second one that she passes to me. She runs her finger over the lip, smiling fondly.

She often smiles while talking about meeting Ophelus, and I do my best to hide the way my stomach turns and my hands tremble. The man she loved and the man who raised me for slaughter are two different people, one of them not even a person at all anymore. I do my best to remind myself of that, but there are times when panic climbs my throat and latches around my heart. A ripple forms in the cup of water I am holding.

"Do you know what name they were going to give me?" I ask suddenly, clearing my throat.

Emilie stills, her eyes drifting to the floor. "Astria. After the seventh sun."

"Astria." *Miracle* in the old tongue. "Do you think... Do you think they would want me to go by that when I meet them again?"

Emilie smiles tightly this time, and grasps my hand. "I think they love you for who you are, not which name you take. You can always ask when you see them."

I don't know how I feel about changing my name. It has been mine for twenty years now, the one thing that Irene did not give me and could not take away. A kindly maid chose it, said it suited me. Irene did not care. I do not know if she would have named me at all if it weren't for that nursemaid. Astria is nice—it feels like home, but yet so unfamiliar. Like it should be mine, but I've lost it to time.

If my parents wanted to call me by that name, I would not say no, but hearing it from the lips of Rowan, or Kya? When Vera was on Tanja's dying lips...

Perhaps it can be a middle name. And when the kingdom is saved and it is written in history books, the name will be Verosa Astria Iales. Not Verosa Elyce of Krycolis. Elyce was Ophelus's mother's name, and it fit like a misshapen shoe.

Verosa Astria Iales.

Kya saunters into the room, a smile on her pretty face and fresh red paint stained on her arms. Amír found more of the paint last week and Kya was finally able to redraw the intricate swirls this morning. Her face still seems foreign, even after all these months without the red makeup she usually wore, especially that which outlined her golden eyes.

"Someone's in a good mood," I remark with a smile on my lips.

Her hair swishes over her shoulder in a dark cascade as she settles on the arm of the chair I rest on. "I am. We found another town. Torin brought some survivors in from it—three women, a man, and two children. We are going back tonight to survey the damage and see if we can't find anything else."

I feel a tightening in my core, like someone snapped a restraint. The darkness I've kept mostly well leashed calls out in furious, howling voices. I've run out of the sacrifices I kept from Mavis last week. I did my best to ration them out and release that power only when it felt like it would swallow me whole, but it gnaws at my insides and demands a release now. My blade feels heavy in my pocket, alongside a note I also swept from the mercenary queen's desk.

"What city?"

"It's at the base of the mountains a little to the east. Niombe."

I'm familiar with the city. When Blaine used to list the crime report to the king each week, most of it came from there. It's a small town, better off than the likes of Adil and Belam, but still not as good of a living as the inner city.

The city burns a hole in my pocket, an address scribbled across the paper with a name attached.

"Can I come this time?" I try as inconspicuously as possible. "I fear I may die if I do not leave soon, though Emilie has been wonderful company and my only lifeline."

"Your only lifeline, huh?" Kya counters with a devious smirk. She smacks my shoulder. "I see how much my friendship means to you."

"You know I love you."

"And I guess you can join, but only because you're cute when you beg."

"Is that so?" Amír crosses her arms, a playful smirk teasing at the corners of her lips as she leans against the doorframe.

Rowan and Torin stand behind her, their faces equally masked with amusement. Kya whispers a response I cannot hear over the rushing in my ears. I shift my eyes away and think back to the list, of who waits in Niombe.

In her desk, Mavis kept a little book of names and addresses of men who have committed unforgivable crimes and escaped the iron fist of the law. Some had been scratched through already. Some names I recognized, either from their crimes or their obituaries. She had shown me the book a few times before and I took it upon myself to snatch a page from it. I've read the names on the list so many times that they're committed to memory. Niombe is home to a man named Lars Farleson. He paid off the judges to escape his sentence for murdering a young girl.

Men like him, Mavis warned me, generally aren't first-time offenders. He might have evaded justice for this one girl, but there were most likely countless others he harmed. His face is burned into my mind from the newspaper clippings—round jaw, thick brow, a bit of a bulge in his right eye. He has a telltale birthmark, a red smudge under his right ear. If he is alive, I'll find him near or still in the town. Or with Torin.

The third option is less favorable, given the mess it may leave behind and the trick of sneaking past my friends and the rebellion. But I can do it. Months of training with Kya have given me the stealth, and Mavis's dark magic has done the rest.

"We leave in an hour." Rowan lays his hand on my arm and leans down to press a kiss atop my head.

Emilie smiles when he takes her empty cup from her hands. He offers her a new one, but she refuses, saying she's not so old she cannot get it herself.

Kya elbows my side as I walk by to grab my gear and I respond by bumping into her with my shoulder. She lands with a small thud against the doorframe and laughs, a sound that chases me all the way to my room.

SPRING HAS FINALLY ARRIVED in the Hills of Siva and the warmth of the sun has begun the journey of melting away months' worth of snow and ice. While flowers and grass sprout up from the melted patches, I know it will take at least another week for all the snow to melt completely. The ice is thick, the lakes solid enough for our whole group to stand on them without a groan or threatening to crack. The summer heat that will come to the mountains in a few weeks will take care of that, but for now, we will enjoy our gentle spring.

The snow crunches under the heel of my thick-soled boots as we march towards Niombe. The air is heavy with humidity and before long, sweat clings my hair to the back of my neck. I fold my cloak into my sack, allowing my arms to swing a bit more freely at my sides to break through the stagnant air.

Gold casts the sky as we approach the town, the dying rays of light painting each dilapidated home and the weather-worn roads. Fresh mounts of dirt line the town in disorderly rows.

"They buried the bodies quickly," Amír notes.

Torin only received word of the town this morning, so they must have worked all day to bury who they could before the sun set.

"Report back if you find anymore," Rowan commands.

We all respond with a brief nod before setting off for our respective quadrants.

Any time we go on a raid, each of us is given a section. We travel on our own, as we're less likely to be spotted by enemies if we move by ourselves rather than in a large herd. Each of us is beyond capable of handling whatever threat is thrown our way, but we still take precautions. I had casually slipped in that I would take the farther quadrant once we arrived and began to divvy out roles. Usually Rowan or I are stationed near the back of the town in case of an attack, so no one marked this as unusual.

The first house I search is nearly empty, save for a few vials of medicine. I reach for my leather-bound notebook only to find it not resting at my hip. I frown. I must have left it back at the inn. Making a mental note instead, I trek to my second home, finding a few more useful items. Then, when I can be certain no one is watching, I head for the address that has been burning in my pocket all day.

The house is untouched when I arrive, not even the rebels have gone through it yet. It rests in the furthest corner of the town, just far enough away that they wouldn't have had time to go through it fully with all the bodies they had to bury at the front of the town. Tomorrow, they will sweep through it again and bury the rest.

My dagger is drawn when I enter, the tip poking through the entryway before any part of my body does. I hold it on the offense, clearing the entry first. When no Kijova or soldiers attack, I allow it to lower and begin my search.

Dust falls from the cabinets I open, clearly untouched long before today arrived. I settle for making my way to the back of the house. A distant buzz fills my ears and grows with each step I take towards the final room of the home.

The flies got to my victim before I could.

I kick the body's head back with the toe of my boot and hiss at the sight of the red birthmark below his ear. Lars was dead long before I arrived, and it was by his own hand, judging by the pills and bottle sitting next to his decaying hand.

My head lolls back and I inhale deeply, the scent causing me to gag. Fresh bodies are one thing to get used to, but once decay sets in, there is no iron stomach that can handle the smell. I glance down at the man, his eyes closed and face not pinched with fear like the rest. He died too easily.

The darkness in my blood calls out to that of his that now pools from his nose and the small holes the bugs have made in his flesh. My knife sings of its own accord, and before I can realize what I am doing, his thumb has been severed.

The rest of the fingers come off intentionally. If the sick bastard didn't pay for his crimes in life, then he will in death. At least now, his body may be useful, providing weaponry to take down the king and save the kingdom. This disgraceful alternative is better than anything he could have offered in his miserable life.

The final finger hits the others in the pouch with a sickeningly wet thud, and just as I contemplate whether or not to get over my fear of tongues, a dark, feminine voice calls out from behind me.

"'114 Mirrors Lane, Adil. Two trousers, one pair of boots, and a cloak.'" Kya speaks quietly, her eyes never leaving mine when I spin to face her. My gaze trails to the journal in her hand—my journal. "'937 Browns Road, Belam. A pair of gloves, three blankets. 506 Falls Road. One shirt, two vials of medication, one piece of ginger root. 892 Drowny Court, Kian. Four socks, and one spare sock.'" The assassin's gaze hardens to the point of stone, a single tear welling in each like water breaking through a worn-down dam.

My hand stills on my blade and I rise, leaving the body to rest.

"What happened to you?" she whispers. "There is no way in this world or the next that the girl who kept track of even a single sock that she had to take would ever go as far as to dismember the dead."

I will myself not to look at the body, not at his open eyes or the fly-torn skin. Certainly not his fingerless hands, the damage that I myself did. But Kya looks. Kya looks at all of it and sees everything, as she always does, before turning that pensive golden gaze back on me.

My fingers curl around the dagger in my hand, squeezing until my knuckles go white and pop. "He was a rapist," I hiss between clenched teeth. "Don't ask me to show his body respect in death when he didn't respect *anyone* in life—not their bodies and not their lives."

"This isn't about him. I couldn't give a damn about him or his body. He deserves the death he got, but this isn't about him. This is about you and who *you're* becoming. Because let's be honest, you only took from him because you could justify it in your mind, but if you found any body mutilated enough, you'd take from it all the same. I don't—"

"You don't *what*?" I snap.

"I don't know you at all if you're willing to go this far," she breathes, her voice barely above a whisper. Her face is haunted, her lips pressed into a thin line and her shoulders barely restraining from shaking.

Guilt gnaws at the corners of my stomach and almost forces my lips to mouth an apology, but something stops me. As much as I fight against it, I can feel the darkness work its way up my throat and ply those lips open. "Then you don't know me," I say, the words bitter on my tongue. "This is a *war*, and I am trying to do my part. If that means getting my hands dirty, then so be it. I thought you of all people would understand that."

Involuntarily, my gaze falls to her arm, the red paint nearly completely gone thanks to the humidity and sweat. Ink is not exactly the type of luxury one finds while the world is ending, and while Amír just found some, I know she uses it sparingly, touching up the intricate whorls with dye from crushed berries when we can find them.

I hit her shoulder with my own as I brush past, but she reaches out with serpentine precision and latches her fingers around my wrist. She applies pressure, gentle enough as not to bruise, but hard enough to get her point across.

"There are still lines we do not cross. I have my lines, Amír has her lines, we all have something that keeps us grounded so we don't become monsters." Her lips peel back in an uncharacteristic snarl. "Do you know why we took you in? Why you were the exception? Darling, it isn't because Rowan thought you were hot. He could've trained you and rid us of you, we didn't have to let you in. Hell, he could've fucked you and left you if that's what he wanted. Have you ever wondered why *you* were the exception when so many coveted the unattainable position of the fifth Nightwalker?"

The fifth. A spot previously occupied by Mavis until she betrayed them. A spot no one could fill, until I came along and they welcomed me with open arms. I'm too embarrassed to admit aloud that the thought never crossed my mind. I never wondered what set me apart. My whole life, I have been used to being handed what I want. I never had to think about what would happen if I wasn't special. Because I was and I am. The last mage, the last known pureblood, the heir to the throne, the only child of the king—or so I thought.

Kya's eyes are golden flames as she speaks, her dark brows pinched upon her lovely face, now so full of rage and sorrow. It feels like sin to see someone as beautiful as she is so broken. "It is because you had a good heart. You were kind regardless of the situation and you had morals. You were light and brought out the humanity in us, humanity we thought we had lost. Now look at you. You've lost yours. I know what that is like, I have been there, and I'll be damned before I let you lose yourself too."

I take one look at her, one good long look, before breaking free of her grasp. "Then you're damned."

I find the other Nightwalkers outside when I step through the door into the wintry night air. My breath fogs as I shiver, Rowan immediately coming to press close to my side. Kya steps out moments later, her face downcast.

All it takes is one look for Amír to whirl in my direction, her fingers tapping the holster at her side. "What did you do?"

"Amír."

"No. What did she *do*?" the gunslinger spits, her hands running along Kya's shoulders and arms, her fingertips dancing over the thick tunic she wears.

Kya shrugs out of her grasp and begins the trek homeward. "Let's just get going before any worse monsters arrive," she murmurs under her breath.

Blaine shoots me a worried glance as my breathing hitches, but says nothing as he follows after her. Even Rowan shifts away. The movement is brief, and to anyone else, unnoticeable, but I feel the absence of his warmth immediately.

My heart rises in my throat, but I follow behind them obediently, the pouch hanging at my hip heavy in more ways than one.

CHAPTER 30
VEROSA

*M*onster. The word is clearly written across each of their faces as the Nightwalkers stare at the soiled pouch at my hip. Given the new stain on the cloth and the horror on Kya's face, it doesn't take long for them to put the pieces together. Despite it, Rowan returns to my side, his heat a constant blanket of comfort beside me.

We walk in silence under the cover of darkness. *Monster.* The word reverberates in my bones. With each heavy step, I can feel it settling deeper into my soul.

Monster.

Another thudding step.

Monster.

The darkness forces its way up my throat and wraps around my heart. The stars do little to light our path and even Rowan's reassuring weight pressing against my side isn't enough to assuage my growing panic.

The brush rustles to my left—the side unguarded by the blond mercenary. I fling my dagger out, gripping it with sure fingers and nearly cutting him in the process. My heels grind into the muddy ground, slick but surefooted.

"There's nothing there," Amír snaps.

Rowan draws his sword and stands with his back to mine. "Wait."

Amír glares at him but makes no move to disobey his command. Then a distant whistle.

I hardly have time to dodge the arrow before it strikes the tree behind me. The wood splinters, the shards embedding themselves into my skin. I can hardly feel it as my feet are moving and my grip on my dagger adjusts.

"Everybody get down!" Rowan calls out.

Our ambushers take this as their sign to spring from the trees. Their forms are pale and gangly, but they are men, not Kijova or any other beast. Some faces I recognize, others I cannot beneath the cover of grime and darkness. They are the other nobles Gadsden allied with, those who chose to side with the king in exchange for their lives. Their numbers are small but they are heavily armed and in better physical condition than we are.

I duck behind a tree just as another arrow rings out and slices through my tunic. Warmth spreads down my arm and I grit my teeth against the flaring pain. Rowan throws a look of concern my way in the dark, but I am already moving. Gripping a finger ripped from my pouch, I summon a dark flame and force it into the shape of a spear.

But the darkness does not hold its form. It rages from my palms, shapeless and relentless as it seeks out our enemies on its own. The dark flame consumes their forms, leaving only their scream on the wind before their ashes scatter in the snow.

The remaining assailants blanch and shout for a retreat, but are met only with a flying dagger or a bullet.

Yet even as the last of our enemies fall, the darkness still forces its way out from me, sucking on my blood and strength. I offer two more sacrifices in hopes of satiating its hunger, but it does nothing to weaken the steady thrum as it drains my energy. I fall to my knees, the melting snow biting through my trousers. My own name rings in my ears, a voice like Rowan's or Blaine's calling it.

My shoulders begin to sag, the ground pulling me towards it. With the last of my strength, I close my fists and picture the darkness surrendering. I shove it into a box in the back of my mind and call it all back into my body or force it into the air.

The darkness begrudgingly listens and I fall to the ground, my back barking with pain upon impact. The hand I split open throbs, any injury I've sustained since meeting Mavis suddenly reappearing in the form of phantom pains.

My eyes burn and squeeze shut as sweat trickles into them. Strong hands are shaking me, an equally stern voice commanding me to open my eyes. I blink and force them open to find Amír looking over me. Her red hair falls over my face, the white streak dancing just above my brow. Her marbled skin pinches as she glowers, but nonetheless, the gunslinger hoists me to my feet and allows me to lean on her. Rowan stands near the tree line with Kya and the others, his face the palest I've seen it.

I hardly remember the rest of the walk back, my memory foggy. Darkness claims me for a few moments as I slip in and out of consciousness. The only sure memory I have is of Amír's hands holding the brunt of my weight.

My mind only clears once we reach the inn and the gunslinger unceremoniously dumps me on the couch. She hisses something under her breath to Rowan that leaves the man uncharacteristically silent.

He stumbles over, his face still white as if he has seen a wraith on the walk home. "Are you alright?"

He's trying. I can see how clearly the words strain him. He's asking because he loves me, and because he wants me to know he still loves me. But what I did, what he's seen... It's hard to put it plainly. There's no other way to say it.

I part my lips to respond, but only a startled croak emits. The sound seems to trigger something in my body that leads to violent coughs and convulsions.

Rowan's eyes go wide, and as if on instinct, he unfastens his cape and throws it over me. "I will go get some water. Stay here," he commands.

Had I any voice, I might have responded that there is nowhere for me to go, nor could I move if I want to. But nothing but a whimper emits, so he is off to find water.

Blaine and Torin shuffle in, their faces drawn. Blaine settles heavily on the chair beside me, Torin opting to sit on the arm of the couch and stroke my hair. I question him with my eyes, quite plainly wondering when he arrived.

"I was on my way to the inn when I heard the gunfire. We spoke a bit on the walk home." Then he frowns. "Do you not remember?"

I shake my head, the motion sending heat splintering behind my eyes. Stars dance behind my eyelids when I squeeze them shut, streaking gold and red. Someone tips water between my lips, parting them with their thumb. Rowan's blurry face smiles softly at mine when I open my eyes, looking much more like the man I know. He strokes that thumb across my chin and dabs away my sweat with a damp cloth, allowing me to take small sips when I want.

"Thank you," I murmur, "but can I speak with them alone for a moment?"

Rowan didn't need to see me like this, not when I know how much it is costing him. Hesitance coats his mannerisms, but he stands nonetheless, and passes the cup off to Torin before leaving the room. Blaine hooks his hand under my arm, the other flying to the small of my back as I attempt to reach a seated position.

"I'm scared."

"No shit. You scared us too."

Torin glares at Blaine for the remark but offers to me in a more gentle tone, "We were worried *for* you. All I saw was you in the snow and you looked like a ghost."

"It was out of control," I offer with a shuddering breath. "The darkness. I couldn't stop it. I thought... I thought..."

It almost killed me. Despite the sacrifices, despite my blood, it almost killed me. Fear is smothered by a mask of rage. Mavis is blessed, not even a pureblood, and yet she can wield such power without anything like this. Do I just need more training? Am I not good enough?

Blaine's gray eyes are iron as they peer over his straight nose at me. It isn't fair how he can still look like he has been chiseled by the gods while being infuriated. My face goes all red and my voice pitchy. I never stand a chance in an argument.

Torin's nimble fingers have woven a small, mindless braid at the bottom of my hair. He promptly unbraids it then creates two instead before undoing those as well and taking to twirling the hair around his finger. His voice is smooth and charming, not too unlike the charm he's used on his many admirers. The manipulator's voice, yet it is honest when speaking to me. "You are pure light, Vera. In a world of chaos, the darkness is going to try to smother you."

I take another shaky breath, my ribs rattling with the minuscule motion. "I think I've been consumed by the darkness for so long that it's starting to call back. What happens if I let it?"

"Then we all die."

Torin bristles. "Blaine. With respect, fuck off."

The former captain only shrugs, his shoulders square and his mouth forming a taut line. Even without his title or his armor, he cuts an imposing figure.

"It's true. If she fails, we die. This is war. I don't have time to make jokes and metaphors. She sorts this power of the pureblood shit out, or none of us stand a chance." He snarls when he catches Torin's scowl. "What? Can you suddenly kill a Kijova? How about an army of them? Last I checked, she's the only one who can."

"He's right," I admit, my shoulders slumping.

The two men stare at my face, slack-jawed and borderline pale.

"What?" I finally snap.

"I just never thought I'd hear those words come from your mouth. Ever."

"I can admit my faults, thank you. It feels like that's all I've been doing lately."

It is true. I've been failing as far back as my memory goes. I failed Irene constantly, not that I cared about that anyhow. I failed Blaine, then I failed him again when he returned to war. Then Tanja, the Nightwalkers, Mavis, now the only family I've ever known.

I promised them an answer. I promised them I would find the key to unlocking this power and save them.

How am I supposed to save them if I can't even save myself?

I DOZE off not long after. I awake a few times during the day to hushed voices and golden light streaming through the window. Someone moves me to my bed at some point, but I continue to doze through the entirety of daylight, only awaking to the sound of an owl outside my window.

Rowan sits at the foot of the bed, his elbows braced on his powerful thighs. His head hangs low like a man in prayer, though I know him better. I'm drawn to him as if on instinct, crawling forward and looping my arms around his shoulders.

"You're awake." Not a hint of tone laces his voice. Just pure exhaustion.

I push a kiss into his shoulder before resting my chin between the juncture of his jaw and clavicle. "I am," I whisper, not even sure what to say. My voice is gravelly with disuse, my mouth dry and tongue heavy. I can feel his chin bob as he nods.

"You and Derrín were supposed to leave tomorrow at first light. To find the Oracle."

Shit. I nearly forgot, too consumed by the thought of avenging those girls through Lars's death, girls whose faces and names I never even knew. I packed my bags days ago and they rest in the corner of the room, leaning against the doorframe.

"We will still go. Clearly, I am well rested."

My joke falls on deaf ears as Rowan shudders. "You used dark magic."

"I did."

I can feel each breath he takes as he forces them to be even, feel his shoulders stiffen beneath my touch. He leans forward and rises, forcing me with him. Though there might only be a few inches between us, the distance in the air presses heavy against me. My feet stay rooted to the floor, the rest of my body threatening to follow suit.

"Even after... after all it's... Dammit. This is harder than I thought."

His distress presses steel into my heart and I step forward, wrapping my arms around his center again. My head rests against his chest, listening for that heartbeat. It seems to drag beneath my touch.

"You deserved better, so I became better. For *you*." He runs his hand through his hair as he looks at me. Tired, he looks so tired.

Gripping tight to his sleeve, I plead with him. "I know."

"And what of what *I* deserve?" He moves out of my grasp, and my heart begins to race. Control is slipping out from between my fingers faster than I can grapple for the pieces.

"What?"

"I deserve better than this, Vera. I don't deserve for you to play with my heart. You know what dark magic did to my family, *to me*. And yet you still..." His jaw clenches. "I can't keep doing this, whatever this is."

My heart lurches into my throat. "What are you saying?"

"I'm saying that if this is how things are going to be, then I'm done. *We* are done."

The pain of the statement forces me to double over myself. My fingertips press into my chest as if I can force the broken fragments together. I've considered many things since I've returned, and a life without Rowan is not something I thought to picture. Rage creeps into the crevices of my soul, rebuilding a wall from the rubble of the one I tore down.

I laugh drily. "You will see me as your equal or you won't see me at all."

"I do, Laei... Why do you think I'm telling you all this?" Rowan runs his hand through his hair, taking a step back. Widening the berth between us. Something in that one simple step lights a fire in my chest.

"Oh, so when *you* act like this, it's fine, but when *I* do, suddenly, I'm a monster?"

"You've changed," he murmurs warily.

"So what if I have? Things are different now, Rowan. I've seen people die. People I love die!"

"So have the rest of us, Vera. We aren't here for fun. We are all trying to protect the people we love. That's why I—" He pauses, his gaze downcast and breathing labored.

"That's why you *what*?" I spit back, too pissed off to care for the pain in his voice.

"That's why I'm trying to stop you."

My heart stills in my chest, the sound of blood rushing filling my ears as I weigh his words. *Because when I cut you, he bleeds.* That's what Mavis said.

Space. I need space and time alone. This is a choice I have to make, to save everyone, and I can't do that if he's here stopping me.

"Nothing good comes from dark magic, Vera. Hell, it's in the name! *Dark* magic!" Rowan shouts at my turned back as I begin to walk towards the door.

Shut up. Stop making this harder than it is, I plead mentally before I whirl around to face him again. "You told me yourself that Raonkin wasn't evil, that it was Deungrid, so why are you trying to stop me? *She's* the victim here." *I'm the victim here.* "The Oracle can help us."

"I know that, but it still exists. The curse—it catches up with you, and not even you can outrun this."

Back and forth. Each word we trade like new lacerations on our hearts. We cut deep enough to wound, to bleed, but never to kill. And gods, we know how to hurt each other worse than anyone else.

"And you'd know, wouldn't you?"

Stop. I need to stop before it's too late, but I can't.

His eyes darken.

"We still haven't talked about that, you know. Or anything you've done, really. So stop playing all high and mighty with me when you've been lying this whole time."

"Everything I did, I did to protect you. What would you have done if you saw Blaine then? You would've made things worse for both of you."

"And I would've left the palace that night and no one would have died," I snap, narrowing my gaze.

The bitter and ugly truth. If he had simply told me where Blaine had gone, I would've left early to help him. I would've been gone before Ophelus was ready. No one would have died. *Tanja* would not have died. I force myself to swallow the lump in my throat and press my forehead against the cool stone wall.

Every muscle in Rowan's body turns to stone. He stills as if the chill of the room has seeped into his blood and frozen him from the inside. It has always been his instinct to fight his way out of conflict and he has never been the type to be good with his words. He's never needed them before now and he's trying. Gods, is he trying.

He runs his tongue over his lips and when he speaks again, the words are strained. "I understand."

"You understand *nothing*," I hiss. "Nothing at all. Are you the only one able to kill a Kijova? Are you the supposed chosen one who has to save everyone? I have the whole world on my shoulders, Rowan, and there is no one who can take that away. No one who can even share or begin to understand that."

His lips part softly in an expression I recognize quickly. I saw it every day in Mavis's compound when the others saw past their fear to notice the loosely fitting clothes and my wobbly steps. Pity. This deep, embedded sadness that they know they cannot save me from this fate, no matter how desperately they want to.

Because they still think I am too weak to handle it.

Even though the anger in the room has dissipated, I force ice back into my words, fighting my instincts to erase any bit of progress we have made. "Besides, isn't this what you wanted? What you trained me for?"

A blink, and the pity is gone. I can practically see the walls go up, the barbs of defense lacing his tongue. "I was training you to be able to defend yourself."

"Really? Is that what all those missions were for? You made me this," I spit with as much venom as I can muster and beat my fist into my chest. "Congratulations, you have your weapon."

"I've made mistakes," he pleads, but there's a bite behind his words now. Even as his voice grows watery and his hands shake, there is something darker lurking beneath. Something that calls to my own darkness. "But all I want now is *you*."

He may think he means those words. Looking at him and knowing him, I believe him when he says he believes that. But he doesn't. He wants who I was before he broke me. Before he and Mavis and Lucius and this whole world decided to fuck me over.

"You don't get to judge me for the blood I've spilled when you put the knife in my hand."

His gaze is hard, but I force myself to hold it. Force him to understand.

"I'm going. I won't expect you to be awaiting me when I return."

Then a pause at the door.

"Goodbye, Rowan."

CHAPTER 31
VEROSA

I don't know where I thought I was going when I left my room, but I am far too angry to turn back. No, it is not anger. It is fear and sorrow and pride. These force my feet to move forward until they melt back into anger and I find myself standing outside a specific door.

Rowan was the one who helped change my mind on the blessed and the cursed, who showed me that the only fundamental difference between us is something as trivial as blood color. So how can he expect me to believe him again now that he says we are not equal? Not in ability, anyway.

Because the shadow show in the forest proves him right. Because I was completely out of control and was going to be killed. If I hadn't by some god found the power to settle the darkness, it would have engulfed me. The curse is real, and as unfair as it is, that is the key difference between the cursed and the blessed. Why must it be that way?

I knock once before opening the door.

"Hi," I whisper softly as I enter the dark room.

A beat of silence, then the near-silent sputter of a match as the flame transfers to a candle. The light traces the form of a simple bed, a few books, and the man I've come searching for.

Blaine sits at the edge of his bed, one leg resting on the worn wooden frame. He cuts an imposing shape even in the dim light, his hulking form seemingly shrinking the rest of the room. His face softens by a fraction. "Hey," he responds with the same tender softness that mine had.

Each footstep echoes through the room, the rest of our motions silent as if our bodies are terrified to break the quiet peace. His shoulders square and muscles tense as I settle next to him, my knees pressed against his thigh.

"What are you doing here?"

The hell if I know. Something like a thread tugged my feet until I found myself standing outside his door, dawn not yet brushing against the sky. Perhaps it was anger, or that constant longing for the comfort of familiarity. Whichever it was, it brought me to Blaine.

"Why are you up?" I ask instead, leaning my head against his shoulder.

He stiffens for a moment before relaxing, allowing his hand to rest in the space between our thighs. Not close enough to be holding or touching me, but enough so that each time I shift, I can feel his knuckles scrape against my leg.

Blaine laughs lightly, holding up the book in his hands. "Just needed to occupy my mind."

He doesn't need to say why. He's grown more distant in the past few days since we announced Derrín and I would be leaving to find the oracle. It is not the type of distant it used to be back when we were in the palace. Then, it was cold and forced indifference. This time, the space between us is filled with longing, tension, and dare I say regret.

I inhale sharply, shattering the quiet. "I can help."

The words slip past my lips before I can realize what I am saying. What I am doing.

Blaine watches my motions with deadly stillness as I idle closer. I feel no warmth as my skin meets his, no shocks to fleck my skin with gooseflesh. I push myself closer to him, my torso tightly pressed to his.

My lips move against his jaw, sending each breath he takes rattling through my skull. My fingers reach up to his lips as he clenches his jaw, restraining himself even now as I offer myself wholly to him.

His breath ceases to warm my face as he inhales sharply. He's holding his breath. The sight of him so unraveled by our close proximity should ignite that old heat. It doesn't. Maybe if I just...

I'm halfway on top of him now, my lips only a breath away from his. He smells like before the world went to shit. Spice from the local bakery. Some earthy scents from the days we would run from the inner palace. Home.

My lips brush against his, and as I am about to move a hair further, his hand clamps over my mouth, shoving me just far enough away. My back hits his mattress, his body kneeled over mine. His breathing is ragged and his gaze dark. The muscles in his arm tense as he holds me there. Close enough to hold and yet far enough to be out of reach.

"Don't kiss me," he murmurs huskily. "Not while you're still thinking of him. I won't be your replacement because you're pissed off that you can't have what you want." His voice should be filled with rage or desire, but there is only sorrow in his dark eyes as they bore down on me.

I swallow thickly, and he flinches as he feels my lips brush against the hand that covers them. Slowly, he lowers it and I breathe deeply.

"And what if I want you?"

I can feel his body go rigid, even at the blatant lie. I'm in too deep to feel burning remorse or guilt. Blaine pauses only for a moment before he moves with the stealth and precision of a predator. His lips cover mine and swallow my gasp as my back arches from the bed to bring myself closer to him. His mouth guides mine, taking more than giving while waiting for me to catch up. I lift my hips as his tongue sweeps my lower lip and across my teeth. Claiming. Possessive. His hands grip the back of my head, pulling me further into him while his other arm wraps around my waist. His body presses into all the places that used to make me gasp as he takes more and more of me.

But I feel nothing.

Only an aching emptiness remains as Blaine plants a final kiss to my swollen lips. He glowers at me, a mix of passion, sorrow, and finally, that cold anger.

Regret settles low in my gut and I scramble to sit up straight, righting my clothes and gasping. "I'm sorry. I shouldn't have, I— I don't know what I was doing."

"You felt cold."

"What?"

"Whenever my fingertips traced your ribs, you used to gasp and squirm. When I took the initiative, you'd practically be a puddle in my arms. Now you're stiff, just going through the motions. You feel nothing when I kiss you, but I feel everything. I am completely consumed by you. Your scent, your feel, your taste. You burn hotter the tighter I hold you, and yet I can't let go. I can still see that future for us," he growls, his anger giving way as tears prick at his eyes. "I love you and you feel nothing. Don't toy with me. Don't make me hate you."

I can see it too when he says it. I can see the dreams we planned, the life we built for ourselves within fantasy. And yet his face is blurred each time and the dream is just out of my grasp. I should want this. I should have...

My chin dips and he presses his forehead to mine.

"I'm sorry. I—"

"Don't. You've made your choice, and while I respect that, you must respect that this isn't a choice for me. I can't choose to stop loving you because it is who I am. I won't wear you down with my affections. I won't mention it again. So long as you're happy, I can live with it. But know this— when the day comes that you die, I will still feel it in my bones and I will mourn you not as a friend but as a love. I've followed and waited for you for a thousand lifetimes, and I will wait a thousand more. I am yours, even if you are not mine."

By the end, he's spiraling, just saying whatever words come to his mind. He rises and stalks towards the door, the darkness obscuring his face.

I move to my knees, my hands outstretched in a silent plea, though it seems far too late. "Blaine, I didn't want to hurt you."

"You can't. Not anymore."

"You're my friend—"

"No. I'm not."

I stand behind him now. He's only a pace away. Just one small step and yet he's never felt further. Not even when I was jumping out of windows and he pretended not to know me did he feel so distant.

"If you're not my friend, and you're not my lover... Then what are you?"

Blaine pauses for a moment as if considering this before he runs his tongue over his swollen lips. The single step it takes to cross through the doorway shatters my heart. As he leaves, he parts with one final condemnation, one that I know will reverberate in my bones for years to come.

"I'm your soldier."

The ground bites my knees as I fall, dry heaving but unable to be sick. Let him be my one that got away. My enemy. My murderer. Anything but my soldier, for I've seen far too many soldiers die now for something as foolish as love.

BY THE TIME I pick myself off the floor, daylight has begun to stream weakly through the curtains. The sky is hardly pink when I drag myself to my room to change, Rowan thankfully already gone and Blaine nowhere to be seen. I slip my sweater on and two pairs of socks, shoving my only other pair in my pack at the last minute. Derrín and I agreed to travel light, given that we could encounter a Kijova at any moment. Only one spare pair of clothing, a few weapons, and even less food. We decided we could hunt along the way and forage the rest of the time, lest any meals weigh us down or perish. I pull my thickest pair of pants on and tuck Tanja's ring under my sweater, but not before kissing it once.

I turn back, and at the last second, grab my dagger, the one Rowan gave me with the rose hilt. It settles heavily in my pack next to the rolled-up map and compass where Gadsden's blood marks the location of the oracle. Nausea roils in my stomach, but I shove the bile back down my throat. I don't know when I will eat a full meal again, and I refuse to lose last night's dinner to the image of a greasy man such as the former duke.

The stairs creak beneath my feet and I can hear the sounds of people sitting below me. Kya's worn face is the first to greet me. I can see her repressing her anger and sorrow, attempting to forgive a wound that is still too new just in case I don't make it back. I love her for it and loathe myself more than I thought possible.

I almost hope that I don't make it back until I catch a glimpse of Emilie's face. Her pretty features are swollen and her eyes red with poorly concealed tears. I see my mother's face in hers, then my father. If they are alive, they will need their daughter, and I need to live to save them. I square my shoulders and reach out.

Her fingers interlace with mine and she kisses my palm. I lean into her touch before throwing my arms around her, enveloping her shaking frame in an embrace. When I pull away, her countenance is resolute, the face of a woman who has lost everything already. Everything but one thing. Her light. Her son.

Derrín throws a pack my way. "We will eat on the road. I've already said my goodbyes." Kya squeezes his hand one last time as he passes, then he is gone out the door.

Amír makes her way over, giving Kya time to steady herself. "Anything we should look for in particular when we search Irene's study?" the gunslinger asks, leaning on the wall beside me. "Or anything you want from home?"

Home. It feels like such a hollow word compared to what I've found here with these people. Or rather *had* found, before it all fell apart.

"No," I say softly.

The mercenary nods, her movements tight with emotion. She clasps a hand on my shoulder as Torin approaches. "Don't get yourself killed out there."

I allow myself a small smile. "I'll do my best," I say as she slips away.

Torin's own lips lift in a smile that I'm sure is weaker than my own. In all honesty, it looks more like a grimace once paired with his uncharacteristically pale face and fidgeting hands. I reach my arms out and envelope him before he can say anything. His knees buckle and his fingers dig into my back. He probably hates this more than all of them, wishing he could go instead.

"I'd ask you not to go but..."

"You know me too well," I finish for him, pulling back to study his features like it is the last time. "So you know I can't handle another goodbye."

Torin's eyes swell with unshed tears. The last time we parted like this, we both thought it would be the last we saw of each other, and soon after, the palace fell and we thought for certain the other had died. I can't handle that thought again, not after all we've been through to find each other.

He grips my forearms, my wrists, my fingers, then he drops my hands. "Then this isn't goodbye."

"If you have a cheesy line after that sentence, I'm walking out the door right now."

He laughs, a warm and lovely sound. "No cheesy lines. Just a promise."

"Ah, and there it is!"

The warmth in my chest is tight, like if I breathe too deep it might pop. I cannot tell if it is sorrow or happiness, or maybe a bittersweet mixture of both.

My eyes flit to Kya. "I have an apology to make."

Torin's gaze trails mine to where the assassin leans against a wall, pretending to not be looking on.

The scent of cinnamon lingers on Kya's skin as I approach her, even months later without access to the perfume she used to wear daily or any of the rich spice. I swear it must have seeped into her skin or very being at this point. The ghost of the scent covers my senses like a blanket and I sigh deeply through my nose.

"I assume I am the first on your list of apologies today," she offers with a bit of bite behind her words.

I shuffle my weight to my other foot and inhale again. "I suppose I deserve that."

"What is this really about, Vera?" Her amber gaze pierces through my foggy thoughts, hot with anger and betrayal. "You don't need to redeem yourself."

I bite my lip to keep from growling out, and instead, grip her elbow, lifting her painted arm. I place my fingers strategically, careful not to smudge the hard-to-come-by paint. "The same reason you wear this paint every day. And maybe so I can hate myself a little less by trying to fix things instead of making them worse. So please, I'm sorry." Then, when she doesn't answer, "I won't use dark magic again. We will find another way. I won't lose you over this."

"And if the Oracle says it is the answer?"

"We will find another way," I repeat, lying through my teeth.

Kya stares on as if she can sense this. She, of all people, should understand my desperation, my purpose. My revenge may be dirtier than hers, but I've still probably killed less men than her.

She sighs, relenting, and wraps her arms around my neck. "Take care of Derrín for me."

"Yes, ma'am." I offer a mocking salute.

She wipes at her eyes before joining the others in the kitchen and I head towards Derrín.

Dawn is slowly ending and the sun's rays begin to warm the earth. The snow outside glistens against the light—beautiful, deadly.

I pause just outside the door. Still no Rowan.

A dark shadow casts over the rotting floorboards beneath my feet. I look up to meet Blaine's iron stare, his face softening considerably when he sees the worry on mine. My heart aches within my chest. I don't deserve him, I never have. I open my mouth, but he silences me with a raised hand that falls on my arm.

"Don't apologize."

"I owe you one though," I argue.

He smirks a bit, clearly in agreement. Still, he doesn't demand anything, just shakes his head with a faraway look in his eye. "We've owed each other a lot of things in our lives, Vera. We can call it even."

"I wish I could love you again."

A small, sad smile. "I know. Just tell me, was there ever another chance, even the slightest?"

His eyes are hopeful even though we both know my answer.

Even after last night, something about his anger has softened his heart. My thoughts flit back to what Kya said about Amír. She is angry because she is kind. Something tugging at my heart tells me Blaine is the same. He throws up the soldier's front because he has seen death too often for it not to remember him. He hardens his heart, waiting for the day it comes for him so that it will not hurt the rest of us. But he is still in there, my Blaine who loved poetry and whose laugh warmed the world.

My fingers trace the side of his face that the shade touches. "Somewhere along the way, the piece of me that fit with you broke." I inhale sharply as tears prick at the corners of my eyes. "And I don't think we can ever fix that."

His fingers reach up and wrap around mine, holding my hand in place for just a moment before he lowers it, our fingers still intwined. He kisses the top of my head, a silent tear escaping the corner of his eye. It slips into the folds of his smile as he walks past me back into the inn, our shoulders brushing and my hand cold.

I hold it to my chest, sorrow swelling in my heart and threatening to pull me under. Blaine and I finally have found our ending and I've made my goodbyes. All this stalling for nothing when the face I wanted to see most is nowhere to be found. It was foolish and I should know better.

Finally, I move to take a step forward when familiar arms wrap around my midsection.

"You come back to me alive," Rowan says gruffly, his words laced with a mix of anger and another emotion I can't quite place. "I don't care if you come back and run a knife through my heart or never speak to me again, but you come back alive. Don't die trying to be a hero. You don't need to forgive me, you just need to live and live well."

The first tear spills over, still hot with anger. I hate him so much that I love him. I hate that too. Only a choking sound comes out when I open my mouth so I close it again, just allowing myself to bask in his presence for a few seconds.

A moment later, I feel him press his lips to the top of my head. "I love you." And then he is gone, disappearing into the shadows again just as daylight streaks across the sky.

Derrín says nothing as I all but storm up to him, my pack slamming angrily against my back with each step. He follows my lead as we allow the compass to lead us east into the thick of the trees.

"Come on," I hiss between clenched teeth. "We have an Oracle to find."

CHAPTER 32

ROWAN

A sense of dread follows me as soon as I wake alone in my bed. For a moment, I panic before I realize that Vera wasn't taken, she left. And I let her.

Hours later, as I sit astride a gelding gifted to me by the rebels, that dread grows. I've both walked and ridden this trail many times and know that if I had veered right four miles ago, we would have reached the compound. Amír and Kya glanced that way, as well, but no one said anything.

Blaine and Torin lead the pack, with four rebels following them. I follow behind them with the two women at the rear. Roiden might have promised a peace pact, but I am nowhere near trusting him enough to let his men behind me for even a second.

I follow the track ahead, the snow melted, thankfully, as to not give away our tracks. Spring is upon Krycolis's cities, even if it is not yet in the mountains. Any moment now, the road will fork and we will take the path to the left and follow it all the way to the palace—to my father—and if we are lucky enough, answers that could change the tide in this war.

Despite Roiden's skepticism, Vera is convinced we can make

blessed weapons, and given the fucked nature of our world, I am inclined to believe her. The gods made a balance, even if they did not want one. With cursed weapons, there must be a blessed counterpart.

Or an abomination such as a hybrid weapon. Maybe *I* am the weapon.

My knuckles groan and turn white as I clutch the reins. I can hear every whisper of a breath that leaves the gelding's nostrils, can feel the vibrations of him chewing on his bit as it rubs against the corner of his muzzle. I can hear the racing hearts of the rebels before us and feel the way the wind shifts to make space for us. I can see the way the light refracts and if I wanted, I could throw myself high enough from the horse to reach one of the higher branches on the trees. Any other blissfully ignorant fool might call this a gift. I only see the curse of a reminder.

Now it is time to face the maker of this reminder and all the painful memories I've begun to recall. I can still see his face, unplagued by time and dark magic. His face was narrow but handsome and kind. I have his smile—not his mouth, but his smile. It is enough that I never want my lips to lift in any semblance of a grin ever again.

He held my mother gently and would sing to her even though her voice was lovely and his was shit. He taught me how to hold my wooden sword and my mother a gun. He braided ribbons in her hair and read me books and was a good father. He was good to us. And he ruined himself for us. And gods, I hate him for it.

The palace comes into view sooner than I would have liked, though I am only aware of it when I hear Torin swear under his breath. I lift my gaze to find the source and my dry response hitches in my throat.

As if some god wielded an axe against the stone, the palace is completely cleaved in two, a deep ravine splitting down the center. All the towers but two have completely crumbled, leaving the queen's tower, and a lone watch tower that stands over what used to be the knights' quarters. Blaine's face blanches and Torin's eyes water. Unrequited pity strikes my heart at the thought. This used to be their home, for better or for worse.

Blaine steels his features first and addresses the other man. "Seb was certain there would be a guard rotation at noon?"

Torin nods his head, though deep, penetrating sadness still taints his features. "Yes, and they're running thin given Ophelus's experiments and the little control his pets seem to have. The nobles have no more men to donate and those that ally with him have been forced to take shifts. If you do encounter anyone, they most likely aren't trained as well as us in weaponry."

A silent command rests over the group. Kill anyone you find.

We tie the horses just outside the southern wall, their dark bodies covered by the boughs of the overarching trees. Kya slips beside Torin and the rebels, picking her way over the rubble to follow the path laid out by Seb. Torin lets her lead, relying on her stealth and jumping each time she reemerges from the shadows until they are completely out of view. While they find and free the remaining survivors, Blaine, Amír, and I will find Irene's study. Blaine comes as a guide and I find myself assigned to him in order to be a secondary. In truth, I know it was elected so that I had a lesser chance of running into the king. Amír follows suit, likely to keep me out of trouble, or to help us blast our way out should we encounter it.

If I thought the outside of the palace looked strange, then the inside is unrecognizable. The tapestries have been torn from the walls, deep claw marks tearing through them and even through the weathered stone. The decadent flooring has cracked and splatters of blood streak against all surfaces—gold, silver, red. All the colors swirl together in a macabre display. Blaine swears lowly but says nothing else, even as he crosses two fingers over his heart.

We creep along the walls, pausing every so often to listen for a familiar growl or the footsteps of two fallen kings—or rather, king and emperor, as Amír would correct me if she could hear my thoughts. Our breaths mingle in the cold as we wait to hear from death. Blaine's motions beside me are stiff as he forcibly lifts his leg higher than usual to avoid the announcing drag. Amír's fingers twitch at her side and she palms at the gun hanging low across her hip. I keep my eyes trained on my surroundings.

My hybrid blood allows me certain abilities the average person does not possess. I can feel the slightest shift in the wind to sense when an attack is coming. I can quiet my steps and breathing enough to be silent and hide among the shadows to be invisible. It is different from how Kya masks her form with shadows. Her ability is derived from her own merits, her skills and practice. Mine comes from what runs through my veins, yet I rely on these abilities now as I study the inside of the castle.

The empty, whistling corridors. The bloody walls seeming to close in ever so slowly. I imagine this must be how the palace looked to Vera every day she lived within these towers. Hollow and dismal. The perfect prison for someone like her.

Blaine traces everything with those eyes, his features sharpening like a brewing storm. He does his best not to look at the blood, instead peeking into various rooms. We pass some that I am familiar with, but ultimately, the whole palace has become a labyrinth of half-crumbling walls and broken bodies. Amír closes the eyes of the few dead we find and Blaine crosses two fingers over his heart. I keep watch, waiting for the telltale rattle of Kijova or Lucius's assured step. None come.

"Be honest, do you know where we are going or are you running blind around these corners?" I bump Blaine's shoulder with my own as I pull ahead, equally lost.

"Well, you stayed here a few months. If I'm so blind, perhaps you could help," he grinds out between clenched teeth. His knuckles are white at his side and I want to push, but Amír shoots me a glare that tells me I know better. The captain stalks ahead, bumping my shoulder now with greater force than I used on him.

I bite back a bitter laugh. "Get a grip."

"You know what I'm doing."

"And I don't have time for it," my second responds, ever the compassionate type.

I wonder if Torin and Kya have found the survivors yet. Wherever they are, they must be faring better than we are.

Amír forges ahead, her gait careless and swaggering. "Come on now, we haven't got all day," she hisses, stepping out into the corridor.

With lightning proficiency and speed, Blaine's arm wraps around her midsection, pulling her back against the wall. Her gun slams into his thigh and his hand flies to her mouth to smother her gasp. I still every muscle in my body and strain to listen. A few moments later, the sound reaches me—a hesitant set of footsteps. Someone who is lost or...

Lucius steps out from around the corner, dressed in his royal regalia. He looks nearly the same as he did all those months ago, his perfect hair still smoothed away from his face that is turned from us. He pauses, and Blaine's grip on Amír tightens. I lay my hand against the hilt of my sword.

Lucius turns his face to us. It is only through years of practice that I am able to withhold my gasp and stay steady on my feet despite the monster before me.

Lucius's hands are completely black and tipped with claws, the darkness slithering up his forearms before the bulging black veins disappear beneath his skin. His complexion is pale, nearing blue. His face, though still handsome, has been marred by bruises and dripping gold-flecked blood. His eyelids have been cut—no, *burned* off, leaving nothing but poorly healed nubs at the top of his eyes.

His white and silver eyes. His dark irises have been burned past recognition until only silver clouds cover the milky white canvas.

Amír stiffens in recognition and our eyes meet. We've seen this handiwork before. We both know who did this to him.

"Vera," Blaine breathes softly as the emperor disappears from view. "What did you do?"

CHAPTER 33

ROWAN

I don't believe in the gods, but something divine intervenes in allowing Lucius to pass us by without sensing our unwelcome presence in the palace. He rounds the corner as Blaine swears, leaving us completely unnoticed, but the chill in the air still permeates.

"He didn't look like that before, right?" Amír interrogates.

Blaine shakes his head and a muscle feathers in his jaw. "No."

No seems to be a simple way of putting it. *No, Amír, the former prince did not have burned eyelids and monster arms. Thank you kindly for that astute observation.*

The gunslinger presses a glare to the side of my head that makes me wonder again if she can read my thoughts. "I'm guessing our little tyrant is responsible for the burned eyes?"

A nod.

"And those claws?"

"Those would be from the experiments Seb warned us about. The king," Blaine finishes with a grim look.

Lucius didn't walk through the corridors. He glided with an otherworldly grace. His shoulders were squared and chin raised as if he still bore a crown, and yet his elbows seemed angled just slightly the wrong way, those dark veins reaching up for his throat and heart, and he sniffed the air with primal instincts. He is more monster than man now.

"Part Kijova, part man?" Amír asks.

"No," I respond. "This is something entirely different."

The air is pregnant with tension to the point of near suffocation. A distant scream rattles through the walls that sends our feet moving.

Blaine is the first to forge forth, tapping our arms with the back of his hand. "We need to move."

I share a glance with my gunslinger. We both noticed at the same time how Blaine's eye twitched and the vein in his neck constricted when the fallen prince walked by. They weren't reactions of a man afraid, but of rage. Had Lucius stood still a second longer, Blaine's sword might have been buried hilt deep in his neck and his blood would have sent every Kijova in the kingdom after us.

Months ago, while Blaine was still recovering, Amír weaseled the information from Kya on why he was crashing with us, drunk as he was. I offered her a few details to keep her off my back, but her lover filled in the rest of the gaps. The Nightwalkers might not have asked Blaine about the duel, but they all were aware of both it and its ending—the ending that left Blaine's honor disintegrated and him turning to drink. That day was a shift not only in the former captain, but the prince and Vera's minimal affections for him.

Amír takes up the middle as I pick up the rear. We fall into position easily, her trusting my heightened abilities and me trusting her nature-given ones. We push onward behind Blaine, slowly making our way to the queen's study.

After passing through the same corridor four times, Amír kicks aside a piece of rubble in frustration. She pushes her hair from her face and glares daggers toward me and the former captain. "You spent months here." She whirls from me to Blaine. "And you lived here for years! How do neither of you know where we are going or how to find one damn room?"

"In case you haven't noticed, this whole place has collapsed in on itself. Most of the hallways we can't pass through, and those we can are crawling with undead guards," Blaine snaps, his fingers fidgeting at his side.

He has been sober for a month now, since the night Vera was kidnapped. Hints of the man Vera must have known are showing through the rage and stress, and I must begrudgingly admit that I like the person I'm meeting. I tend to like him more when he argues with Amír on our behalf. Saves me from yet another headache.

The two bicker as I peer around the corner. No undead guards or Kijova linger in the halls, so for now, we are safe. We won't be for much longer if they keep shouting at each other like this. My face swivels to the left. What was *that*?

Buried beneath their harsh whispers, the soft susurration of a feminine voice lingers. It wraps itself around my senses, lulling me to comfort. Without bothering to look for dangers, I follow it. My gunslinger and Blaine immediately stop and follow as I slip around the corner down a new hall. The temperature begins to drop and my breath fogs before my face.

"Rowan. Where are you going?" Amír's voice crystallizes in the air. She shivers, yet despite the obvious cold, I feel nothing.

Blaine's countenance is grim and he whispers something to her that I don't catch. Her own expression hardens and she dips her chin, no more questions asked or complaints voiced.

This way.

Her fingers dance along the handle of her gun, a rhythmic tapping blending melodically with the sweet voice that beckons. Blaine's dragging limp scrapes along the stone, the final notes of a perfect blend. My heart slows and my shoulders drop. This peace, this calm, it is lovely.

"—like this. We should snap him out of it," Amír hisses beneath her breath, jarring some of my senses back.

Where am I going?

"We can't. We won't find it otherwise."

"You've seen this?"

"Vera."

"Oh."

Follow.

The calling is louder now, growing in urgency and causing my feet to move faster. We fly across the floor, missing every rotation of undead guards by just a hair before we stop before a door. Its finely etched wood is worn yet pristine, the bronze door handle still shining, not yet dull with use. My hand reaches for it of its own accord when Amír steps before me.

The barrel of her gun points straight at my forehead, a warning. "Dark magic."

These two words douse ice down my spine and I leap away from the door as if she actually shot me. Irene's study stands before us, as the dark force around it called me to it. It wants me to open that door.

Suddenly, our mission feels less appealing.

The bit about Blaine knowing and having seen this before with Vera—it all makes sense. The magic called to her not because of the blood flowing in her veins, but because Irene wished her harm. Because Irene wanted an excuse to leave her for dead that winter night. The same way she wanted me dead from the moment I entered this world. If my mother were here, I am sure the call would be much louder and demanding than the sweet voice I heard.

"You let it bring us here," I hiss, hurt flashing across my features.

Blaine nods in patronizing understanding and I find myself rescinding my earlier statement about liking him. "We had no choice. You were the only one it called to."

"Right," I grind out. "And I'm sure I have no choice but to slip some whiskey in your cup tonight."

Blaine grinds his teeth and closes his fist around the hilt of his sword. The pain of this betrayal hones on Amír, the one who should've understood. I find nothing but cool and unflinching resolution on her face. No signs of guilt. No shame.

"Fucking... move." I shove her aside and throw the door open. It halts of its own accord before it slams against the stone, a silent whine of magic the only proof of the dark force surrounding us.

The study is open and untouched, as if it was frozen in time the day Irene died. Given the stories I've heard, that wouldn't surprise me in the least.

Mounted on the walls are hundreds of papers, most covered in dark runes or spells, some are maps that have been slashed through. I fear for those left untouched. Racks of vials with decaying organisms lean against the far wall. Amír picks one up, the reddish-brown liquid inside sloshing unsavorily at the disturbance. She puts it down and rubs her fingertips along her pants.

Blaine rifles through Irene's desk with stiff motions, his eyes avoiding a skeletal hand on display. A rusted ring lays on its finger. I avert my gaze and take to combing through the loose-leaf papers atop a bookshelf in the corner.

"Anything?" Amír calls out.

I shake my head.

Blaine groans. "There's so much shit in here, I forget what we're even looking for."

"Anything on blessed weapons."

"It's just a figure of speech." The former captain throws his hands in the air and I drown out the rest of his irate response.

The room is dim, lit only by torches and a single window. I

forgo my search in the bookshelf and approach that window, a shiver creeping up the back of my neck. With careful hands, I push the glass panes open and jump as they creak.

A cool, fall breeze caresses my skin and prickles gooseflesh across my exposed forearms. I dare to lean out a little further and drop my gaze to the ground. A tall and withered tree stands near the base of the palace, dried and dead wisteria vines climbing the stone near the roots. Branches reach skyward, save for the portion of the tree closest to the window—the dead portion the size of a small child.

My heart hammers in my chest. The drop must be at least twenty feet and she was only a child...

A heavy hand settles on my shoulder and I jump. Blaine grimaces when he traces my gaze to the ground below and quickly shuts the window.

We both take to sorting through Irene's desk drawers together. I rifle through papers then pass them his way, allowing him to check for anything my tired eyes might have missed. I pretend I cannot feel the gentle caress of the wind on my neck, nor the way that window beckons me to come and lean out just a bit further.

"You were the one who found her that morning, right?"

"I was."

"Was she..."

"I thought she was dead," the Vari man answers honestly. "She was so small and her skin was so blue. Her eyes had frozen over and the frostbite stole most of the flesh on her fingers. The healers said if she wasn't a pureblood, she wouldn't have survived and even then, it was a miracle. None of us knew she was a mage at that point."

I inhale sharply and take another step away from the window. "Was that the only instance like that?"

Blaine's eyes darken and he unconsciously rubs at his aching leg. Vera told me some of her history with Irene, but we all know there's more that happened between her and Irene than anyone will ever know. Some things are too terrible to utter and risk it reentering the universe. Blaine is my only link to her childhood, and her only savior in those times.

"No."

"I found it!" Amír's strong voice breaks through the silence. A wad of papers crumple in her fist that she hoists in the air before folding it and placing it in the satchel she carries. We nod towards the gunslinger and make for the door when a low rumble shakes the foundations of the palace.

"Still not earthquake season," she whispers.

Not a moment later, dust and rubble falls in the hall, the stones of the floor beginning to crack. The door to the study snaps shut and the rumbling within the room ceases.

The three of us share a single glance and thought. The room has been left untouched, not because it has been frozen in time, but frozen in dark magic. Irene was powerful enough to cast a spell of this magnitude and have it live over ten years after her death.

We wait a few moments before Amír opens the door again to find the hall has completely caved in. Small stones clatter at her feet. She promptly picks one up and throws it at the wall of rock. Blaine lifts her away by the waist and slams the door shut as the larger stones begin to fall her way.

"Well that was helpful," he deadpans when she smacks his arm.

"It's no use, we will have to go out the window," she elaborates when Blaine and I both stiffen. "I packed picks to jam in the stones just in case we had to scale the wall to get in. We aren't jumping, so you two just need to pretend this is any other window for the two minutes it will take to get down, okay?"

This challenge proves to be easier said than done as I wedge the first pick into the stone. My shoulders groan as I lower myself with only the strength of my upper body. I drop an arm lower to place the next pick and it slips out of the crevice, leaving me hanging from the wall by one arm.

A small stone hits Amír in the forehead and she looks up to glare at me.

"Sorry."

"Sorry," she mimics my tenebrous voice. "*Laei.*"

Blaine seems to fare far better than I am as he lowers himself above me until we are next to each other on the wall. On my second try, the pick holds and I lower myself a few feet lower. We are nearly halfway down the crumbling stone now.

"Tired?" he jests, even though I can see the sweat beading along his brow.

I grin through gritted teeth and quickly lower myself again. "Never. You?"

"I could do this all day."

"Less peacocking, more climbing," Amír barks.

We silently lower ourselves further. Her feet touch the earth first, right as another wave of power shakes the palace. My picks slip from the crevices in the stone and Blaine nearly laughs as I fall the last five feet to the ground. The impact robs all air from my lungs and the rocks bite into my back.

"Rowan, how good to see you embracing the dirt," Torin quips, standing over me while Blaine gently lowers himself to the ground.

Kya stifles her smile and the knights behind them pretend to not see me sprawled across the ground.

"You are such an ass," I croak when I raise myself to my knees. "What the fuck is with these earthquakes?"

Torin and Kya's grins drop immediately and my assassin helps me to my feet. Once standing, I take in the sparse group of knights they've managed to rescue. They stand a haggard bunch, only ten or so of them. Their clothes hang loosely from their skeletal forms, their cheeks and eyes gaunt and hollow. Scruff lines their jaws and they lean against each other or the rebellion members to stay upright.

"Ophelus has been running experiments on Lucius under the guise of regaining his sight," Kya says softly, crossing two fingers across her chest. "Ver fought back when they took her. He has a gnarly bite scar on his hand." I don't miss the hint of pride in her voice, nor do I ignore my own pride. I want to say it was our training that allowed her to survive, but I know that it was purely Vera. I never gave her that fiery spirit, only allowed her to hone it as a weapon.

My gunslinger frowns. "What kind of experiments?"

Amír doesn't need to wait long to hear an answer as another rumble shatters the ground, the thunderous sound only rivaled by the piercing scream that comes from somewhere far too close. It doesn't sound like Lucius. Hell, it hardly sounds human.

"He's turning him into a weapon." Torin ushers us towards our mounts with a grimace. "A mix of death and man."

We help the knights onto our horses, all of us riding double to fit. The rebellion may have provided us with horses, but even they do not have twenty to spare right now. We were lucky to get the ten we did.

Blaine blanches. "That'll kill him."

"It already has." Torin's face pinches. "There's something else that's been living in him since Vera's ball. The first experiment took place after you left."

The thought should startle me, but rather, it brings a form of comfort. The man who coveted Vera and shattered Blaine is dead. There is no man left, only a monster. Men come with guilt, but I have no qualms killing a monster.

I mount my horse quickly, untying her reins from the post we left them at as I go. Her ears flick back and forth as I settle in the saddle, a haggard knight sitting in front of me. Pulling a rope from my saddlebag, I tie the man to me, lest the exhaustion forces him to pass out and fall off the steed. Once we start moving, we won't have the luxury of stopping until we reach the rebellion.

The earth around us stills in anticipation. Not even the breeze dares to disturb the branches of the trees above our heads. The birds have ceased their chirping, the steady thrum of insects quieting until there is only the soft clicking of icicles melting amongst the snow.

As I sink my heels into the stirrups, a booming voice breaks the peace and sends fear crippling my heart.

"*Rowan!*"

My hands still on the reins, the leather slipping from my grasp. That voice. I know that voice, despite no memory of hearing it. I've yet to regain all memories from before Irene's death, only wisps of recollection. A scent, a tangible feeling. Sometimes a full scene but never a voice. But I would know that voice anywhere, even if it called for me in death.

This is the first time I've heard my father say my name, and he's not even my father anymore.

Ophelus stands atop a broken tower, his face gaunt and twisted with a mix of fury and relief. His hands twitch at his sides as if he doesn't know how to use them anymore. Shadows envelop him in wisps, tendrils of that darkness curling up his arms towards his neck. He outstretches a single hand towards me while I sit fixed atop my horse, completely choked.

"Rowan!" Kya shouts. "Rowan, *go!*"

Her startled cry draws my attention back to the present as the rumbling growls draw closer. I shake my head clear of any sorrow. All of their lives hinge on the fact that I live to get them out of this. I can't afford to get lost in sentiment or my own grief.

I swallow the lump in my throat and dig my heels into the

mare's belly. She squeals and pins her ears, but obeys with a small kick, taking off into a gallop.

"Rowan."

I hear his voice now as a whisper, soft and paternal. It is the sound of summer picnics and afternoon in the sunlight. A homage to days of laughter and unbroken promises, and if I dare say I've ever felt it, joy. It was a time where I didn't have to struggle to survive, or watch the light fade from my mother's eyes each day, even though she tries her damned hardest to be strong.

A single tear plops along the bridge of my nose before it is carried away by the whistling wind. The man who sits before me groans and I clench my jaw.

These are the people I have to protect, that my father failed to protect. *This* is my job and responsibility now. I do not have the luxury of simple pleasures such as love and nostalgia. This is my job. *This* is my purpose. I am the shadow he created, here to save the people from him.

Deep down, I know I am no better than him. Deep down, I know I am the monster he created, and that goes deeper than blood. That settles in my bones, in my existence.

It is time the monster comes home.

CHAPTER 34

VEROSA

The last time I dared to venture outside the safety of a stronghold was the fateful trip I took with Mavis, Neris, and Emi. The trip that ended in me murdering Gadsden and learning of the Oracle in the first place. The trip that flipped the switch in my mind towards darkness. That told me I had to be willing to do anything to protect the ones I love.

The trip taught me of my own failures. Tanja's death wasn't my fault, I know that now, yet I am failing to realize it in my heart, just as I failed to save her. In that way, doesn't that make her death my fault?

I try to push the thought from my mind. Emilie has been working on that with me. Reminding me that I am not able to save everyone and that grief is only a shield so long as it is not a sword. I like to pretend I don't know what she means.

Derrín walks ahead as the sun settles low in the sky. The golden light catches on his tight coils. He hums to himself and picks at his bandages as he walks. Barely five words have been spoken between us. Frost and ice still settle over the grass with some sparse patches of snow, making the footing wet and slick as we walk.

"There's only a few more miles now. We will stop for the night outside the Bone Wood, then go around it tomorrow," he calls from ahead, his face buried in a compass.

A shudder seems to run through the valley we are in. The Bone Wood. A crimson stain across an otherwise pristine map.

Spindly tree trunks the color of milky, pale bone crawl towards the sky in the Bone Wood, the wood completely smooth, unlike any other tree bark. If one were to take a knife to the trunk or carve a letter into it, the tree would bleed a sticky crimson sap that stains the clothes like blood. The wiry branches bear crimson leaves that block out the light, creating a grotesque ambiance resembling constant carnage.

It is not the atmosphere that strikes horror in the heart, but the bodies that enter and never return. Rumors of monsters once men haunt those trees, and those monsters are the reason the sap runs red.

"Why can't it be a haunted beach for once?" Derrín complains loudly. "A nice beach with warm sun and waters. Why is it always some creepy forest or mountains?"

"At least we won't have to run through sand. If it were a haunted beach, that would be a problem." I allow myself to lighten my tone. The previous horror curls off my spine as he tuts his tongue.

"That is true. I have weak ankles."

A dry laugh breaks the silence. I've always liked Derrín well enough, yet I never got to know him as well as I have the others. We've gotten to talking comfortably now since we left the inn yesterday morning. Our first night was tense, but something about the glow of our fire broke through our awkward conversation. The more time I spend with him, the greater I enjoy his company. He is blunt yet well meaning. He works well with the others and yet is so vastly different. Each of them, different pieces welded together over time.

Kya might be the exact opposite of her twin and the irony is not lost on me. Where Kya is sweet and sensual, Derrín is honest and just... not. Kya's emotions are always high, whether that be anger or joy. Derrín shows his emotions rarely, and dully at that. Yet he is quick witted and funny in his dry humor and the brilliant things he says plainly. Rowan and Amír may be strategizing geniuses, but Derrín is mechanical. Sometimes, I catch him staring at something for a second too long and know that if asked, he could create a better version of it.

"Do you think the stories are true?" I call out. "About the Bone Wood?"

Derrín doesn't hesitate for even a second before responding, "No. Sure, magic does weird things to people, but history has never shown it being able to turn on people without them using it themselves. It is just another story to keep enemies out of our borders. The sap is a phenomenon, sure, but judging by the lack of sunlight the trees see, it would make sense that..."

I listen to him ramble on, using words larger than I can comprehend as I fall into step beside him. The sky is clear above us, not a single puffy cloud dotting the horizon. Derrín's prattle fills the silence and eats away at the dread that had begun to settle. He throws out words like *photosynthesis* and *chlorophyll* and I understand those, but the rest might as well be a foreign language. It might actually be and the mechanic is just toying with me, but I welcome the distraction either way.

"Have you seen Lucius since he tried to sacrifice you?"

Never mind.

"No."

"What do you think would happen if you did?"

"I would kill him."

"Okay."

Our versions of small talk must be different, but I pay him no mind. Rather, my mind drifts to the face that haunts my nightmares—the prince turned emperor that hunts us now. My ex-fiancé, and someone I once cared for.

I cannot pinpoint the exact moment I felt a shift in Lucius's demeanor. He still seemed kind and caring up until the duel with Blaine. At first, I thought he was merely jealous of Blaine and what we once shared, but going as far as having Rowan spy on us...

I felt my faith in my image of Lucius shift, and I'm not sure if I ever knew him at all. Maybe the boy who named his horse Jacques because it was a fine and noble name never really existed. The boy who liked my smile and was the first to draw a line severing me from Irene.

The potential truth in that is more painful than his betrayal.

Without warning, Derrín halts and throws his pack on the ground. "Here," he says, then props his hands on his hips. "This will do."

I glance around, searching for any sign of horrifying trees or rolling mist that moves of its own accord. Cannibalistic monsters, too, but thankfully, those are just as out of sight as the rest of the Bone Wood.

"I hate to question your intelligence—"

"Then don't."

"But this doesn't look like the Bone Wood," I finish with a hint of ire in my voice.

Derrín sighs then sets to rummaging through his pack before producing the map still marked with Gadsden's dried blood. Amír marked it with ink as well, just in case the blood flaked off entirely.

"We are here, and the Bone Wood is here, just over a mile away. Is here sufficient, or did you want to sleep right outside a forest potentially filled with monsters that feast on your flesh?"

That nagging sense of horror reclaims its spot curled around my heart. It squeezes like a serpent, pushing its venom through my veins. "I thought you said you didn't believe in that."

"I ran the calculations in my mind and there's a tenth of a percentage point of a chance that it could be real once compared to all the other things we've seen born of magic, and I don't like those odds. Do you?"

"Here, it is," I decide.

He nods in confirmation, then sets to gathering firewood. I take the time to study our map and surroundings. The Oracle should only be a day's trip away on foot, but an ugly red smear on the map blocks our path. With the Bone Wood in our way, we will have to trek through the mountains that barricade our borders, adding another five days onto our journey. We are prepared to make the trip, both in terms of mentality and provisions, but I cannot truthfully say that I am looking forward to the journey.

A ghost of a hand flutters across the back of my neck. I reach to clasp it only to find the wind dancing in my hair. I inhale sharply through my nose and force my breath out from my mouth. I've long since given up on believing in ghosts, but wraiths are a different story. Goosebumps prickle across my skin at the memory of Mavis crashing through the brush, bloody yet alive after our encounter. My thumb grazes over the thin white scar on my wrist. The blood bond no longer throbs, but the scar remains.

Derrín returns before my memories can consume me, a welcome distraction that allows me to shove the thoughts to the back of my mind again. He settles beside me and drops the firewood before pulling out a gadget from his pocket. I hold my hand over my chest. He glances over with a knowing look, Any other of the Nightwalkers might have let it go, but not Derrín. Derrín has to push as always.

"Repressing your emotions is just going to make the burnout worse."

I take to setting up our fire instead of responding. The sun has begun to set, the days growing slightly longer now, though still not as long as what they might be in the city.

"You're just doing the same thing you and Rowan have been doing for months, and look how that ended."

The sparks refuse to take to the wood as I strike the flint.

Derrín's gaze never leaves his device that he is fiddling with, still refusing to let the conversation go. "You aren't handling her death well," he states plainly.

"Oh, fuck off. Like you'd take it any better."

The spark catches and the log bursts into flame.

How long is it going to take for them to stop comparing me to how I used to be? How long until they stop hating me for how I choose to handle my grief? How long will it take *me*?

"I have and *do* handle it better, actually." The mechanic furrows his brow as his machine sparks. The electric ember catches on his tunic and he swears. "I still blame myself for my sister's death. If I hadn't refused to kill, maybe all three of us could have made it off that island. You don't see me vomiting every five seconds or turning to dark forces."

My limbs freeze and all I can do is gape at the Nightwalker. I had nearly forgotten about the twins' sister. My heart rises to my throat and I swallow my apologies. "You blame yourself?"

"I wasn't good with a sword and I couldn't bring myself to hunt. There were no fruits or herbs grown on the island, the whole place was designed so that you had to kill something, one way or another. I was a dead weight." Derrín cuts a red wire with a sharpened stone. The machine sputters for a moment and he grins. "The only thing I could do to help my sisters was make their weapons. Anything they brought me, I could work with. I let them kill for me."

"And you don't feel guilty at all?"

Derrín pops out his bottom lip and shrugs. "I'll always feel guilty over Natara's death. I'll always have to deal with the fact that if I didn't have this aversion to killing, then maybe I could have saved her, but I know she wouldn't want that. I've made peace with my guilt. It's the only way you can keep going in a world like this."

"That hardly seems fair," I groan, rolling onto my back and sounding wholly like a spoiled child.

Derrín sets the trinket aside and tucks his hands under his head. "No, I suppose it isn't."

The stars are slightly obscured by the rising smoke from our fire. A few embers leap into the air, ash falling back down in its place. I stretch my palm skyward, relishing in the slight burn as they press against my sensitive skin.

"What do you think we will find when we get there?' I ask, lolling my head to the side.

Without missing a beat, Derrín deadpans, "A crap-ton of Kijova probably."

"Stop."

"And a bunch of creepy monsters. Spiders, probably very large spiders." He shivers despite the heat of the burning fire. "I hate spiders. Why do they need so many legs?"

"They've got a lot of eyes too."

I laugh as the mechanic blanches, his nose crinkling with disgust. He may not be sarcastic like Rowan or witty like Torin, but there's something sharp and humorous in his dry honesty. It's refreshing.

As I stare at the sky, my mind clears in the silence, allowing my anxiety to dissipate with the crackling fire.

"To be honest, I prefer it out here." Derrín stares at his scarred fingers. "These monsters don't pretend to be anything other than what they are." Something haunted comes over his features then as he stares into the fire. The flames dance in his watery gaze like the reflection of a battlefield, haunting his every mannerism.

"You know, Kya never told me how you two came to be with the Nightwalkers." I nudge his leg with the toe of my boot.

For a moment, he doesn't say anything. Just when I begin to fear I have said the wrong thing again, Derrín parts his lips with a shuddering breath. "It was after we escaped the island. We landed at the port on the southern Krycolian border. We were young and Varium was all we knew, but even then, we weren't stupid enough to go back. So those nobles sent hunters after us. They didn't want their secret operation being exposed. The king sanctioned it so they wouldn't face any repercussions, but their reputation would have taken a hit. A foolish thing, reputation is. Worth enough to end two young lives."

A weight settles in my gut at his words and how simply he says them. Not like he believes them, but acknowledges that they're a fact to someone out there.

He continues anyway, his face to the stars. "The night we became Nightwalkers, the bounty hunters found us. There were seven of them and we were just kids, and Kya... she only had this small knife. She told me to run, so I did. That's how I found Rowan."

"Then what happened?" I'm not sure I want to know the answer.

Derrín inhales sharply, then admits quite plainly, "Rowan had to get her a new knife."

The weight of his words hang dead in the air and settle in the silence between us. The logs crack, sounding unnervingly like snapping bones. I shake the thought off. It is only my nerves at being so close to the Bone Wood mixed with the horror of the twins' story.

"I'm glad you're here," I answer honestly. "I don't think Kya would understand what I'm trying to do. I'm just trying to save everyone."

Derrín chews on the stalk of a blade of grass then frowns. He spits the greenery into the dirt and folds his arms beneath his head. "I understand, but that doesn't mean I approve."

"Good to know," I sigh.

I suppose understanding is all I can hope for at this point. None of them can fully grasp the pressure I'm under. This apocalypse is all my fault, and now I am the only one who can stop it. I'll use whatever means necessary to keep them safe, and yet to them, I'm a villain.

"You should start valuing yourself more," Derrín casually drops in before curling up on his side. "You don't have to throw yourself away. You just act like you are nothing. That is what hurts them." I consider this for a moment before he adds, "And all the stupid stuff you've been doing too. Human sacrifice, looting dead bodies. Not cool." A certain degree of gravity coats Derrín's voice, but I can hear the hints of dark humor commingling in there. The bit of him that still believes I'm capable of redemption reaching out.

I nearly laugh. A broken, rattling sound settles in the back of my throat instead, something like a sob. I lean back against the trunk of a tree and flip my dagger into my palm. "I'll take the first watch."

"I was planning on you saying that."

I scoff and roll my eyes, but say nothing else. Soon, it is only me, the stars, and the sound of Derrín's soft snores filling the air. My head lolls back for a moment before I rise and search for a high ground. I leave my pack of sacrifices by the fire.

CHAPTER 35

ROWAN

The survivors are taken to the med bay the moment we reach the rebel base. The idea of leaving the former king's men with the rebel group sit like stone in my stomach, but we don't have the resources to save them and Torin has assured us they will be fine. As the former captain of the guard, I assume he knows what he is talking about, as he now walks daily through this pit of vipers.

The Nightwalkers rest around a fireplace in a spare apartment area Roiden reserved for us. He expressed his condolences that he could not be here to tend to us, but sent Lyra in his stead. Blaine pushes through the door, returning shortly after going to check on his mother, who, as promised, found a place for herself in the furthest corners of the rebel compound.

The older woman wears her hair loose this time, and the softer look makes her appear more aged than she is. A dark form of sadness coats her mannerisms as she cares for Amír, stitching up a laceration from an arrow fired as we fled the palace. Kya holds the gunslinger's hand, more for her own benefit than

Amír's. The redhead does not complain, neither does she look as the needle slides in and out of her flesh.

"This is going to scar," Lyra offers.

Amír tosses a playful look to her lover, even through the pain. "It won't be the first or the last I receive." Then she adds, "Thank you for your kindness."

I nearly snort at the nicety. The words "thank you" hardly leave my second's lips, and when they do, they are usually sarcastic.

"Anyone else on the verge of death?"

No response.

"Good to know."

"You didn't have to come all the way down here." I try my hand at being polite. I've avoided Lyra ever since she walked through the door.

You have her eyes.

Those words have been clouding my mind ever since I met the woman. Somehow, the rebellion leader's wife knew my mother, knew her well enough to recognize me without a last name. Even knew my last name, something not even the Nightwalkers knew.

With my memories now returning, I have a good grasp on many things. The day Irene attempted to take my life. My father's face and love before the dark magic took over his mind. My mother's friends and the company they both kept before we ran. Lyra does not appear anywhere in these memories. Not even her name.

"I know."

Amír pretends not to listen to the conversation. Her eyes flit to mine and my lips peel back in a slight snarl. She raises a brow in challenging, but turns away as Lyra approaches.

"I suppose you want to have a talk."

"You knew who I was."

Lyra settles deep into the chair across from me and stretches back with a groan. "Of course I knew who you were. You're

Rowan. The only living hybrid and future king of Krycolis." She says it so sweetly, so simply. It is like the first night I met Vera, when she tried to worm her way out of danger with sweet words and wit that matched my own. Beneath Vera's voice, though, was an edge. There was a silver tongue hiding beneath the honey of her words. With Lyra, there is just emptiness. The kind that rattles in the ribs where a heart should be. The type that never stops bleeding.

"You knew my last name. How."

Not a question. A demand.

Lyra sighs. She isn't an assassin or a runaway princess. She may be the wife of a rebel leader, but she does not have the same tight lips of one. I can see it in her eyes. She is tired, and willing to tell me anything. The wall crumbles with a few well-placed blows. "It is my maiden name," she finally admits with a small smile. "How is my sister?"

I've come to expect the worst of the world. If you expect disappointment, you will never face it. Very few things in my life have truly shocked me. The event is a rare enough occasion that I can count the number of times on one hand. The first was finding Kya and Derrín, Kya with a bloody knife in hand, standing over four grown men while Derrín huddled behind her. Then learning my father is the king, the third was thinking Vera was my sister.

Learning my aunt is Roiden's wife, or learning I have an aunt at all, will have to be my fourth.

"She's... alive."

Lyra's face falls a bit, not enough to break the newfound glow in her features at the mention of my mother. She's alive—that brings hope. My lack of description is the culprit for her disappointment.

"Are you going to say anything else?"

"Why did she never mention you?" I press.

"Emilie has a habit of not talking about things that make her sad. She doesn't even know I am alive, it's been so long. I was gone before you were born, married to Roiden."

She's right. If my mother thinks her sister is dead, there would be no way for her to bring herself to even speak about her. The pain would be too much. She'd bury it.

"And why wouldn't you say anything? If you knew, you were breaking her heart."

"You think I could get back?" she hisses under her breath. "Look at the silver in my husband's hair, boy, and the little I have in mine. Do you see how things are run around here? Use that brain she gave you and put it together. Not to mention the fact that you're the king's son. Under different circumstances, Roiden would have killed you already, and that would have killed her more than my disappearance."

The Nightwalkers' stares burn into my spine and sweat pricks the back of my neck. Lyra is speaking lowly, but the room is small. Even the crackle of the fireplace cannot mask her words. Their gazes are questioning, waiting for their next command. Their next move.

I have none.

I sit, letting my head fall into my hands and stare at the ground between my knees. It always comes back to me. No, not even me. My father.

The scars across my wrists burn. They burn with the same searing pain that they did the day I tried to claw my veins from them. The same ache in my heart that told me the universe knew I should never have been born. There are laws against hybrids for a reason. We are too powerful.

Abominations.

Lyra's chair screeches against the floor as she pushes it back and rises. She offers the others water before settling by the fire and talking with them. I should be there with them, offering them comfort and hatching a plan to free her from the rebellion. I don't move.

A hand settles on my shoulder, then a shadow falls over my legs. I look up to find Amír standing before me and Blaine's hand clasping my shoulder.

"Get your ass out of that chair and come tell us what the fuck to do," my second pushes, pulling me to my feet. "When Vera gets back, we will need to have a plan so she can save the world and shit."

Blaine laughs a bit at that, the most honest sound he's made all day. He releases his grip but dips his chin in respect. I don't need or dare hope for anything more than that from the man.

Kya scoots over on the small couch and tucks her knees to her chest to allow space for me. I settle on one side of her, Amír taking the stool in the middle. She spreads out the parchment we found, despite telling Roiden we didn't find anything in the queen's study.

"Well, I'll be damned." Torin whistles. "Vera was right."

Detailed with multiple sketches, clear instructions for how to form a blessed blade are scrawled across the parchment in what can be recognized as the late queen's loopy handwriting.

"It seems simple enough," Kya notes. "I mean, Derrín has done much more with much less, and these things don't seem hard to find. Sure, we will need to wait for them to get back since he will have to forge it and it says we need a drop of pure blood in the waters when the iron cools. Not to mention the incantation, but..." The assassin trails off, her eyes gleaming with a hope that has been absent for so long.

Amír rolls the parchment up, storing it safely in her pouch. "Think we can make bullets out of this?"

I laugh, the sound foreign but welcome. "Like she said, we've managed worse."

The gunslinger grins at that.

"You know…" Torin smirks that lopsided smirk. "You actually look quite lovely when you smile."

Amír's lips flip downwards in an immediate scowl.

Blaine insists he meant no harm by the comment, but Torin is already sliding further away when he sees Amír's fingers strum against the holster of her pistol.

Lyra smiles fondly in my direction, suddenly looking painfully like my mother.

I make a silent vow now to protect this fragile peace. Once Vera returns, I will tell her everything, and she can make the choice to stay or leave. *Her* choice. I won't take it away from her. I won't be like everyone else in her life, hiding the worst of things from her like she is still a child. And I will free Lyra, kill my father, and fix this broken kingdom.

The world told each of us we are broken in some way, simply because we look, act, or love differently. So fuck the world.

Amír loops an arm over Kya's shoulder. Blaine nudges at Torin.

I look to my aunt. "He will be dead before your hair turns silver," I promise.

A wicked gleam forms in Lyra's usually demure gaze. "I know."

CHAPTER 36
VEROSA

Derrín sleeps soundly through the night, not a single threat to disturb his rest during my watch. I sit alone in the dark for maybe an hour before sleep pulls at my eyelids.

No. You have to stay awake.

My traitorous body ignores my commands as darkness creeps into the corner of my vision. With each moment awake, I can feel my heart begin to drag.

Sleep, it coos. *Sleep.*

A soft hand brushes my bangs from my face as my eyelashes flutter against my cheekbones. Sunlight streams through the canopy of trees overhead and the morning birds chirp along merrily. Shit.

Shit.

"Easy. Everything is fine," a low voice calls as I scramble to my feet.

Bewildered and mind still spinning, I glance over my shoulder. Lucius sits with his back against the trunk of a thick tree, his fingers plucking at guitar strings. The melody is soft and caresses the wind that carries the tune to me.

My feet move of their own accord towards him, stopping only a foot away.

The dress I wear is soft and clean, something Tanja would have chosen for me. I remember now—she left it on my bed for me this morning before rushing off to the florist with Ruby. They were picking out flowers for her wedding today and she didn't trust Ruby to not put lilies in the bouquets.

Lucius's fingers halt on the strings as he sets the instrument in the grass beside him, his lips lifting in a charming smile. I allow myself to sit on the ground in front of him, settling on the blanket he left sprawled out.

His dark eyes close for a moment, his smile still morphing his mouth. "The weather is finally getting nice again," he notes offhand.

I hum in agreement. It feels too soft and the sound is lost to the hum of insects in the air, not that I mind. My chest feels light as I gulp deep breath after breath to the point of dizziness.

Lucius laughs, a lovely sound. "Why are you breathing like that?"

"The air feels light." I smile back, toothy and wide. "I feel like I haven't been able to breathe in months."

The prince's smile falters for a moment. Had I blinked a second later, I would have missed it, but I didn't and I don't. Rocking back on my elbows, I tilt my head to the side, my bangs falling in front of my face.

Lucius reaches forward, hesitant, and pushes them back behind my ear. "I've missed this," he murmurs.

"Me too."

I don't know why my words are tainted with sorrow, or why this yawning hole of loss begins to gnaw at my core. I've missed Lucius. Why have I missed him when he is right here?

"Do you think you could have fallen in love with me?"

His voice is low, but a rushing fills my ears. Two words echo in cacophonous refrain. *My love. My love. My love my love my love my love.*

It all boils down to love.

A splitting pain cleaves my memory open as the scent of blood and flashes of violet light resurface. That lightness in my chest fades all too quickly and the air clogs my lungs. Before I even realize it, I'm on my knees coughing, blood splattering on that soft, ivory-colored dress.

"No," I hiss between blood-smothered lips.

"Why?"

"Because you killed her. You tried to kill *me*."

I do not know how many times I need to say the words before they stop sounding hollow. Before they stop stabbing my heart with their truth. Their existence.

"But if I didn't have to, could you have loved me?"

The softness of his voice douses my body with cold shock. His tenebrous tone caresses my flesh like a lover, podding and questioning but hesitant. As if it, too, is holding their breath.

"I could have," I admit, hardly noticing the silver tear plopping on my cheek until his thumb brushes it away. "If not for…"

Lucius's face turns to stone and he finishes my thought, "If not for Rowan."

"Don't say his name like that."

Surprise lights both our features at the teasing bite in my voice. It was supposed to be sharp and cruel, but comes out more like the gentle chiding of a lover.

Lucius smiles again and it reaches his eyes this time. There is something so soft and wonderful in it, my heart aches. "You know we aren't that different, Verosa."

"We are nothing alike."

"Maybe not from your narration, no, but view it as an

outsider, or from my perspective." He is gentle and patient with his words, despite the buds of rage blooming in my chest. "I loved you, Verosa. And I still do, but I love my mother more. I sacrificed the person I love most in the living world for the person I love more than myself. To others, that sacrifice could deem me a hero."

"You're not a hero."

"No, we aren't. But what of the men you're killing now for peace? The darkness you're unleashing?" He lays my hand flat across his chest and lets me feel his heart beating beneath my palm. It is steady, yet quickens when our gazes lock. "Look into my eyes and tell me you wouldn't damn this entire world for the ones you love. For your Rowan, or Tanja."

A lush green aura drifts over my senses, calm and understanding that smothers the embers of anger threatening to burst into flames.

His face is youthful, no scarring or charred flesh like in my other dreams. This is the face of the boy I could have loved. Because yes, there was a time I could have loved Lucius.

"But you still lied to me."

His eyes darken in confusion, so I continue.

"You lied when we met about your mother. You implied that she had just died, but I went to the funeral years ago. How can I trust you when you lied from the beginning?"

Something pitch black forces his jaw to clench as this newer aura moves in like smoke over his features. The clouds begin to gather above us, dark and pregnant with rain.

The prince's shoulders square, his linen tunic straining against his powerful muscles. "I didn't lie."

"But—"

"You attended the *queen's* funeral. My mother was a consort and I was passed off as the queen's legitimate child. So I *do* understand you, Verosa. Better than anyone ever can. I understand your rage that manifests as this desire for freedom. I understand every step you take and how you keep yearning for something more than the love you were given. I understand." His eyes narrow to slits. "My *mother* didn't even get a funeral."

I must be gaping because Lucius hooks his thumb under my jaw and closes my lips with his fingers before continuing with a low growl.

"It happens all the time. How the hell did you think Ophelus wound up on the throne? The previous king fell in love with a cursed woman. She became his official mistress when she came to be with child, only for the baby to be born cursed, not a hybrid." A dry laugh. "The queen had already died from the shock when she discovered her 'loving husband' had a consort, and he had Ophelus's mother put to death for treason. Left without an heir, Ophelus became king, only to kill his father for the murder of his mother. Sound familiar?"

Rowan.

My Rowan born from a vicious cycle of bloodlust and hatred between fathers. Our whole kingdom has been born from it. Now we must end it.

"I would never sacrifice someone innocent to bring someone else back." Lucius's fingers fall from my lips when I pull my jaw from his grasp. "You're too far gone to be anything like me."

Another vicious laugh comes, this time as the first drops of rain hit my face. I shiver, not from the cold, as my gown is soaked and Lucius runs a hand through his wet hair. He pushes it from his face and dips his chin in a serpentine glower. Beautiful. Dangerous. Entirely different from the man I was speaking to just moments before. I take a step back. Then another.

"I don't know how that boy managed to break through, but he's made quite a mess of this. Perhaps I should just kill you now." The thing inside Lucius slurs every "s" as he staggers my way, his hand palming the sword at his hip. His eyes flash milky white for a moment. "I warned you, I owned you. I own *all* of you, and you disobey me?'

As his words become further slurred, I cannot tell who he is speaking to. Me... or Lucius.

My bare feet slip in the mud as I back up. This is my dream, dammit, I should be able to wake up. My heels hit the waters of the moat and as I twist my spine, I am met with the sight of the crumbling palace, bodies hanging from the towers.

"Verosa," Lucius gasps. His face is buried in his scarred hands, his gait stalking. He's only three paces away now. Two. One. His hand rests on my sternum then brushes right to hover above my heart.

The wind picks up, lightning streaking the sky behind him until the world is howling.

"Verosa, run."

Then he shoves my chest, *hard*, and I spiral into the murky waters.

A low, rumbling sound comes from within the woods, then the distant sounds of screams. I leap to my feet, my fists out and ready. Awake. I am awake now and the screams are not in my mind anymore. They ring clear through the forest, guttural and raw. The sleep clears from my eyes and the haze dissipates just as the scream is cut short, leaving dead silence in the air.

My feet move before my mind does, one hand flying to the dagger at my side and the other to Derrín's shoulder. It is the same feeling I felt when I ran towards Rowan instead of safety the first night we met. The sense of duty that runs deeper than lessons with Eida and blood. The feeling that broke my heart when I turned my back to it and tried to run.

Derrín is half conscious and still blinking sleep from his eyes when I take off towards the sound—towards the people and potential Kijova. He kicks some dirt over the fire and takes off after me.

The screams came from the woods surrounding us and I follow it blindly. I hardly notice the way the trees thicken until not even moonlight guides the way. I follow on instinct, even as Derrín trips blindly over roots and stones.

Then a clearing. A clearing up ahead. I rush forward when a hand grasps my elbow.

"Vera. Be very quiet."

Derrín's voice breaks the fog and I crouch down behind a bush beside him. I blink and my vision clears. In the distance, I can see a streak of red and white.

The Bone Wood.

But before the wood is something much more monstrous than rumors meant to scare armies. There are bodies, or rather, *parts* of bodies strewn across the clearing. Silver, gold, red. The blood paints the grass, the spray range so vast that some runs off the trees beside us in rivulets. I flick my gaze towards the low growling sound and lace my fingers around the hilt of my dagger.

Shit.

The face staring back at mine is torn straight from the pages of Irene's favorite story, straight from my childhood nightmares. The elongated snout raises to the darkened sky, those slitted nostrils flaring. Its claws dig into the earthy ground, slicing through mud and stone as if it is nothing more than butter. Those slanted eyes open and I find myself caught in the stare of the Ricor.

"Do you know what that is?" Derrín whispers between bated breaths.

I can barely dip my chin in acknowledgment, too frozen in fear and whatever dark power it possesses. Judging by the carnage surrounding it, the Ricor does more than just eat the tongues of naughty children, as the story goes. Limbs and headless torsos that have been shred to ribbons litter the ground. The repugnant smell of blood and death overwhelms my senses, and it takes

Derrín's hand on my arm to shock me back to the present moment.

I jolt, and the Ricor snarls.

"Run," I hiss, already springing to my feet. "Run!"

We take off not a moment too late as the Ricor rocks back on its haunches and launches itself towards where we were just hiding. A bone-chilling clicking sound comes from the back of its throat. Unlike the scream of the Kijova, it is breathy and high enough pitched that it rattles my eardrums.

"What *is* that thing?" Derrín pants, his dark face reddening with exertion as we sprint to wherever our feet are taking us. The Kijova do not like water, so we always knew we could head for a river. The Ricor, however, has no such known weakness, none for us to exploit.

"Did Kya or Natara ever tell you the story of the Ricor?"

Derrín blanches but shakes his head.

"Ah," I hiss between gritted teeth. "I always forget you had a loving, not fucked in the head family."

"Can't you use your magic on it? Blind it or something?"

I clench my jaw so hard it pops. I haven't felt even the slightest whisper of my power beneath my skin since leaving Mavis. Whatever damper she placed on my abilities still holds now, and no recitations or rituals have been able to bring it back.

But we don't need light magic to defeat a creature of darkness. Sometimes the only way to smother darkness is to be the greater darkness.

I spot spindly white trees ahead, fog drifting out from between those skeletal trunks. I recognize those from images within a book on Rowan's desk and shiver. The Bone Wood. Right now, it might be our only option.

"Get to the Bone Wood and stay behind me."

"What are you going to do?"

"Something you won't like."

Derrín clicks his tongue but says nothing else as he eyes the absence of a gore-speckled pouch at my side. I abandoned my sacrifices by the fire when we ran, but I don't have much of a choice. It is either risk death by the hands of the curse or a sure death at the teeth and claws of the Ricor.

I settle for calling from the well of darkness that has taken hold inside of me. Derrín's gaze narrows and he curses, something I've never heard him do before.

I dig my heels into the ground right at the tree line and spin around to face the thrashing beast. It's only a few paces away now. I have only a few seconds to act before Derrín and I are both dead.

I unfurl my fist, my hand throbbing where the flesh split open weeks ago, so strong that I cry out as that dark power surges from it. Derrín grips at my shoulders as I sink to my knees. The darkness shoots out in several small skeins towards the beast and I swear vehemently. *Control.* I need to control it or we are doubly dead.

With the last of my strength, I force it into one smooth blade. At the last second, the sharp edge buries itself in its neck, slicing clean through its thick spinal cord and rotten flesh. The large head falls with a heavy thud in the mud-crusted snow, black blood like oil melting the ice and powder around it.

When using dark magic with a sacrifice, the ritual felt fulfilling and filled me with need simultaneously. But I was in control. I never felt that burning as the darkness consumed me entirely. Now, my whole body throbs and my vision goes blurry while starving need ravages my senses. I need to use that power again, need to feel its darkness call.

And yet it might kill me to do so.

Derrín yelps as I fall forward into the snow, my eyes heavy lidded and barely open. My hand burns with blinding pain as if I just split it open once more. I can feel phantom pieces of bark grate against my bones, my flesh screaming as the trunk tears through layers of tissue and muscle.

Vaguely, I feel his hands hook underneath my armpits and haul me into the mist. Pale and spindly roots greet my blurred vision, the fog obscuring the majority of the forest floor. Derrín grunts as he props me up against one of those skeletal trees. The last thing I see is his worried face before the sweet lull of darkness pulls me under.

CHAPTER 37

VEROSA

The first thing I notice when I come to is the low-burning fire and the scent of smoke that floods my senses. Derrín crouches beside the small flame, rocking back on his haunches when a smoldering twig cracks. The sound slices through the silence, rattling the tree canopy. I find myself gazing skyward, searching for stars or any sign of what time of night it is. I am met with nothing but a thick layer of bone-white branches and the occasional crimson leaf. One of them falls slowly towards the fire, flickering before catching flame and burning to nothing but ash.

I am awake, not in another dream or vision. That is what I have opted to call my last visit from Lucius. It was undoubtedly a vision. Somehow, the fallen prince managed to break through the hold the darkness had on him and warn me about the Ricor. He saved my life. The thought makes my head throb and I push those thoughts to the back of my mind if only for a moment.

Slowly, I push myself upwards on my elbows. Every muscle in my body feels leaden, my limbs barely supporting my weight as they hang heavy from my sockets.

The mechanic rises from his spot by the fire, the golden glow leaving his face as he follows me into the shadows. He says nothing as he rests his hand on my lower back, helping to ease me into a seated position. Nor does he say anything as I thank him for taking first watch, or when he walks back to sit by the fire alone. His silence is more smothering than that of the forest.

I force myself to rise at least to my knees, then my hands before finally standing shakily to my feet. Derrín sawed off tree branches and wove them together in a form of makeshift cot that he laid me on. The small care saved me from losing any more body heat to the earth during this frigid winter. I try to remember this as I attempt to brush the sticky red sap from my arms and hair. That may never come out.

"Are you hurt anywhere?" I ask softly, my voice harsh with sleep and my tongue stone in my mouth. I run it over my teeth. It tastes like ash.

"No."

"So you do speak! Here I was, afraid that the Ricor had gotten your tongue."

"Now is not the time for jokes, Verosa," Derrín hisses, the most vile sound I've heard the man make. His shoulders slump inwards as he curls in on himself, his jaw hard set and mouth in a firm line.

I flex the fingers of my still-burning hand. "No, I suppose it is not."

Derrín scoffs, and when his face turns to mine, I bite my lip to keep from crying out. His eyes are red-rimmed and puffy, and a hollow rage ravages his features. I've seen his twin wear that look before, but never him. Never kind and quiet Derrín.

"Do you have any idea what you've done?"

My eyes roll so far back into my skull that I fear I may never find them again.

The bitter hiss Derrín makes as he sucks on his teeth tells me he might not have liked that choice of action so much. Not that it was any more a *choice* of action than a reaction or reflex. Always what I've done. Always the sins I've committed.

"Enlighten me," I purr.

Disgust flashes across his face.

I raise an eyebrow, daring him to question me.

His lips pull back in a sneer. "You've killed the light in you," he whispers. "There's nothing left. You can't use your power, your hand has never healed. You took that darkness into your soul and you let it smother you."

My jaw loosely drops, my breathing coming out in short puffs. Damn him. Damn these twins and their ability to see through the front I put up.

Initially, it may have been Mavis and the overwhelming presence of dark magic that dimmed my powers, but even then, I could feel the faintest spark of it thrumming in my veins, like the whisper of an old friend brushing across my skin, flowing through my blood. Now, my hands feel cold and numb. That once constant warmth has gone from my body, my soul. All that is left is this yawning darkness that seeks for more incessantly, begging and stealing more than I can bear to part with. It has killed the light.

"I'm fine."

"No," he says firmly, "you're not. The curse may kill the light from everyone, sure. But you're not everyone, Vera. You *are* pure light. It is in your blood. Your very creation. You kill that light and..." He trails off, but I get a clear enough picture.

I don't need him to tell me what I can already see. I am sleeping through the night and finishing my meals without a trip to the bucket. And yet I cannot walk up stairs without heaving for breath. My clothes still fall from my frame, my face gaunt and haunting.

"I will find another way to save everyone," I murmur, my bruised bones far too weary to pick a fight with my only company.

I settle myself beside the fire, my chin resting on my knees as I tuck them to my chest. "The Oracle will know. I'll do what I must."

"But who is going to save *you*?" Derrín brushes by me with just a whisper. "Stupid. Stupid..." The mechanic curls up on the sticky bone leaf, not caring for how the red sap sticks to his clothes or his thick hair. He props his arm under his head, tucking himself into his cloak. His eyes pinch shut as if feverish, but he says no more as a disquieted sleep pulls him into dark unconsciousness.

The crackling logs fill the void where his voice used to occupy. The flames dance lowly, a sultry yet somber dance that eats away at the wood until only black ash remains. Embers fly skyward, flickering against the white and crimson canopy like red stars. Grayish filaments fall where the embers rise, stinging my palm slightly when I extend my hand to grasp for them. The slight hurt does nothing to mar my pale skin, nor does it compare to the dull burning within my other hand.

I cradle my injured fist to my chest and grimace. The ground is dry when I allow myself to lay on my back. Small snow flurries fall just outside the Bone Wood, yet none make it through the branches, no matter how sparsely covered some patches may be.

The scent of blood clings to my nose and clothes, consuming my senses entirely until I fight the urge to gag.

The Ricor was always my worst fear as a child. That night, ten years ago, when the fall shattered my leg and the snow hazed the sky away into a dark gray blur, it was not wolves I feared. I was less than a good child. I didn't listen, I broke into Irene's study, I deserved every bit of pain, I thought. The Ricor should have come for me. It should have killed me.

I learned afterwards that fictional monsters were not the ones I should fear. I should be wary of those that wear a crown and those painted lips that call me daughter. But the Ricor hadn't killed me that night, and I banished any thought or fear of it from my mind, convinced of its fictional reality.

Until now.

That beast was certainly not an illusion, nor were the bodies that it left in its wake. The image of its maw snapping shut over that man's throat, the fur shrouding its muzzle matting and stained red. I shake my head as if that can clear the guilt and horror from my mind.

Did Ophelus create it because he remembers Irene reading those stories to me when I was a child? I doubt he actually listened when we spent time together, but that only leaves a more horrifying realization.

The magic pulled the creature from the pages. The king shoots power any which way, and the darkness chooses its form on its own. Was the Ricor pulled from those fairy tales, or were those stories written about a time that already came to pass? None of our history books note any monstrous entities aside from the Kijova, even the banned books that are stored in Irene's study.

I lift my hand and spread my fingers far apart, as if trying to grasp the falling embers as they are blocked from the sky by a tide of crimson. Red sap drips from the leaves and their stems, a blood rain perpetually misting the forest.

A sticky, scarlet glob plinks against my cheek, just narrowly missing my eye. My fingers ghost the sap, feeling the way it clings to my flesh. There have been many stories about the Bone Wood, all to keep enemies from entering the kingdom if the mountains failed.

Quickly, a thick fog rolls in, smothering the fire and tangling with my hair. I bolt upright, my joints popping and muscles groaning with each motion. My hand finds the dagger at my hip. I palm the weapon for a second in debate before flipping it into my grip. The thick gray mist coats only the ground, rising up to about my knees. It rolls in waves, like the white caps on a lake on a windy day.

I shuffle my feet in the dark, kicking out slightly until I find Derrín's sleeping form. I dig the toe of my boot into his ribs and he shoots up with a yelp.

"Fog?"

"Fog doesn't move like this."

Realization dawns in his eyes before I finish my words. He reaches for Rowan's sword and shoves his back against mine.

If stories are coming to life, then the last place we want to be is in the Bone Wood.

"You don't think—"

Derrín is unable to finish his thought when the first of my fears crashes through the brush, its elongated fangs snapping and talons poised to rip out our throats.

The Infected are just one of the many nightmare-inducing horrors the poets wrote about residing in the Bone Wood. Unlike the Ricor, they are human in shape, and unlike the Kijova, they are not born of dark magic, despite once being human.

No, they are born of an original clan that lost their way attempting to invade Krycolis. Trapped for eternity in the Bone Wood, they had no choice but to turn on each other. The gods, enraged by this sacrifice of humanity, deemed that any who ate human flesh would be cursed with eternal bloodthirstiness and rage, doomed to forever wander the Bone Wood, tormented by the sight of blood-like sap and bones, but never any real flesh.

And as luck would have it, Ophelus brought them to life too.

I sink my blade to the hilt in the soft of its jaw, recoiling at the sickening squelch as I drag the blade back out through the rough skin. The Infected drops to the ground, dead. The same oily, black blood that the Ricor had pools under its head. At least these are easy to kill, if you can get past their human appearance. I whirl and slam my dagger between the fangs of another Infected, its mouth only mere millimeters from my neck. Too close—they're getting too close. I spare a glance over my shoulder to check on the mechanic, only to find Derrín using Rowan's sword to block attacks, but he pauses whenever he attempts to strike.

"Derrín," I call over their unholy screeches, "they're not people."

"But they were!"

"They're not and haven't been for thousands of years, and they're going to kill you if you don't kill them first."

The mercenary raises his arms as if to strike, but freezes on the spot, leaving a vulnerability in his form. An Infected spots his belly, now unguarded, and dives fangs-first towards it.

I whirl before him, ramming my dagger through the back of his skull. Oily, black blood splatters over my hand, my face, and the intricately carved hilt. I tug on the blade. It won't move. Hissing fills my ears and flaming pain shoots through my leg as an Infected's claws rake through it. I flinch in time, sparing myself from any muscle damage, but the wound bleeds furiously, drawing the attention of all the monsters.

"Fucking... fuck," I hiss between breaths. "Derrín, give me your sword and get my dagger."

Derrín's eyes go wide at the sight of my gold blood mingling with the snow, mixed with the black. His throat constricts and his mouth drops open in a soft "o." "You're hurt."

"Yes, and we are going to die, so give it to me."

Numbly, he passes me the sword, and not a second too late, I lop the head off of an Infected careening towards us. I swing the blade in wide arcs, casting fatal blows upon the depraved beasts two at a time.

A cool and familiar metal handle is pressed into my hand, though slick with greasy blood. Derrín stays huddled behind me as I fight now with both dagger and sword, stabbing my opponents when they come too close and slashing long range when I have the time. I work in a circular motion, protecting Derrín, as well as myself.

We continue on like one of the training exercises back in the palace. After Rowan abandoned me on the ballroom balcony, I made the knights train with me, taking on three or four at a time. Those knights were skilled, and while they initially did not wish to harm their princess, they soon lost such qualms as I tore through their ranks. The Infected are bloodthirsty and fueled by unending rage, but they are clumsy and blinded by their strengths. Their shrieks of rage are music in the wind as I deliver blow after blow, kill after kill.

However their rage fuels them, mine is only draining my already run-ragged body, not to mention the insatiable nagging of dark magic at the base of my skull. It squeezes my senses, blurs my vision, slows my heart rate. Something sweet and distinctly iron drips down the cleft beneath my nose and onto my lips.

The trees begin to spin. One more—there's just one more infected. Then Derrín is safe.

I sink to my knees as the last of the monsters leaps.

And it dives onto Rowan's sword that Derrín ripped from my grasp and jabbed before I fell.

The creature falls to the side, its inky blood helping it to slide clean of the blade. The mechanic sheaths the sword at his hip with a green face, taking great care not to stare at the gore-speckled blade. He wipes his hands on his trousers, then extends his hand to me.

"I refuse," he grinds out, "to watch another sister die."

CHAPTER 38
VEROSA

As we stumble out of the Bone Wood, the mist recedes, clinging to the darkness of the trees. I glance up at Derrín to find him staring at the dark blood on his hands. He catches my stare and matches it with a haunted expression.

Silence rattles through the brown grass, the breeze that picks up dry despite the slick of ice surrounding us. I lean against Derrín as I limp, my leg screaming with each motion. Derrín's grip on my arm is a vice as he all but drags me beside him.

"You're doing great, just a little further," he murmurs every so often, as if his words of affirmation can stop the blood from seeping through my torn calf.

I look down once to assess the damage and my head begins to spin when I see my own gored flesh hanging off the muscle like strips of meat in a butcher's market.

Derrín grips me tighter, noticing the same thing. "Don't look," he commands. "You're going to be fine."

"We have different definitions of fine," I try to say, but the words die on my tongue.

After a short while, Derrín deems it safe enough for us to stop and patch my wound. We only made it a mile or two from the Bone Wood, but are now far enough from it that we shouldn't have to worry about coming across any more infected.

Red clouds dot the horizon as the mechanic pulls the leg of my trousers up, then promptly vomits. I pull my leg out of the way just in time, then scream between clenched teeth at the searing pain that rattles my bones.

"Let me do it," I say once Derrín finishes his retching. I attempt to take the medical kit from him, but he holds it tight in his white-knuckled grip.

He fishes a needle from the kit and some thread, his face going paler than before. "No, I can do this."

"It's not that I don't think you can, but you don't see action a lot. It's okay if this is too much."

He runs his tongue over his dry lips and wipes the corner of his mouth on his sleeve. "You need to be stitched up."

I allow myself to look down at the wound and dig my fists into the muddy ground. Some of the lacerations are deeper than the others and will definitely need stitches, but others are shallow, just skin hanging from the wound. That skin will never heal, instead just rotting where it hangs. I grimace and grip my blade, beginning to wipe the dagger off on the cleanest part of my shirt.

"I need you to start a fire first," I hiss through clenched teeth.

Derrín's face slackens, almost thankful to have something to do with his hands that doesn't involve stitching my necrotizing flesh back together. His hands still shake, though noticeably less as he strikes the flint until a dry branch catches flame. He keeps the fire small lest the smoke attract attention, but soon enough, the flames are hot enough for what I need to do. Once the blade is clean, I hold it to the flame, letting the fire purge any remaining bacteria. Derrín watches with a void expression in his eyes.

Then without warning, I bring the blade down in a flash. A

scream tears loose from my throat as I slice through my flesh, cutting the dying pieces from my leg. I repeat the process while Derrín rushes forward, his face a mask of horror as I strip all the loose flesh from my body.

"What the fuck are you doing?"

"The skin is dying, and the edges will die too before those stitches heal. You can't stitch dead skin. Now move."

I sob unabashedly, pain dulling my senses until there is nothing but the steady slash of my knife. I steel myself against the pain and fear as I plunge the dagger back into the fire, then lay the flat of the blade against the shallow wounds. The sizzling scent of burned flesh mingles with the snow as I scream until my voice dies in my throat.

But I'm not done. I can't be. The wound will get infected and if I'm dead, I can't save anyone. I can't be the answer.

"Fuck, fuck, fuck." I repeat the vulgar word like a prayer as I take the needle from Derrín and holds it above the flame, too, repeating my previous process. I've never had a problem with needles before, but now the curved bow of the tiny thing strikes a new fear in my heart.

"Have you done this before?" Derrín's face pinches.

"Yes, many times," I lie.

I've never done this before. But something in the way Derrín's face relaxes tells me he never has either. So he returns to sit by the fire, laying Rowan's sword at his side and staring into the flickering golden flames.

I grit my teeth and slide the needle in, ignoring the mix of pain and the sensation of something foreign entering my body. My calves tighten, the muscles trying to push the needle and thread from my skin. Silent tears streak my face, mixing with the sap, blood, and dirt. I do my best to force the muscles to relax.

The stitches are crude, but I am done soon enough and cleaning the wound with the cleanest patch of snow I can find. I think back to Emi placing snow on my injured hand by a small fire like this. Laying her head in my lap.

I squeeze my eyes shut, taking a deep breath. "How're you doing over there?"

No response.

"You know, it was either that monster or me. I can't say I'm in a position to dole out any moral awards at the moment, but if it counts for anything... thank you."

Nothing. Not even the tiniest flicker of emotion crosses his face.

I've seen this in soldiers who have just returned from war, saw it in Blaine's face when he lost the duel against Lucius. It is the look of a man haunted by what he had to do to survive. The one who kills a bit of the humanity in himself for the first time. That would have been me all those months ago if Rowan hadn't been there to keep me grounded.

I settle on the ground beside him, ignoring the barking pain in my leg. I try to situate myself in a position that hurts the least, and that winds up being cross-legged and leaning into the mechanic for support. My head rests in the crook of his shoulder and I can feel each breath he takes, shallow and quick.

"You know, the first time I killed something, it was a person. A boy, maybe sixteen years old. He was a rebel and—"

"Vera, I am going to need you to shut up." Derrín's voice is gravelly and mechanical, no hint of the heart I know is breaking within him.

I close my mouth and just sit there, having used all my energy to settle beside him.

The Bone Wood is a red and white smear on the horizon, a stain on the map just far enough to be safe but close enough to see. We've left a trail of bodies where we've been so far—the Ricor's victims, then the Ricor itself, now a dozen or more Infected. Derrín can't even touch raw meat since it looks too much like the animal it used to be. He can hardly look at it until it is cooked and arranged beyond resemblance. This must be killing him.

He finally speaks again after some time. Six words that streak pain through the cavity of my chest like an arrow: "I was able to do it."

He was able to kill something. Realization washes over me in horror. It is not guilt for the Infected that he feels, but his true sister. The one he wasn't able to kill for when it mattered. But he was able to kill now, for me, and that just proves he was capable all along. He just didn't when it mattered.

His head lolls to the side and his cheek plops against the top of my head. His breath rattles in my ear and my hand finds his, squeezing tightly. Three times. *It's okay. It's okay. It's okay.*

"Your sister is going to flip her shit when she sees the scars we come home with," I finally say after the silence becomes too heavy.

Derrín's breathing hitches and he stares down at his unwrapped fingers then laughs, the sound splitting the dead air. "She's going to kill us both," he agrees.

I nudge his shoulder with my own. "It's not too late to go back into the Bone Wood."

"Remind me that I had that choice when we see her again."

A slight shuffle later and Derrín is standing, offering me his hand once more. He pulls me to my feet and loops my arm over his shoulder. I lean heavily against him, unapologetically grunting at each step. Derrín tells me I sound like an old man and I threaten to burn his ass to a crisp.

Our camp and rest forgotten, we plow forward into the night towards that incessant tug of darkness.

"What do you think this place will look like?" he asks after a while. "More monsters, spiders?"

"Yes, lots of spiders, Derrín."

"I knew it. We hadn't seen any yet and I thought we were too lucky."

I snort at that. Luck is surely something that must exist in this universe, but it doesn't give a damn about us. "Maybe the Kijova ate them all."

"That's stupid."

"*You're* stupid."

Derrín raises a single brow as if questioning my choice of comeback. I will admit it was not my finest, but not my worst. I stick my tongue out at him. Maybe not my worst, but definitely my most childish of responses.

He reaches up and yanks on my tongue, an action I wasn't expecting.

I yelp and lean away, falling on my ass. "You're fucking weird, man." I spit on the ground and he laughs, this time, a hearty sound. It warms my heart enough that I can forget the pain in my leg and ass where I just slammed onto the cold ground.

I pull myself to my feet this time, too stubborn to accept his help. My wounds may keep me slow, but I grit my teeth and walk on my own anyway, even as tears prick the corners of my eyes. Derrín fishes through our packs, having elected himself mandatory bag holder given my condition, and produces a few strips of dried fruit and bread, passing me one of each. I gratefully accept and eat in silence, trying to ignore my whirling mind.

According to Mavis's map, we should only be an hour or so from the Oracle. The Bone Wood was a shortcut that we hadn't intended on taking due to the rumors surrounding the place, but it shaved several days off our journey regardless.

The mountains surrounding us grow steeper until we find ourselves in a valley, the dark and hulking figures of the steep cliff edge blocking the new day's light from sight. Dim light guides our path, coming from where I do not know. Suddenly, I find myself missing my light powers more than ever. Will I ever get them back, or was Derrín right? Have I finally killed the light? I try to shove the thought down, as I've gotten so good at doing lately, but it remains in the back of my mind. Taunting me.

"Hey, Vera?"

"Hmm?"

"I was right."

I trail his gaze to a junction in the cliffside. At least seven dark shapes mindlessly wander, their elongated arms dragging against the ground. Their talons spark when they hit the stone in front of the cave mouth. The Kijova meander together, almost in a pack, standing between us and what I can only assume is the Oracle.

I crouch down behind a boulder, studying the clearest path past the monsters. Derrín settles next to me, placing his hand atop the boulder. Then he shrieks and waves his hand, nearly tipping over and alerting every Kijova of our presence. I grab his elbow to steady him and he hisses in rage and panic.

"Spiders. Evil spawn of hell..."

I nearly snort in amusement at the mechanic's creative insults that he slews at the tiny arachnid. He settles quietly a few moments later, squatting beside me to study the cave entrance. A few of the Kijova mingle just before it, the remainder patrolling the woods. The cave mouth is sealed shut, save for a crack. Derrín will need to open it in order for me to slip in and find the Oracle.

Then a tug in my stomach. Not the pull of dark magic, but a familiar burning sensation. Something I thought I'd lost pulling me towards the Oracle. Hope flutters in my chest and I test it out. My veins in my wrist begin to glow. Silencing the light quickly, I turn to the Nightwalker, suddenly more confident that we can actually pull this off.

"Do we understand the plan?"

Derrín raises his hand, but I cut him off.

"I asked do we understand, not do we agree."

He huffs and brings out the small blade I gave him this morning. "Kya is going to be mad."

"She will have to get over it. Fingers bleed more."

Derrín will have to slice his finger to draw the rune on the stone while I take care of the Kijova and clear a path for his escape while I enter the cave.

"Let's go."

Derrín nods and I don't waste a second before sprinting down the hill, sliding to a stop in front of one of the beasts. It hardly has time to raise its claws before my fists are up. I call forth that well of power and...

Nothing. No light. No darkness.

I try again, demanding light to come forth, but nothing happens.

I hear Derrín cry out behind me. I hear his warning moments before the blow hits, and manage to jump to the side right as those claws rake the dirt where I stood moments before.

"Use your powers!"

"I can't!" I shriek in a panic. I thought I felt that light, I'd been able to make a small spark back in the Bone Wood, and a few moments ago, I glowed, so why can't I make it now?

A panicking realization settles in my stomach. I really *might* have killed the last bit of light in me. That bit of light was the last of it warning me to turn back, but I ignored it.

Pushing past the dull ache in my chest, I face the beast before me. "Fuck it," I grumble, unfurling my fingers.

I ignore how Derrín shouts as I raise my hand. A dark wave emits, temporarily slicing the Kijova in half and stunning me with pain.

"We don't have long before they reform, and this magic is unstable without a sacrifice. I'll do the best I can, but once that cave is open, run. Don't wait for me."

Derrín's face is pale as he drags his finger along the stone. A crimson and silver trail follows the path his digit takes and before long, the rune is finished. The ground rumbles and debris falls from the cave as the entrance groans in opening.

"Run!" I shout as I cut down the last Kijova while the first one begins to reform.

The mechanic looks between me and the beast, hesitating for just a moment.

I push a ripple of power his way. "Now!"

The magic is enough to set his feet running towards the hill again. "You have twenty-four hours and then I'm coming back!" he shouts as he crosses the hill to safety.

I can make that work.

The stone screeches as it grinds in closing. I force oxygen to my burning legs with each deep breath I take and will my feet to move faster. With only a sliver of time left, I launch myself from the ground and fall through the opening. My shoulder barks in pain as it makes contact with the stone floor. A sickening pop comes as the joint dislodges from its socket and hot blood begins to seep through the tear in my tunic. I hiss in pain as I roll onto my back, surrounded by the dark.

I sob through clenched teeth and call for light. "Lumis." Even the words refuse to bear power. I fish through my pouch with my good hand, pulling out a match and using my hands to find a torch along the wall. Thank the Laei Derrín remembered to grab our gear as we ran. Once the torch is lit, I set to the second task— resetting my shoulder. I bite down on the leather strap of my sack as I grab my wrist and pull. The crack resounds in the cavern as I scream against the leather, tears pricking the corners of my eyes.

My blood should heal the wound soon enough, if the Oracle is of any help at all, so I forgo turning my only shirt into a sling and pluck the torch from the ground. The flame sputters slightly as I rise and inspect the walls. There is only one path to follow, and I allow the cave system to guide me. I don't have time to think on the absence of my powers. I have twenty-four hours to get the Oracle to agree to teach me and learn how to save everyone.

No pressure.

Every so often, the cave rumbles and debris falls from the ceiling. I pray there's no cave-in ahead or behind me, or I may be forced to find an alternative exit.

A distinct smell fills these caves. Something between musk and floral, but disgustingly fragrant. I swallow hard to avoid gagging and force myself to breathe through my mouth.

Somewhere within the system, I can hear water trickle. I feel hope pricking at my skin. If there's water, there is generally life of some form. An Oracle may be a godlike figure, but they must need to eat and drink all the same.

That is the hope I cling to as I quicken my step, marching towards the sound. I try to keep my mind from wandering to whatever squelching substance I am stepping in. I slip for a moment, stiffness arching through my spine.

Soon enough, my efforts pay off and I blow my hair from my eyes just as a dim light appears at the end of the tunnel. I take off somewhere between a walk and a jog, though perhaps it appears more as a limp. I find myself in a large room lit only by a few flickering torches, the lights a dim lilac. A figure sits cross-legged in the center of the cavern, their eyes crusted shut with years of disuse.

I don't need to call out for a response or to question who they are. I know.

"I was wondering when you would show yourself, pureblood," the Oracle says slowly.

CHAPTER 39

VEROSA

The Oracle sits in the center of the room, an aura of darkness surrounding the figure. My own darkness calls me closer. Beckoning. Longing. I heed the call, stepping closer until their face becomes visible.

Weathered skin coats a youthful face, the deep color taking on an unnatural purple hue. Violet eyes snap open, framed by a thick set of dark lashes. Inky black streaks like war paint slide down their cheeks, causing their long, dark hair to stick about their face.

The Oracle of Raonkin is darkness incarnate, but not only that —they are a woman. Or at least, they present as a woman now. Legends have warned that they will take on whatever form they please given the century, a rumor which aids in their elusive nature.

I step forward, allowing those amethyst eyes to drink me in. I know this is unnecessary, as they could sense me the moment I entered their territory. My darkness calls for them, tendrils of power emanating from my being. I swallow thickly and step forward to accept my fate.

"Verosa Iales of Krycolis. Darkness slayer, the last blessed mage. Blood bridge—no, they do not call you that yet." Their voice is a dry rasp, as if they have not used their tongue in thousands of years. "You have gathered quite a few titles. Lived a few lives. Which one are you now?"

"I come only as Verosa."

"Verosa. An old name of a long-dead dialect. Do you know what it means?"

I do. I've known the irony of the meaning of my name since I was a child. Irene never failed to remind me, and now these haunting dreams finish her job.

"Truth."

The Oracle's lips peel open in a smile. "Truth. Light. Purity. It is all the same. You don't feel you fit the title?"

"The title is what I *need*." I raise my voice, emboldened now. "I need to know the truth. I need to know how to end this war. How to kill the king."

That smile twists into something cruel and sadistic. The echoing cacophony of crunching bones fills the cave as the Oracle stands. Bones snap into place while they rise and stalk my way, a withered hand already reaching for my face. A razor-sharp fingernail grazes my cheek, painlessly drawing blood. "A daughter of my master's enemy seeking my assistance in killing her son. Your hubris makes you foolish, girl. Return home. There is no place for you here."

"There is no home, not anymore. He has done wrong to people of *both* gods. He kills without discrepancy. I come to cease the bloodshed."

It takes me a moment to realize before my gaze trails back to those violet eyes. With a gasp, I notice something I had failed to before. There is no blackness within the purple—they have no pupils. The Oracle is blind.

"Do you?"

"Do I what?"

"Truly come to cease the bloodshed?" they ask, stalking even closer somehow.

I fear if I breathe too deeply, I might inhale their dusty skin right off those decrepit bones.

"Many men have come to see me through the years. Humans, you all seek the same thing. Power in one shape or form. Some ask for the guide to money or love, some political positions. You all seek some kind of power, and all for your own selfish gain."

"I come for the people. Not myself."

The Oracle motions for me to sit, and I oblige.

"Do you even understand the weight of those words?"

Their question is left lingering in the dank cave air as the shuffling of paws on stone draws my attention. A dark cat circles by her feet, occasionally rubbing against her knees before it plods its way over to where I sit and crawls to purr in my lap. I stroke its back with soft hands and coo.

The Oracle watches blindly, those violet eyes never blinking. "You don't recognize him?" they ask, then lean back. "Interesting."

I frown and stare at the creature. "Should I?"

Before the words leave my mouth, the Oracle snaps their withered fingers and the cat leaps into the air in a cloud of blackened smoke. I barely have time to jump up before a familiar black stallion stamps his hooves against the stone ground where I sat moments before.

"Vestíg," I breathe.

Vestíg tosses his head in the air, shaking out that long mane. Powerful, corded muscle ripples beneath his dark coat and he snorts into my palm.

"It's not just anyone who can catch the attention of a minor god, let alone the favor of one."

I am sure they do not need their sight to know that my jaw has dropped to graze the floor. God? I was taught there are only two gods, neither of which would ever curl up on my lap.

"Deungrid and Raonkin each have many children. The scriptures won't tell of them because, unlike their parents, the minor deities do not receive followers. The only gifts they received from their parents are their immortality and power."

Vestíg tosses his head one more time before dissolving into a cloud of darkness and reappearing as a panther. He snarls. *Hello again, Verosa.*

I jump, and the Oracle laughs, a dry, heaving sound.

So the god speaks. I press the flat of my palm to his snout, feeling his cold breath skitter across my skin. "What does your true form look like?"

Something between shadows and nightmares. No mortal can withstand the sight.

Shuddering, I picture the Kijova. I cannot imagine anything worse than that, and yet what he claims... I swallow thickly, afraid of what answer this question might heed. "Are you responsible for these dreams that have plagued me all these months?"

The little god hisses. *I have kept the worst of them from you.*

"Some of what you've seen have been images sent by the fallen prince," the Oracle interjects. "Vestíg has kept none of those from you, only those that are dreams."

My heart stutters in my chest as I retract my hand. A minor god taking interest in a mortal. I know how the stories end—death at the forefront of all epilogues.

Vestíg shifts again, this time merely staying as a darkened smoke, swirling through my fingers and weaving through my hair. His body forms a crown atop my head and a skein of darkness wraps around the base of my throat. *Queen of the shadows and daughter of light.* His voice rings out through the cave before he bursts into nothing more than dust that evaporates in the wind.

The Oracle cracks open their eyes and allows their energy to focus on me. Their assessing prowess coats my every cell and ushers my mind under the cover of darkness. Panic grips at my heart for only a moment before it subsides.

The Oracle rises, shaking their head. "Pesky god, telling me what I already know." They tut their tongue as they start down a darkened path. "Well? Come, then. We have much to do."

CHAPTER 40
VEROSA

The Oracle walks with sure feet while I stumble in the darkness after them. I do not feel the same swell of power I felt when they assessed me earlier, now that they are not relying on that sense to guide them. They shuffle their feet by muscle memory and stroll through the dark cave halls.

I hold my shoulder in place, gritting my teeth against the pain as I trip over a loose stone. My stitches must have torn, judging by the wet warmth dribbling down my leg and the biting pain shooting up from my calf past my knee. The air hangs heavy, unnervingly thick with moisture, like the Hills of Siva are right before torrential rain. No gray clouds dot the mold-speckled cave ceiling. No winds rip through my haggard body. The storm is the tattered form leading me through the dark, those violet eyes unseeing.

I almost make a joke about the blind leading the blind, but they pause, the lack of footsteps rattling in the caverns.

"You're fairly quiet for someone who came all this way for a few paltry answers," they note offhandedly, now walking again.

They take a sharp right and I follow, my clavicle hitting the stone wall and barking with pain.

"I wouldn't call ending a war and needless slaughter *paltry*," I grit underneath my breath, "but you're awfully quiet for someone who is supposed to have all these answers."

The Oracle ducks and I am not left wondering why for long when a wet root smacks across my face. Spongey moss splatters, leaving a sticky residue. For my own sanity, I do not wipe it away or even pause to consider what it might be.

"Such a sharp tongue. Use that to stop your war."

"Trust me, the war would be over by now if it worked that way."

"It hasn't been much of a war, only a slaughter."

I exhale through my nose, stopping hotly. "Are you going to tell me what I need to do to prove myself or are you just going to take jabs at my pride?"

I can hear Amír's sharp voice in the back of my head. It melds with the tenebrous growl of Blaine's, creating a wicked subconscious. They snap at me that perhaps insulting the one being that holds a tie to the gods and answers of the future is not my wisest move. They caution me against anger in more cruel terms. How curious that now, the reprimanding voices in my head are theirs and not my own.

The Oracle laughs, a dry, heaving sound of sand on stone. Not quite rough enough to be gravelly, but not soft enough to be anything other than rock. They offer no other response, but knock twice on the wall that is apparently before them.

The stone peels back, now grinding stone on stone, a far worse sound than their laugh. Light blossoms as the gap between the wall and the cavern widens until it envelops us both. A secondary room sits nestled in the corner of the earthly hall, already lit by flaming torches that I know must have been lit for my benefit.

"I am used to the unseeing," the Oracle says with no hint of empathy or explanation in their voice. They take to crouching on their knobby knees and feeling around in the dirt. I extend my hand and they swat at it. "Don't pity me, girl. School that from your heart."

"Fine, I'll just be a bitch and leave you in the dirt."

"Good. You're learning." Something like a smile lifts the corners of their dry lips. The skin stretches in a sickening manner and just when I believe it may crack and bleed, it stretches further.

A sour feeling settles in the pit of my stomach and I cover my mouth with the back of my hand. While the Oracle may resemble a human of sorts, they in no way are human. Perhaps the purple-tinged skin and violet eyes should have clued me in, but somewhere along the way, familiarity crept in and stole reason.

The Oracle shuffles in the dirt, resting their weight entirely on their heels. They swirl across the floor like some spider-ape mix and drag their heels through the dirt. Where the skin should tear, it doesn't. The dirt smears and creates some rune not too different from the one Derrín drew on the wall outside. They jut their chin towards their creation.

I take a step forward but pause, my foot hovering just above the center. "Someone is coming for me in twenty-four hours," I say, suddenly feeling quite small, like a child warning a long-known friend how long until their mother collects them.

The Oracle snorts and I take that as my sign to put my damn foot on the runes.

Smoke covers my eyes and lingers behind my eyelids even as I blink. The startled scream that should've erupted from my throat hitches and my hands fly to the column of my neck. My heartbeat thrums through my bones and I sink to my knees.

This is how I die. This must be.

And just as it becomes unbearable, the smoke clears. The burning subsides. My heart resettles in my chest.

The land around us is green and the Oracle sits cross-legged under a large oak tree. They stroke a panther that has its head resting in their lap. Vestíg yawns and stretches out lazily, resembling more of a house cat than the large form the little god chose to take.

"I apologize for the dramatics," they say, not sounding sorry at all.

"Where are we?"

"Outside the palace, of course."

A young girl's laugh rings through the clearing, and I whirl towards the sound.

The Oracle shrugs. "Ten years ago."

A girl maybe half my age crashes through the brush. Her tanned skin glows in the midday sunlight, warm and golden like honey. Lively chestnut curls bounce free around her face, her hazel eyes pure sunlight. She smiles just as brightly, the sound of her laughter constricting my heart within my chest until I fall to my knees.

A second girl follows closely, her dark hair braided in a crown atop her head. She huffs and falls behind quickly, a young boy having to prop her up. Her leg is still bruised and her skin far too pale, but by gods, the sunlight feels divine and she is not going to stay locked in that infirmary any longer.

The healers took most of the pain away, but she still needed to stay in the med hub for two weeks, even with their expertise and powers. But Tanja begged, and she, Blaine, and another boy named Torin convinced her nanny to allow Vera out for just an hour. They stole jelly tarts from the kitchen and tied them into a bedsheet that was now sticky and stained.

The children disappear around a corner and I watch them until my eyes strain and blur.

"Why?" I croak. Emotion doesn't lace my voice. It smothers it. It has me swaying on my feet, and I feel myself longing to follow, even as I stay rooted to the spot.

The Oracle watches curiously. Their power numbs some of the pain, carries it away on a dark wind. They speak slowly after a long pause and Vestíg ceases his purring. "I wanted to give you one good memory before we begin."

I swallow thickly, the laughter now an empty hollow behind my eyes.

"I wanted to remind you, and give you a chance to remember."

To remember the light. The words don't fall from their tongue, but I hear them all the same. In some ways, Derrín and Rowan were right, but in others, they were wrong. *The dark cannot smother that which is light.* The dark magic didn't kill the light in me, but it did repress it. The one who has been killing it was me all along. In smothering Tanja, in trying to forget her and blame myself because the pain was just too much. Because the truth was far more worse than a half-believed lie.

The thought forces me to my knees and a gasping breath from my lips. Death is so sickeningly final. And a part of me thought that if I bottled all my rage and grief, it could delay the inevitable. I feared that if I opened that part of my heart, I would have to come to terms with what I wasn't able to face yet—the fact that no amount of tears or revenge can bring her back. That no matter how many men I kill or in turn people I save, she will still be gone. And I will be here, left with nothing but a memory.

Tanja is gone.

But the light is not dead. It cannot be killed, not so long as I live and as she lives in me.

"Ah, so not all hope is lost." The Oracle smiles, a nearly tooth-less grin, save for one remaining canine. "Good. We start now."

Before I have the chance to question it or even pick up the pieces of my heart that just shattered on the earth, a weight slams into my back. I spin on instinct, flipping to face the threat. A shadow-clad beast snaps its fangs at my throat.

It has fangs, I note. And a body. A body can be destroyed, where shadow cannot. It rears back for only a moment, but I only need that singular moment to tuck my knees into my chest then kick it with both legs when it comes down again. The beast skitters to a stop a few feet away and I take the moment to look up at the Oracle.

The gloriously green and sunlit meadow outside the palace has been replaced with marble columns and stone seats. The Oracle and Vestíg sit atop the dais while I stare up at them from the center of the royal colosseum. Vestíg does not deign to show his face, but his shadows take on a more humanoid form now, even as they shift and slither about.

"I thought you were supposed to teach me!" I call up to the dais, fury wrought anew.

"I believe in learning on the job."

Duck, a deep voice in my mind commands.

The Oracle swats at Vestíg for "cheating," but I do as he says. The air whips my face as a second shadow beast tears its claws through the space I previously occupied, just narrowly missing my throat.

"Your rage is blinding you." The Oracle sounds... bored. Or disappointed. Maybe a mix of both.

A low growl of frustration rises in my throat. I prepare to bark out a snarky response when I feel pain ripple through my lower back. A third monster's claws rip through close enough to my spine to be worrisome. This simulation that the Oracle has created allows my previous wounds to be healed for the time being, but the newer wounds still hurt and bleed the same. From the corner of my eye, I spot a fourth beast appear, then a fifth and a sixth.

Then a dark presence overcomes my senses. Not smothering, but protecting.

The Oracle whines in complaint, but Vestíg pays them no mind.

Focus. Rage is not a weapon. It steals your energy, but like all energies, it can be manipulated.

I take a deep breath and when I exhale, the darkness is gone and I am surrounded now by seven shadow monsters. I shoot the Oracle a dirty glare.

They shrug, as much of a response as they will deign to give me.

Focus. Right.

The ground rumbles with each step, the ground shifting until I can feel it deeper in my bones the closer the monster gets. The air shifts slightly to make room for the space now occupied, and the wind sings through the talons as one of those clawed hands encroaches.

I spin on my heel and it misses, not by luck.

Each step is in sync with the world around me. The wind shifts as I dance to the side. One monster surges while I avoid another. Just like how it was back in the training arena with Torin and the guards. They were easier as I knew their patterns and their training, but even shadow beasts have patterns. Kijova have patterns. In a few moments, it is easy to pick them up and avoid then offer a counterattack.

The last of the beasts hits the ground, their shadows drifting skyward as dozens of bodies now rest around my feet. I step over one and offer the Oracle a bow.

Something new sparkles in those violet eyes. Excitement, maybe?

No.

Hope.

"Well done, pureblood."

"Verosa," I reply, beaming despite the blood and sweat coating my body. "My name is Verosa Iales. Daughter of the light. The last blessed mage. The blood bridge and whatever the fuck else you called me."

If shadows could smile, Vestíg would be grinning. No, his face would be completely split by the smile judging by the smug energy radiating from him.

The Oracle laughs again, that horrible, dry sound. Then, with a snap of their fingers, the arena disappears from view, leaving us in a library now. "Don't think things will be so easy, blood bridge."

CHAPTER 41
ROWAN

Roiden has been breathing down my neck since we returned empty handed from our palace raid—empty handed only to his knowledge, and save for the few men we were able to rescue. I have been to visit them a few times now, staying as long as I can bear. One of the men passed the first night. I was unable to look any of them in the eye after that, too ashamed that if maybe we had gathered just a day sooner, the man might have lived. Torin says they are all grateful and none of them blame me, and I believe him. But how can I not blame myself?

The wood creaks above my head and dust settles in the air. Another spy on the roof. Another sign of Roiden's growing distrust. It has only been three days, but the man has sent countless a spy to the inn. I'll give credit where credit is due—the bastard is right in his distrust.

Amír and Kya are settled in the corner when I stalk downstairs. Kya's fingers make quick work of her boot buckles despite the rust from months in the mountains. Amír finishes polishing her pistol and begins on Kya's many blades, slowly handing them back one at a time. The assassin rewards her with a peck on the cheek as she stores the blades in her old assassin's suit. The knives disappear amidst the leather as if they were never there. But I know if she were to so much as flick her wrist, she could send them flying at will.

"There's another spy on the roof. Give me a heads up before you go so I can distract him while you two sneak out from the cellar."

Amír mock-salutes with a blade. "Yes, sir."

"They're not very good," Kya murmurs under her breath. "They shouldn't even be called spies if they're going to have such heavy footsteps." The assassin pulls a face, insult highlighting her pretty features at the thought of being lumped in with the amateurs Roiden sends.

"His 'insolent signs of rightful distrust' is more of a mouthful than 'spies,' so excuse my shortcut," I quip.

The men haven't been trained and don't have the innate talent my assassin has. They are mainly farmers or poor men from the outskirts of the city that survived the initial onslaught. They were raised to trek through sewers and stomp to scare off the rats, or tramp through fields on weary feet all day. None of them possess the quiet agility Kya has, and her pride has taken a direct hit at even being slightly compared to the men.

She lolls her head back with a groan and my mother sympathetically pats her shoulder, entering the room with Blaine in tow. She passes a tied leather pouch to each of the women, along with a full canteen.

"This should last you a few days," she offers.

They accept both gratefully as Amír passes the final espa back to Kya.

"Thank you, Emilie. But I hope we will be back by nightfall tomorrow."

"The trek should only take half a day, assuming we do not run into any trouble. We gather the iron and go. In then out," Kya agrees, still accepting the provisions, nonetheless.

"And you come back if you encounter anything you can't face. If there's Kijova or the king's men, you retreat. We will find another way," I remind them. Even still, I see the rebellious spark in Amír's eye. She won't back down, even if a Kijova has her in its gaping maw. Retreat is rarely ever an option. Kya, however, places her hand on the redhead's arm and nods.

Then out the window, I spot a flash of blond. The spy had ruddy brown hair when I saw him this morning, and judging by the consistent creaking, there hasn't been a rotation. The outlines of three figures slowly emerge from the tree line behind the inn. Just out of sight, for now.

"Shit," I swear.

"Dammit, Torin," Blaine huffs.

We lock our gazes, and soon, I am pushing through our little group, heading for the door. "You two leave now. I am going to draw the spy to the front. Blaine, go with them and bring Torin and his guests through the back while I distract our friend. If he is taking the back entrance, my guess is Roiden doesn't know about these visitors."

My crew agrees, springing into action. My mother follows suit, preparing to bolt the door from the inside if necessary, just as we practiced. Roiden is still unaware that my mother is with me, or that I have one at all, and I'd prefer to keep it that way. Every time Vera's name leaves my lips or my Nightwalkers enter his compound, he has something over me. My mother is the final card he would have to play to take me down, and I can't risk that. Not with all these lives hanging on my shoulders. *Their* lives.

I step into the grass, some of the dew flinging from the stalks to the toe of my leather boots. Spreading my arms skyward, warmth envelops my body, bathing my limbs as the sun's glow touches everything. Spring has come. The only spring Krycolis ever sees is in the mountains. No doubt if we were still in the inner city, we would be swamped with the heat wave that crests the kingdom almost immediately once the last of the frost melts. Winter is quick but harsh, moving through as swiftly as it comes. Summers are just as extreme, with scalding heat waves ravaging our borders for the majority of the year. Spring exists only in these high altitudes, and fall lasts for a few weeks at most before the cycle begins again.

My dagger reflects the light back into the sky as I unsheathe the weapon. I make a show of brandishing it, then stalking off towards the trees before me, praying the spy takes the bait.

He does.

His breath is harsh upon my neck as we trek deeper into the greenery. The sunlight, now distant, blots against the ground through the thick layer of foliage. He attempts to stay in the trees, but his clumsy footsteps alert not only myself but every woodland creature that still breathes of his presence. Once far enough in that the retreat should allow the others time to enter the inn, I spin, the knife in my hand flying into the tree trunk behind the spy. The cool metal edge clips his ear, crimson and silver blood blooming immediately.

"Tell Roiden that trust goes both ways. If he wants to keep sending his dogs into my territory, I will send my assassin into his."

The mention of Kya causes visible terror to flash across the man's face and he rushes into the woods, a new stain on the fold of his pants. I pull my knife from the tree, grunting at the bit of flesh still on the blade.

Two haggard yet familiar faces greet me, along with Torin's sheepish one once I return to the inn.

Finneas crushes me in an embrace, the suffocation welcome after months apart. The large man stands tall, not much of a change in his physique since I last saw him. He has lost a bit of the softer flesh that surrounded his gut and arms, but the loss has only emphasized the bulk of his corded muscle. His freckles have multiplied greatly, despite the paleness of his winter-fresh skin, but there is a sharp gleam in his smile. The same soft brutishness that I've known the man to possess has not been damaged in the slightest.

Aiko's arms replace his the moment the man releases, though she is noticeably more slender. They shake as she holds me, as if she does not have the strength to hold them up that long. Yet she grips me tighter, her fingernails digging into my shoulder. Her face is gaunt and her clever eyes near wild as they search the room. "Where is my daughter?"

Blaine and I fix Torin with a strong glare at the same time, the Vari man all but shrinking into the wall. Apparently, he hadn't found it necessary to wait for the rest of us to break the news to the nobles on who their daughter has grown to be, but chose to not explain that she is off on a perilous mission that might cost her her life.

It is my mother who answers, her golden hand coming to rest on Aiko's pale arm. "Verosa is with Derrín in the heart of the mountains. She has gone to consult an Oracle on the future, specifically on how to end the war." She doesn't say to kill Ophelus, but the weight is there. She also does not mention the trials, or the fact that she and Derrín will be close to the Bone Wood—far closer than I prefer them to be.

Finneas frowns, seeing through it but choosing not to push, not as his wife collapses onto the couch. "When will she be back?"

"A few days at the latest. She left two nights ago."

The rooms lays thick with a heavy silence. For the first time in a while, no sarcasm bounces from the walls, or at the very least, an argument. The cold settles in our bones despite the spring sun, only the groaning of the wood as the weight of the silence presses against it filling the room.

After a short while, Aiko balls her fists and parts her lips in a breathy whisper. "I would like to speak with Rowan."

The "alone" is silent, but the others leave, nonetheless.

Finneas comes to sit next to his wife and motions for me to sit on the stool across from them. "Tell us everything," he commands. His face is weathered and his arms laced with scars that must run deep into the muscle. Without his smile and twinkling eyes, he looks like the feared warrior he once was. He looks exactly like the type of man who would kill another suitor for his wife.

So I tell them everything with an honesty I didn't know my black heart still possesses.

Aiko listens with the intensity of a hawk, her deep blue eyes boring into my soul. Her lips purse to taste any lie I might dish to them, but her jaw relaxes when she finds none. Finneas holds her hands in one of his. His other is empty, as it has been for twenty years.

"So everyone else who has gone to see this Oracle has never returned, and yet you let her go?"

"You've met her, Aiko. There was no *letting* her do anything. She could either go with my support or go with my disapproval, but she was going to go either way."

The woman inhales, her shoulders hunching as she buries her face in her hands. Her inky black hair falls forward, shrouding her face. The portrait she paints is so distinctly Vera that it causes a spear of hot pain to pierce my heart.

Finneas lays a large hand on her back but she shakes it off. The woman rises and wraps her arms around her midsection, her eyes lined with silver. "I won't fault you for her choices, but I need a moment before I make you think otherwise." Each word is strained, as if she is holding herself back even now.

I can only dip my chin in respect and acknowledgment. When her footsteps recede beyond even my hybrid's earshot, I allow myself to slump forward. My shoulders nearly touch and my spine curves as guilt lays siege on my being. I can feel Finneas's stare and his lingering question.

"Can you tell me about her?" His voice is soft in juxtaposition to his large figure. "I only really met her the once, and she wasn't exactly conscious the whole time. We didn't get to speak the second time before your mother stole her away." The man cringes at how it sounds, and it forces an equally dry and brief laugh from between my lips.

"Honestly, she told us who she was from day one," I admit. "She's grown up quite a bit, but she is still the same spitfire that puts me in my place."

Finneas beams with something like pride at that, and I continue.

"She's got this strange view on the world. She sees things as they should be, rather than what they are. She can't seem to draw a line between the two. Yet she's not the beam of sunshine everyone would expect her to be. She's got a short temper and an even shorter leash on her tongue. I've never heard such colorful insults in all my life."

The older man booms with laughter, the sound rattling the windows and my ribs. "She gets that from her mother. The cleverness, that is. She probably gets her temper from me," he admits.

"But..." I inhale sharply. Finneas deserves to know the truth. "She's not the same as when you met. Her best friend sacrificed herself for her life, and it changed her. She's done things, horrible things to other people. She's learned dark magic and lost all sense of boundaries and morals. She's not the innocent baby you lost all those years ago. She's changed."

I barely scratch the surface of her sins as I recount just some of what Vera has done. To her credit, some was for survival, yes, but the thought of dark magic caressing her palms sends a shiver through my body. The hairs on the back of my neck stand at attention and Finneas halts me by raising a large hand.

He rocks forward, resting his elbows on his knees. When he speaks, his voice is rough, like sandpaper on oak. "When someone took our baby, I didn't sleep. I didn't eat. I just took care of Aiko as best as I knew, then I went searching for her. During the day, I'd knock on doors and ask as kindly as I could if anyone had seen anything. Warrants went out that way, but at night, I would break into any home I knew had a baby or heard one crying in. I would search for her in every screaming face, but none of them were her. I never would have thought..."

I remember hearing about this from the gutters. A man who would break into homes, noble and poor, cursed and blessed alike. He would break in but never steal anything and would leave gold for the families to repair their doors or windows. I had my suspicions, but no one was able to pin any blame on the man, until now.

"I did far worse for my daughter, and would go even farther if it meant I could take this weight from her shoulders. Aiko has done the same in her own ways, things neither of us dare speak about lest it finally catch up to us and Vera takes the fall. You say you would do anything for the ones you love, but you never know just how far you would be willing to go until the one you love most is taken from you." He sighs, then stares hard into my eyes. "You do not love someone in spite of their flaws. If you love them that way, you cannot call it love at all. To love is to accept completely, the saint *and* the murderer. Whoever my daughter has become, I will learn to love her how I know best—completely." His hand rests heavy on my shoulder. "You can guide them towards the light, but how can you force them out of the darkness when you're shrouded in your own?"

"That's a fancy way of saying don't be a hypocritical asshole."

"If you'd rather I say it that way, then fine. Don't be a hypocritical asshole." His gaze hardens. "I don't care who you are to me or to her. Love her right or don't love her at all."

I've lost count of how many men I've killed. How many innocents. The children I've indirectly slaughtered as I try to push my evils to the back of my mind. We've all tried to justify our sins and condemn hers because we feared she would become like us.

Love is not always good. It is dark and twisted even more so than hate. Hatred knows boundaries, while love knows none. Of the two, it is clear which is the more lethal weapon, and which one has poisoned more men.

"There's something else you haven't said. You're hesitating," Aiko drawls from the doorway. She drapes herself across the frame, leaning into it for support. Her eyes trace my direction lazily, but there is a sharp awareness beneath the façade.

Verosa called her a silver fox in passing once, and I laughed, not only because it was an odd description but because it was accurate. She is clever and unassuming, a lethal combination.

"Lyra."

Aiko blinks once, then twice. She moves into the room with feline stealth and closes the door. She brings her face close to mine, close enough that I can smell the mint upon her breath. "She's alive?" she breathes.

"Alive and married to the leader of the rebellion," I respond lowly. "It's interesting that you never ran into them, considering you were hiding near their base."

"How do you know that?"

"Winter mint only grows near the base of the mountains in that region."

Finneas beams and clasps my shoulder again, nearly knocking me over. "That's my boy."

Aiko does not share his pride, though the slight upward curve of her lips tells me she acknowledges it. "What is she doing married to him?"

"I don't know," I admit, "but it didn't sound like she had much of a choice. Any light you can shed on this situation?"

I can practically see the gears shifting in Aiko's mind. She's filing through a life of memories from over twenty years ago. A time before I existed, before the world went to shit. "She's your mother's younger sister. She was about fifteen when she went missing, your mother was twenty. This was just under a year before you were born. You were not quite an expected blessing."

"What a polite way to call me a mistake."

Aiko ignores my slight and continues. "Your grandparents were dead by the time your mother was fifteen, leaving her with a child to care for. She viewed herself as solely responsible for Lyra, so imagine the grief when one day, she left for school and never came home."

Look at the silver in my husband's hair, boy, and the little I have in mine. Do you see how things are run around here? Use that brain she gave you and put it together.

"So Roiden *took* her."

Aiko's face is grim and her mouth a hard-set line. Finneas's fists shake at his side.

"Most likely."

I expected her response, coming to my conclusions and not quite requiring her confirmation, but the two words still send nausea roiling through my stomach nonetheless. "I've promised to get her out."

"I'm sure you have."

"And I'm going to tell my mother."

"Don't," Aiko interrupts. "Not yet. If it wasn't for your father, your mother would've chosen to leave this earth after Lyra went missing. If it wasn't for finding out she had you to live for, she would've..."

I press my eyes closed, harder and harder until the stars in the black turn red and streak across the darkness in my vision. I can feel the air shift as Finneas rises, feel his every footstep through the legs of the stool. He paces closer to the window, slamming his fist against the stone. When I open my eyes, I find that the sunlight drifting through the window has cast his freckles in gold, just like it does Vera's.

Secrets like these tore us apart. I thought I was protecting Vera by keeping Blaine from her, and I was wrong. I cannot forget the hurt that flashed across her face at the duel when I told her what Lucius asked of me. It cuts deeper than the moment she came to after Ophelus and Lucius tried to murder her, when she found Blaine sitting at the foot of her bed, none of us surprised to see him there. The first cut into her trust was unexpected. She had full faith, and that faith was sliced away until she didn't question it when I revealed I had Blaine all along. I was met with silence for days, then we moved on like nothing ever transpired between us.

"No, she deserves to know. I don't intend to fail in bringing her home. I *won't.*" I keep my voice level and firm, a tone I do not usually take with the two adults sitting across from me.

Aiko's gaze is challenging, her eyebrows furrowed and her face all hard lines. I see so much of Vera in them both now. Her eyes and calculating glare. Finneas's smile and furrowed brow. Vera's nose scrunches the same way his does when they're deep in thought, and she throws her head back to laugh like Aiko.

Aiko's shoulders drop and she nods, once. "Let's bring her home then."

CHAPTER 42

VEROSA

The last shadow disintegrates in a strong burst of light. My skin is glowing, my veins bursting with light with each motion I make. The magic caresses my senses like an old friend, longing filled with relief at its return. The part of me that craved dark magic has been satiated with the abundance of light that bursts from my every pore. I am not filled with light.

I *am* light.

The Oracle claps, a slow and languid motion that rattles the chandelier above my head. The ballroom fades from view and I find myself in the library seated by the window I used to hide by with my friends.

"No more trials?"

I've killed countless shadow monsters by now, each in a different place of my memory, each one possessing skills that are my weaknesses, each one bearing a different face. Afterwards, the Oracle says something to Vestíg, asks me a question with a shrouded meaning, then transports us elsewhere.

"Just one, but it will wait a moment." The Oracle passes a mug my way. It is filled with molten chocolate.

I take a slow sip as the first snowflake hits the window.

"You still have questions," they note with a wiry smile.

I purse my lips and nod. I've defeated several monsters, faced countless memories, and yet questions still burn in my mind. Questions with answers only they have. "Life is supposed to be a balance, and yet we can only use light magic? Why not dark magic?" My fingers tighten around the mug in my hand. "When I use light magic, it feels fulfilling, like an extension of myself. But the dark magic is different. It is wild, and without a sacrifice, it feels like it is tearing me apart. That doesn't seem like a balance to me."

The Oracle considers this if only for a moment. Vestíg winces as they shift that sightless gaze my way. "You assume everything was designed for men. You humans tend to think the universe was made for you when really, you were an afterthought. Dark magic is able to be wielded by gods. Men just are not... durable enough for such power."

"What do you mean?"

"You humans like attaching names to things you cannot understand. Good and evil, light and dark. There is no good or evil magic, there is only magic in its various forms. What you call dark magic is the same as your light magic, just a form that is not suitable for humans to use. You make up your stories and warnings. You do anything but accept the truth that not all things were designed for you. This 'dark' magic is a more archaic form that was meant to be wielded by gods, not men. Sure, you have found a way, but all you're doing is letting the power tear your body apart."

I pause, my hand throbbing at the reminder of the power I let overtake me. A blush coats my face. I hadn't considered it that way. "And you aren't a god?"

They shake their head. "I am neither god nor man. Only a messenger."

Well, that couldn't be less helpful.

"I have a question for you now, pureblood," they say after a long pause. "You fear the snow and the dark, yet not heights. Why?"

It is a question I have gotten a few times in my life, especially after my stunts where I willfully jumped out of windows rather than falling. I fell from Irene's study and broke my leg, something that should have killed me, yet I fear what came after—the snow, the darkness beckoning. It has chased me all my life, yet still, I jump. I push past the boundaries that others deem the more appropriate lines to draw.

"I never feared the fall," I finally admit. "It was free. I was weightless and it was wonderful, so how could I fear something that gave me what I wanted?" I swallow thickly and take another small sip. My fingers reach out of their own accord, the pads of my fingertips pressing against the cool glass. "I feared the end. The moment it all caught up with me."

"You cannot outrun death no more than you can outrun time," is the Oracle's response.

I grimace even as I acknowledge the truth in them. The weight. I've cheated death all my life. One of these days, the darkness would smother me and there would be nothing but unending cold. I don't know if I believe in the afterlife, and I panic if I think too long about it. The unknown is something that goes against the core of my curious nature, and the thought of having to face it for eternity one day...

My breaths come out in panicked gasps. No man can outrun death, not a king or a pureblood. Only a god. For a moment, I look upon Vestíg with something like contempt. This fear is something he would never know. He and the gods that made us.

"Why do you come now to save the people you turned your back on?"

"Because I was wrong to run from my problems, and it cost

me the thing I loved most," I finally admit. Even my best attempt at selflessness is rooted in my selfish nature. "We were all given a purpose by the gods, right? I was supposed to be queen, and I failed, so they punished me."

"Do not think it is so simple," the Oracle says, reaching into their cloak. "You were a child who was hurt by those who were supposed to protect you. Running became a habit. But you've come here to break that habit. Why?"

I think back to the people I've loved and those I've lost. The Nightwalkers who have shown me their despise within their love indiscriminately, and the people in the palace who put their faith in me. Even Lucius, who might have been the first person to truly see me for who I am. Who endured the most of my hatred for it.

"There are people I love who are better than I am, and I refuse to fail them again."

Silence.

Then the Oracle lays a small vial in my lap. Their face is passive, but I can feel the shift in the air. It is not quite the same storm that was brewing when I entered, more the gentle silence after rainfall where the sky knows it lost something. Reverential, and nearly regretful.

"What's this?" I ask, bringing my eye to the bottle. I nearly drop it, but Vestíg catches it before the vial can shatter and spill the poison everywhere.

Poison. The Oracle handed me poison.

Krycolian Viper venom mixed with pure cursed blood, to be precise.

The silver liquid sloshes against the side of the vial, the sweet scent of the venom filling the air. It is potent enough to drown out the dank scent of the mold in the cavern now that we have returned from the visions the Oracle trained me in. The pain of my wounds has returned, my shoulder still hanging limp and my calf still bleeding profusely. The pain is lessened and I lift my hand not holding the vial.

"The final trial."

Light dances between my fingertips and I choke back a sob.

"The final test is death."

I spring to my feet, Vestíg's shadow following my every motion. His form winds itself around my arm as if sorrowful. I shake him off, panic gripping at my chest. "No."

"Blood bridge."

"*No*," I hiss. "All of this was not for nothing. If I die, then that is what will happen. The kingdom will fall. My friends will die. I'm sorry, did you miss the part where I'm the *only* one that can kill the Kijova?"

The Oracle speaks slowly, as if weighing each word. "Then don't die."

Death is the final test, but I shouldn't die?

As if sensing my question, the being continues, their violet eyes darkening like twilight. I swear for a moment, I can see stars in them, the last stars I might ever see.

"The poison will kill you, if the gods deem you unworthy. The venom preserves the body, but the poison will kill it. However, with my assistance, your soul will live, trapped in your body, unless the gods intervene."

"What the fuck is that supposed to mean? 'Unless the gods intervene'?"

"The final trial happens in your mind. A guide will appear in the darkness, a manifestation of the worst parts of you. Unlike my training, this manifestation will be real. If it is a Kijova, it will be real. If it is a person, it will be their soul. They will guide you to the answers you seek. If you survive and the gods deem your soul worthy to live, then your soul will return to your body and your body will return to life. If you fail..."

"I *die* die."

"Yes."

I weigh the bottle in my hand, watching the silver liquid slosh against the sides. This much cursed blood is enough to kill twenty men twice my size. Not even my pure blood could attempt to save me from this much poison.

I uncork the bottle with my thumb and let the cork fall to the floor. My gaze rises to the Oracle in questioning. "And this will show me what I must do to save everyone?"

The Oracle nods. "Look for the guide. They will be the physical manifestation of the darkest parts of your soul. Only they can lead you to the answers you seek. You must conquer them first, or your soul will die with your body."

Vestíg curls around my shoulders. Somehow, the shadows seem desolate, as if already in mourning. He rubs affectionately against my cheek while the Oracle stares on in wonder.

"I've never met a human quite like you, blood bridge."

I ignore their comment, my racing heart all but drowning out those last words. I tenderly run a finger down the length of Vestíg's shadowy form. "Protect Derrín for me, please? He will be on his own for the way home now."

I will.

I swallow the lump in my throat and with shaking hands, raise the poison to my lips. The blood burns my lips upon contact and singes my mouth and throat. The glass shatters to the ground, slipping out of my hand almost immediately. My hands fly to my throat as I croak. All air evades my lungs and I fall to my knees.

"Vera?" I can hear Derrín calling from the hallway. "Vera!" His feet reach my vision by the time my back hits the stone. His arms wrap under mine and lift me to his chest. His scarred fingers brush the hair from my eyes and press into my throat for a pulse. His gaze finds the silver-flecked broken glass and his eyes widen in horror. "No, no, don't you dare. You're not allowed to leave me too." His tears drip from the bridge of his nose against my cheek.

I try to smile, but comes out as a grimace. I never knew death would be so painful. I can feel each of my organs as they shut down, I realize in a panic. I am unworthy. My time is running out.

Blinking back tears, I shakily grip his hand. "I love you."

I say it so he knows it is for him, but also for the others. It is all I can say, all I can do.

I say it for Kya, who has shown me kindness above all else. For Amír, who taught me to survive and loves me in her own way. For Blaine and all we were, Torin and all we've lost. And for Rowan, who has to know that I have loved him in this lifetime more than all else, and will find and love him in the next.

I have my regrets, as any dying person does. I regret not being able to tell my parents that I love them to their faces, as anything more than a poor girl they took pity on. As their daughter. But this... this will have to be enough.

The ghost of a hand brushes my bangs from my face and a soft voice lilts a whisper to my ear. *You were never meant to survive. You were designed for this since the day you were born. A sacrifice to the king, to the gods, and someday, to men. You were the one born to die.*

Why do the gods choose to grant clarity to men in their final moments when it is too late? Once they've already damned us all. Even as the thought passes through my mind, I know no gods are to blame. My undoing is truly of my own design.

Death is not swift nor kind to me, but I do not regret raising that vial to my lips. Convulsions wrack my body, and Derrín's hands shake where he tries to hold my shoulders still. Even as he holds me to him, I can feel his warmth fading, or rather, my ability to feel him. At least with the numbness coming, the pain lessens. Blood pours from my mouth, my nose, my ears. The poison has burned my vocal cords and distorted my voice to where it is no longer my own. I can feel the skin on my lips boil and peel back.

And yet a small part of myself thanks the poison, and is grateful my fight is finally over.

A soft voice reaches out and brushes its fingertips across my freckles, down the bridge of my nose. *Vera.*

"I love you," I repeat again with my last breath, even as Derrín's screams rattle my bones, and I let the darkness pull me under.

CHAPTER 43
ROWAN

Sunlight bathes my mother's peaceful face when I approach her. I slept on my decision to tell her about Lyra. Too much commotion has occurred in the past two days with the Ialeses coming home and I haven't found a moment to confront her about my new knowledge. This morning, however, Aiko found me and called me a pitiful coward.

Now here we are.

Finneas comes to stand behind me while Aiko settles beside her and takes her hand in hers. She squeezes them, the gentleness of the action drawing my mother's gaze to my solemn face.

"What, my Noiteron?" She smiles, strained even to my eyes.

I drop my chin to my chest and inhale deeply. How am I supposed to tell her what I know without breaking her heart? What if I fail, and worst of all, I fail her?

Finneas's heavy hand falls on my shoulder. Aiko's on my wrist. Even now, knowing they are Verosa's parents and the threat Finneas made earlier, they are not afraid to stand by me. To stand in as the full family I never was gifted by blood.

Forcing my features to soften and my nerves to steel, I meet my mother's worried gaze. "Lyra is alive."

I want to tell her everything, to tell her how we met, how she knew me because I had her eyes. I want to ramble on and on and promise her that I will bring her sister back. That I will bring her home to her and kill the man that stole her.

But her mouth drops open.

And she screams.

She screams a great, shuddering sob and collapses into her hands. Aiko holds her shoulders to her chest as she convulses. I sit still, mute until silence befalls the room.

Horror fills my chest cavity—horror at the thought that I caused this, that I don't know how to fix it. My mother may have weakened over the years, but still remained strong in a way that shadowed her former self. She's never once sobbed before me, not to her knowledge, anyhow, and surely never screamed.

My panicked gaze shifts to Aiko, who is trying to comfort her, rocking her back and forth like a child. She's inconsolable, and just as I am about to reach for her hands, she falls silent, the shrieking stopping just as quickly as it started.

No one moves, not even daring to blink or avert our gazes.

My mother sits up. Dries her eyes.

And smiles.

The sight is more horrifying than the guttural screams that were just wrought from her body.

"Emilie," Aiko speaks slowly in a low tone, "what's going through your head?"

"My son has lost his mind," she says, her voice barely above a whisper. She stares at me with red-rimmed eyes, clear yet distant. "I must help him."

"No, Emilie, he hasn't. Lyra *is* alive. She was taken, but she is alive and Rowan found her. He's going to bring her home when it is safe for both of you." She and Finneas exchange a look both sorrowful and guilty. They know the loss Emilie is going through. They lost their daughter and were told after twenty years that she had been found, so they must have had similar reactions. They must have been lost and confused and shocked.

But they had each other.

My mother has no one. No one but me, someone she has always felt the need to protect above all others.

And this is the final straw. That light I have been terrified of going out, that I fight daily to keep burning, I have been the one to snuff it out.

I sit frozen on the stool as Aiko leads my mother away, that hollow smile still cemented on her face. She doesn't protest as Aiko brings her to a room and lets her lie down. She hardly even glances my way.

And I just freeze.

The same way I froze when Vera used dark magic and almost killed herself. My muscles constricting and refusing to follow the instincts I've instilled in them since taking up the mantle of Noiteron. Of the king of mercenaries. Every time it mattered most, I couldn't move. I was too paralyzed by fear of love lost.

The same way I froze when Mavis drove that knife into my thigh.

Aiko rests a hand on my shoulder and I jump. I hadn't even realized she had returned.

"She's sleeping."

"I broke her. You were right. I never should have told her anything."

"No," Aiko says sternly, her hands gripping my arms. She rests on her knees in an attempt to be eye level with me, but the action forces her to crane her neck upwards, her height betraying her. "She would have had a worse reaction if we just brought Lyra home without telling her. She would have shut down just like this and then when she came to, she would be angry. No, she would be furious that we did not tell her that her sister was alive. You did the right thing."

"Okay."

"Rowan."

"Hm?"

"You did the right thing," The older woman speaks each word slowly, rolling the syllables off her tongue as if tasting their weight. She says it again, more weighty now.

Finneas claps my arms and helps his wife up when I sigh in relent. Just in time for the front door to open.

"No spies today?" Amír's voice calls from the door. Her shoulders sag as she dumps four filled packs of what sounds like iron ore to the ground. Kya follows behind her, carrying four more bags that she drops with equal gladness.

"None since you left and I threatened to send Kya after them." I force a grin onto my face as I embrace them both.

Finneas peeks into the sacks and whistles lowly. "Solid iron ore. I need to start training with you both again."

"You're always welcome to join, Finneas." Kya beams broadly. "So long as you aren't afraid of getting your ass kicked."

The man laughs, the hearty sound filling the chilled void of the room with warmth again.

Aiko moves to embrace both the women before seating them both at the table in the kitchen. "Have either of you eaten yet today?"

Amír hesitates and it is all the other woman needs to notice. She pops her hands on her hips and whacks the gunslinger's arm, eliciting a yelp. "Girls! It is nearly sunset and you've been gone since yesterday morning. Food is in order. Now."

Kya giggles under her breath and Finneas helps rub out Amír's weary shoulders. Her left has always bothered her more than her right, something to do with her father. That's all she has ever told me. I suspected once that Kya knew the reason, but when I confronted her about it, she revealed she didn't know, not that she would ever tell me if she did.

Aiko begins making something in the oven when Kya falls silent, despite being mid-conversation with Finneas. The older man glances at her curiously, but she only holds up a finger. "Someone's coming," Kya states without rising. She twists her neck to face the window and squeals. "They're back!" She sprints out the door without waiting for anyone else.

We know if the distance weighed heaviest on any of us, it was the assassin. Derrín rarely goes on missions on his own, let alone missions to places no one has ever returned from.

Amír chuckles, but we can all see the relief written across her face. The anxiety and consistent wonder of whether or not they would return has worn on us all.

Aiko pales and her eyes well up. "Vera?" She drops her spoon, forgoing the meal she was cooking for my two mercenaries.

Her husband moves to meet her, his lower lip trembling and hands shaking. Finneas squeezes her hands as the tears begin to stream. "Oh, Laei." Her husband holds her elbow and the two breathe deeply before following Kya out the door. The moment they've been waiting for for over twenty years waits for them just past the porch.

Another figure appears, summoned by Kya's gleeful shriek. Blaine approaches my side, sighing in relief at the spots on the horizon slowly coming into view between the trees.

We spoke briefly after Vera left. He told me he kissed her, and although he apologized, we both knew he didn't mean it. Not to me anyway. He felt more sorry for himself, because while he will never say it, we both know he believed for just a moment that she could have loved him again. He did not throw up his walls this time and did not turn to drink. He told me how his mother had fallen into similar habits when he was younger and how when she was clean, she made him swear to never fall into the same trap.

She told him about his grandfather, then great-grandfather. He promised, and while he didn't know where she was, the shame at breaking that promise helped steer him away from that path. His mother and Vera.

Blaine rests a hand on my shoulder. "You two will get through whatever is going on."

I offer a weak smile in response. "I hope."

And for a moment, it seems true. For a moment, I can see a future for us, one where we win this war and find the life we wanted from the beginning.

Until Kya's scream shatters through the small peace.

Without waiting, we sprint towards the sound. The sunlight blinds us temporarily, but what I see is one figure in the trees— no, two figures. One standing.

Derrín carrying Verosa.

The mechanic's skin is bruised and dirty, his dirt-stained face streaked with dried tear stains. His fingers have cracked open and begun to bleed from the strain of carrying her. He carried her all the way here.

He falls to his knees, his head to his chest as he lays Vera before Aiko and Finneas. "I'm sorry."

Aiko pauses a moment, gasping for air as she raises a hand towards her daughter. She pauses just before her pale skin, as if afraid she could shatter her. Then she wails, a sound that slices straight through my core as she falls over Vera's body.

I approach slowly, a fog shrouding my motions. At some point, my hand reaches for her face. Her mouth is slack and coated in blistering burns. Black snakes through her veins, stretching towards her heart beneath her skin. And her eyes —*gods,* her eyes. They lay open still, pitch black throughout, with whirls of silver.

Cursed blood.

Derrín presses his fingers over her eyes, closing them, but it is too late. Aiko screams over her body, holding her to herself as if it is the only thing keeping her from dying alongside her. Finneas folds himself over as if shot, an expression written across his face that I know will haunt me for the rest of my life.

I feel my heart shatter beyond repair as I lean over and close her eyes, then press a kiss to the back of her hand. I hold it to my face. It is cold. Something that was so warm, so loving even as it touched the blackest soul this kingdom has seen...

The first of my tears stain her skin as Finneas pulls Aiko away, her screams still piercing the air. He holds her tightly, still trying to shield her from the reality of it all.

I lift her into my arms, her inky hair falling as her head lolls back with no resistance. Was she always this light? Did her heart and soul truly weigh so much? "Open your eyes, love," I plea with broken breath. "Just open your eyes for me."

Because when she opens her eyes, they will be every shade of blue and lit with laughter. She will tell me in a hundred different ways how stupid I am, then how much she loves me in a million.

Her lips parted, the wind ruffles her hair. The world keeps moving, the sun still falling. Vera does not wake.

The war is so far away now. Mavis. My father. All of it seems so small now, holding her body. What all was once so light and warm is now stiff and cold in my arms.

An irrevocable truth rings through us all as the light begins to die.

Verosa is dead.

CHAPTER 44

VEROSA

I should have expected death to be cold, but still, the frigid winds douse my system in shock. Can someone who has died feel shock?

I also should have expected the darkness. I should have expected the worst. I was foolish in that I did not.

The nurses told us of the Etherworld when we were all just children running around the palace. They told us the Etherworld consisted of a paradise known as the Heavens, or a place of eternal torment known as Hell. They swore to us it was true, and having nothing else to believe in, we trusted them.

I've been holding on to this hope that Tanja is in the Heavens and not trapped in eternal darkness. If it is just unending dark, I pray there is no consciousness to exist in the darkness, just a void. Even as the thoughts cause my heart to race and panic to climb my throat, I hope for it. Because this—an eternity of nothing but cold darkness—is eternal torture, and surely the gods couldn't be so cruel.

The darkness envelops my form as I force my limbs to move, both sticking and yielding to my motions. Each step I take further into the void, the feeling grows familiar. My breath crystallizes before my face, the first sight beyond darkness for what feels like eternity. I follow each tendril of mist as my eyes begin to burn with the cold. My tears freeze to my face and I force my limbs to move.

"We are *not* doing this again," I hiss through clenched and chattering teeth. "You don't get to put me through this again!" I scream in frustration, but the cold only grows until I fall to my knees. "So what? You've killed me just to kill me again? Get on with it then! Send me to Hell!"

My own voice echoes back at me, followed by a slow, quiet tapping. The sound grows until I recognize those clicks. Fine leather heels on stone and quartz. Rhythmic. Poised. Cold.

The one time the gods listen to me...

The pale, heel-clad feet stop before my face and I bite my cheek.

I raise my gaze and force my shaking features into steel.

"Hello, Mother."

Irene smiles, her face not a single day older than the day she died. Her lips curl wickedly as she sees where I kneel before her. A well-manicured finger traces my jawline and she tuts.

"Hello again, Verosa darling."

About the Author

Haydn Hubbard is a North Carolina native who spends most of her time daydreaming of worlds filled with love, magic, and occasionally dragons. The King's Queen is her debut fantasy series and the first of many to come. When Haydn is not writing, she can be found competing with her horses in any local coffee shop or anywhere where there is a dog.

For more information visit her website at https://hhubbardauthor.com

instagram.com/hhubbardauthor
tiktok.com/@Hhubbardauthor

ALSO BY HAYDN HUBBARD